The highest praise for
Jane and the Unpleasantness at Scargrave Manor

"Splendid fun!"—*Star Tribune*, Minneapolis

"Happily succeeds on all levels: a robust tale of manners and mayhem that faithfully reproduces the Austen style—and engrosses to the finish."
—*Kirkus Reviews*

"Jane is unmistakably here with us through the work of Stephanie Barron—sleuthing, entertaining, and making us want to devour the next Austen adventure as soon as possible!"—Diane Mott Davidson

"Well-conceived, stylishly written, plotted with a nice twist . . . and brought off with a voice that works both for its time and our own."
—*Booknews* from The Poisoned Pen

"People who lament Jane Austen's minimal lifetime output . . . now have cause to rejoice."
—*The Drood Review of Mystery*

"A light-hearted mystery . . . The most fun is that 'Jane Austen' is in the middle of it, witty and logical, a foil to some of the ladies who primp and faint and swoon."—*The Denver Post*

"A fascinating ride through the England of the hackney carriage . . . a definite occasion for pride rather than prejudice."—Edward Marston

"A thoroughly enjoyable tale. Fans of the much darker Anne Perry . . . should relish this somewhat lighter look at the society of fifty years earlier."—*Mostly Murder*

"Jane sorts it all out with the wit and intelligence Jane Austen would display. ★★★ (four if you really love Jane Austen)."—*Detroit Free Press*

Jane and the
Man of the Cloth

~Being the Second Jane Austen Mystery~

by Stephanie Barron

BANTAM BOOKS

NEW YORK · TORONTO · LONDON · SYDNEY · AUCKLAND

This edition contains the complete text
of the original hardcover edition
NOT ONE WORD HAS BEEN OMITTED.

JANE AND THE MAN OF THE CLOTH
A Bantam Book

PUBLISHING HISTORY
Bantam hardcover edition / February 1997
Bantam paperback edition / December 1997

ISBN 978-0-553-57489-0

Published simultaneously in the United States and Canada

Bantam Books are published by Bantam Books, a division of Random
House, Inc. Its trademark, consisting of the words "Bantam Books"
and the portrayal of a rooster, is Registered in U.S. Patent and Trademark Office and in other countries. Marca Registrada. Bantam Books,
New York, New York.

PRINTED IN THE UNITED STATES OF AMERICA

OPM   14   13   12   11   10   9

Dedicated with love to my sister Cathy,
who always gave me the best books;
and to my sister Jo,
who taught me to read

Editor's Foreword

When Jane Austen traveled to the Dorset coastal town of Lyme Regis in the late summer of 1804, she returned to a part of England she had first visited the previous year and that she is thought to have loved. She chose Lyme and its peculiar blend of fishermen, retired naval officers, and fashionable pleasure seekers for a pivotal passage in her final novel, *Persuasion,* published posthumously in 1818. Her affection for the town's steep streets and bracing Cobb (a stone breakwater encircling the harbor of the same name), the secretive wilderness called the Pinny and the high downs beyond, shines through the scenes she set down on paper over ten years after the action of this memoir.

For *Jane and the Man of the Cloth* is exactly that—a memoir of Austen's detective adventures in Lyme in the late summer of 1804. Austen scholars have long been frustrated by their lack of knowledge about this period in her life, since only one letter written from the town survives in the collected correspondence. In that lengthy note to

Cassandra, Jane talks of many people and events that will become familiar to the reader of the present volume. We listen as she discusses Mr. Crawford, with whom she had danced the previous evening at the Thursday night Assembly; the servant-man James and his lanthorn; Miss Armstrong; the Schuylers and the Honourable Barnewalls—"bold, queer-looking people, just fit to be Quality at Lyme"—and the mysterious man she names only as *Le Chevalier,* who divided the winnings of a card game with her mother. The details are tantalizing, because they are fragmentary—and yet powerfully suggestive of the richness of the author's visit to the Dorset coast.

At long last, the full story of Jane's extraordinary Lyme experiences may be shared with the world, in the form of this diary account, one of many discovered among the long-lost Austen journals currently undergoing restoration and editing in the United States.[1]

Although the events Jane Austen describes in the following pages are surprising enough, it is possible that they serve to elucidate a personal episode in her life that has been the subject of much conjecture and debate. Years after Jane's death, Cassandra Austen, Jane's older sister and closest confidante, told her niece Caroline that the writer was involved in an unfortunate love affair with a clergyman whom she had met during a seaside holiday. The young man died or otherwise disappeared before an engagement could be formed, and since Cassandra was notoriously closemouthed regarding her sister's private life, neither the gentleman's name nor the exact history of the affair have come down to posterity. Various Austen

[1] For a full account of the journals' discovery, readers are directed to the Editor's Foreword in the first volume of the Austen collection, published by Bantam Books in May 1995 under the title of *Jane and the Unpleasantness at Scargrave Manor.*

family members recorded conflicting explanations of the episode—which Caroline Austen termed Jane's "nameless and dateless" romance—and the facts appear to have been garbled with time. It has been suggested that the clergyman's brother was a doctor, whom Cassandra visited years after Jane's death; or that the unknown suitor was in fact the Reverend Samuel Blackall, an acquaintance of Jane's for many years previous to this period. Constance Pilgrim, in her book *Dear Jane: A Biographical Study of Jane Austen* (Pentlands Press, Durham, 1971), goes so far as to suggest that the writer's mystery lover was Captain John Wordsworth, a naval officer and brother of the poet William Wordsworth, who was lost with his ship in 1805, and that they met in Lyme Regis as early as 1797—a theory described as "fanciful" by George Holbert Tucker, another Austen scholar. Some have asserted that Jane met the unknown clergyman while traveling with her family in Dorset during the summer of 1801; others place the encounter closer to 1804.[2]

Jane and the Man of the Cloth offers one possible answer to the debate. Austen's acquaintance with both Geoffrey Sidmouth, whom she believed to be the notorious Reverend, and Captain Percival Fielding—as well as Sidmouth's friendship with the medical doctor William Dagliesh, whom Cassandra knew and might well have visited in later years—make it likely that the writer's "nameless and dateless" romance occurred in Lyme in the late summer of 1804. To offer further evidence here would be to spoil the tale for the reader; so I shall allow Jane to speak for herself and leave it to the reader to determine the truth of matters.

In editing this volume, I found that Geoffrey Morley's

[2] For an excellent survey of the "nameless and dateless" romance theories, as well as a rich portrait of Austen's milieu, see George Holbert Tucker, *Jane Austen the Woman*, St. Martin's Press, 1994.

1983 work, *Smuggling in Hampshire and Dorset: 1700–1850* (Newbury UK: Countryside Books), was very nearly indispensable. I would offer it to readers who wish to know more about Free Trade and the Gentlemen of the Night. Novelist John Fowles, who has lived and worked in Lyme for many years, is the author of *A Short History of Lyme Regis* (Little, Brown & Co., 1982), a concise but thorough summary of the town and its past.

Stephanie Barron
Evergreen, Colorado

Jane and the
Man of the Cloth

Chapter 1

The Perils of Travelling Post

3 September 1804
at High Down Grange,
on the Lyme road

~

IT IS A TRUTH UNIVERSALLY ACKNOWLEDGED, THAT THE EXPECTATION of pleasure is generally preferred to its eventual attainment—the attainment being marred, at its close, by the resumption of quotidian routine made onerous by the very diversions so lately enjoyed. But as I gaze upon the tortured aspect of my dearest sister, her head bound round in a makeshift bandage, her pallor extreme, and her features overlaid with suffering, I must declare all such nice distinctions the indulgence of a frivolous mind. For how much more melancholy still, to find pleasure usurped entirely by the advent of disaster! To have no chance of mourning the *end* of good times, by observing them waylaid and truly routed before they had even *begun*! And Cassandra's is the sort of misfortune one never anticipates, being met in unhappy accident—the chance of a moment decided it; and the course of our long-awaited pleasure trip to Lyme is thrown utterly to the winds.

But I write entirely of outcomes, and am quite heedless

of causes; a testament to the discomposure of my mind. I shall step back, the better to govern the tumult of my reason, and endure again the horror of those moments that left my dear one insensible in a stranger's bed.

Bath being unbearably hot this August, and my father's health indifferent, we determined to exchange our rooms in Town for more salubrious ones along the coast. We had little inclination to try the bustle and vulgarity of Ramsgate,[1] though my brother Edward *would* take a large establishment there; Brighton was not even to be spoken of; and so to Dorsetshire we would go, and to Lyme Regis in particular, having made a several-weeks' trial of its delights the previous autumn. No coaching inn should be good enough accommodation on the present occasion, however; none of your Three Cups or Golden Lions would do for us—no, the Austens of Bath should travel in style, and take furnished lodgings. A cottage on the water, where my mother might gaze at the sea, and consider her Naval sons, and my father might indulge his passion for botany in walks along the shingle, should do very well. Cassandra and I meant to be happy with frequent turns about the Cobb,[2] and even more frequent dances in the

[1] The Austens had visited Ramsgate during the spring or summer of 1803, prior to their first visit to Lyme that September. Jane disliked Ramsgate intensely; and when she wished to place a fictional character in a compromising position, she often sent her to Ramsgate. Georgiana Darcy was nearly seduced by Wickham there, in *Pride and Prejudice*, while in *Mansfield Park*, Maria Bertram endured a loveless Ramsgate honeymoon before her adulterous affair with Henry Crawford. —*Editor's note.*

[2] Jane refers here to Lyme's Marine Parade, known in her day simply as The Walk; it ran along the beach fronting Lyme's harbor, and out along the ancient stone breakwater, both of which are called the Cobb. —*Editor's note.*

town's pretty little Assembly Rooms; our memories of the place were so cheerful, in fact, that the plan met with immediate approval. Bath was forgotten; Ramsgate consigned to those of little sense or taste; and Lyme became the object of all our fondest hopes.

Being possessed of a fortune that no longer admits of a private carriage, but finding ourselves above the meaner conveyance of mail coach and stage—the former being adjudged too swift and precarious for my father's temper, and the latter too crowded and vulgar for my mother's— we were forced to adopt the only alternative, a post chaise initiating in Bath, with horses changed daily *en route*. Having descended towards the southern coast by way of Shepton Mallet, Somerton, and Crewkerne, as recommended by *Paterson's*,[3] we were even yet embarked today upon the final stage of our journey, with a new postboy, hailing from Lyme, mounted before; when the appearance of a murkiness upon the horizon gave rise to general alarm. Our fears were rewarded, as such fears generally are, with the sudden convergence of a gale above our heads; and the fierceness of the wind and rain that then ensued was indescribable.

Though it was not much beyond six o'clock, the light had failed utterly, leaving the interior of our coach in a grey dimness through which the faces of my sister and mother, seated opposite, shone palely. Cassandra, who is ever indisposed by the motion of a carriage, and who, after long days of travel, was at the last extremity of her endurance, was in very ill looks; and her temper could hardly be improved by the proximity of my mother, whose

---

[3] *Paterson's British Itinerary* was the road bible of the traveling gentry from 1785 to 1832. Written by Daniel Paterson and running to seventeen editions, it detailed stage and mail routes between major cities, as well as their tolls, bridges, landmarks, and notable country houses. —*Editor's note.*

general alarm at the fearful neighs of the horses as the storm built wrathfully above our heads, and the postboy's resultant curses, had taught her to seek comfort in a fierce pinching of Cassandra's hand within her own. I observed the whitened knuckles of her grip, and silently thanked the force of chance that had placed me beside my father.

"We shall be overturned! I am sure of it! Overturned, Mr. Austen!" my mother cried.

"Now, my dearest," my father said, in a tone of gentle reproof, "you must not give way to womanly fears. The Lord looks after His own."

"Then He must be looking after them in Town," my mother replied, in some exasperation, "for He is assuredly *not* along the Lyme road at present. We shall be overturned, and all of us killed, and I should like to know what you will say *then*, Mr. Austen. I am sure you shall be very sorry you did not listen to your wife!"

"Now, my dear," my father said again, and took up once more his book.

A fearsome jolt then occurring, I was thrown abruptly against the coach window, and seized my chance to gaze out upon a storm-tossed world. The pitted road, but poorly maintained in the best of times, was awash in muddy water; the adjacent trees lashed into silvery indistinctness by the combined effects of wind and rain; and no relief apparent in the lowering density of cloud. I drew back to the relative comfort of the coach's interior, and attempted to calculate the distance remaining. We were some hours removed from Crewkerne, where we had spent the previous day and evening, not being prone to Sunday travel;[4] and should even now be breasting the long hill into Up Lyme. Was not the carriage rising? But

---

[4] In Austen's time, traveling on Sunday was considered disrespectful to the Sabbath. —*Editor's note.*

as this very thought struck, a yet more bone-rattling shudder seized the coach's frame, as though a great beast had taken us up in its jaws and tossed us about for sport. I cried out, and was rewarded with a look of terror from my mother and a squeak of pain from Cassandra, whose hand was no doubt suffering under the effects of her companion's anxiety.

"Overturned, Mr. Austen!" the good woman cried, and half-stood as though to throw herself upon her husband's breast.

A great crash from the road ahead, and a lurching of the carriage; then the screaming of horses, and a tumult that could only be due to chaos within the traces. For the world to revolve an hundred degrees, was required but a moment; and when I found the courage to open my eyes, the floor was become the coach's ceiling. A most ludicrous position, particularly when viewed through a quantity of muslin, the result of one's skirts being tipped over one's head. I lay an instant in utter silence, feeling the rapid patter of my heart and the laboured nature of my breathing; and was relieved to find that both continued in force.

A grunt from my father roused me.

"Sir!" I cried, endeavouring to secure him amidst the murk and confusion. "May I be of assistance?"

At that, the coach's nether door was seized and opened—by the postboy, no doubt—and my father, whose main support the door had been, tumbled from the vehicle. Hardly a dignified antic for a clergyman of three-and-seventy, but followed by the still less-seemly exit of his younger daughter, her skirts in a tangle about her knees. The relief, however, at being freed from such a world gone topsy-turvy, was beyond every indecorous attempt to achieve it; I drew a shaky breath and tested my limbs, heedless of the fierce rain that pelted my cap. My father, having been helped to his feet by the postboy (a burly fellow of some five-and-thirty, one Hibbs by name), was seized with a coughing fit. The poor man's senses were little assisted when Hibbs thought to pound upon his back, and I hastened to intervene.

"Father," I said, taking him by the arm, "I trust you are not injured in any way?"

"Only in complaisance, my dear," he replied, with the ghost of a smile, "and that has been decidedly shaken. I shall be forced to attend your mother's every warning, by and by—a triumph, I fear, that she shall not know how to sustain."

My mother! I turned in an instant, and peered back within the carriage's depths—and oh! What a scene I then descried!

My beloved sister lay wan and lifeless, in a heap of crushed muslin against the coach's farthest wall—the wall that had received all the force of impact in the conveyance's upheaval. My mother was attempting to shift Cassandra towards the open door—which, given the tossing of the coach, was well above her head; but the poor woman lacked the strength for it, and was reduced to tears as a consequence.

"Stay, madam," I cried, and leapt for the postboy.

The man Hibbs saw the necessity in a moment; and lifted Cassandra to safety so swiftly and gently that I was all but struck speechless; the condition of the poor sufferer being of paramount importance, however, I offered broken thanks and turned to her comfort, overcome by nameless dread. So much lively beauty, reduced to deathly silence! It was not to be borne. My beloved sister was carried to the shelter of a tree, and my father's cloak propped on a few sticks above her, in an ineffectual attempt to shield her from the rain.

My mother's wails declared her incapable of use; my father was consigned to comfort her; and I turned to Cassandra to see what ill I might find.

A great bruise o'erspread her temple, and in feeling about her scalp, I was rewarded by a grimace of pain flitting across her countenance, and a warm trickle of blood upon my fingertips. I chafed her wrists, and called her name; implored her, in desperation, to awake; but she continued insensible, lying at the verge of the road like so much cast-off clothing. The horror that seized me then! I shudder to recall it. I was the closest to despair I have been in all my life—and so resolved upon action. To *do*, when one is very nearly past hope, is the sole means of relief. I turned from Cassandra and looked for the postboy.

"Hibbs!" I shouted. The tumult of the storm continued unabated, making all attempt at conversation a dubious affair.

"Yes, miss," the man rejoined, turning from the wreckage of his rig.

"My sister cannot remain here."

"Don't know as she 'as much choice, beggin' yer pardon, miss. The horses be gone, and the coach a fair ruin. Then there's the matter o' that there tree," he said, tossing a look over his shoulder.

I regained my feet and peered ahead into the tempest. A massive trunk indeed lay full across the road, barring further passage. How unfortunate that it should be *before* us, rather than behind. But I comprehended, now, the reason for the horses' terror and flight. We were any of us fortunate to be alive.

"We cannot hope to shift it?"

Hibbs shook his head in reply. "And with the nags run off—"

"Then we must fetch assistance from some neighbouring farm," I said with authority, and cast about me into the gloom. Misfortune could not have chosen a more desolate place to befall us. As far as the gaze might reach, the high downs rolled unimpeded to the sea. But wait—

"Is not that a light, away there in the distance?"

The postboy shrugged, and his brows lowered. "Happen it is. But you'll not be finding help for the young lady at the Grange."

"And why ever not?"

"They're queer folk."

"Queer or no, they cannot refuse to help a lady in such distress," I replied firmly, and turned to my father. Heedless of the rain that had completely soaked his hat, he stood at a little distance from my mother, who was bent over Cassandra in an attitude of despair. My sister's condition, I saw at a glance, was unchanged. With such burdens of infirmity and age parcelled out among them, they should none of them be left too long in darkness and storm.

"Sir," I called, crossing to my father, "the postboy and I intend to seek aid from the farm whose lights you espy at a little distance. We shall hasten to return."

"But, Jane—my dear—had not *I* better go?" my father enquired doubtfully, and when I would insist, he added in a lowered tone, "For it cannot be proper to send you off into the night in the company of such a man. A complete stranger, and a hapless one, I fear; only look to what an impasse he has brought us!"

"But thankfully, Father, he calls this country home; and may be of service in appealing to the inhabitants of the farm. And as to going yourself—would you leave three women alone and unprotected, on such a road, in such a state? Better that you should stand with my mother, and comfort her when you may."

I turned from him before he could reply—for, in truth, help should be long in coming, did my father go in search of it. He is an elderly gentleman whose pace is slow on the smoothest of roads, and in the best of light; and I paled to think of him attempting the downs in the present hour.

"Come along, Hibbs," I called to the postboy, who

stood muttering under his breath over the ruin of his harness. "To the Grange it is, as fast as our feet may carry us."

I SHALL PASS OVER IN SILENCE THE RIGOURS OF THAT DAMPENING walk; how endless it seemed, the lights of the Grange receding ever before us through the rain; how our ankles were turned, and our clothes snagged, and our legs thoroughly wearied, well before we came to the narrow track through the meadow that led to a neat gate, and a stone pathway running up to a massive oak door, lit only by a smoking lanthorn. High Down Grange—for so, I have learnt, is its full name—was at one time a modest farmhouse, though now turned country manor; the home of a gentleman, by all appearances, while maintaining still its purpose as a center of agricultural endeavour. The house was wrapt in quiet, despite the storm, the fierceness of which had driven all sensible folk within doors; and my relief was so great, upon gaining the stoop, that I nearly sank to my knees in gratitude.

The baying of a dog—nay, several dogs—announced our arrival, and then the beasts themselves rounded the corner of the house like a pack of wolves, slavering for our throats. I confess that I screamed, and clutched at poor Hibbs, who thrust me behind him and menaced the curs with a stout cudgel—taken up some time past as a walking stick, but performing now a dearer service.

"Jasper! Fang! You there, Beelzebub! Heel! *Heel*, I say!"

The commanding voice came from the doorway, now streaming with light as the sturdy oak was unbarred. A lanthorn held high revealed a gentleman's face—though a countenance most harshly-drawn, under a windswept mop of black hair. The master of High Down, I presumed; and masterly enough with his dark brows heavy and knit, his eyes glowing and fierce, and his nose as sharply hooked as a bird of prey's. A man of middlish age, perhaps five-and-thirty, arrayed in knee breeches and a white shirt quite open at the collar, his stock being put aside as though he were in the act of retiring. His countenance was suffused with a most ungentlemanly rage—the violence of his great dogs, it seemed, being mirrored in the spirits of their master.

"Who the Devil are you?" he cried, with a glower for the beasts, now cowering at his feet, and a glower for ourselves—and so Hibbs and I were welcomed to High Down Grange.

"Miss Jane Austen, of Bath," I replied, in a tone that betrayed a quaver.

"Miss Jane Austen of Bath, and her merry man," our host said caustically, with a look for poor Hibbs. "And what in God's name brings you out on such a night? Some unholy pilgrimage?"[5]

"A gentleman of better breeding and greater charity might have saved such questions for the comfort of his drawing-room," I retorted, my patience thoroughly spent. The rain, though diminished to a fine drizzle, was still as wet; and its continued descent upon my drenched cap and shawl did nothing to improve my temper. "We are clearly driven to your door by the utmost extremity, sir, and if any alternative served, should never have troubled you longer—for you are undoubtedly lacking in the sensibilities of a true gentleman, and the assistance of a common labourer should be given with greater goodwill, I am sure."

"Undoubtedly," he said, and though his lip curled cyn-

---

[5] We may presume Geoffrey Sidmouth to be referring, here, to Chaucer's *Canterbury Tales*, in which the character of the Wife of Bath figures. Jane's mention of the town must have sparked the allusion. —*Editor's note*.

ically at the word, my tart rebuke appeared to soften him a little. His choler drained away, and I thought him about to speak in a more measured tone, when a small sound caused him to turn, and the rings of light emanating from the lamp he held shifted and welled like a tide of water across the darkened courtyard. I turned, and started in fright, and reached again for Hibbs's arm; for we were held at bay by the business end of a very imposing blunderbuss, levelled in the hands of a stable boy—of malevolent intent, to judge by his aspect.

"Put up the gun, Toby," the master of High Down said gently. "You need not be threatening a bedraggled woman. She looks harmless enough."

"She ain't no woman, Mr. Sidmouth, sir. She's a *lady* to you." Hibbs's hands were clenching and unclenching at his belt. That he kept a pistol there, for fear of highwaymen, I well knew; and that he had left it with my father, the better to safeguard the ladies, I surmised he very much regretted.

"Be off wi' ye," the boy said menacingly; but he lowered the blunderbuss, with evident mistrust. "Ye're no more'n a pack o' spies, ye are. Be off, 'fore I blows ye down the lane!"

"Toby!" Mr. Sidmouth—for so I assumed him to be, as Hibbs had named him—strode swiftly from the doorway to the boy's side, with nary a glance for ourselves. He pried the gun from Toby's hands and turned him towards the back of the house, from whence he had appeared. "Tell Mary we've company, and then fetch Miss Seraphine, there's a good fellow."

"Run 'em off, Mr. Sid," the boy said, by way of reply. "They're here as 'formers, I'll lay my soul on't."

A sound bussing on the bottom was his only answer, and the master of High Down turned once more to face us. "My apologies," he told us. "The boy has yet to learn his manners."

"You astonish me." My tone was dry. "And with such a paragon as yourself for instruction?"

In the lamp's glow, Sidmouth's mouth tightened, and the black brows lowered over his eyes. I felt sure that in a moment he should drive us down the hill with the butt of the gun, but instead, he drew breath and managed a smile. "Your reproof is well-placed, Miss Jane Austen of Bath," he said. "I fear I have shown myself to disadvantage upon first meeting. Do not, I beg of you, take the instant for a portrait of the man. And now, I trust, you will do me the honour of entering High Down Grange? For it rains"—at this, he cast a look towards the heavens—"undoubtedly it rains." There was an air of immense satisfaction about the man, that I was at a loss to understand; but mindful of my sister's plight I wasted not another thought upon Mr. Sidmouth and his mysteries, and followed him into the house.

It is a simple-enough affair, rather reminiscent, at first glance, of dear Steventon,[6] in its exposed beams and whitewashed walls. I imagined the upstairs rooms would have sloping floors, and dormer'd eaves, and all the comfort of age and use to recommend them—and as I sit here now, writing by the light of a single candle, in one such a room, I find my conjecture immediately proved. It is a house made for laughter and song and the fresh-blown scent of roses in the doorway; and that it is sadly lacking in all such delights, I readily discerned. For High Down Grange has been subject to decided neglect—the result, perhaps, of having no mistress. Geoffrey Sidmouth is a single man, prone, as are all such fellows, to thoughtlessness with regard to his surroundings, and to an over-

---

[6] Austen's childhood home, the parsonage at Steventon where she lived until May 1801, would be regretted and missed for most of her life. —*Editor's note.*

active benevolence towards his hounds, his horses, and his hunting. Or so I surmise.

The drawing-room eloquently bespoke the want of a lady's attention, in its shabby fittings and dusty aspect, and I wondered, as I stood uneasy upon the hearth, at the aforementioned Mary—was she cook, or housekeeper, or merely a slovenly attempt at both? And who should *Miss Seraphine* be?

"Allow me to introduce myself," Sidmouth said, in closing the door and crossing to the fire. "I am Geoffrey Sidmouth, and High Down Grange is my home—at present. I take it from Hibbs being your attendant, Miss Austen, that you are a traveller in these parts; and that his regrettably poor driving has unhorsed your equipage."

Hibbs glowered from his place near the doorway, all the anger of his outraged reputation hot upon his lips; but Sidmouth silenced him with a glance. "I have reason to regret that driving myself," he mused. "I am surprised you have the courage to show your face here, man." With that, the master's eyes found the postboy's and their gazes locked for an inscrutable instant; an instant that ended in Hibbs hanging his head.

"Go to the kitchen until we have need of you," Sidmouth said; and Hibbs quitted the room without another word.

The master of High Down motioned me to a worn chair by the fire, and as I hesitated, surveying the soaking fabric of my gown, and certain it should leave a mark, he made a gesture of impatience and took me by the arm in a most forward manner. I had begun to regret poor Hibbs, when Sidmouth thrust me abruptly towards the seat. "Forget the matter of your dress," he said, not ungently. "It shall be changed as soon as possible for another. Now, tell me of your affairs. You travel alone? From Bath to Lyme is a great distance for a lady, and without even her maid."

"Indeed, sir, I do not," I said, all the memory of my recent trouble rushing full upon my mind. "I travel with those dearest to me in the world—and overcome, like myself, by a great misfortune. Having changed horses at Crewkerne, and acquired Hibbs as postboy, we thought to make Lyme this very e'en—and should have done so, but for the storm. We were, as you have surmised, overturned; and I fear my beloved sister is injured as a result. She lies even now upon the verge of the road, and I am come to beg your assistance; for she cannot remain there. We are lost without your aid, Mr. Sidmouth, and every minute must be precious in such a cause."

To his credit, Sidmouth made for the door with alacrity, crying harshly for the stable boy Toby as he did; and I was allowed the sensation of exquisite relief, in having accomplished my mission without further enquiry, and in being able to enjoy the comforts of the chair by the fire, despite my sodden dress and aching feet. In an instant, the master of High Down had returned, followed by the unfortunate Hibbs.

"I am sending this fellow and Toby in search of your sister immediately, Miss Austen, with the instruction that they are to convey her hither. There were others in your party, I believe?"

"My father and mother, sir, of advanced years."

"I fear you shall none of you make Lyme tonight. Hibbs tells me of a great tree, to which he credits the chaos of his horses, that lies across the road and bars all passage." The curl in Sidmouth's lip as he spoke these words, told all his opinion of Hibbs's excuses. "Your family shall be borne to High Down, and the hospitality of this house extended gladly to all."

"Thank you, sir," I said, with a bow of my head. "You are very kind, and we are much obliged to your goodness."

"Think nothing of it. I would that I could do more.

And now, my man," he said to Hibbs, as we heard the sound of a carriage being brought round to the door, "be off. Do everything to assure the Austens' comfort, since you have already assured their distress. There are lap robes and warm bricks in the carriage."

"It may be that a waggon should serve better," I broke in. "It might more easily cross the downs, should the road hither prove impassable. And, too, when I left my sister, she was as yet insensible from a blow to the head. She may be incapable of mounting the carriage steps, and my father is no longer strong enough to lift her."

"The carriage will have to do," Sidmouth said shortly. "There is not a waggon to be had tonight. Hibbs must serve, should any lifting be necessary."

I wondered at such words, and at the obligations which could engage a farm's waggons in such darkness and rain; and wondered still more at Sidmouth's failure to go to my sister himself, when necessity pled so powerful a cause. But he turned away from me, and paced before the fire, seemingly lost in contemplation of the flames.

"Cannot we send to Lyme for a surgeon, Mr. Sidmouth?" I enquired anxiously, as a new thought struck me. "My sister, I fear, is gravely injured; no care should be spared, that might prove her salvation."

"A surgeon is utterly impossible."

"But why?" I was astounded. "I know that a tree bars the way into town, but could not a single horse pass where a larger conveyance might not?"

"Did we send for the surgeon the entire night through, Miss Austen, we should assuredly find him already called out."

"But you cannot know this for a certainty!"

"I fear that I can. I fear that I *do*." At that, Sidmouth braced himself against the mantel as though overcome by some powerful emotion, and I was utterly silenced.

The painful pause in our discourse was broken by the

turning of the doorknob, and the silent entrance of a woman so beautiful, that had I not heard the name Seraphine spoken already by Sidmouth himself, I am certain it should have sprung unbidden to my lips. There was *that* of the angel about her, in the graceful movement of her carriage, and her liquid gaze, and the unbound glory of her golden hair, that inspired one to imagine wings fluttering in the shadows to her back. And of a certainty, her appearance was not quite of this world—for though her face bore the lines of nobility, her clothing proclaimed her neither housemaid nor lady, but a common labourer of the fields. She was arrayed in a simple gown of nankeen, such as a milkmaid might wear; stout boots that had seen much use; and a flowing red cloak. An unlit lanthorn of a curious design—tall and cylindrical, and possessed of a spout—was in her right hand.

"There you are at last," Sidmouth said, with a touch of impatience.

The angel made no reply, but awaited his command.

"This is Miss Jane Austen."

Her gaze turned my way, as cold as the breath of a sepulchre. Then she looked her enquiry to Sidmouth. To my surprise, he broke into a torrent of French, a language with which I am somewhat familiar; but the rapidity of his speech left me quickly behind. A few words only I caught—*dogs,* and *the bay,* and perhaps *the men;* and then Seraphine was gesturing towards me, her lovely face overcome with suspicion, and Sidmouth abruptly silencing her with a word. That it was an incomprehensible one to me—*lascargon*—made no difference to the angel. She turned on her heel in a swirl of red wool, and was as swiftly gone; and I drew a deep breath, and looked for an explanation to Sidmouth—who clearly intended to offer me none. His face was once more to the fire, and his hands clasped behind. As if sensible of my gaze, he roused himself, and met my eyes with a single long look; then he bowed, and made for the door.

"Mr. Sidmouth!" I cried.

"Yes, Miss Austen?" He halted in the very act of exiting, and offered a lifted eyebrow.

"This is a very singular household indeed," I burst out.

" 'Singular' does not even begin to describe it," Mr. Sidmouth replied, and left me to myself.

I HAD NOT LONG TO AWAIT THE RETURN OF THE GRANGE'S CARRIAGE, and my anxious feet had sped me to the courtyard well before the horses were pulled up, and the coach door flung open, and my dear Cassandra laid gently on a settee before the fire. She was as colourless as a ghost, and I might even have believed her to have expired, but from the composure of my father in attending her.

Sidmouth materialised in the drive with a sturdy farm woman behind, the very Mary whose slovenliness I had conjectured; she bore a steaming basin and a quantity of torn cloth, for the preparation of bandages, and I was soon relieved to find her possessed of a quiet efficiency. When she had bathed Cassandra's wound, Sidmouth himself bent over my sister with an air of command that would not be gainsaid. His fingers probed the bones of her skull, and passed with delicate knowledge along her temple, so that she winced in her delirium, but showed no other sign of discomfort. My poor Cassandra! So lovely still, despite her suffering, that even Sidmouth could not fail to be moved!

"Mary," he said, extending a hand for a cloth and wringing it over the basin, "she will need some brandy first and then some hot broth. Beef, I think. Fetch those and your smelling salts directly."

The woman silently departed, and the master of High Down proceeded to test the waist of my sister's dress, so that my mother made a small movement of distress, and my father laid his hand upon hers. "The gentleman knows what he is about, my dear," my father said quietly. Then, to Mr. Sidmouth himself, "You have experience in such matters, I believe?"

"I do."

"You were in His Majesty's service at one time?"

I saw the direction my father's thoughts were taking; and applauded his perspicacity. Sidmouth's actions looked for all the world like those of a camp doctor, accustomed to crisis in the field. But the gentleman himself did not reply directly.

"Her ribs are intact, for which you may be thankful," he said briskly, and reached for a length of calico to dress Cassandra's temple. "She is not out of danger—we must await the outcome of the night to proclaim her truly safe—but I think it likely she shall only want strength for some weeks, and suffer from the headache. I venture to predict, that barring a relapse in the next few hours, she may recover entirely."

My mother gave a faint cry, and staggered backwards; my own relief was not to be described; and my father silently joined his hands in an attitude of prayer. To all of this, Sidmouth made sardonic witness, a faint smile about his lips. At Mary's reappearance, brandy was administered, and smelling salts applied; Cassandra's consciousness returned, and with it a bewilderment that brought tears to her eyes—and so we were borne away to bed.

HOW EXTRAORDINARY IS THE HAND OF FATE—ITS ACCIDENTAL miseries, its directed salvations. My father bears Cassandra's trouble well, and is even now gone peacefully to his bed; he has seen much that is worrisome in three-and-seventy years, and trusts to the goodness of Providence. My mother is less sanguine. She starts, and weeps upon our bedroom stoop, and wrings her hands for lack of anything better; and permits the grossest fancies to unnerve her sense.

"But do you think her quite *at ease*, my dear?" she enquired thrice this last half-hour, her ravaged countenance peering about the door-frame.

"She *shall* be, madam, as soon as she achieves some quiet."

"Perhaps my wool wrap, placed over the coverlet? For cold is ever a danger in such cases, as you will remember. Miss Tate was carried off in a matter of hours, for want of extra bedclothes, and Miss Campbell in but a week, for having got wet through in a sudden rain; and how her mother survived such a cruel mistake, I shall never comprehend."

"I assure you, madam, that everything will be done to sustain Cassandra's comfort," I replied, stemming my impatience with difficulty. Having heard of the untimely ends of a score of young ladies among the Austen acquaintance, my tolerance for my mother was at its close. "Do you seek the chamber Mr. Sidmouth has provided for you, and rest easy in the knowledge that should we require you, you shall be summoned directly."

Though all benevolence in her distress, my mother is overcome by such tender emotions in gazing at her dearest daughter, that I fear she should prove of little aid to Cassandra, in any hour of extremity. Better that I should sit watch by my sister alone, and my mother find some comfort in sleep's oblivion. But it required a full quarter-hour, and the recollection of the fates of both young Master and Miss Holder, who met their ends some three years past, before she would at last seek her bed.

Cassandra is stirring now, and calls my name; I set aside my pen and journal and reach for her hand. A touch alone suffices; we two are so familiar to each other, from the happy intimacy of our minds and hearts, that at the pressure of my fingertips upon her brow, her troubled mind relaxes. A moment more, and she slumbers deep, the pain of injury forgotten. I regain my seat, and take up my pen and modest book—formed, according to my habit, from a sheaf of paper sewn quite through and trimmed to manageable size. A stout book, for the stoutest of thoughts; and of considerable comfort, in serving as confidante when no living mind may answer.

All around us the eaves of the old farmhouse creak with the violence of the wind, but the intimates of High Down Grange are lost in storm-filled slumber—no sound emanates from the shuttered rooms, so that I might be the last soul alive, left here at the edge of the world. Beyond is darkness, and cliffs, and the depthless sea; England is to my back as I sit by Cassandra's bed. And so I cross the room to peer out at the unknown, stretching before me like all the days I have yet to live; and can discern nothing beyond my own wavering reflection in the window's glass. A shiver—of foreboding, perhaps—at the hidden landscape, and I would turn away to find comfort in candlelight. But a sudden flare in the darkness below seizes my gaze; I peer more closely, my eyes narrowing, and discern the bob of a lanthorn. A lanthorn just come up over the cliff's edge in the distance, and toiling even now towards the Grange itself. A curiously-shaped lanthorn, perhaps, with a protuberant spout, of a utility unknown to me? Clutched in an angel's ethereal hand, while the other flutters at the nape of a flowing red cloak?

Chapter 2

The Understanding of Eliza

5 September 1804
Lyme
~

AND SO WE ARE AT LAST COME TO LYME, AND TO OUR VERY OWN Wings cottage—a smallish affair of a house tucked into a hillside, with *two* ground floors—one in its proper place, and the other at the top of the house containing the bedrooms and a back door opening onto a greensward behind. The house fronts upon a busy block of Broad Street, a location *not* entirely as our imaginings had made it; for where we had looked to gaze upon the sea, and throw open our casements to its gentle roar, we are instead meant to be happy with a partial view of the Cobb, and that only from the garden at the house's top. But the sitting-room is pretty; and the bustle of traffic at the foot of town, and the eternal cries of muffin men and milk carters climbing its precipitously steep main road, little more than we should have heard at home. More to the point, we are free at last of High Down Grange.

We were obliged to presume upon Geoffrey Sidmouth's taciturn hospitality for the sum of two nights and a day—my dear sister Cassandra's condition permitting of no removal to Lyme so early as yesterday morning. We saw little enough of the gentleman himself during our tedious sojourn, however—he being occupied with the concerns of his estate, and much out of doors in their pursuit. It was to Mary I applied for the necessities of the sickroom; and she provided them with alacrity and good sense. Of Seraphine I neither saw nor heard a word—in any language—though I found myself listening betimes for the whirling passage of a long, full cloak.

It was not until yesterday's dinner hour, in fact, that my own care for Cassandra allowed me to descend the stairs; and I was then to discover that the Austens partook of the meal alone, the master of High Down being yet abroad, and no one able to say when he should return. In a similar state of independence we claimed the drawing-room that evening, and finally retired; and it was well after midnight that a bustle about the gates, and all the noise of a courtyard arrival, bespoke the end of Sidmouth's day.

We could not but be grateful this morning, however, in learning from the postboy Hibbs that some part of the master's activity was motivated by a concern for our affairs. A team and dray he had rousted, in the early hours, for the removal of the tree from the Lyme road; and our coach ordered repaired by a blacksmith fetched from town for that purpose. All this, before departing on some business of his own, of which we learned nothing.

We were to see him once more, however, as we assisted Cassandra somewhat shakily into the coach, and settled ourselves with bated breath in a conveyance we had little reason to trust. My mother was clutching at a handkerchief, in readiness for tears should the carriage disintegrate before her very eyes; and my father, who had seated himself beside Cassandra, was engaged in patting her hand in a comforting, if absent-minded, fashion; when I was startled by a voice at my elbow.

"Farewell, Miss Jane Austen of Bath, though I believe

we shall meet again," Mr. Sidmouth said. "Indeed, I shall be sustained by the hope of such a meeting's being not too long delayed. Your health, Miss Austen," he continued, peering in the carriage window at my sister, who nodded faintly; "and to you both, sir and madam. Godspeed to Lyme."

"Less of speed, and more of care, I truly hope," my mother replied tartly, with an eye towards the carriage front and the unseen Hibbs.

The master of High Down smiled faintly. "The fellow knows it is as much as his life is worth, to come to ruin again. I have told him so—and what I say, he believes."

With a nod, and a slap to the coach's side, we were sent off; and more than one of us breathed a sigh of relief, I am sure. There is something hard and sharp about Geoffrey Sidmouth, that commands attention, and quickens the pulse, however much he would soften it with the air of a gentleman. He is a man much accustomed to being obeyed, I suspect; and to enjoying the power of making those around him do as he likes. A difficult manner to endure for too many days together, however bewitching in moments.

THE ROOMS WE NOW POSSESS ARE SUCH AS ONE TAKES WITH GOOD grace for the space of a few weeks, though they should never do for a twelvemonth. Dressed in foxed paper peeling as a consequence of salt air, the house is meant to be enjoyed as briefly as possible—the majority of one's time in a seaside town being spent out of doors, in pursuit of schemes of pleasure. Cassandra's delicate state, however, will confine her yet a few days to her room; or so we are assured by the surgeon's assistant, one William Dagliesh. He is but lately in the employ of Lyme's venerable surgeon and coroner, Mr. Carpenter, and sees to many of that gentleman's patients—Mr. Carpenter having little time to spare, we are told, from his chief passion—the excavation of fossils.

He appeared on our doorstep not an hour after our arrival—sent, so he informed us, at the direction of Mr. Geoffrey Sidmouth, who appears to be one of his particular friends. Mr. Dagliesh is a young man of perhaps thirty, well-made and possessed of a cheerful countenance easily read—too easily, perhaps; for at the sight of Cassandra, reclining in all the interesting attitude of one lately blessed with suffering, her pallor heightening the beauty of her features and her languorous spirits suggesting a certain mystery about her person, the surgeon's professional solicitude became marked by something verging on the mortifying. He flushed scarlet, and lost his tongue; and could so imperfectly meet Cassandra's gaze, as he held her wrist to feel her pulse, or touched her forehead to judge of her fever, that his performance was painful to contemplate. On several instances of his speaking low, we were forced to request that he repeat his words; and this further embarrassment of circumstance completely unmanned him. Though I had seen him to possess a voluble and easy manner at his arrival, it was entirely unequal to the proximity of so much loveliness and distress, and I doubted that we should make any sense of the good surgeon's diagnosis, when once it did come. To aid him in regaining his composure, therefore, I determined to distract his sensibilities; and so embarked upon a topic of some idle interest to myself.

"We sorely missed your command of things medical, Mr. Dagliesh, on the evening of my sister's accident," I began. "I understood from Mr. Sidmouth, however, that we should not have found you at home on Monday, could we have sent to Lyme for your services. *I* was willing to attempt any distance or trouble for my sister's good, but that Mr. Sidmouth assured me you should already be called out."

The poor man turned an even deeper hue of scarlet, and muttered something unintelligible into his collar.

"But perhaps he meant only that your Mr. Carpenter was engaged and we should have found you at liberty."

"I fear not," Mr. Dagliesh replied.

"You have, perhaps, a standing engagement on Monday nights?" I persisted.

He turned to me then, a slight frown of consternation creasing his brow, and his eyes roving the room as if in search of an answer. "I was detained by a confinement," he replied at last; "one that encompassed some thirty hours. Mr. Sidmouth knew me to be so involved, as a consequence of my having broken an engagement we had formed the day before, to dine together that afternoon at the Three Cups. I fear I did not send to him in time, and he rode into Lyme to no purpose. He must have been returned to the Grange only a little while, when you appeared on his doorstep."

"He has told you, then, of our unfortunate evening?"

"Indeed. He related the particulars only yesterday, when he engaged my services for—" At this, he glanced at Cassandra and was ruined again.

"Mr. Dagliesh," my sister said faintly, "is there aught you might recommend for the relief of pain? For I confess that my head aches quite dreadfully; the slightest sound or movement deranges it; and the throbbing has quite robbed me of sleep."

The surgeon jumped up, aflame with the delight of his purpose; declared that he should go himself to the apothecary, Mr. Green; and urged Cassandra to remain quite chary of visitors, whose noise and attention should undoubtedly do her more harm than good. Then, bowing his way towards the door in all the confusion of newfound ardour, he would have struck the far wall had I not gently seized his arm, and guided him to the hall; whereupon he turned and bowed in *my* direction, assuring me all the while that Cassandra should enjoy a complete recovery.

It is impossible for me not to value anyone who sees the excellence of my sister; and so I pitied and liked him, and showed him to the street with thanks as heartfelt as they were desirous of cloaking my inner mirth.

"You have made a conquest, my dear," I announced as I regained Cassandra's room. "You must endeavour to find your feet in time for tomorrow's Assembly, since poor Mr. Dagliesh will be quite undone if you fail to appear."

"It must be impossible," she replied, her eyes turned upon some inner pain; "the thought of all motion and music is repugnant to me."

"And if you truly wish to secure Mr. Dagliesh," I added reasonably, "by all means, remain elusive. Disappoint his every hope. Make yourself so scarce that he shall come to believe you a lady encountered in a dream, forever out of reach, and thus, forever to be desired."

"But you shall have the Assembly," Cassandra observed, ignoring my raillery from long familiarity with its nature. "Pleasure at least shall not be denied to you, dear Jane. And since I cannot go myself, you might have the wearing of my pink gown. I should be the happier to know it is of use."

"Pink is a color decidedly unsuited to the redness of my complexion, as you very well know," I replied, as I drew wide the window curtains, so that my sister might gaze upon the waves beyond the Cobb. "I suspect that you make a present of the gown, Cassandra, in order to scare away my suitors, and win them all for yourself."

"I had entirely forgot your blushes." Her voice faltered. "I fear I have been forgetting altogether too much. A consequence of the knock, perhaps. Do you think it a permanent one, Jane? Am I to be made quite an idiot by the heedless driving of an heedless postboy?"

"You are *not*," I said, perching at the bed's foot. "And would you have me attend a ball while my dearest sister lies confined by such cruel woes, as the forgetting of my blushes? You are too good, Cassandra, to think so ill of me."

"Indeed I am not, Jane!" she cried, sitting up against the pillows perhaps too rapidly, and wincing. "I have caused difficulty and trial enough. You *must* go, and carry my father with you. James shall light your way with his lanthorn, there being so little moon."[1]

James is our new manservant, acquired, like the portraits of ships that adorn our walls, with the house.

"Very well," I said, shifting myself from her bedside at the sound of voices below. "I shall attend the Lyme Assembly tomorrow e'en, *and* wear your pink gown, if only to encourage your envy. I intend you to be quite wildly green, Cassandra, at all my good times; and so encourage you to quit this room as soon as ever you may. For if I am not very much mistaken, my dear, Henry and Eliza are even now at the door; and no one can be abed while Eliza is underfoot. The noise of her chatter alone should banish sleep for a fortnight."

THERE WAS NO WONDER IN THE APPEARANCE OF MY BROTHER HENRY and his wife, Eliza—who, as well as being my sister[2] these six years at least, has ever been my cousin, and as fond of calling Henry's family her own, *before* she could claim the rights of a daughter, as she has been ever since. Indeed,

---

[1] It was customary in Austen's time to stay at home on evenings with little moonlight, and accept engagements for those nights when the moon would be full. Travel along unlit roads could otherwise be quite hazardous. —*Editor's note.*

[2] In Austen's day, relations by marriage were generally referred to as relations of blood. Although the term *in-law* existed, it was more of an affectation than common usage. —*Editor's note.*

we had parted from the Henry Austens not many weeks before, during their annual visit to Bath, and the scheme of joining us in our travels was undertaken one morning in the very Pump Room.[3] Both declared themselves wild to see Lyme; and very little more was necessary for the achievement of it. Eliza's craving for diversion is so constant, and her enjoyment of pleasure so honest and thorough, that my brother finds it necessary to avoid present tedium, by engaging in relentless plans for future delight; and so, in constant expectation of improvement to her spirits, Eliza makes a tolerable business of living from day to day.

"My dearest Jane!" she now cried, as she threw open the bedroom door. A swift embrace, as from a small whirlwind, and she had moved to my sister's bedside. "And *poor, dear* Cassandra. Does your head ache very much? Am I disturbing you dreadfully? No matter. We shall have you to rights in little time, I am sure of it. You cannot do better than sea air, you know, for all manner of illness; and if *that* does not cure you, we shall whisk you away to Farquhar. He is quite the rage in London, I assure you, and has done wonders for my complaints—though I *did* commit the *bêtise* of addressing him as '*Doctor,*' on our first meeting, when it should have been 'Sir Walter.' "

"You have cut your hair, Eliza," I said faintly, in some wonderment; and, indeed, her lovely dark head was quite shorn all around, and worn in a mass of curls. A peach silk turban, with a jet-black feather, topped the whole.

"Quite *à la mode,* is it not?" she rejoined delightedly,

[3] The Pump Room was the social center of Bath, where many of the residents and visitors congregated daily to drink the medicinal waters pumped up for their refreshment, and to stroll about in close converse with their acquaintance. To be seen in the Pump Room of a morning, and in the Upper or Lower Assembly Rooms at night, was indispensable to the conduct of one's social life. —*Editor's note.*

twirling her sheer muslin gown upon the drugget for our edification. "Or should I say—*à la guillotine,* for that is what they call it in London. Having cheated the infernal machine once already,[4] I thought nothing *now* of parading my lovely neck. I quite recommend it to you both. The sensation of lightness, in ridding oneself of masses of hair, is indescribable."

"For my part, I thank you, but no," I rejoined gently, with a scandalised glance at Cassandra. We both of us have dark brown tresses that reach well past our knees; in truth, I can almost stand upon my hair, and my sister's is little shorter. I should feel worse than naked, did I part with it; I should suffer almost as from the loss of a limb. But Eliza met with, and let slip, most things in life with equal carelessness; and I could say in all honesty that the coiffure's gruesome style became her. I had never known her to adopt anything that did not.

"Eliza, my dear, you see how we are fixed," said my mother as she walked briskly into the room. "You see how unbearably cramped we are. We cannot hope to keep you, nor Henry. You *are* intending the Golden Lion, I suppose?"

"Naturally, madam," Eliza replied, and pecked my mother upon the cheek. "I have only just settled it that dear Jane shall walk with me there, that we might spare Cassandra our chatter. Her head aches fearfully, you know, though she never says a word."

"There, my love," my mother said with a start and a look for Cassandra, "I was almost forgetting. The young man who attended you earlier—Dervish, was it?—"

"Dagliesh," Cassandra supplied.

---

[4] Eliza's first husband, the French comte Jean Capot de Feuillide, was guillotined in 1794. Eliza retained her title of Comtesse de Feuillide even after she married Henry Austen, out of habit and a liking for its aristocratic air. —*Editor's note.*

"—begged that I should give you draughts of this green-bottled stuff whenever the pains take you." My mother adjusted her spectacles to peer at a slip of paper she held in her hand. " 'Two spoonfuls in warm water,' so Mr. Dawdle said, and seemed quite anxious I should get it right. He repeated it above three times, as though I were a woman of little memory and less sense. The meadow flowers were *not* to be steeped, as I had at first thought, but are to brighten your room."

"Flowers, Mother?" I enquired, looking behind the door.

"Oh, Lord," she breathed, "here I've left them below, when I thought to come up expressly for the purpose of setting them at your bedside. A lovely posy they are, and picked by Mr. Dawes himself. I believe you have made a conquest, my dear."

"Though she cannot recollect of *whom*," Eliza whispered, her eyes sparkling with fun.

"Madam," I called after my mother's swiftly retreating back, "do not neglect to bring hot water and a spoon, for the administering of Cassandra's medicine!"

FROM OUR COTTAGE TO THE GOLDEN LION WAS A PALTRY DISTANCE, and at my expressing a desire to stretch my legs a little— for, in truth, I had been so much taken up with my sister's care, that I had not spared a moment for the town—Eliza declared herself ready to try the Cobb, and accordingly, we joined arms and set off down the length of stone Walk, heads into the sea wind.

The Cobb is a massive rampart that effects to create a harbour, where none should otherwise exist, the seas surrounding this stretch of the Dorset coast being quite prone to sudden storms that eat away at the land. There are some who profess to remember land-falls about the town—sudden shiftings in the cliff, that cause earth and houses and all to slide into the sea, a most fearsome manifestation of Providence. But whatever its purpose, the Cobb is chiefly of use in being walked upon—by all manner of people, at all times of day. There are stairs ascending to the breakwater's upper edge, that only a foolish child or a brave fisherman should attempt;[5] but the lower, broader way is recently improved, and a walk along its stones is ideally suited to the exercise of a lady. Here Eliza and I braced ourselves against the blow, which tugged and swept at her feathered turban, and brought an exhilaration to both our strides. What glory, in facing once more the sea! What life, in its billowing waves—everchanging, ever-roving, to lands and climes of which I know nothing! When I gaze out at the endless horizon, I know a little of my brother Frank's days, in the blockade off the coast of France, or Charles's as he dreams of the East Indies;[6] what freedom such men possess, who call the world their home!

But at the thought of France, I was seized by a memory and a notion at once.

"Eliza," I said, as we ploughed ahead against the wind, "how great still is your command of the French language?"

"As great as my enjoyment of it, Jane—which is to say, excessively good."

"I had observed it to find its way into your conversation."

"Oh, *that*, my dear—when one has a reputation for liveliness, one is forever ejaculating bits of French and

---

[5] Austen probably refers here to the stairs she later used in her final novel, *Persuasion*, in which Louisa Musgrove falls in jumping from one level of the Cobb to another. —*Editor's note.*

[6] Francis Austen, born between Cassandra and Jane in the order of the Austens' eight children, and Charles, the youngest child, were both officers in the Royal Navy. Frank Austen would end his life as Admiral Sir Francis Austen, Admiral of the Fleet. —*Editor's note.*

Italian. It passes for breeding, in some parts of town. But you cannot mean *bêtise*," she said, as if suddenly struck. "Even *you* must know it to mean a stupidity."

"I thought it a *faux pas*," I rejoined, with a hint of dryness, at which Eliza laughed aloud.

"How I have missed you," she cried, patting my arm. "You must come to London this winter, my dear, and throw yourself in the way of some dashingly handsome murderer, so that I may have the enjoyment of following in your train as you go about exposing the man's vileness. In fact, *à propos* of vile men, I have several we might pretend are murderers, and expose for the fun of it. Nothing has been so delicious, I assure you, since you ended the Scargrave business so tidily. I have been quite overcome with *ennui;* but then, I always am in the summer. One so *wants* a little scandal, now and then, that one is almost tempted to make it oneself!"[7]

"Now, Eliza—" I cautioned.

"Oh, never mind, *chérie*. Unmixed felicity is rarely found in life, but your Henry knew when he married me that I was unaccustomed to control, and should probably behave very awkwardly, did he attempt it; and so, like the wise man he is, he makes *my* will his own.[8] And thus we get along quite happily."

"I am relieved to hear it."

"Of course you are. You mistrust the married state so well, you have never ventured near it yourself—and may be forgiven for assuming it to be the ruin of all those around you."

"I deserve neither such praise, nor such censure,

---

[7] Eliza refers to the first of Jane Austen's detective memoirs, *Jane and the Unpleasantness at Scargrave Manor.* —*Editor's note.*

[8] Eliza de Feuillide used words very similar to these to describe her marriage in a surviving letter written from Ipswich in 1798. —*Editor's note.*

Eliza!" I cried. "I should gladly have assayed the estate, had it been offered by a gentleman for whom I could feel sincere affection. But in cases where such affection was possible, the gentleman did not offer; and when it was the reverse, I could not accept."

"I am very sorry for it, Jane," Eliza replied soberly, "and for the unconscious cruelty of my words. I meant but to make a sport of men, in holding them up to your supposed derision; but I ended by wounding *you.*"

"Let us think no more about it," I replied, mortified at my own susceptibility; were my feelings regarding my single state, at the advanced age of eight-and-twenty, so exceedingly raw? But I shook off such thoughts and returned to my first subject. "Regarding your mastery of French," I said. "Can you give me the sense of a particular word, did I attempt to repeat it?"

"I can but try."

"Very well. I believe it was *lascargon.*" A French word spoken in the drawing-room at High Down Grange.

Eliza's brows lowered over her eyes with a pretty air of penetration. "But that means nothing, my dear Jane. You cannot have got it right."

"Think, Eliza. What *might* I have heard?"

"*Lascargon. Lascargon.* I suppose it might have been *les garçons*—the boys—or *La Gascogne,* a woman from Gascony, a province of France."

"That could very well be!" I cried, considering Seraphine. "But why did he not simply call her by name?"

We had achieved the end of the Cobb, and were thrust quite far out into the sea; a drenching plume of spray burst and churned against the rocks at our feet, and in the distance, a cutter sped by under full sail, its stern harried by seabirds. The breeze off the waves was decidedly stiff; and after a summer of Bath's closeness and poor drains, the smells of a city given over to medicinal waters, I revelled in Lyme's freshness, and breathed deep.

Eliza was not so sanguine. "Jane, my dear, I am all to pieces in this wind," she declared, turning about with a hand to her turban, "and your confusion of pronouns has quite worn out my patience. Let us turn round, and find our way to the Golden Lion, while you explain yourself."

And so, as the shadows of afternoon grew longer on the Cobb, and the gulls wheeled and dipped above our heads, I told Eliza of High Down Grange, and the mysteries of a lanthorn on the cliff edge at night.

"And you cannot place the girl Seraphine's purpose in the household," Eliza mused, her eyes upon the stones. "She seems neither a domestic nor a lady. Well! There is only one possibility remaining! She is his little French lovebird—though why he dresses her in sacks, and sends her about the shingle at night, I cannot undertake to say. You have once again found yourself the company of a rogue, my dear Jane, and we must know more of his character before such questions may be resolved."

"I do not think you have the right of it, Eliza," I protested. "Seraphine had not the look of a mistress."

"And what is *that*, in your understanding? An open vulgarity, a blowsy aspect, a decided want of taste? I assure you, the *chère amies* I have known—including my late husband's—were hardly as the novels have painted them." At my expression of horror, Eliza threw back her head and laughed. "I shock you, Jane; I am sure that I shock you; but, after all, that *is* my purpose in life. I continue to exist merely for the upsetting of Austen conventions. And when are we likely to encounter this most intriguing gentleman? At the Lyme Assembly?"

"I should not think Mr. Sidmouth prone to dancing. He wants the sort of easy temper that finds diversion in frivolity."

"Perhaps," Eliza replied. "Perhaps. But I would charge you to take care with your appearance on the morrow, in the event Mr. Sidmouth comes."

"You cannot believe me to wish for the attentions of such a man!" I protested.

"I can, and I do. Your air, when you speak of him, is hardly easy; and you were ever a girl to find the eccentric character more engaging than the open. You delight in *mystery*, my dear Jane; and Mr. Sidmouth has piqued your interest. Admit it! Your reddened cheeks even now bespeak your susceptibilities."

"Indeed they do not." My voice was sharp—but then, I *was* rather mortified. "They are merely brightened by the wind."

"I could find it in my heart to believe you, my dear," Eliza said comfortably, "did not the wind blow to our backs at present."

I HAD REASON TO PONDER ELIZA'S WORDS WHEN ONCE I HAD SEEN her safely into the care of her devoted maid, Manon, and her little dog, Pug, in the rooms Henry had engaged at the Golden Lion. I was returned once more to the street, and only steps from my cottage gate, when a brief scene unfolding near a shopfront opposite, drew my curious eye. A flash of a scarlet cloak, a stream of unbound blond hair, and the angelic features of Seraphine—and behind her, Mr. Sidmouth, his brows drawn down in an expression of angry contempt. Another man—a common labourer, and quite astoundingly tipsy, by his wavering appearance—was lounging in the shop doorway, an unattractive leer upon his face. That he had only just unburdened himself of a phrase of abuse, I read in his countenance; and knew Sidmouth's anger to be the result. Seraphine, to her credit, appeared unmoved. *Her* noble head was high, and her carriage graceful; she moved, as always, as though possessed of wings. I bent my head, much intrigued by what had passed, but desirous of drawing no attention from their quarter; and in a moment I had gained the safety of the cottage door. One further glance sufficed to tell me that the intimates of High Down were turned the corner; and I breathed a sigh of relief. But why? Why this emotion at the sight of *him,* and in *her* company? A man of whom I know next to nothing, and have even less reason to think well of; a man so little likely to prove congenial to my sensibility or expectations? The ways of the mind and heart are sometimes past all understanding.

Except, I am reminded, for the Elizas of this world.

Chapter 3

The Salty Gibbet

6 September 1804

~

CASSANDRA AND I WERE ROUSED FROM SLEEP AT DAWN BY THE HUE and cry of a large party of men; and when I had stumbled to the window, and o'erlooked the lightening Cobb,[1] I found them to be racing back along its length in an attitude of urgency. I might have spared a thought, in my fuddled state, to wonder at such a noise; but, in truth, I merely felt all the strength of honest resentment, in being roused so early by a party of brawling fisherfolk. Though I have lived more than three years in Bath, and must be accustomed to the sounds of a city's daybreak, I have not yet forgot the felicity of early-morning birdsong, and the gentler down of the country. And so I gaped, and glared once more upon the beach, in the direction from which the men were running—and started where I stood.

For the first rays of a rising sun had picked out the end

---

[1] Austen probably refers here to the beach that fronted Lyme's harbor, which is also called the Cobb, though not to be confused with the jetty of the same name. —*Editor's note.*

of the stone pier, to reveal erected there a scaffolding ominous in its outlines, even from the distance at which I beheld it; and depending from its crossbar, what appeared to be a bundle of clothing, swaying dejectedly in the stiff breeze off the sea. It must—it could not be other—than a parody of a man; a straw form, perhaps, for burning in effigy—or so my bewildered thoughts insisted, as I gazed with palpitating heart. For if it were truly a *man*, then he could not be otherwise than hanged. And how a man should meet his end in so extraordinary a manner—in a place I well knew to have been free of a gibbet only the previous afternoon—was past all understanding.

As I watched, a wave rose up and broke whitely against the rocks, drenching the crossbar's nerveless form, and the cries of the fleeing fishermen drew nearer.

"What is it, Jane?" came Cassandra's sleepy voice behind me. "A fire?"

"Nothing so general in its destruction," I said slowly, "though perhaps as inexplicable."

WHEN I HAD DRESSED, AND BADE THE HOUSEMAID, JENNY, TO SUPPLY Cassandra with tea and toast, I slipped on my bonnet—which was Leghorn straw, quite new, with an upturned brim and violet ribbons—and ventured out of doors. I had told my mother I wished to purchase a pair of gloves, my own being unhappily spotted from the effects of Monday night's rain; but, in truth, I intended to find what the townsfolk might tell me, of the body at the end of the Cobb.

I opened the picket gate, and turned onto Broad Street, making my way with care towards the linendraper's on Pound. Harding and Powell's is a bow-fronted building with a cheerful entry, much frequented by the Austens the previous year; indeed, the fifteen yards required for Cassandra's pink muslin, which I should wear this very evening, were purchased in the shop. But beyond the delights of its lengths of silk and lawn, its ravishing soutaches and braids, its pretty little bunches of purple grapes, ideally suited for the adorning of a straw hat with violet ribbons—the shop was the centre of gossip, according to the temper of its principal clerk, a fellow by the name of Mr. Milsop.

A bell tinkled prettily as I thrust open Harding's bottle-green door and stepped inside. The interior was pervaded with a peculiar mixture of scents, of the sneeze-inducing variety—part camphor, part dried roses, part good new cloth. I glanced quickly about, and found my eye drawn to a sprigged muslin *exactly* the colour of clotted cream, a shade I may pass off with a fair measure of success; but turned away with some regret, mindful of my errand.

A group of three very fine ladies was gathered at the counter, desirous of service—or perhaps of conversation; for I perceived the very Milsop, waspishly thin, and resplendent in a sky-blue tailcoat, striped breeches, and stiff white cravat, one elegant hand at rest upon the counter's edge, and the other holding high a quizzing glass,[2] the better to study his fair audience—with the occasional glint of sunlight, in catching the glass unawares, completing the dazzling effect.

And thus we have the caricature of our age—a gentleman of weak understanding, who apes the *form* of gentility in an effort to supply his want of *substance*. But I was not to be afforded further moments for contemplation, or assays of philosophy; the bell had drawn notice; I was seen and—to my great surprise—remembered. The paragon stiffened; the quizzing glass dropped on its silken cord; and condescension gave way to beatific pleasure.

[2] This was a long-handled lorgnette, with a single magnifying lens, that hung about fashionable necks. —*Editor's note.*

"Can it *be*? Is heaven so benevolent? Do I see before me the very Miss Austen—Miss *Jane* Austen—who brightened the tedious hours of an endless September past; whose delicate step, and dulcet voice, could lift my heart with her every visit—whose taste remains so far above *Lyme,* that I wonder at her repairing once more to these sadly dismal shores; whose understanding, penetration, and cunning ways with hat-trimming are not to be equalled? Or should I say,"—with a sudden recollection of the aforementioned audience—"equalled only by the ladies who stand before me now? And by her *own* sister as well, the lovely *Miss* Austen—but can it be?"

To stem a further efflorescence of this kind, I hastened forward, the embodiment of womanly virtue, and extended a gloved hand to Mr. Milsop. It was decidedly spotted, and a delicate frown twitched about the draper's eyes as he bowed gallantly low.

"I am come, as you see, Mr. Milsop," I began, with a nod to the ladies, whose company had parted coolly for my admittance, "under the direst necessity of a new pair of gloves. I was incommoded by a dreadful storm Monday last; and my things were all quite ruined with rain and mud. But I trust you shall have something that will answer."

"Answer? *Answer?* I have gloves that are *ravishing,* Miss Austen, gloves whose charms could never be denied. Silk gloves, in lilac and peach blossom; doeskin gloves, in day and evening lengths; knitted silk, or knitted cotton— Ah!" he cried, bending low over a counter and pulling open the glass, "*these,* perhaps? Or would silk serve better?"

Held out for my inspection were a delicately-netted pair, of the finest cotton lace. "Valenciennes," Mr. Milsop said, with the profoundest satisfaction; "and very dear."

"Then I fear they shall *not* do, for a seaside resort, where one is much exposed to the elements," I replied, with regret. "Such dust and sand, as fly about these streets, should have them soiled in a moment." I scanned the counter's array, and selected a pair of simple cotton gloves, undoubtedly the cheapest on offer in the establishment, and very like the ones I presently wore. Mr. Milsop's face fell; but he rallied, as was his wont, and found a virtue in simplicity.

"Such retiring taste—such a repugnance of show! Not for Miss Jane Austen the vulgarities of Spanish lace; *she* is the very soul of delicacy! I *quite* agree. Indeed, I *applaud* your choice. With consideration, one sees that no other glove in the world could be so suited to your hand. That will be four shillings."

There was a murmuring behind me, while the little show of exchanging coins occurred; and with a pricking of my ears, I knew the three ladies whose privilege I had displaced, were discussing the very incident of which I wished to learn more.

"His face was quite ghastly," said the eldest—a bold, queer-looking woman in her middle thirties, with the accent of an Englishwoman raised in Ireland. *That* accounted for the boldness, and perhaps the queerness as well—which must be said to have begun with her height, which was considerable, and her dress, a vivid green and white drapery in the Greek style, which swooped low across bosom and back, and was held at the shoulders by polished-steel clips in the form of heraldic arms. *Quite* unsuitable for day, unless I am hopelessly behindhand in my fashions; but her independence of attire was exceeded only by that of her slanting dark eyes, which roved everywhere, and drew back from no one.

"You cannot mean to say you *saw* it, Mrs. Barnewall!" ejaculated one of her companions—a sharp-featured girl of perhaps four-and-twenty, with ginger hair and an incompatible taste for pink.

"*Saw* it—alas, I had not the pleasure. I had the news of

my tyger,[3] who ran up to the gibbet when he should have been holding the horses.''

"The violence of the lower orders is not to be credited," the ginger-haired girl observed. "Why, only last week, Father ordered a tenant of ours be hanged; for you know that Father is a justice, and the man had poached one of our deer. Only imagine! So brazen! But it was an example, for the fellow had seven children, and his widow is turned out; so that now I fancy our deer shall run unmolested in the park.''

"For heaven's sake, Letty," the youngest of the three rejoined faintly, "do not *talk* so about the odious Cogginses. It quite turns my stomach; and you know I have not been at all well today. I think I shall have some of that yellow muslin, with the scattered border; I am sure it should improve my spirits immeasurably.''

"You have spent your purse already, and Father shall have my head for it," ginger-haired Letty replied; and tucking her sister's arm beneath her own, she exited the shop in all the complacency native to the possessor of a deer-park, however many unfortunates might be hanged to ensure its continuance.

"Mr. Milsop," the bold Irishwoman said, with an eye my way, "you have not been very kind. In fact, I must quite accuse you of cruelty. You have extolled the virtues of this lady to everyone who might listen; and yet, you deny us the felicity of an introduction. I am sure you mean to keep her acquaintance all to yourself, for fear that she shall like others better, and desert you.''

"My *dear* Mrs. Barnewall!" the counter fop cried. "It would be an *ecstasy* to make *two* such examples of womanly

[3] A tyger was a small boy arrayed in livery, almost as a mascot, whom the fashionable set employed to ride on the exterior of their carriages. —*Editor's note*.

excellence, known the one to the other." And before I could demur, he had turned to his office with alacrity.

"Miss Austen, may I introduce to your acquaintance Mrs. Mathew Barnewall, of Kingsland. Mrs. Barnewall, Miss Austen—of Bath, was it not?"

"Your faculty for placing your patrons is indeed remarkable, Mr. Milsop," I replied, and shook Mrs. Barnewall's hand.

"Bath! How delightful! You are a native of the place?" that lady enquired.

"I am not," I replied, "and, in truth, I cannot think of anyone who is. But that is to be expected, when one makes a pleasure-place a home."

"Indeed. You trade one pleasure-place for another, I see, in visiting Lyme."

"Ah! But the two are so different! The one merely *called* a pleasure-place, from convention and long familiarity; and the other, so infinitely capable of inspiring real happiness!"

I could not keep the admiration from my accent. Lyme is a town that has become dear to me, for reasons I cannot fully explain; unless it be that the smallness of such a place, particularly after its season has closed, offers a peace and solitary beauty I cannot find in Bath or London—a peace denied me since my removal from dear Steventon.

"You think such a village charming, then?" Mrs. Barnewall said, with obvious disbelief.

"Certainly there is little to admire in the buildings themselves," I conceded; "but the remarkable situation of the town! The principal street, almost hurrying into the water! The pleasant manner in which the Cobb skirts the bay, and the beautiful line of cliffs stretching to the east!—These are what a stranger's eye will seek, and a very strange stranger it must be, who does not see charms in the immediate environs, to make her wish to know Lyme better!"[4]

"But the people are so coarse, in general; one rarely encounters good society, beyond the doors of the Assembly Rooms. At this time of year, the town is overrun with common labourers and fisherfolk; and the degradations to which one is subjected! You have heard, I suppose, of the hanged man."

"Only a little," I said coolly. "But men may be hanged anywhere, I believe. I had understood it to be quite a common thing in Ireland."

"But in such a manner!" my new acquaintance cried. "The placement of the gibbet! The placard hung about his neck! The binding of his hands and feet! The mutilation of his features!"

"Of all *these,* I had not heard," I said, with greater interest. "There was a placard, you say?"

"Assuredly, my dear girl." Mrs. Barnewall advanced rather too rapidly to terms of intimacy for my taste, but in search of further particulars, I ignored her familiarity. "My tyger told me all of it. 'Done for as he did,' the words read, in ragged letters; and it was hung about his neck with a bit of fishing twine, of the sort such folk use for their nets."

"How very odd!" I said thoughtfully. "One supposes such violence to be the result of a bitter feud among the fishermen."

"Undoubtedly," Mrs. Barnewall replied, and loosed her parasol. "I trust, Miss Austen, I shall see you tonight at the Assembly. Not that it is worth the trouble of attending; neither so very good company, as to be called select, nor so very bad, that one might fancy it dangerously excit-

---

[4] These words, slightly modified and expanded, make up Austen's principal description of Lyme Regis in her final novel, *Persuasion.* —Editor's note.

ing. But when in Lyme, it may be termed a delight, for want of competition." And with a nod for Mr. Milsop, she took her leave.

"What a very singular lady," I said.

The draper stiffened and surveyed me narrowly with his quizzing glass. "The Honourable Mathew Barnewall is to be a viscount. He is heir to extensive estates in Ireland."

"And yet, even *that* does not explain his wife, my dear sir." I drew on my new gloves with a smile, and left the spotted pair on Milsop's counter.

IT WAS AS I APPROACHED WINGS COTTAGE THAT A PROCESSION FROM the Cobb neared where I stood, and I pressed hard against a neighbouring building so that they might more easily pass. A glimpse only of their sad burden did I have; but it was enough to nearly overpower me. Do not think, however, that it was the corpse's starting eyes, or its lolling tongue, or what Mrs. Barnewall had airily termed a "mutilation"—in this instance, a knife slash that opened one cheek—all these, I could have withstood. But the source of my faintness upon viewing the hanged man was entirely of another order. For I had seen these features and this fellow before—and only the previous afternoon, as he lounged in the doorway opposite, hurling what I believed to be drunken insults at the angelic Seraphine. The man had appeared to earn Geoffrey Sidmouth's contempt on that occasion, and possibly his rage. But as the body slowly passed, I wondered with a chill in my heart whether his impertinence had cost him even dearer—whether it had won him, in fact, the brutal manner of his death.

Chapter 4

Le Chevalier

7 September 1804

~

THE LYME ASSEMBLY ROOMS SIT ON BROAD STREET, AT BELL CLIFF and Cobb Gate, and their windows so o'erlook the sea, that when one is twirling in the midst of the floor (and well supplied with negus),[1] one might almost believe oneself aboard ship, and borne on the crest of a wave. Or so Captain Fielding observed; and as he is a Naval man, albeit lame in one leg and now retired, I must take his observations as more generally apt than most.

But I run ahead to the middle of the play, and neglect to draw open the curtain and set the scene; and so I give you the Reverend George Austen, attired in a shabby if respectable black tailcoat of uncertain vintage, his younger daughter by his side in her borrowed pink feathers, entering upon the Assembly at the stroke of eight o'clock. Henry and Eliza intended joining us later, believ-

---

[1] Named after Captain Francis Negus, this was a warm punch made of water, sugar, and sherry or port, and frequently offered at balls. —*Editor's note.*

ing the hour far too early for fashion; but I rejoiced to find the majority of Lyme society less nice in their distinctions, and the rooms already quite full, and of a happy mixture of ladies and gentlemen—the former being generally of that middle age that assures them either married or safely beyond susceptibility, and the latter retired Naval officers. Lyme has proved so attractive to the seafaring set, in fact, that a coterie of Naval families has settled in the cottages lining the streets of town; and their society seems at once so self-sufficient, and so cheerfully *good*, that one quite longs to marry a daring commander of the Red or White,[2] if only with a view to settling in Lyme some twenty years hence.

But perhaps Captain Fielding has influenced my views.

"What a fearful crowd, my dear Jane," my father remarked, in his vaguest tone, as though only just emerging from the leaves of his book. "Had not we better return to Wings cottage, and the society of your mother? For the crush is heavy, and we know no one." And he would have turned for the door, had I not seized his arm, and urged him firmly into the room.

"There are not above four-and-twenty couples, Father, and you know that in Bath we are commonly burdened with thrice that number. We cannot *know* anyone, unless we *meet* someone; and for that, you know, there is nothing like an Assembly."

"I wish your mother might have come, Jane. I wish I had insisted."

My mother remained at home, administering spoonfuls of medicine from Mr. Dagliesh's green bottle to a suffering, though improving, Cassandra.

---

[2] The Royal Navy was divided into three squadrons—the Red, the White, and the Blue. Austen's brother Frank, for example, advanced to become Admiral of the Red, before his promotion to Admiral of the Fleet at the age of 89. —*Editor's note.*

"I think, sir, that you will like the card room. I am sure that whist is to be played there. Shall I conduct you thither, and claim a chair?"

"But what of yourself? You will be all unchaperoned!"

I stifled my impatience—and stilled my foot, which *would* tap in time to the music, the orchestra having just struck up the first dance; and considered the Reverend's delicacy. Despite having almost nine-and-twenty years, I remain for my father a chit of a girl, and shall claim such attentions as long as he is able to give them. But on a sudden thought, I searched the gay throng for the one woman whose acquaintance I might claim in Lyme, the better to still my father's fears. I had only to look for the peevish young ladies met with that very morning at the linendraper's—and there I very soon found her, standing a head above her companions and arrayed in a cloth-of-gold costume cut along Egyptian lines, with a circlet of rubies in her black hair. She had a gentleman on either arm—*one* of whom must surely be her husband.

"There, Father!" I cried, turning him in the proper direction. "I see my acquaintance, Mrs. Barnewall. She is the wife of the Honourable Mathew Barnewall, of Ireland, whom I understand is to have the viscountcy of Kingsland."[3]

"Barnewall, do you say?" my father replied doubtfully. "She looks rather like an actress."

"My dear Miss Austen," Mrs. Barnewall cried, swooping down upon me from her considerable height, and bearing with her several of her party; "how lovely you look. As fresh as a rose from an English hedgerow. Does

[3] Mathew Barnewall was at this time only a claimant to the viscountcy of Kingsland, and his right to that title and inheritance was not yet determined by the House of Lords. It is unlikely that Jane Austen was aware of this dispute when she met the Barnewalls. —*Editor's note.*

not she look lovely, Captain Fielding? I am sure you admire her. So much loveliness cannot be resisted, even by *le Chevalier.*"

The man to whom she spoke was neither in that first youth, as to be called callow, nor so advanced in years, as to appear beyond the temptation of so daring a woman as Mrs. Barnewall; but he had the grace to look discomfited by the lady's effusions, which could not help but recommend his character to me. He bowed low, and offered a smile, and asked if he might beg an introduction. At which point, I found myself indebted to the bold Mrs. Barnewall for the chief of my pleasure that evening.

She looked first to the ladies in her train. "The Miss Schuylers, of Shropshire, I believe you have seen already, Miss Austen," she said, "but may I have the honour of presenting Miss Letitia, Miss Susan, and Miss Constance Schuyler to your acquaintance."

The first and second were familiar; the third, their youngest sister—left behind, it would seem, on the morning's visit to Mr. Milsop.

I nodded; the other three bowed; and there our mutual interest ended.

"They are also privileged, in being able to call Percy—Captain Fielding—our cavalier."

At my expression of enquiry, Captain Fielding looked diffident, and would have turned away, the better to avoid explanation, but Mrs. Barnewall intervened.

"There!" she cried. "Was ever a man so perverse in accepting praise! I assure you, Miss Austen, that Captain Fielding comes by the name through nothing dishonourable, as his countenance would suggest. But I shall leave you to tease him about the story, and so give you grounds for conversation; for one *must* talk in the dance, and I am sure he means to ask you."

Captain Percival Fielding is of good height and very well-made, with fair hair, a quick blue eye, a sudden smile, and the ruddy countenance of a man accustomed to being and doing in all weathers. That he is possessed of a wooden leg joined just below the knee detracts not at all from his charm; if anything, it adds a certain dash to his otherwise commonplace appearance. His impediment certainly *impedes* him very little, as I was to learn in the course of the evening; for tho' he forewent this first dance in order to make my acquaintance, to enquire as to my engagement for the next, required but a moment; and for my acceptance of his offer, only another.

"And I believe this is your father, Miss Austen? For we have not been introduced," Mrs. Barnewall said.

I hastened to amend my stupidity, and made each known to the other; and was made acquainted myself with the gentleman on Mrs. Barnewall's *other* arm, who was no more the Honourable Mathew than the Captain. A Mr. Crawford, an elegantly dressed gentleman of undistinguished countenance, balding head, and perhaps five-and-forty years—a widower possessed, so Mrs. Barnewall tells me, of a prettyish sort of place called Darby, out east along the Charmouth way.

"We were just speaking," Mrs. Barnewall said, "of that dreadful business on the Cobb."

My father looked vague.

"The hanged man, Father," I supplied.

"Ah, yes—dreadful business, dreadful." He looked a trifle dismayed—at a lady's advancing the topic, I imagined, rather than the topic itself.

"They say he must be one of the Reverend's men, and killed by a rival," the ginger-haired Letty Schuyler remarked.

"And *I* heard that it was the Reverend did the deed," her sister Susan rejoined scornfully, "because the man betrayed his trust."

"But what of the flower?" Captain Fielding objected.

"Flower?" I enquired, all attention to every detail.

"A white flower was found near the hanged man," Mrs. Barnewall supplied. "It is the talk of all Lyme."

"A rose, was it not?" This, from Letty Schuyler.

"No, no!" her sister Constance cried. "It was a lily. I have heard the Reverend intended it as a sign, but know not *what* it signifies."

"But should a man of the cloth be likely to commit murder at all?" my father cried indignantly. "We are *not* in Rome, where all manner of evil may be perpetrated in an odour of sanctity. The Church of England may be charged with many faults—a laxity of moral purpose, betimes, and an unbecoming luxury, on occasion; to such faults any *human* institution may be prone. But the taking of a life! I profess myself quite shocked that you may credit the notion, and toss it about as a commonplace among yourselves."

"My dear Reverend Austen," Mr. Crawford said with a knowing air, and great good humour, "you quite mistake the Miss Schuylers. They speak not of a clergyman like yourself—ho! ho! a very good joke *that* would be—but of a notorious scoundrel who devils these parts—the very Reverend, who is famed for bringing contraband goods from France, and supplying all of England with his wares."

"A smuggler!" I cried. "I had not an idea of it!"

"Indeed, Miss Austen," Captain Fielding replied, "the Dorsetshire coast has ever been prey to the evil. The Reverend is merely the latest ringleader of an ancient trade indeed. The Gentlemen of the Night, as such fellows presume to call themselves, have long plied the coves and secret harbours of the very waters beyond those windows." And with a bow to the ladies, he added, "I must declare myself quite of the Miss Schuylers' opinions."

"But which?" the youngest, and the prettiest, enquired with a winning smile. "For you know, Letty and Susan cannot either of them agree."

"I think either equally possible, for the Reverend's hand is certainly behind the gibbet," the Captain diplomatically replied.

"And I, Fielding, cannot see the sense of it," Crawford broke in. "The man's livelihood depends upon his discretion. Why, then, take the fellow's life in so public a manner? Would it not have been better to settle the score in privacy, and in the dark of night? A man might be thrown over the side of a swift galley, on a run from Boulogne, and no one the wiser. No," the good gentleman continued, sliding a hand into his ample waistcoat pocket, "I think the gesture too public. The scaffold was quite deliberately placed at the end of the Cobb. We might almost think ourselves recalled to Monmouth's time.[4] There is more here than meets the eye; the hanging was meant for an example. A message has been sent."

"But to whom?" I enquired.

"There's the rub of it. And *from* whom?" Mr. Crawford's balding pate began to shine with the honest sweat of his enthusiasm.

"I still hold to the Reverend," Captain Fielding said stubbornly.

"But *who*, my good man, is *he*?"

"You mean to say that the miscreant has never been seen?" my father interjected, with some astonishment.

"Not a glimpse or a whisper has anyone had," Mrs. Barnewall said exultantly. "The man is said to operate in such disguise, that even his lieutenants may not know him in daylight, much less the Crown's drunken dragoons. On

---

[4] Crawford is speaking of James, Duke of Monmouth, the bastard son of Charles I, who sailed from France to Lyme in 1685, intent upon toppling his uncle James II from the throne of England. His revolt was suppressed, and twelve men of Lyme were hanged on gibbets erected in the shallows of the beach where Monmouth landed. —*Editor's note.*

this depends his success; so that nothing is more guarded than the Reverend's identity."

"I thought to have seen him once," Mr. Crawford said, turning to my father, "at my fossil site. A party of men beached a boat just below the cliffs, and commenced unloading a cargo. But the cargo turned out to be fish—and there is nothing very contraband about that, you know."

Amid general laughter, my father's interest was swiftly diverted by the mention of fossils; and the two men were soon engrossed in a discussion well-suited to the interests of them both. I rejoiced in the discovery of Mr. Crawford—a man of little physical distinction, being of short stature, decided rotundity, and middle years, but possessed of an intellect that must be pleasing to my father. I had not the opportunity of knowing Mr. Crawford better, however; for as with one thought, the two older gentlemen moved towards the card room, still talking of botany and cliffs, and the Reverend Austen did not reappear for the majority of the evening.

"Lord!" Mrs. Barnewall cried. "I am perishing of thirst! And *where* has my husband got to? Playing at loo, again, and playing high, I've little doubt. Come along, Letty, and preserve me from boredom. I am sure you should like a glass of wine as much as me."

And with a nod on my side, and several insincere simpers on theirs, the Barnewall retinue moved towards the supper room in a swirl of trains and delicate shawls.

I found myself quite alone with Captain Fielding, and under the pain of the moment, cast about for a topic; several were adopted and discarded as unsuitable; and though my curiosity was raised, I resolved *not* to ask for the meaning behind *le Chevalier*, since the Captain had appeared so little inclined to discuss it. But I was saved all the trouble. The music began, the Captain bowed, and we moved into the dance.

"You have been in Lyme before, I think," he began. "I

am sure that I observed you in this very room, some months ago."

"It is exactly a twelvemonth since I visited Lyme," I cried, all astonishment. "How came we not to meet before?"

"I was little able to *dance* before this summer, Miss Austen; and you will observe that I manage it now with a very poor grace," the gentleman replied, with a wry look for his game leg.

"You were wounded in service?"

"Off Malta, in '99; a brush with the Monster's forces.[5] I was unlucky enough to be on the gunnery deck at the very moment a cannon came loose; and the full force of a thirty-two-pounder rolled over my leg—which was, as a consequence, removed on the spot."

At my sympathetic ejaculation, he returned a smile. "In one fell swoop I went from Post Captain to millstone about the necks of my men. I was fortunate, however, in having a First Lieutenant of the first water; and we prevailed before the night was through."

I thought of dear Frank, and dearest Charles, and shuddered despite the heat and noise of the rooms—for how much danger and horror might they even now endure, far from home and the expediency of news; they

---

[5] "The Monster" was the common appellation for Napoleon Buonaparte. Captain Fielding probably alludes to the seventeen-month-long British, Russian, and Neapolitan blockade of French forces holding Malta in 1799. The final French surrender in March of that year was marked by a daring escape attempt on the part of Admiral Denis Decrès, who barely survived to be named Napoleon's Naval Minister in 1801. The nearly 1000 men on his ship, the *Guillaume Tell*, were hardly so fortunate; Decrès gave up his opportunity to escape in order to attack the British fleet single-handedly, and lost 500 men under fire. Badly wounded himself, he was taken prisoner and released after the Treaty of Amiens in 1801. Presumably, Captain Fielding lost his leg in the midst of Decrès's attack. —*Editor's note.*

might yet be killed, and we know nothing of it for weeks or months. My depth of feeling must have been written upon my countenance, for Captain Fielding's voice noticeably softened.

"You cannot be so moved on a stranger's account," he said, with concern. "Someone dear to you is similarly engaged in battle, even now?"

"My brothers," I replied. "Perhaps you know them. Commander Charles and Captain Frank Austen, of the Red."

"I was of the Blue, I fear," Captain Fielding replied, "and though I may have heard the name of Austen, I cannot in honesty claim acquaintance with your brothers. They are presently at sea?"

"Frank is with Rear Admiral Louis, in the flagship *Leopard* off the coast of Boulogne. They are blockading there, and constantly exposed to enemy fire. I fear for Charles less; he awaits his transfer to the East India station."

"But a storm or misadventure may strike as readily there as in the heat of action." Captain Fielding's tone was pensive, and I felt all the injury his brave spirits must endure, in being forced into retirement at the very moment hostilities were renewed. "You may look for their rapid advancement, however," he said, thrusting aside regret and affecting a cheerful air, "now Buonaparte is likely to invade. Many brilliant careers are forged in battle."[6]

"You think an invasion likely, then?"

"You will have heard that the schoolgirls of Portsmouth keep blankets under their beds, equipped with

---

[6] The Peace of Amiens, negotiated in October 1801 and broken in May 1803, brought peace to France and England only briefly. A year later, in May 1804, Napoleon crowned himself emperor of France, and hostilities between the two countries continued until 1815. —*Editor's note.*

tapes for hasty donning, lest they be routed from their rooms in the dead of night," he replied, "and what schoolgirls plan with conviction, must not be subject to question."

I rewarded this attempt at humour with a smile; but indeed, so close to the seas of the Channel as a glance through the window revealed me to be, I could not be completely sanguine.

"With your brothers to defend us, Miss Austen, I am sure we have little to fear," the Captain said gallantly. And so we continued through the dance, each blessed with the pleasantest associations regarding the other, and anxious to share the burden of our hearts.

Talk of war and the Navy, however, soon gave way to the subject of the Captain's tenancy of a country house some two miles distant, on the Charmouth road, and of our own Wings cottage.

"You came then, only a few days ago!" he exclaimed. "How fortunate that I did not neglect to attend the Assembly, and thus lose some part of your time here!"

I smiled, and turned aside out of embarrassment, for the genuine ardour of his expression proclaimed his delight. But in turning thus, I espied a gentleman standing patiently behind me, awaiting a word.

"Mr. Dagliesh!" I said with a nod. "I am happy to see you."

"The pleasure is mine, Miss Austen," the surgeon's assistant replied, and bowed, with less animation, to Fielding. "Forgive me for overlistening your conversation—it was unintentionally done. I crave only to learn how your fair sister mends."

"Decidedly well, under your careful attention," I replied. "She should have accompanied us hither, had I not wrested her prize gown from her grasp, and forced her to keep to her rooms."

"I am glad to learn that she prefers retirement to premature activity," Mr. Dagliesh said earnestly. "Had I found her present tonight, I should have urged her return to bed. She should not be abroad for some days yet; far better that she rest, and heal her wound—"

"—And gaze upon the flowers you so thoughtfully provided for a sickroom," I told him archly. The figure requiring me to turn my back upon the surgeon, I was spared the sight of his flushed cheeks by the exigencies of the dance.

"Please extend my compliments to Miss Austen," he said, and with a click of the heels and a bow, moved on.

"You are acquainted with Mr. Dagliesh?" Captain Fielding enquired, with a slight frown and a penetrating look.

"The acquaintance was forced upon us, by a misadventure that befell us as we entered Lyme," I replied. "Though the gentleman is so open and cheerful, and his intentions so well-placed, that I cannot consider the acquaintance burdensome."

"Assuredly not—though I could wish him to belong to a more reputable set."

"You know something to Mr. Dagliesh's disadvantage?" I enquired, all curiosity. "Then pray reveal it, Captain Fielding, I beg of you! For I believe him quite susceptible to my sister's charms, and would not have her thrown in the way of a scoundrel."

"Of Dagliesh himself, I can say nothing ill," Fielding conceded. "It is of his friends—of the people with whom he spends the better part of his idle hours—that I would take issue."

"You mean Mr. Sidmouth!" I spoke with all the energy of conviction, and a desire to know more.

"I do," the Captain rejoined, with something like relief at being spared the necessity of broaching the man's name. "I have observed that gentleman's ways for some time, Miss Austen, and I cannot like them. I should hesitate to introduce any lady I held in true esteem, to their pernicious influence. But how do you know of Sidmouth?"

"He is another whose friendship we did not seek. We were overturned in a violent storm near High Down Grange Monday e'en. My poor sister, I fear, was gravely hurt, and even now suffers from her injury."

"But that was you!" cried Captain Fielding. "*You* were of the unfortunate party! My own house lying not above a half-mile from the Grange, I had occasion to see your coach righted by a team and dray the following morning, and wondered, as I passed on my way into Lyme, what rude events had occasioned such misfortune."

"And had we but known, we might have sought shelter from *you*," I observed. "Fate is a fickle mistress, is she not? For instead, we toiled up the hill to the Grange, and met with an uncertain welcome, and some very odd inmates indeed, in whose bosom we were forced to reside for some two days."

"I regret it," the Captain replied, with feeling. "Could I have spared your dear family from such an inhospitable abode, I should have done all that was in my power. But I was not to be allowed, and Sidmouth was afforded the pleasure of your company."

"He did not seem to find it a *pleasure*," I said. "Indeed, he spent as much time out of doors as possible, the better to avoid us."

"You may consider yourself fortunate, Miss Austen. He is not a man to entertain for many hours together." After a little, with an air of hesitancy, he asked, "You met the Mademoiselle LeFevre, I suppose?"

"I could not undertake to say. A woman I *did* see, who I think was called Seraphine; but as she was never properly introduced, I cannot tell you if she was the same."

An expression of anger suffused Fielding's countenance, and he seemed too overcome to speak; but finally, with a little effort at a smile, and a quick glance of the eyes, he unburdened himself. "I must apologise, Miss Austen, for the violence of my feelings," he told me; "but I cannot observe that gentleman's treatment of his cousin, without some indignation and general outrage."

"His cousin!"

"Indeed, a cousin from France, who first fled the deprivation of her estates, and the murder of her family, in the old King's time. She has been resident in England some ten years, and under Sidmouth's care."

"But it seems impossible!" I cried. "I thought her no higher than a servant, from the manner in which she was dressed, and the air of general command he enjoyed in her presence."

"I fear that you saw nothing out of the ordinary way," the Captain replied, his lips compressed. "Sidmouth rules her frail life with an iron hand; and she is so far dependent upon him, as to make her prey to every degradation. I very much fear—I have reason to wonder—if she is not *entirely abandoned* to his power, Miss Austen, in a manner that no honourable man should tolerate. To consider *his own* advantage, when he was charged by her dying father to protect *hers*, is in every way despicable; but I must believe him to have sunk even as low as this. I pity Mademoiselle LeFevre; I am stirred by the outrage she daily endures; but I cannot intervene. I have not the cause. Not yet."

I was overcome by this confidence, and all amazed at the depravity it bespoke; and though I wondered a little at Captain Fielding's imparting so much of a rumoured nature, to a lady and a virtual stranger, I silently applauded the fine sensibility that encouraged his indignation, and felt a warmth of respect for his concerns. Of Seraphine LeFevre, I thought with renewed pity, and of Sidmouth, with contempt.

Our dance coming to a close with the Captain's last words, he bowed gravely and I curtseyed, somewhat lost in thought. My gallant partner then suggesting we should repair to the supper room, I gladly took the arm he offered me, being somewhat out of breath from the double exertion of conversation and dance, and allowed myself to be led in search of punch and pasties.

Fielding shook his head. "The man's charm is considerable. I am sure—I cannot but assume—that you felt its force yourself. Consider then how the people of a town, who feel only the *public* benefits of association with such a man, are more generally likely to forgive his private sins. Sidmouth has spent such sums on the betterment of Lyme, as to ensure his place in the hearts of the Fane family and their creatures, who all but control the town;[7] he cuts a handsome figure at the Assemblies; his taxes are paid, his tithes collected—and if he continues to form a part of a roguish set, much given to gaming and general drunkenness in its hours of idleness—so be it."

"I am shocked," I cried, "shocked and saddened. Men who have much power for good, seem always that much more tempted to evil; and that it should be the reverse, in the eyes of Providence, holds but little sway."

"My dear, my most excellent Miss Austen," Captain Fielding replied, with some emotion; "you have given voice to my very thought. I hope our two minds may be always in concert."

I thought then, with a rush of foreboding, of the hanged man at the end of the Cobb, the scene I had witnessed the previous day, and my own doubts of Mr. Sidmouth's motives. I suspected another incitement to

[7] Captain Fielding here refers to the Earl of Westmoreland and his family, resident in Bristol but controlling Lyme's two parliamentary seats through corrupt voting practices. The Fanes dominated Lyme for roughly a century—from the 1730s until the Reform Act of 1832, when the borough was reduced to one MP. In 1867 it was disenfranchised completely. (See John Fowles, *A Short History of Lyme Regis*, Little, Brown & Co., 1982.) —*Editor's note.*

murder—one that had nothing to do with the notorious Reverend or his smuggled goods. But to voice such fears and suspicions, even to Captain Fielding, on the strength of so little, must be impossible; the ruin of Mr. Sidmouth's reputation—nay, even his life—might hang upon such idle talk.

It could not do harm, however, to probe what more Captain Fielding might know of the murky affair.

We had secured refreshment and moved towards the settee at one end of the room, before I took up my subject.

"Lyme seems particularly prone to such grotesqueries of character as Mr. Sidmouth displays," I observed, as I settled myself delicately upon the edge of a cushion. "The hanged man on the Cobb, for example. It was a very *singular* example of crudery, was it not?"

A look of surprise from Captain Fielding, and a hesitation; for a Mrs. Barnewall to raise such matters, might be acceptable, but for a Miss Austen to broach them, apparently was not.

"Poor Tibbit," he answered at the last, as he eased himself next to me and extended his game leg before him. "He leaves a wife and five children, and all ill-provided for."

"You knew him then? How tragic! And nothing is known, I suppose, of his murderers?"

"Nothing." The Captain offered me a glass of wine, his fingers grazing my own. Unless my eyes misgave me, his hand trembled at the touch. "The fellow was a scoundrel, of course; he has turned up at my home a thousand times, to labour in the garden or mend a stone wall. The sort of idler who can be hired for a few pence, in the performing of odd jobs—which sums are as quickly dissipated at the Three Cups, as turned to his children's account. Tibbit shall not be missed, even by his wife."

"But is that reason to ignore the manner of his end?" I

enquired gently, as I took a sip of punch. "Is not the death of even the slightest creature of weight in the scales of justice?"

"Oh! But of course! If you would look for a *reason* in his death, Miss Austen, you need search no further than the manner of his *life*. I will wager that if Bill Tibbit did not meet his end at the hands of the Reverend, then it was through some fellows he double-crossed, in an affair of devilry; and though the local justice were to question the entire village, and solemnly record their protestations of innocence, and preoccupation with their affairs on the night in question, he should not arrive at the truth of it. No, Miss Austen"—the Captain said, drawing me back towards the ballroom as the musicians recommenced— "the scales of justice are balanced already. Bill Tibbit knows why he is dead, I warrant; but that *we* shall ever know, is quite unlikely."

IT WAS SOME HOURS LATER, AS I WAS RESTING IN THE COMFORT OF AN alcove settee, having danced with Mr. Crawford, and a few of Captain Fielding's brother officers (who had gone in search of negus), that Mr. Sidmouth arrived. Mindful of all that the Captain had told me, I felt some little trepidation upon perceiving the master of High Down; a confusion of disapprobation and dislike, which warred with my appreciation of his appearance. For indeed, he showed to greater advantage in his dark blue tailcoat and cream-coloured breeches, than he had in an open shirt, standing in his doorway on a rainy night. The fine figure, the aquiline line of his nose, the dark glow of brown eyes, the sternly commanding countenance—all these cried out *nobility* where I now knew there to be only the vilest propensities. He divested himself of hat and walking stick, drew on his white gloves, and commenced to scan the room, as though in search of acquaintance; and an expression of glad alacrity encompassing his features not long thereafter, I assumed he had found it. A brisk step, a bow—and I was to see him exert his charms upon a slip of a girl, not above nineteen, and very pretty at that. She was accompanied by an older, shrewish-looking woman, dressed all in mourning, whose aspect held less of warmth in regarding Mr. Sidmouth; and at their being joined presently by Mr. Crawford, I presumed the ladies to be of his household. But I had not time to observe their conversation, for behind Mr. Sidmouth stood Henry and Eliza.

I judged from the animation of the Comtesse's countenance that she had succeeded in scraping acquaintance with the master of High Down Grange. Her cheeks glowed, her eyes snapped, under the recent influence of his brusque regard; and Henry's brow bore a faint crease, as though already wearied by this rival for his wife's attentions.

"Jane!" Eliza called, as she tripped on her small feet, encased in red satin slippers, across the room. Her bobbed brown head was adorned with pearls, and a cameo locket circled her neck on a length of dark red ribbon; her dress was of cream sarcenet, very fine for Lyme, and trimmed in the same rosy hue. Her gown slipped well down upon her arms, showing to advantage her excellent shoulders and bosom, in a manner that was all the London rage, but which must have afforded dear Henry some anxious moments. What artistry the maid Manon employed to keep Eliza so bountifully displayed, and yet still *clothed*, never failed to amaze me.

"I have met your roguish suitor," she confided, as she pecked me on the cheek, "and I applaud your taste. He will quite do for a heartless flirtation."

"Do you imagine yourself to voice *my* intentions, Eliza, or your own?"

"Now, do not scold me, Jane. You know me too well to

imagine I should steal your beaux. I am five-and-thirty at least."

In fact, she was three-and-forty, some ten years older than my brother Henry; but with a woman such as Eliza, whose beauty and spirits defy attempts to cage them, the flow of years is best left untallied. It may be that she had long since forgot to consider the anniversaries of her birth, and sincerely believed herself on the flow tide of forty; what is certain, in any case, is that age had no power to repress her.

"Mr. Sidmouth is *not* my beau," I replied with asperity, "and I may say with feeling that I hope he never may be. I have heard such things of him tonight, Eliza, as confirm my worst suspicions. I believe him *now* to be the very worst sort of fellow, and must thank Providence for having allowed us to come to so little harm while under his roof."

"Oh, pshaw!" Eliza rejoined. "I see you are determined to sink me in respectability. I will *not* have it." She settled herself beside me and glanced quickly about the room, a sharp-eyed bird. "And with whom have you been dancing? For it can only be another man who would strip Sidmouth of his good name. Only one anxious to win your affections would attempt to assassinate his character."

"I must disagree, Eliza," I said drily, "for it seems calumny is more properly the province of women. Men have other weapons, that may carry mortal injury; but a lady may use only words."

"Unless she employs poison, as she did at Scargrave," Eliza said, sidelong, "but then gossip may be considered one of the most lethal of *those*, I suppose. I will not be convinced, Jane. A rival for your interest has torn Mr. Sidmouth's reputation. *Do* admit."

"And there he comes," I replied, as the gallant but limping form of the Captain appeared through the throng, "bearing a cup by way of peace-offering. Will you dance, Eliza, or have you the time to be acquainted with Captain Percival Fielding?''

But she was denied the opportunity to answer.

"Miss Austen of Bath," Mr. Sidmouth said at my shoulder. "You look very well this evening."

I turned, intending to cut him with a glance—but that glance, in revealing all the power of his manner and appearance, instantly overwhelmed me. I settled for a wordless nod, and took refuge in averted eyes.

"Do I presume too much—or may I have the honour of this next dance?"

I opened my mouth to declare myself already engaged, when the change in Mr. Sidmouth's complexion stopped the words in my mouth. His gaze was fixed by something beyond my head, and as I watched, his countenance was suffused with colour, then paled to a deathly white.

"Mr. Sidmouth," Captain Fielding said with a bow, and handed me a glass of negus.

The master of High Down nodded almost imperceptibly, turned on his heel without another word or look for me, and thrust his way back towards the opposite side of the ballroom.

"Well, my dear," Eliza said wryly, "he saved himself the misery of your refusal." She glanced at Captain Fielding, as if in hopes of an explanation; but she was to receive none. He bowed, and smiled, as though unaffected by the recent scene, and looked to me for introduction.

Recovering myself, I made the fair Eliza known to the Captain, and the two were soon engrossed in conversation. But I found I was little suited to following its conduct; my eyes would too often search the room, and find him first in close confidence with Mr. Dagliesh, and then upon the arm of one of the Miss Schuylers; and so, vexed with too contrary a nature, and torn between wishing for, and fearing, a renewal of his address, I went in search of my father; and departed the Assembly not long thereafter.

"WELL, MY DEAR JANE, I AM QUITE INDEBTED TO YOU," SAID THAT good gentleman, as we walked the length of starlit Broad Street behind our man James and his lanthorn. "Crawford is a most excellent fellow! Such industry, in the pursuit of science! Only think—he has engaged a team of men, for the express purpose of digging for fossils! We are to visit the site on the morrow. You must certainly accompany me, and your sister, too, if she is able."

"Fossils, Father? I cannot profess an interest in bits of old stone."

"Now, now. Did they have the lettering of ancient Rome upon them, you should moon about their ranks in reflection of fallen glory, and think yourself a lady of Caesar's time, and indulge in every romantic fantasy open to a girlish heart. I know you, Jane. You merely want persuasion. Consider the smallest invertebrate, impaled for eternity upon the rock, as a minor centurion, and you shall suffer the visit in good grace." We walked on some moments in silence, while I considered my plans for the morrow—which had encompassed nothing of a fossilised nature—until my father overthrew all my complacency.

"Yes, fossils are quite the rage in Lyme, I understand," he said. "Even Mr. Sidmouth intends to be of the party."

"Mr. Sidmouth," I said, faltering.

"But of course," my father replied. "He is a man of great sense and intelligence, so Mr. Crawford says."

"Mr. Crawford!" What *could* the retiring widower, of kindly if balding aspect, have to say to Mr. Sidmouth?

"I hope you do not intend to repeat *everything* I say, Jane. I may have attained a venerable age, but my memory is equal to the length of a conversation. I wish that I could say the same of your dear mother's." My father halted at the gate of Wings cottage, peering absent-mindedly at our stoop. "Have we come home so soon, James? Have you found the number directly?"

"That I have, sir—number ten, as you'll see." The manservant raised the lanthorn in a swinging arc that sent light and shadows at a run across the cottage's facade.

"And so Mr. Crawford and Mr. Sidmouth are on such excellent terms that Mr. Crawford may praise his understanding," I mused, as I preceded my father up the path. "I should not have considered them the most likely of friends."

"Indeed. I am assured by Mr. Crawford that we could not have chosen a better place to overturn and that there is nothing like Mr. Sidmouth for decency and good sense. Quite the prop of Lyme, from what I understand." My father pushed open the gate and motioned for me to precede him. "I quite look forward to knowing him the better—for I confess I did not think much of your Mrs. Barnewall, Jane, nor all her pretty little friends. More form than substance, hey? And so pronounced a taste for rubies as she displays must always be suspect."

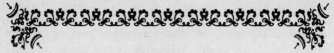

Chapter 5

The Surgeon, the Captain, the Rogue, and His Carriage

7 September 1804, cont.

~

I AROSE RATHER LATE THIS MORNING, DUE TO THE FATIGUES OF THE previous evening, but still well before my fellows in Wings cottage; and so I availed myself of the interval until breakfast to take a solitary ramble along the Cobb. I found it cleansed by the tides of its sinister associations; the scaffolding had disappeared, and with it, all hint of intentional evil. The stones at my feet were awash in early sunlight and cold spray; and I walked briskly, glad of the calls of seabirds, and suffused with pleasure at the turning season. September is a month of paradoxes—part decaying summer, part incipient autumn; and the complexity of its character decidedly suits my own. Not that I believe the deeper nature to be more *worthy* of study than the simple—but complexity is assuredly more compelling to the student than transparency. Captain Fielding, for instance, could be likened to June—forthright, warm, and easy. Mr. Sidmouth, however, is neither summer nor its frigid counterpart, deepest January; he is a November of a month, or perhaps a March—that mix of sudden sunlight and chill wind that keeps one always alert for change.

So I mused, as I walked; and did not neglect to ask whether one should be better suited to a lifetime of June, than an eternity of November—a question I deferred answering until another day.

At the Cobb's end, I halted, and eyed uneasily the marks of recent building; did I close my eyes, the shape of the gibbet should be revealed as etched upon my veiled sight, and the spray-drenched form of Bill Tibbit depending from its ominous bar. Such a fearsome structure could not have been *carried* to this place—even at night, its progress from town should be remarked—and so, at a thought, I gathered up my skirts, removed my right glove, and crouched down to search the rocks at waterline. A few moments' groping sufficed; an iron ring was revealed to my hand, and the manner of Tibbit's dispatching confirmed. Flakes of rust were smeared across my palm—I blessed the foresight that had removed Mr. Milsop's perfection of a glove—and that the flakes were but lately displaced, I quickly discerned. A boat's painter had disturbed the iron ring, in being recently tied up at the Cobb's end, and the vessel's burden then shifted to the stones, no doubt in the very dead of night. A little time indeed might prove sufficient for such a hanging, and poor Tibbit's cries had surely gone all unheeded at this distance from the town.

I paused a moment, to ease my aching muscles—such bending and reaching, while wearing tight-laced stays, can only be called exertion—and glanced back at Lyme. An increase in activity along Broad Street heralded the advancing morning; I had better make my way back to Wings cottage. And so I bent to the stones once more, and leaned quite far over to gaze at the ring in the rocks, and saw then the marks of paint.

But of course! When a simple wooden boat is moored

near the jetty, the tide *must* drive it against the stones, particularly if its crew is bent upon the destruction of one in their midst, rather than the preservation of their vessel. And so the dinghy's prow had scraped against the Cobb, and left its telltale mark. A dark green, a very bottle green, and common enough in its way among the fishing boats of Lyme. I should be unlikely to discover the Reverend's vessel—if the murderer *was* the Reverend—from such a signature. But the smear of green remained a grim reminder of the night's vile work, all the same; and one I should hold close in memory.

THE IMAGE OF THE BOBBING GREEN BOAT, ITS MUFFLED OARS AND menacing figures outlined against the darker night sky, persisted in my waking thoughts the remainder of the morning. As I sat at the little Pembroke table in the Wings cottage sitting-room, attempting to write, I was so often forced to draw a line through my words, that I became quite vexed and threw down my pen.

"The story does not come to your liking, Jane?" Cassandra enquired gently. She was reclining upon the settee, with a view of the street beyond our gate, and the two of us quite filled the tiny room. My father and mother had gone to stroll up the hill, in search of Henry, whom we hoped should accompany us to Mr. Crawford's fossil site. I had taken out my small sheets of writing paper, folded in half in preparation for composing,[1] and begun

---

[1] If one can judge by the appearance of Austen's extant manuscripts—*Sanditon*, for example—she made a habit of writing on small sheets of folded paper, which could be readily hidden if a visitor intruded upon her privacy. These sheets were then assembled in book form, and the pages hand-sewn through at the fold. It would appear she is speaking here of her unfinished work, *The Watsons*, which Austen scholars believe she began sometime in 1804. The manuscript paper bears an 1803 watermark. —*Editor's note.*

to work at Emma Watson, while Cassandra trimmed her hat.

"I am *not* in congenial company, Cassandra—and so the conversation comes with difficulty. I have just got Emma home to her father's house, and into a pony cart on the way to a ball; and as she is quite low in spirits, I find myself in a similar state. It is not a condition conducive to composition, I fear."

"On her way to a ball—and in low spirits?" my sister rejoined with some amusement. "Then she cannot have sprung from *your* pen. An impostor has had the writing of it, Jane, while you danced the night away in the Lyme Assembly. For I know your portraits of young ladies are always drawn from life. Elizabeth Bennet should never be so low, when faced with the prospect of a ball."

"But then Lizzy is blessed with resources not commonly granted to frivolous beauties," I rejoined. "She is almost as clever as myself. Emma Watson's portion must and shall be different. She cannot be Elizabeth Bennet; it is impossible that *two* such should fall from my pen—but neither is she an empty-headed girl, unformed and filled with nonsense. She is a sober young woman, tried by the perversities of those she holds most dear, and faced with the prospect of a future all unprovided-for."

"She does not sound very droll," Cassandra observed. "She sounds unfortunately like ourselves. I fear she shall disappoint."

"Then disappoint she must!" I cried. "For I cannot always be writing of Fortune's darlings—those dowerless chits whose beauty and understanding conquer the most mercenary of fellows. No, Cassandra, in Emma Watson I *will* have the truth of a penniless woman's prospects."

"Then she is not to marry? I thought her destined for Lord Osborne."

"Lord Osborne!"

"But I forget. Even *you*, dedicated to truth, would not

have a woman marry a man she did not love, merely to ensure her future." My sister's gaze was too indulgent; and I knew her to be laughing at me.

"Very well—Emma *will* marry—but do not laugh, Cassandra, I beg of you!" I protested, as she threw back her head in delight. "One cannot end a novel without marriages all around. Emma shall marry, though never Lord Osborne. For, you know, we *must* marry."

"Do you speak of ourselves, Jane," Cassandra enquired, sobered at once, "or merely of the plight of women in general? I do agree that it appears the only role of dignity accorded to us—the sole method of securing fortune, position, and respectability in society—but I cannot say that *merely this* is enough to recommend the state."

"For you, dear Cassandra—never." That I thought of poor Tom Fowle, dead these seven years, and with him all my sister's affections and hopes, I need not underline.[2] From her expression, I knew her overcome by a similar sensibility. "And for myself—I could do very well single. A little company, and a pleasant ball now and then, would be enough for me."

"If one could be young forever," Cassandra said quietly. "I *might* have married, had I never lost Tom Fowle— but then, very few people marry their first attachments."

"Better to stay unmarried than to marry for anything *but* attachment, Cassandra. You cannot believe otherwise; I am sure you cannot."

"But you know, Jane—you know better than anyone—

---

[2] Cassandra was engaged in 1795 to marry the Reverend Thomas Craven Fowle, son of the Austens' lifelong friends, and a protégé of Lord Craven, whose naval expedition to the West Indies Fowle felt obligated to join that same year. He died of yellow fever in San Domingo in February 1797, aged 29. He left Cassandra a legacy of one thousand pounds. She never married. —*Editor's note.*

that it is very bad to grow old, and be poor, and laughed at. And my father will hardly support us forever."[3]

"Well!" I cried, "let us make the most of our time, while he still does! We are in Lyme, Cassandra; we are young; we might yet simper at Mr. Milsop as he measures out some lace, or glance sidelong under our parasols at an idle fool of a fellow on every street corner. There remain to us yet your blushing surgeon, Mr. Dagliesh, and the lame Captain Fielding. Let us exert ourselves, though summer wanes, and try what Fortune offers!"

I had no sooner voiced this battle cry, than the very gentlemen mentioned were shown in by the housemaid Jenny, her heart-shaped face and glad blue eyes all wonderment at the surprise of it. A morning visit—and the very morning after the ball![4] *This* was singular behaviour indeed. But perhaps, I thought, as I thrust my writing paper under a book, kept upon the Pembroke table for just such a purpose, not so very singular for Lyme. The common ways of society are *not* to be expected in a town whose general air is so easy.

"Mr. Dagliesh," I said, rising in greeting, "Captain Fielding. I have the honour to present my sister to you, Captain. Miss Cassandra Austen."

Fielding bowed his fair head, and smiled his warm smile, and was so exactly as my description had led Cassandra to expect, that she met him with tolerable composure. Mr. Dagliesh, however, was in a pitiable state—now waxing red, now waning white, as his eyes sought any resting place but my sister's face. His discomposure, and some hint of its cause, reduced Cassandra to a confused

---

[3] This conversation with Cassandra regarding marriage must have impressed Jane, because it eventually found its way, in amended form, into *The Watsons* manuscript. —*Editor's note.*

[4] Only intimates of the family were accustomed to visit before noon, while acquaintances usually paid calls before dinner. —*Editor's note.*

silence; and that he might mistake her air for one of disdain, was all the more probable.

"You are abroad very early, sirs," I said, offering them each a chair. "Late hours must agree with you."

"For my part," Captain Fielding protested, "I should not have come near Wings cottage for anything—but I encountered Mr. Dagliesh on my way, and he declared himself bound to come, for a report on his fair patient; and I was then very ready to accompany him."

"And we are the happier, in knowing ourselves able to greet you," I replied, with a look for Cassandra, "for in another hour, we should have been gone. We are to visit Mr. Crawford's fossil site with my father."

"Capital!" Captain Fielding cried. "Old Crawford can be tiresome regarding his particular passions, but never in such a landscape. You shall enjoy it exceedingly. Did business in town not claim my attention this morning, I should be spelling for an invitation myself."

"I thought to find Sidmouth with you, Miss Austen," Mr. Dagliesh broke in, with a quick look for Cassandra. "I met him not an hour ago, on his way to this very house."

At the mention of the name, my unruly pulse *would* quicken; and being unable to meet Captain Fielding's eyes, and incapable of speech, I sought comfort in silence.

"I assure you, Mr. Dagliesh," my sister replied after an instant, "we have seen nothing of Mr. Sidmouth. Though I should dearly relish the opportunity; I had not the strength to thank him as I ought, the day we parted from High Down Grange."

A short silence fell at this; and I seized the moment to observe Captain Fielding, the better to know his thoughts. That Mr. Sidmouth was an intimate at Wings cottage must make him wonder; and yet his face bore no outward sign of concern. He seemed not quite at ease, however; he was not glad in Dagliesh's company. Though it may have been my imagination supplied what Nature failed to do.

"I might yet have the pleasure of joining you, all the same," the Captain said then, as though continuing a previous thought; "I might persuade you both to drive out in my barouche[5] when you tire of your visit to the cliffs. Crawford's pits are not far off my road home. When my business is concluded, I shall venture your way, and enquire if a drive is pleasing."

"You are all consideration, Captain," I told him. "I am sure a gentle turn in the sea air should do Cassandra a world of good."

"And what is your opinion, Dagliesh?"

"I do not think her quite recovered. Indeed, had I been asked, I should have advised against even the trip to Crawford's," the surgeon replied. He folded his arms across his chest, and studied the worn drugget, his countenance gaining a most mulish aspect. "The jolting of a carriage can only revive her injuries. It is not to be thought of."

"Oh, come, man!" Fielding cried with impatience. "She is in the bloom of health. She is quite obviously well. Are not you well, Miss Austen?"

"Indeed, I feel myself to be not indisposed," Cassandra said, faltering, with an eye for Mr. Dagliesh. "I grow quite weary of sitting always within doors."

"And how do the roads, Captain Fielding, that you intend traversing? Are they rutted and poor, such as should incommode my sister?" I enquired.

---

[5] A barouche was considered quite fancy in the first part of the nineteenth century. It had two seats facing each other, and held four people comfortably; the landau top folded back in the middle, to make it an open carriage often used for country outings. It was drawn by anywhere from two to six horses. —*Editor's note*.

"The roads are capital,"[6] he said with a dismissive wave, "and my barouche even better. You shall not suffer the slightest jolt, Miss Austen, I assure you. Dagliesh cannot know anything of the matter; he is hardly accustomed to the sort of conveyance I own, and mistakes its effects for his own poor trap."

The intended rudeness of the remark struck home; Mr. Dagliesh coloured, bit his lip, and as abruptly rose.

"I see that I have offered an opinion where none is wanted," he burst out. "I shall take care before offering the same again. My compliments, Miss Austen, Miss Jane Austen."[7] And with the briefest of nods to the Captain, he quitted the room, to our surprise and dismay.

"A touchy fellow!" Fielding said, with a hollow laugh; but his words were drowned in some commotion from the hallway, and the sound of men's voices too indistinct for comprehension. Another moment of suspense, and the door was thrown wide to admit a caller, and a gentleman—none other than Mr. Sidmouth!

Captain Fielding turned—saw him—and turned away. He had declined to offer any greeting, and the insult *must* be felt. Mr. Sidmouth, however, appeared insensible of Fielding's very presence, and maintained his careful expression of good breeding. That he maintained it with difficulty, I guessed from the rapid flexing of his fingers, and clutched my own hands involuntarily.

---

[6] Captain Fielding probably refers to the relative *newness* of the roads. Lyme was inaccessible to wheeled traffic until 1759, when a turnpike was built leading into the town; all land transportation prior to that date was done by pack horse. —*Editor's note.*

[7] In the presence of several members of an untitled family, it was customary to address the eldest child by the title *Miss*, or *Mister*, with younger siblings distinguished by the title and their first names. Thus the ordering of rank was preserved; similarly, the eldest would pass in and out of the room before the next youngest child in age, and so on to the youngest. —*Editor's note.*

"Mr. Sidmouth!" I cried, in some anxiety of spirit. "You honour us indeed, with so early a visit!"

"I must apologise if my presence has in any way disturbed the course of your morning," he replied, with a glance for Fielding. "I am come to enquire of Miss Austen's health, and should have settled the point with the housemaid at the very door, did not I encounter Dagliesh, and learn that you were even now entertaining a visitor. It is a pleasure indeed, Miss Austen, to find you in such good looks. I trust you shall be journeying to Mr. Crawford's today."

"Thank you, Mr. Sidmouth. That I am present at all, I am sure is due to your good offices." Cassandra spoke all the warmth of her gratitude; and I saw Fielding's surprise. That *she* bore no reservations towards Geoffrey Sidmouth was evident in her attitude of eager attention; that I had imparted nothing of all he had told me, to my dearest sister, was clear in her unguarded thanks.

"I did nothing any person of feeling and decency would not do," Sidmouth replied, taking the chair Dagliesh had vacated. In sitting, he adjusted it slightly so as to place Fielding at his back. "I am rewarded entirely by finding you much improved, under Dagliesh's care. He is a surgeon's assistant of some ability—and should have been a physician,[8] I believe, had his fortune been the greater. With time and Mr. Carpenter's careful instruction, however, he is likely to possess such a practice and home as will make all apology unwarranted."

"Considering the many cases you put him in the way of, I do not doubt it," Captain Fielding said drily. "You might almost be taking a finder's fee."

[8] Surgeons were considered common village tradesmen rather than educated professionals, such as physicians, and their wives could not be presented at Court, while physicians' wives could. —*Editor's note.*

Sidmouth sat back, his face grave and his lips compressed. Cassandra looked conscious, and coloured.

"Indeed, Mr. Sidmouth engaged Mr. Dagliesh's services on my sister's behalf, Captain," I interjected, "and we are heartily glad he did so. For as strangers to Lyme, we could not have had the choosing of a surgeon; and Mr. Sidmouth's valuation of his friend has been amply proved, in Cassandra's regained health."

"I am very sorry—I did not intend—that is to say, I knew nothing of it," Captain Fielding stammered, in some mortification.

"I wonder if that is not often the case," Mr. Sidmouth rejoined quietly, his eyes upon mine.

Captain Fielding rose with some effort on his game leg, and reached for his hat. "I must beg leave of this pleasant abode, Miss Austen," he said, with a bow to Cassandra, "and hope that my business does not detain me too long. I look forward to this afternoon."

"This afternoon?" Mr. Sidmouth enquired, stiffening.

"Indeed." Captain Fielding looked all his satisfaction. "I am to drive the young ladies about Charmouth once they have done visiting Crawford's fossil site."

Mr. Sidmouth consulted the large pocket watch that hung from the chain of his waistcoat; and very handsome it was, too. "Then you had best be about your business, Fielding," he replied smoothly, "for you should not wish to find the party gone upon your arrival. I came, it is true, to enquire after Miss Austen's health; but having been assured of its excellent tendency, I am free to broach my second errand." He turned his attention to Cassandra and me. "I am come in Crawford's barouche expressly to fetch the Miss Austens, and their father; we are all to be of the party, Fielding, you see. Quite a delightful affair; and it *is* a pity you shall miss it."

The transformation of Captain Fielding's face was singular to behold, but there was nothing to be said; and with a bow to myself, and the barest of nods for Sidmouth, he turned for the door. It being evident that the entry was never to be without bustle, the poor Captain encountered my father and mother there, only just returned from the Golden Lion; and upon hearing them successful in their errand, and Henry and Eliza behind, I knew Mr. Sidmouth should be rewarded in his scheme. My father was only too happy to be saved the trouble of hiring a rig; the offer of Mr. Crawford's barouche was gladly accepted; and so, with an air of suppressed triumph not unwarranted by events, Mr. Sidmouth helped my family to their places. My mother alone remained behind, declaring herself untempted by the prospect of rocks, and extremely dirty ones at that; and not all the attractions of a ride in an open carriage, in delightful weather, could persuade her.

"And the barouche is filled, besides," she pointed out, as she came to the street to wave goodbye. "I do not think that Jane shall find a place."

"I am afraid the interior *is* very much occupied," Mr. Sidmouth said, surveying the four faces turned expectantly my way, "and I should not like to worsen your sister's delicate health, by incommoding her further. It seems you have but one choice, Miss Jane Austen—to remain at home, or ride up front with me."

At my hesitation, he approached, and added in a lowered tone, "I was denied the felicity of a dance last evening, for reasons I shall not ask. You cannot be inclined to disappoint all your family, who wait upon your decision. Do I presume too much, Miss Jane Austen of Bath—or will you do me the honour of sitting on the box?"

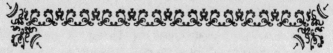

Chapter 6

Pits and Pitfalls

~

THE DRIVE WAS HARDLY A LONG ONE, FOR MR. CRAWFORD'S FOSSIL site was among the cliffs below Charmouth about two miles from Lyme, and indeed, but a stone's throw from the heights of the Grange. And so, the penalty for coward- ice being the loss of such a pleasure party, I bowed to Fate and allowed Mr. Sidmouth to hand me up onto the ba- rouche's box, and waited stiff-backed while he settled himself beside me, and took up the team's reins. I had never before had the occasion to watch a gentleman drive four-in-hand, and must declare myself quite fascinated; his strong, broad fingers in their leather driving gloves seemed endowed with a particular sensibility, that read the intentions of each animal's mouth almost before it was itself aware of them. As we headed east up the long coastal road, however, the team picked up speed; and the effects of wind and motion so high upon an unprotected seat almost unnerved me. I would not allow myself the indulgence of giving way—no feminine shrieks, no pitiful hands clutching at Mr. Sidmouth's arm—but rather maintained a stoic appearance as I swayed beside him; and if my jaw was clenched and my fingers knotted, I pray he was too intent upon the road to spare either a thought.

"How fortunate that the weather is fine," he said, after a time, "and yet, not *too* fine—not so very dry that we should have a cloud of dust before and behind. One wants a little rain at night, when one embarks upon a plan of driving."

"Mr. Crawford is very good to think of us, and to endeavour to afford so many so much pleasure," I said.

"Crawford is always bent upon pleasing. It is his chief fault."

"His fault! Can goodwill and generosity ever be so considered?"

"When they lead to obligation, I believe they can," Mr. Sidmouth replied. "Cholmondeley Crawford is a wealthy man, and may have the pleasure of doing as he likes; but some of those he entertains, cannot afford to treat him in a like manner, and the mortification of it goes unnoticed by the man himself. If the distinctions of rank have any value, it would seem that they should be preserved, if only to prevent embarrassment."

"If this is a fault, then Mr. Crawford has chosen wisely," I cried. "I should rather be charged with doing too *much*, of being *too easy*, than of being above my company. Pride is a quality I abhor beyond all things. However justified by the accomplishments of the possessor, it renders the power to do good, onerous when once bestowed. We none of us like condescension when it is offered."

"Very true. Condescension, and officiousness—the unwonted interference of others in our private affairs."

He spoke with an edge of bitterness, as if at a painful recollection; and unbidden, Captain Fielding's face arose in my mind. His opinion of Mr. Sidmouth was so very bad; and yet, so kind and generous a gentleman as Mr.

Crawford counted the master of High Down among his intimate friends. It was a puzzle.

"And what is *your* fault, Mr. Sidmouth?" I enquired, bracing my right hand against the seat as the barouche rounded a ragged curve.

"Following my own inclination, when I should consider the needs of others," he said, without hesitation. "You will notice, for example, that I drive to suit myself, rather than in deference to your fear of heights and speed. But having observed your hand clutching at the seat, I cannot persist; I must imagine the rest of the party to be similarly incommoded." He sawed at the reins, and glanced over his shoulder at the four heads bobbing behind; all were engaged in animated discussion, the sense of which was drowned in the tumult of hooves and wheels; and none, to my eye, looked the slightest bit discomfited.

"To follow one's inclination first, is the habit of a solitary man," I observed.

"And how then have I acquired it? For I can hardly be called a hermit."

"I did not mean you wanted a household," I replied. "Only that a household cannot claim the consideration that a family might."

"Ah! The wife and children!" he said, with some amusement. "Yes—I admire your circumspection, Miss Jane Austen of Bath. It is rare for a young lady in my company *not* to broach the subject of marriage within an hour's acquaintance; and you have withstood the test now several days. But I fear my habits are not conducive to a settled life. For domestic bliss, you must search elsewhere."

"I spoke but in the general way!" I cried, mortified. "I meant only to illustrate my point, by describing your situation."

"But you have not described it as you should," he replied. "For I do not live alone. There is my cousin Seraphine."

I must have flushed hotly at the name, for his eyes, when they glanced my way, narrowed shrewdly.

"You have heard something to her discredit. I am sure of it."

"Of your cousin I have heard little—and that, only praise. But of yourself, Mr. Sidmouth—" I faltered, and searched for a means of carrying on. "I hear such conflicting reports of your character, that I confess I know not what to think."

"If you would draw my likeness from the opinion of men such as Percival Fielding, you cannot hope to capture it truly."

"Captain Fielding appears all that is honourable," I replied, stiffening.

"Appears! Aye, he *appears* to be a great deal." At this, Sidmouth laughed with contempt, but his countenance was decidedly angry. "He has sunk Mademoiselle LeFevre before the eyes of all Lyme. The sorrow Fielding has caused—the pain—I tremble to think of it, Miss Austen."

"How *can* you speak so!" I said, my attitude all indignation. I clutched involuntarily at the seat's edge as the barouche began to descend towards the Charmouth shingle. A broad sea vista was spread before us—breathtaking in the extreme—but I was too intent upon my thoughts to give it proper notice. "*You*, Mr. Sidmouth, who should have been your cousin's protector! You—who are responsible for reducing her to misery of the acutest kind! I wonder at your encompassing a man so honourable as the Captain—his motives all disinterested, his aims merely just—in the ruin of Mademoiselle LeFevre! Your own sense of decency, Mr. Sidmouth—of respect for the duties of a gentleman—must cry out against it!"

His countenance paled above his bitten lips, and his gaze, levelled as it was over the horses' heads, became stony. "I would beg you to speak no more to me, madam, of Captain Fielding," he said. "You cannot know what is toward between that gentleman and myself, and I shall not stoop to deriding *him* to others, as it has suited him to serve me."

"I am glad to know you retain *some* claims to the honour of a gentleman," I replied tartly; and so we pulled up before Mr. Crawford's fossil works, in silence and some confusion of emotions the one towards the other.

"My dear Mr. Crawford," my father exclaimed, as he advanced upon that gentleman with hand extended, "I quite revel in this opportunity to view your pits! What industry, on behalf of science! What energy, towards the greater glorification of God!"

Mr. Crawford stood in his shirtsleeves (for the day was decidedly warm), his bald head shielded by a monstrous hat. The redness of his countenance testified to the energy with which he had been stooping and carrying the small articles of stone laid neatly to one side upon a blanket; and the weariness of the two men employed in his behalf, who worked deep in a quarry hewn from the cliff face with picks and trowels, spoke eloquently of the labour undergone. The heat was intensified by a smallish fire ignited near a bellows, where Mr. Crawford's men might repair such tools as required attention, on a crude sort of forge; and all about lay piles of rubble, the detritus of scientific endeavour.

Eliza and Henry were admiring the view from the shingle; Mr. Sidmouth was attending to the horses; and so Cassandra and I followed my father towards the day's burden of treasures. There we found the two ladies of the Crawford household ranged on either side of a blanket, in the process of unpacking a hamper.

"Miss Crawford! And Miss Armstrong!" Geoffrey

Sidmouth declared, coming up behind. "How delightful to see you, indeed. I did not know that you were to be of the party. May I present to you the Miss Austens, of Bath."

And so there were introductions all around—and several glances the length and breadth of our simple white gowns from Miss Crawford, who is fully as sharp and shrewish in aspect as I judged her to be the previous e'en. She is Mr. Crawford's sister, and his housekeeper since the death of his wife some years ago; and I judge her to labour under the burden of disappointment, for her pinched and suffering countenance bears the mark of regret. This, and her customary black, give her the general air of a raven, an impression that the harshness of her voice does nothing to dispel.

Miss Lucy Armstrong is their niece, down like ourselves from her home in Bath.[1] She is not above nineteen, with the freshness of complexion and sweetness of temper common in those untried by life. She met Mr. Sidmouth's eyes only with difficulty, and seemed to prefer the study of an ant toiling across the blanket, so firmly did her gaze seek the ground. She was likewise impervious to the slings and arrows of her aunt's tongue—which suggests some greatness of mind, upon reflection, for one consigned to living with Miss Crawford so many months together. At Mr. Sidmouth's moving to join the gentlemen, young Miss Armstrong recovered her faculties enough to attend to our conversation—though not so well as to partake of it.

"Well! And so you are the famous Austens, of whom we have heard so much," Miss Crawford began, as she set out

---

[1] In her letter to Cassandra, written from Lyme Sept. 14, 1804, Austen refers to Miss Armstrong without revealing her Christian name; in another letter dated April 21, 1805, she mentions renewing the acquaintance in Bath. We learn here for the first time that Miss Armstrong's name was Lucy. —*Editor's note*.

forks with the efficiency of a Commander of Foot. Her malicious glance flicked up to meet mine, and as quickly dropped away. "Mr. Crawford is quite full of you, I declare, *and* Mr. Sidmouth. One is reminded of the smallness of Lyme, when the slightest addition to our society is regarded as such an event."

"Mr. Crawford is too kind," I replied. "I am sure he makes all his acquaintance feel equally celebrated."

"Oh! Cholmondeley has no discernment in his society, I assure you. He is forever acquiring strangers on the road, and compelling them to visit these dreadful pits. Such dirt! Such noise! And in pursuit of what? The tracings of a few vanished creatures, too poor to survive, too abject and miserable for consideration. It quite works upon my nerves—though they are shattered already. I attribute the shocking decline in my condition, Miss Austen, to the date of Cholmondeley's embarking upon fossil-collecting; and I have made it a policy not to encourage him in the pursuit. I should never have come *today*, in fact, did not I have the opportunity to meet your dear sister"—this, with a simper for Cassandra—"whose interesting trouble has given rise to such concern among the intimates of Lyme. The poor state of the roads, and the worse state of the drivers! Something *ought* to be done about our modes of private transportation. Though I *do* say, that those who undertake to hire as disreputable a fellow as Hibbs for postboy must take their chances of a bruising. Not that I would speak of it for the world, now your dear sister *has* come to grief. Indeed, I said as much to Mrs. Schuyler only last evening; and she quite agreed."

"But we were not to know of the man's propensities beforehand," Cassandra said gently. "We accepted his services in Crewkerne, where his general character could not be known. When one is a traveller, one must trust a little to Fortune."

"And look where Fortune took you! To the very brink

of death! No, my dear—the only driver worth consideration is one's own coachman, at the head of one's own carriage. I should not *think* to trust dear Lucy to anyone but our Summerfield when she is to come down from Bath, though her father *would* send her post."

"I observe, however, that you trusted *us* to Mr. Sidmouth," I interjected.

"True—but he *would* insist. And when Mr. Sidmouth insists, even *I* find myself overruled. Cholmondeley becomes decidedly bullheaded in the man's presence; there is no managing him. Lucy, dear, do fetch your uncle. He is turning quite purple. This heat and exertion *cannot* be good for him."

Miss Armstrong smiled prettily in our general direction, and floated towards the gentlemen; I say *floated* because of the airiness of her cloud of green muslin, which was quite sheer, and draped to becoming effect across her full bosom. She is a well-grown girl—though petite, like my sister Eliza, and possessed of decidedly red hair, and the freckled complexion that so often accompanies it. But I detect some acid in my description of Lucy Armstrong, and must hasten to retract it. Freckles on the one hand, a pleasing figure on the other—of what importance are such? If I resent her youth and simplicity of manner, it is only because I remember possessing both myself, and fancy I can foretell Lucy Armstrong's future. When, indeed, I know nothing of her fortune, or prospects; merely assuming that both are slight, since she appears in the guise of poor relation dependent for her pleasures upon a spiteful maiden aunt and widower uncle. She might as easily have three thousand a year, and a bevy of suitors waiting to snatch her back to Bath. Much may preserve her from a state such as mine—growing old, unloved, and unprovided-for.

And yet I am only ten years her senior. Only ten years! —Of balls, and flirtations, and new dresses and fashions;

of disappointments, broken hearts, and fading hopes. I shall be nine-and-twenty next Christmas; and Lucy only just embarked upon *her* ten years. I would not wish them to end as mine have done.

I was jolted from my reverie by the appearance of the gentlemen. Mr. Crawford walked somewhat slowly, as though fatigued, and had Miss Armstrong by his side; but to my surprise, Mr. Sidmouth quite monopolized my father's attention.

". . . then you would agree with Bentham,[2] that the question is not 'do animals reason,' but 'do they suffer'?" my father enquired. I started, knowing him to be anything but a Benthamite, and hardly believing him acquainted with that gentleman's philosophy.

"I would."

"Though that places the animals on a par with mankind?"

"I would say, sir, with Kant, that I cannot lay claim to the distinction of being Creation's final end.[3] These very fossils in Crawford's cliffs proclaim us but a stage upon Nature's great journey. We cannot but wonder if we shall

[2] Jeremy Bentham (1748–1832) is best known as a wealthy lawyer of the Georgian period who advocated Utilitarianism: the belief that society should be regulated by inherent principles, much as his rough contemporary Adam Smith (1723–1790) believed economies operated by self-evident market forces. Chief among these principles was that social action should produce the "greatest good for the greatest number"—a frankly democratic notion. Bentham attracted a coterie of "philosophical radicals," who, by 1815, advocated universal suffrage in England. Reverend Austen is referring here, however, to a famous passage from Bentham's 1789 work, *Introduction to the Principles of Morals and Legislation. —Editor's note.*

[3] Mr. Sidmouth is paraphrasing Kant. The philosopher actually wrote that he was unable to find "any being capable of laying claim to the distinction of being the final end of creation." (*Critique of Judgment,* 1790). —*Editor's note.*

be quarried ourselves, by some inhuman hand, millennia hence."

There was a loud *Tsk!* of disapproval from Miss Crawford.

"You would not see them, then, as merely the confirmation of God's great design," my father continued, "as a reflection of Man's infinitely greater powers?"

"Forgive me, sir—but I cannot."

"Well, well! Very stimulating to be sure! We have been debating philosophy, my dears," my father said, as the two men joined us. "I quite wish your brother James were here to make a third in the discussion. I rather fancy, being of the next generation of Austen clergymen, he might fall somewhere between the two poles of Mr. Sidmouth and myself."

"You are determined in disagreement, then?" Cassandra enquired.

"As surely as Lucifer and St. Peter, my dear—though I meant no offence, Mr. Sidmouth, in the comparison."

"As I assumed you to be pleading the part of Lucifer, my dear sir, none was taken." There was a slight ripple of laughter, and Mr. Sidmouth began again with better grace. "I quite applaud your liberality, Reverend Austen. It is rare, indeed, to find a man of the cloth so open in his acceptance of what science tells us. For these very fossils must put paid to the Bible's notion of the world being formed in only seven days; the age of these cliffs, and their silent inhabitants, speak of thousands upon thousands of years' passage before creatures like ourselves walked this earth."

We were silent a moment, in gazing upon the chalk heights, and the excavations of Mr. Crawford's labourers; and it was then that Mr. Sidmouth turned to me, and took my hand. He turned over the palm, and pressed into it a fragment of rock, perhaps six inches across, with the barest impression of a life-form. A shell, it seemed to me;

the remnant of a forgotten sea creature, curled like a ram's horn. The sensation of movement was palpable—whorling away within the rock for thousands of years, adrift in the seas of time.

"What is it?" I enquired.

"The rock is Blue Lias," Mr. Sidmouth said. "Much of these Charmouth cliffs are formed of it."

"And the creature?"

"An ammonite. Though a very small one. Crawford has others, full six feet across."

I looked, and marvelled. (And I am still gazing at it, as I write—having propped the bit on the bedroom dresser at Wings cottage.) "Thank you," I said, looking into Mr. Sidmouth's grave dark eyes. Our discord of the drive appeared entirely forgotten. "It is very beautiful."

"There is something of eternity in it," he said.[4]

IT WAS SEVERAL HOURS LATER, AFTER THE CRAWFORDS' EXCELLENT repast was consumed, and we had listened with as much sympathy as we could muster to Miss Crawford's sad history of her blighted romance with one Jonas Filch—who died of a fever, thus leaving his fiancée to wear black for the subsequent thirty years—that Cassandra and I persuaded Eliza to walk with us along the water. We had left poor Henry and Miss Armstrong in Miss Crawford's grip (while she recounted for their edification the good works she superintended as the head of St. Michael's Ladies Auxiliary), and coursed along the beach. We discovered, to our delight, a small cavern not far from the fossil site,

[4] The search for fossils was well advanced along the Dorset coast by the time Austen visited it in 1804. A local schoolgirl, Mary Anning, would be credited with the discovery of the world's first ichthyosaur in the cliffs between Lyme and Charmouth in 1811, when she was just twelve years old. —*Editor's note.*

its entrance marked with a cairn of stones; but Cassandra lacked the courage to venture inwards, and I would not go alone. I could look for no aid from Eliza's quarter—she was delighted with the cave's discovery, but too concerned with the possible ruin of her apparel to try its interior. "A cavern, Jane, as foetid and dank as Mrs. Radcliffe[5] should make it! Shall we venture within, at the very peril of our lives?"

"You know very well, Eliza, that a heroine must be alone to invite peril," I said; "but let us venture all the same. We may fancy ourselves exposed to mortal danger, and so achieve a modest victory in braving the cavern's terrors together."

But Eliza's attention, as readily let slip as it was secured, had already wandered. She preferred gossip to trials of courage, and made a very poor adventuress indeed.

"I am quite taken with your Mr. Sidmouth, Jane," she declared, having traded the cavern for a seat on a weathered log. "Such tempests of emotion as are graven upon his countenance! First, the darkest of clouds; and then, as if under the influence of a warm breeze, the threat of rain is swept away, and sunlight breaks! Upon first espying his countenance before the Lyme Assembly, I thought it quite ugly; not a single feature may be called handsome. And yet the whole is not displeasing. I could watch the play of his emotions for hours."

"It would appear that you already have," Cassandra observed.

I feigned disinterest, and prodded at some seaweed with a piece of driftwood I had seized for a walking stick.

[5] Ann Radcliffe is best remembered for the Gothic romance, *The Mysteries of Udolpho,* which Austen satirized in *Northanger Abbey.* She was, along with her contemporaries Maria Edgeworth, Charlotte Smith, and Fanny Burney, one of the women novelists Austen read and admired. —*Editor's note.*

The tide being quite low, all manner of sea-life was washed up upon the shore, and every step afforded new wonders.

"And so much the man of the world," Eliza continued, as though Cassandra had never spoken. "I felt myself almost returned to Paris, in the course of our nuncheon!"[6]

"You *were* singularly engrossed." Cassandra straightened up from the sand with a bit of sea-glass in her hands. "This appears to be a fragment of a bottle, Jane—cast overboard from a passing ship. Only think, if it should have fallen from one of our brothers' hands!"

"Mr. Sidmouth is quite an *habitué* of that dear city," Eliza resumed. "It seems he has occasion to travel to France fairly often—or did, before the peace ended."

"Indeed?" I was compelled to attend to her chatter despite myself. "And what could be his reason for such travel? I had understood that those French relations he once possessed were all murdered in the revolt."

"Oh! I daresay he is in some line of trade." Eliza's tone was careless. "Though while the Monster yet holds the throne of France in thrall, all trade is at an end. Mr. Sidmouth and I are quite agreed that now Buonaparte has crowned himself Emperor, and has begun to murder his opponents,[7] the condition of the country can only worsen. I was forced to turn the conversation, in fact, from fear that the gentleman's opinions should become too heated. He grew quite warm in his discussion of French policy, and *that,* with a lady."

---

[6] *Nuncheon* was a common term for food taken between breakfast and dinner—which in the country was usually eaten in the late afternoon, around four o'clock—since the term *luncheon,* or lunch, did not exist. —*Editor's note.*

[7] Eliza refers here to the March 1804 execution of the Duc D'Enghien, who was of royal Bourbon blood. Napoleon had the duke seized, imprisoned, secretly tried, and executed, in the wake of several Royalist plots to dethrone him. —*Editor's note.*

"In trade?" I said, all wonderment. "He certainly gives no indication of it. I should have thought Mr. Sidmouth a gentleman of easy circumstances."

"Even a man with four thousand a year, my dear Jane, may use his property in a profitable fashion." Eliza was all impatience. "I cannot name for you the legions of gentlemen in London alone who serve as Venturers[8] for all manner of commercial enterprise. Their money is their proxy—they may benefit from its utility in the hands of others, and keep their *own* fingers clean of such vulgar stuff as buying and selling."

"How very extraordinary," Cassandra murmured.

I turned to agree with her; and found she was absorbed in examining a fragment of shell. "The whorls and chambers of this bit of stuff—this sea-creature's home—are as fully a work of art as any Italian sculpture. How wonderful is Nature!"

Put out of temper with *both* my companions, I left the water's edge and wandered aimlessly back towards the fossil site. I was required to stop, however, and glance about to find my way; Charmouth beach at such an hour was crowded with pleasure-seekers, attempting the waters in bathing machines, or walking with some difficulty through the heavy drift of sand. I raised a hand to my brow and narrowed my eyes, the better to find a familiar face—and stopped short in my survey, upon sighting what could only be an overturned skiff drawn up on the shingle, quite barnacled and scraped about its exterior, as from heavy use. What paint remained upon its wood, however, was a rich, deep green.

I approached it slowly, my pulse at fever pitch, the thought of the ring at the end of the Cobb my only con-

[8] Venturers were what we might call venture capitalists—titled or simply wealthy gentlemen who invested in others' business ventures. —*Editor's note.*

sideration. Was this the very vessel that had borne the unfortunate Bill Tibbit and his gallows to the stone pier's end? At the skiff's side, I dropped to my knees in the sand, heedless of my muslin, and studied it soberly. Several long scratches were cut deeply into the wood—the result, perhaps, of bobbing against the Cobb in the dead of night, though they might have been acquired in any number of ways.

"Miss Austen," came a voice at my elbow; and I jumped.

"Mr. Sidmouth!"

"Should you like to take a turn upon the waves?"

I attempted a smile. "I confess, it is not my favoured pursuit, though I *am* of a Naval family."

He bent and patted the boat's sturdy prow, from which an anchor, small but mortally sharp, protruded. "*La Gascogne* could never do you harm," he said. "She is Lyme-built, and has performed many a useful service."

"You know the boat, then?" I enquired, its very name having the power to rob me of all complaisance.

"These ten years, at least," he replied with a smile. "When a local fishing family had no further use for her, I took her under the Grange's wing, and seaworthy she has proved. You are certain you do not wish to take a turn? A pair of stout fellows at the oars, and we should be beyond the surf in a thrice."

"My apologies, Mr. Sidmouth," I said, rising with effort, the image of the gibbet before my eyes, "but I fear my stomach is not equal to a ride in such a vessel."

"AND DID YOU ENJOY YOUR FIRST DAY ABROAD, MISS AUSTEN?" Captain Fielding enquired, as his stout ponies jogged up the road from Charmouth. Given the lateness of the hour, we had determined to forgo a pleasure drive, and turn instead towards the Captain's house, there to take tea and a tour of his gardens, of which he was quite proud. "I trust you are not overly fatigued?"

"I must confess to feeling a little exhausted," Cassandra said faintly from her seat opposite. Captain Fielding had settled himself at my side in the open carriage, while Lucy Armstrong held the place next to my sister. Fielding's coachman, Jarvis, sat alone high upon the box; and I felt a twinge of consciousness at the thought of an earlier ride in a barouche-landau, and a more precarious seating. Mr. Sidmouth had parted from us some hours since—to avoid meeting Captain Fielding, I suspected, though the Gentleman Venturer of High Down claimed only pressing business about the farm.

"So much sun, and good food, and cheerful company, *will* prove tiring, I own," the Captain said, with a broad smile on his weathered face. "We are quite surfeited with schemes of pleasure, are we not? Your uncle, Miss Armstrong, is the chief culprit, I fear, in all our cases of exhaustion." Miss Armstrong dimpled prettily at this, but Cassandra seemed to find even so little effort as a smile beyond her powers, as I observed in some dismay. The Captain studied my sister an instant, and must have surmised the same. "We shall not tax you much further, Miss Austen," he told Cassandra, "merely to charge you to enjoy the splendour of the countryside hereabouts, and that, in silence."

And indeed, Captain Fielding could not have spoken with greater justice. The waving golden-green of the high downs in early September was a spectacle to behold; even so late in the day, with shafts of sunlight stretching warm and long towards the sea, haymakers were abroad in the fields, and the picturesque was completed by the introduction in the distance of the occasional hay-wain and stout horse, blowing at the chaff and the flies. To our left, as we progressed northwest, was the grey-blue edge of the cliffs, dropping precipitately to the sea; and then the sea itself, curling and re-forming ceaselessly against the rocks.

"Look!" Miss Armstrong cried. "A cutter! And a fast one indeed! It might almost be racing the ship behind."

"I fear that it is." Captain Fielding spoke grimly. "Jarvis! Pull up!"

The barouche rolled to a gentle stop with the coachman's "Whoa, there, Jezebel. Whoa, Shadrach," and we four turned, as if possessed of one head, to gaze at the horizon.

The cutter was, as its name suggests, a fast little ship of light build and sleek lines; it clove through the waves like a knife through warm butter, making the most of a stiff breeze. Behind it came a heavier brig, flying the ensign of the Royal Navy—and that the one pursued the other, we little doubted.

"They would apprehend it," Lucy Armstrong said, with all the wonder of nineteen. "Whatever for?"

"Wait but a moment," Fielding replied, "and you shall see something curious."

The cutter was nearing the distant end of the Cobb, and the Navy brig was well back; it looked as though the lead vessel should triumph. And then it came round, and almost to a halt in the waters west of the Cobb, and a frenzy of activity on the main deck could be observed.[9]

"They are jettisoning the cargo," Cassandra said quietly. "It must be contraband."

"Exactly." Captain Fielding's voice held only satisfaction.

"Smugglers!" Miss Armstrong cried, her face alight. So even *she* was prey to the romance of the age. Her aunt

---

[9] The cutter Jane describes probably came about near Charton Bay, two miles west of Lyme proper; this was a lonely stretch of shoreline favored by smugglers. —*Editor's note.*

could not approve it; but happily, we were spared Miss Crawford's strictures.

"What a fearful loss this must be, for the captain of that cutter," I observed.

"Loss? That is very unlikely," Captain Fielding replied. "They will have marked the place in Poker's Pool where the casks went down—indeed, they may even have buoyed them just below the surface—and will in due course retrieve them in the dead of night, in smaller boats. Provided, of course, the captain is not impressed."[10]

"Why even attempt a landing in broad daylight?" my sister enquired. "It seems the worst sort of folly."

"Lyme has been known as an hospitable port," Captain Fielding said drily. "The local Revenue men and dragoons are so well-supplied with French brandy—of the sort that is very hard to come by—that more often than not, they are elsewhere engaged when the contraband arrives. Only one of your Revenue men is worth his salt—Mr. Roy Cavendish, the local Customs man—but his duties are too numerous, and his territory too broad, for the effective policing of Lyme. I cannot tell you how many afternoons I have watched waggons come in a long line to the shingle below the Cobb, their horses standing in surf up to their flanks, on purpose to fetch the smugglers' shameful cargoes and bear them into the deep recesses of the Pinny,[11] and thence to the Dorchester road, and

[10] Captain Fielding is referring to the Royal Navy practice of pressing smuggling captains into active service when apprehended. Such seamen were known to be remarkably skilled, from long experience of landing on difficult coasts in bad weather and under cover of darkness; exactly the sort of captains the Royal Navy needed in time of war. —Editor's note.

[11] The Pinny, in Austen's time, was a heavily wooded wilderness a short walking distance from town. She describes it in Persuasion as possessed of "green chasms between romantic rocks, where the scattered forest trees and orchards of luxuriant growth declare that

Bath, and London beyond. But of late Cavendish has been quite pressing in his charge to apprehend such cheats of the Crown's revenues. What you see before you, ladies, is a miscalculation on the part of our Gentlemen of the Night. They did not hear of the Royal Navy's sudden interest in their trade. The brig looks to be the *Renegade*. I imagine she has been chasing that cutter all the way from Boulogne."

"Jane!" Cassandra cried. "Our brother is even now engaged in blockading that very port. Is it credible a smuggling ship could penetrate where so much active vigilance holds sway?"

"There are many methods for winning blindness from one's countrymen," Captain Fielding broke in. "I regret to say it—my years of service in the Blue would urge me to prevaricate—but the truth of the matter is that many who were once in the service of the Crown form the chief part of the smugglers' bands. Who better than a sailor, accustomed to privation and endurance in the worst of seas, to pilot a ship into enemy territory? Who better than a soldier, accustomed to long marches, to carry a barrel of brandy slung from each shoulder several miles through the Pinny to safety? And who better than either, to suborn old friends in strategic places, with the gift of a length of silk or a bottle of rarest cognac?"

"I am all amazement," Cassandra said, with averted eyes. "It is my custom to believe those who serve in the Royal Navy to be among the most honourable of men."

"And in the main, they are, I grant you," Captain Fielding said gently. "Certainly I could not suggest that your

---

many a generation must have passed away since the first partial falling of the cliff prepared the ground for such a state. . . ." There were to be additional land-falls in subsequent years, the most spectacular of which took place in 1839. It was the ideal place for a smugglers' band to meet. —*Editor's note.*

own brothers would be so easily corrupted, Miss Austen. I speak but in the general way, and of the common lot— the ordinary man-at-arms, who cannot look to rise to an officer's rank, and achieve great fortune. One night's despicable work on behalf of such a one as the Reverend could suffice to feed a family for a week."

"The Reverend?" Cassandra looked her puzzlement.

"I am forgetting," Captain Fielding exclaimed. "We were deprived of your loveliness last evening, and *you* of our conversation."

"The Reverend is a smuggling chief," Lucy Armstrong supplied. "His identity remains one of Lyme's greatest secrets. The very cutter below us may well be one of his boats."

We gazed once more at the sea, and observed the Navy vessel come alongside the cutter, which, having abandoned its cargo, now stood off Lyme some little distance with an affectation of innocence; in an instant, the little boat was boarded; and a search of her holds no doubt begun. To my surprise, I found myself wishing her good fortune and Godspeed, and that the officers of His Majesty's ship *Renegade* might find nothing to her detriment. Then abruptly I shook off such fancies, appalled at my want of moral sense. How should it be, that our hearts leap at the sight of anything graceful, fast, and daring, and turn away from the stolid predictability of the tried and narrow way? Only Eve, clutching at her apple, might have the answer.

WE DROVE ON IN A MOMENT, THOUGH MORE THAN ONE OF US craned a neck backwards to observe the progress of events on the cutter's deck; but though we espied the boat itself, the actions of its men were veiled from our sight, and the conclusion of such a story must await another day. Cassandra's eyes were closed, and her pallor such as gave rise to concern in my breast; but believing her to be resting, I chose not to disturb her with unnecessary enquiries. Turning instead to Captain Fielding, I thought to pursue a nearer interest, by probing his dislike of Mr. Sidmouth.

"I had understood you to tell me, Captain Fielding, that Mr. Sidmouth's relations in France were all deceased, and that Mademoiselle LeFevre represents the sole surviving leaf of the family's foreign branch."

"I believe that to be the case," he replied.

"And yet my sister Eliza finds that Mr. Sidmouth goes often to France—or did so, before the outbreak of the latest hostilities. Having been long a resident of that unfortunate country herself, she was delighted to meet with a gentleman capable of offering the latest intelligence regarding Parisian society, something for which she is always longing."

"I am happy to learn that Mr. Sidmouth was capable of offering *anything* that could be described as pleasing," the Captain rejoined soberly. "That he was engaged in conversing with a lady—and a lady of the world, as everything about your brother's wife proclaims her to be—must speak for itself. Sidmouth's charm is always most lively in the company of the fair sex."

"You are aware, then, of his travel?" I persisted.

"I am. It has been many months since I have regarded it with anything but dismay."

"Dismay!" I cried, with a look for Lucy Armstrong, whose eyes were cast down upon her folded hands. Her cheeks were remarkably rosy for one so apparently indifferent to our conversation.

"Indeed." Captain Fielding appeared to hesitate, as if debating within himself; and then the desire to relate his anxieties won out over the impulse towards discretion. "I have reason to believe, Miss Austen, that Geoffrey Sidmouth is engaged in business of a most unscrupulous nature; that he ventures to Paris on behalf of certain nefarious interests whose result you saw only moments ago; that he is, in fact, none other than the reprehensible Reverend of whom the world speaks with such a strange mixture of repugnance and admiration."

"Mr. Sidmouth! The very Reverend!"

"It cannot be," Cassandra said, with some urgency in her tone. Her eyelids had fluttered wide, and two spots of colour burned in her cheeks. "Mr. Sidmouth retains every aspect of the gentleman. I cannot believe so good a man as he proved himself to me, in my time of need, to be so lost to the expectations of society—of duty—indeed, of every moral purpose!"

"I wish that I could share your approbation," Captain Fielding said. He spoke gently to Cassandra, as was his wont, but his blue eyes were cold and hard in his tanned face. I understood, in gazing at him then, what it must have been to answer his commands on a surging deck in the midst of battle. "I have watched his movements for some time. The trips to France are but a part of it; to this, I would add the strangeness of waggons coming and going at the Grange at all hours of the night; the appearance of bands of men who shelter in its barns for a few days only, and then are seen no more; the constant traffic along the cliffs, in the foulest of weather; and the habitual walks of Mademoiselle LeFevre."

"Mademoiselle LeFevre?" Lucy Armstrong said, in a tone of bewilderment.

"Mademoiselle LeFevre," Captain Fielding rejoined. The barouche tilted suddenly, in turning into a private avenue of well-grown trees, and I looked up to find we were come very nearly to the end of our drive. "She is given to walking, as all of Lyme has observed, along the cliffs in her bright red cloak, and on particular afternoons."

"There can be nothing singular in a lady's taking exercise," I objected, as the barouche rolled to a halt before Captain Fielding's door, "nor in the fact of a scarlet wrap, when one is speaking of Lyme."[12]

"There can—and there is—when the lady's constitutionals are followed without fail by the landing of a smuggling ship along the beaches that same night. I am convinced her red cloak is a signal; she wears it for the benefit of the Reverend's cutters, lying offshore, and straining at their sea-glasses for a glimpse of scarlet. At times when the dragoons are particularly active—when they feel, for the sake of propriety, a need to assume an attitude of vigilance, and stand about the town as if ready to arrest us all—I have observed Miss Seraphine to remain within doors for whole days together."

The Captain eased his game leg out of the barouche with the coachman Jarvis's assistance, and, once steady upon the ground, turned to hand down first Miss Armstrong and then my sister. "Having seen the cutter running offshore today, I find it in me to wonder, indeed, if Mr. Sidmouth's presence at Mr. Crawford's fossil pits was entirely without design. From such a point, one might have an unimpeded view of all sea traffic; he could combine a pleasure party with scrupulous observance of his cargo's fortunes."

"But he departed before the cutter appeared," Lucy Armstrong argued. Captain Fielding merely bowed, and gestured her towards the open door, where a housemaid stood ready to usher her within. Cassandra followed, with the faintest of smiles. Her gait was unsteady, as though she moved under the influence of a fearful headache. My

---

[12] Jane alludes here to the whittle—a shawl of red wool traditionally worn by the women of Lyme's laboring class. By the turn of the eighteenth century, however, the tradition was on the wane, as Lyme residents of all classes were increasingly exposed to the cosmopolitan dress of fashionable visitors. —Editor's note.

heart misgave me as I watched; but Captain Fielding's hand was outstretched to receive my own, and I returned to the subject uppermost in my thoughts.

"You have indeed been an avid observer of all Mr. Sidmouth's movements," I said, as I grasped the Captain's gloved fingers and found the carriage step. "I would venture to say that even your place of abode is not without design. With no other object than the closest scrutiny, can you have chosen to settle in a house not a half-mile from High Down Grange. For no other reason than to calculate his ruin, can you have chosen a neighbour so abhorrent to you."

How my heart reacted to this knowledge of Captain Fielding's design, I cannot say. I confess to a confusion of emotions—some all in admiration of his penetration and bravery, and others, having more to do with Geoffrey Sidmouth, that were marked by regret. But I could not deny the calculation of Fielding's words, and the careful study behind them; I myself had spent two nights at High Down Grange, and had seen the red-cloaked girl with a lanthorn bobbing along the cliffs. What had Mr. Sidmouth said to Seraphine, in those few phrases of French? Something about the men, and the dogs, and the bay. And the name of the bottle-green boat on the beach—*La Gascogne.* Presumably a cargo was expected the very night of our precipitate arrival—hence the hostility with which we were met, and the stable boy's levelled blunderbuss. Seraphine LeFevre was undoubtedly dispatched to divert the men and their wares to another place of hiding, for the length of our unfortunate stay.

"You are possessed of a singular understanding," Captain Fielding said, his eyes intent upon my face. We stood thus a moment in the drive while Jarvis remounted the box. "But then, I have allowed myself an unwonted frankness in your company. It may be that our minds are formed for such effortless meeting."

"I am happy to learn that you are not *entirely* languishing in retirement, Captain Fielding," I rejoined, deflecting his gallantry with a smile. "Indeed, I think you are possibly the most *active* former Naval officer I have ever met."

He threw back his blond head and laughed. "You have found me out, Miss Austen. I am, indeed, as yet employed—though on behalf of His Majesty's revenues rather than his seamen. I shall have the Reverend yet—and when I do, I shall be very much surprised if he is *not* Geoffrey Sidmouth."

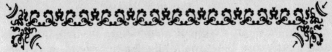

Chapter 7

The Lander Routed

8 September 1804
Dawn

~

I HAVE PUT ASIDE MY FOOLSCAP AND MY EFFORTS TO FORM EMMA
Watson to my liking—a more wrongheaded heroine I
have never encountered, so intent is she upon ceding the
stage to her spiteful sisters and the ridiculous Tom Musgrave[1]—and taken down this journal once more to record
all that has unfolded since yester e'en. I had progressed
only so far, in relating the chief of that tumultuous day,
when Mr. Dagliesh appeared at my brother Henry's dispatching. And so I must set down something of how the
surgeon's assistant came again to Wings cottage.

We had partaken of a little refreshment, and decidedly

---

[1] Tom Musgrave, a charmingly vacant womanizer in *The Watsons*
manuscript, should not be confused with the more finely drawn
Mus*grove* family of *Persuasion*. It was Louisa Musgrove who received a
near-fatal head injury in falling from the Cobb—an event that may
have been inspired by Cassandra Austen's misfortune recounted in
this diary. Austen clearly liked the sound of the name and its varia-
tions; and her godmother was Jane Musgrave of Oxfordshire, a relative of her mother's. —*Editor's note.*

superior tea—an excellent Darjeeling—in Captain Fielding's attractive blue and white drawing-room, and had then quitted the house to observe the last slanting rays of sunlight in the gentleman's garden. Captain Fielding reveals himself as a devotee of the rose, on a scale that rivals the Empress Josephine, for almost the entirety of his grounds is given over to beds of that noble flower—though sadly for us, well past its blooming.

"But this is charming, Captain Fielding!" my sister exclaimed; among the Austens, she is the true lover of the garden and its healthful exercise, and is possessed of a remarkable taste in the arranging of beds and successive waves of seasonal bloom. "Utterly delightful! And in June, when the roses flower, it must be a veritable Eden!"

"Eden must not be considered as approaching it, Miss Austen," the Captain replied. "For *my* garden has no snakes."

"But what energy and industry has been here applied!" Cassandra continued. "And you are not even resident in the place very long."

"No—but where application is steady, and the means exist for the furthering of work, all manner of change may be swiftly effected. I have had teams of men labouring here to rival Crawford's fossil pits. Where we stand this very moment, was only two years ago a pitiful stretch of downs, replete with scrub heath and the occasional fox den."

"Extraordinary," Lucy Armstrong said quietly, and gazed around her with a wistful air. "I remember this place some months ago, Captain Fielding, when you entertained us all at dinner. The roses were then in bloom—and a glorious sight it was." She gave me a brief smile, as though lost in a pretty memory, and moved on down the path with my sister.

Captain Fielding offered his left arm, which I gladly

accepted, and we followed behind. The Captain employs a walking cane when attempting a greensward, and must progress more slowly as a result, so that Cassandra and Miss Armstrong were soon at some little distance from ourselves.

"I venture to hope, Miss Jane Austen, that you shall again walk among these flowers, when their scent fills the air with a headiness unequalled, and their petals suggest a grace that can only be found in your lovelier form," my companion said, in a lowered tone.

I blushed and turned away; for the import of his words was unmistakable. But I affected not to understand him, and said only, "I hope I shall often have reason to visit Lyme. It is a place and a society that has become quite dear to me. To fix one's residence by the sea, is, I believe, to live in the greatest privilege and the most salubrious circumstance."

"You dislike Bath, then?"

"Who can feel otherwise, who is consigned to spend the entire year through, in a place destined for pleasure parties and occasional travellers? The sameness, and yet the constant parting with friends, happy in their return to quieter homes; the bustle, and the self-importance, and yet the nothingness of the town; the white glare of its buildings, the fearful drains, the endless parade of the fashionable and the foolish, hopeful of cures from the sluggish waters—no, Captain Fielding, I cannot love Bath. It is become a prison to my spirit, however gilded the trappings of the cage."

"I regret to hear it," he said slowly. "But you will have some weeks yet in Lyme."

"Yes," I said, recovering. "We intend to remain here through November. I cherish every day, and count out those remaining, as though I turn the rarest pearls along a string."

The Captain raised his fair head, and gazed into the distance, his eyes narrowing. "Miss Austen!" he cried. "Miss Armstrong! We are losing the light, I fear, and must turn back."

"And what is that place my sister has come to?" I enquired, in gazing upon a prettyish little wilderness some yards before us.

"It is my temple ruin," Captain Fielding said abruptly, "a colonnade of stone, in wisteria and hedgerose. Your sister has found it necessary to rest some few moments, but she cannot remain there."

I must have looked my surprise at his terse words, so clearly expressive of a proprietary interest in the *place*, rather than in Cassandra's state; but in a moment, I understood the cause of Captain Fielding's distress.

"I must chide myself for an overactive enthusiasm in exhibiting these grounds—and in so vigourous a manner," he said, "for assuredly the walk has proved too much for her delicate health."

And indeed, Cassandra was slumped upon a bench in an attitude of great fatigue, while Lucy Armstrong searched frantically among her green muslin pockets for what I imagined to be some errant smelling salts. The enquiring eyes of a stone wood nymph, arranged over a little door that stood ajar in the temple's wall, looked down upon the tableau. That the door shielded an area for the storage of garden implements, I readily discerned; for a huddle of indiscriminate shapes, cloaked in sail-cloth, was revealed by the setting sun—and a clever usage it was for a wilderness ruin. Captain Fielding's house is entirely fitted out with such similarly charming notions—reflective, perhaps, of a man accustomed to tight quarters on a ship. I had observed the snug arrangement of his bookshelves and desk, the latter article having a removable surface for writing in one's chair, as we earlier passed through the library; and indeed, little that the Captain owns is designed purely for ornament, or for a single purpose, serving a variety of duties in ways that are decidedly ingenious. I thought of Frank, whose life is similarly efficient in its organisation, and shook my head fondly at my brother's plans to marry.[2] Mary Gibson should make a sad business of Frank's tidy habits.

As we approached, Cassandra raised her head, her countenance suffused with pain. "I have overtaxed my strength, dearest Jane," she said, "and must run the risk of offending you, Captain Fielding, with my plea for a return to Wings cottage."

He turned from securing the door beneath the nymph's head, and cried, "It shall be done with the greatest dispatch. A moment only is required for the summoning of Jarvis. But tell me, Miss Austen—can you attempt the walk to the house?"

"If Jane will support me on the one hand, and Miss Armstrong on the other, it may be done," Cassandra replied, and slowly regained her feet with an air of grim resolution. I hastened to her side and suffered her to rest her weight against my shoulder, my arm around her waist and my heartbeat rendered the more rapid by a fearsome anxiety. A quick glance at Captain Fielding revealed the agony of regret that suffused his countenance; and I knew as though he had spoken aloud, that his mind was a turmoil of recrimination and anger at the disability that prevented him from providing greater assistance. But a lame man, dependent upon a cane for his own support, was hardly likely to serve as a prop for my suffering sister; and

[2] Frank Austen had recently fallen in love with Mary Gibson, a girl of Ramsgate whom Jane found disappointing—she considered her as vulgar as her town. Frank married Miss Gibson in 1805; they had six sons and five daughters before her death in childbirth. —*Editor's note.*

so I left him to sort out his manly feelings in peace, and turned my attention where it was the more necessary.

We had progressed perhaps one half the full length of the garden walk, when Cassandra begged to rest upon a bench; such dizzyness as overwhelmed her, coupled with a throbbing at the temples, nearly dropping her where she stood. I bit my lip, and wished for some greater aid— my brother, perhaps, or even Eliza—while Lucy Armstrong satisfied her tender feelings in repeated enquiries of Cassandra, and the triumphant production of the smelling salts. At last my sister rose, and managed to regain the house; whereupon Captain Fielding sent for his carriage and bade the housemaid fetch some brandy. This last having been administered, Cassandra sat back upon the settee with streaming eyes and a choking cough, unaccustomed as she is to strong spirits; and turned to me with all the terror of her infirmity upon her face.

"Jane!" she cried, though her voice was but a whisper; "I had thought myself completely recovered! It was not so very great an injury; the rest of my dear family suffered little from the coach's overturning; and I am several days removed from the event. And yet my present pain is unbearable. Can it be that I have received a greater knocking than was at first understood? Or that Mr. Dagliesh has mistaken the extent of the malady?"

"Such fretful thoughts cannot improve your prospects for the remainder of our travel home," I said gently, as the sound of wheels upon the gravel revealed the barouche as even then standing before the door. "We will consult with Mr. Dagliesh as soon as ever we may."

Captain Fielding assisted us to the carriage with the greatest concern alive upon his countenance, and urged the coachman to achieve his two-miles' journey with all possible speed, though mindful not to jar the lady. And so, with these conflicting orders settled upon his head, poor Jarvis clucked to the horses, and we were off.

The ride itself was uneventful, being spent chiefly in the sort of silence that only arises from great perturbation of spirit; and I sighed with relief as the barouche began the descent into Broad Street, and the cheerful lights of Wings cottage appeared through the growing dusk.

We were not to be afforded the comfort of an uneventful arrival, however—for Cassandra had only to set foot to paving stone, before crumpling in a faint upon the ground.

AND SO MR. DAGLIESH WAS SUMMONED AT THE BEHEST OF MY brother Henry, who was even then within the cottage awaiting our return, the better to give his fondest adieux—for he and Eliza depart for Weymouth today, to tour the town and observe the embarkation of the Royal Family.[3] From thence they should travel to Ibthorpe, and by a leisurely route return to No. 16 Michael's Place, and their neat little home. But at the outcry and bustle from the very gate, my dear brother rushed to our assistance; and his anxiety was the more extreme, from being motivated by surprise. Miss Armstrong and I were more sanguine, having journeyed in some anticipation of the event.

I may say that Mr. Dagliesh was *very* angry; he regarded us all as having precipitated a dangerous relapse, by our determination to force Cassandra over-early into activity; and he ordered the strictest quiet, the administration of broth, and the application alternately of ice and warm compresses, for the relief of my sister's throbbing temples. The poor surgeon's assistant stood some few minutes by her bedside, holding her wrist between his fingers

---

[3] George III and his retinue made a habit of visiting the Dorset village of Weymouth, where his brother the Duke of Gloucester often stayed. —*Editor's note.*

as though intent upon her pulse; but I knew him to be utterly inattentive to the flutter of Cassandra's heart, so clearly were his thoughts fixed upon the agony within his own.

He departed not long thereafter, in search of some ice from the Golden Lion, and assuring us of his return at the earliest hour of the morning; and it remained only for us to determine the wisest course. The consultation of Dagliesh's superior, Mr. Carpenter, was much canvassed, and rejected by my mother, who had learned something to that gentleman's detriment from a recent Lyme acquaintance, one Miss Bonham, who claimed a persistent nervous fever. Henry at last voiced the thought chief within all our minds—that Cassandra should accompany himself and Eliza on their return to London, that trip being expedited by the amendment of the plan, and a determination to proceed with all possible swiftness towards Michael's Place; for the opinion of a physician, with all the experience of a city practice, should be solicited as soon as possible. My father agreed; my mother lamented and groaned at this loss of her favourite; and I felt a pang at the loneliness I should undoubtedly feel in Cassandra's absence.

"Should not I accompany you, Henry, the better to nurse my sister?" I asked, in a lowered tone, as my mother hastened to the kitchen for a warm poultice.

"Eliza shall amply supply your place, Jane; for, you know, she was many years in attendance upon poor Hastings.[4] Better that you remain to comfort my mother and father." Henry smiled and patted my arm. "Despite the events of this evening, I do not believe Cassandra to be in any real danger; a bit of peace and quiet, and restorative

---

[4] Henry refers here to his stepson, Hastings de Feuillide, Eliza's sickly son. The boy died in 1801 at the age of fourteen. —*Editor's note.*

sleep, shall soon reverse the indifferent state of her health.''

I GAZE UPON HER NOW, AS SHE SLUMBERS STILL IN THE EARLY WATCH of morning, and pray that it may be so. In a few hours she shall be torn from me, and all the delightful prospects of our Lyme visit o'erthrown; I shall have no one but Miss Armstrong for rambling the Cobb, or climbing the chasms of the Pinny, and my solitary visits to Mr. Milsop's glove counter shall be melancholy indeed. Poor Mr. Dagliesh shall feel it acutely, I am afraid—but Cassandra was afforded little time to return him anything but gratitude, for his attentive and solicitous care; a deeper emotion— an emotion capable of displacing the unfortunate Tom Fowle in her heart—would require such lightness of spirit and limitless days as are presently denied her.

And what of myself? Exists there the seed of feeling, that I might try what limitless days and lightness of spirit may do? And if there be a seed—in whose favour planted?

I had occasion to lie awake much of the night in contemplation of the vagaries of the heart—due, perhaps, to the shallow breathing of my sister tossing beside me, or perhaps to the contrariety of my own heart's impulses. I have ever been possessed of too passionate a nature, however I would cloak it in a general appearance of sobriety and sense. It has led me to care too readily and too deeply, for men whose circumstances are utterly unequal to my own—being separated the one from the other by either a gulf in fortune, or a disparity in nature that does not recommend of happiness. Geoffrey Sidmouth belongs most clearly to the latter. A more reasonable woman should give her heart without reservation to the gallant Captain, whose apparent good nature, firm principles, and forthright contempt for all that is ignoble, proclaim him to be the stuff of which England is made. And yet my heart is unmoved by Percival Fielding; I find him possessed of intelligence and integrity, and wish him more blessed by cleverness and good humour.

And beyond all this, is a something *more*—a want of that which I cannot quite define. The Captain speaks and behaves entirely as he ought; and yet I cannot feel that he is open. There is an *affectation* of openness—he was surely frankness itself yesterday, in discussing the smugglers' affairs—and yet I have the creeping certainty that he is open by design, and *that* only when it suits his purpose.

Geoffrey Sidmouth, on the contrary, is neither open nor secretive; that gentleman is merely the master of his own business. *His* emotions are so hardly checked, as to be almost transparent; one will always know where one *is*, though utterly confounded as to *why*. His is an eager, a forthright, temperament; and even in his blackest moments—when I find nothing easier than to mistrust his purpose—I know myself to be in the presence of the man. With Captain Fielding, one is ever in the presence of a caricature. Even his gallantries are studied.

I had reason to consider this but a few hours ago, well before my return to Cassandra's still-slumbering form, and the quieter comforts of my pen. I was awakened, as two days before, by a great hallooing along the Cobb; and with a sickening certainty I saw in my mind's eye the ghastly scaffold raised once more, and the lifeless body awash in surf. At the sound of men's voices I threw back the covers, and hastily exchanged my nightclothes for yesterday's discarded muslin; a moment's thought instructed the choice of stout boots over my usual slippers. It required but an instant to descend the stairs as noiselessly as I knew how, and exit Wings cottage.

I lifted my trembling eyes to the Cobb's end—but not a gibbet was to be seen. Along the wide beach that fronts The Walk came a parade of toiling men, casks upon their backs; and great wains were drawn up along the shingle, with the horses full in the water to their very flanks' height. Feeling rather foolish, but nonetheless thoroughly roused, I proceeded along The Walk until I had gained a better view—and espied two galleys, with crews at their oars, bobbing in the very waters where the smugglers' cargo had been dropped the previous day!

"So they would retrieve it, then, as Captain Fielding asserted," I said aloud, in some wonderment; and was rewarded by a reply of sorts, and from my very elbow.

"At an hour when most women should dread to be seen abroad, you are lovelier than I might have imagined, Miss Jane Austen of Bath."

I swiftly turned, in some dismay and confusion, and found Mr. Geoffrey Sidmouth on the sand below, seated easily astride a black stallion of fearsome appearance; the animal's nostrils flared as it chuffed at the wind and tossed its powerful head. I stepped backwards involuntarily, and clasped my arms together, shivering somewhat from the morning's chill. In an instant Sidmouth had dismounted and secured the horse; and in another, he had divested himself of his cloak and draped it about my shoulders, so swiftly I had not time to protest.

"The breeze is cold off the water at dawn," he said, with an indifferent air. "We cannot have you catch your death, however deserved of your impetuous nature. Dagliesh has enough to do at Wings cottage."

I swept my eyes the length of his powerful figure, and noted that he was in a similarly-disheveled state. His wine-coloured coat was stained with a dark liquid I could not identify, but took to be spirits; his stock was undone, his jaw unshaven, and his hair decidedly ruffled by long exposure to the wind. He might almost have been abroad the entire night through, and be only now upon his road home, and tarrying by the scene at the water's edge; and

with a sudden blush, I imagined the hours of dissipation
now put behind him.

"What brings you to the Cobb, sir?" I enquired. "And
at such an hour!"

"I might ask the same of you, Miss Jane Austen of
Bath." His voice held too much amusement for my fragile
pride.

"I thought to observe another unfortunate fisherman,
hanged for the Reverend's sins," I retorted, "and at the
hullabaloo below my window, ran out to offer assistance."

"Singular," Mr. Sidmouth observed coolly. "Very singular indeed. Most women should faint dead away at the
mere prospect. But then, you are always a singular person-
ality, Miss Austen. It was just such a sense of purpose in
extremity that drove you to my very door, some few days
ago."

For this, I had no answer; and we were silent, observing
the activity below in the fitful light. The sun was not yet
up, and the industrious figures flitted like shadows in a
graveyard. Sidmouth's eyes were narrowed over the sharp
hook of his nose, and his lips compressed; and I wondered, as I stole a glance at him sidelong, whether I stood
next to the very Reverend, in the act of overseeing his
cargo's landing.

"It is a smuggler's goods," I said, with the most casual
air I could effect; "Captain Fielding and I observed the
cutter only yesterday, as it jettisoned those very casks."
For the labouring men were wading through the surf with
a massive barrel suspended from each shoulder, and
heaving them into the carts drawn up to the water; and
despite the weight of the contraband, as evidenced in
their bowed backs, their progress was swift indeed. In but
a moment, I imagined, the last of the waggons should be
filled, and the horses turned towards some safe place of
hiding in the midst of the downs—but would they be wel-

comed by a girl in a sweeping red cloak, her spigot lant-horn[5] held high in the dusky dawn?

"French brandy." Sidmouth spoke as though re-marking upon the weather. "It shall be turned a proper brown in some hole in the woods, and be on its way to London in a very few days.[6] But you look stupefied, Miss Austen—surely you knew that French brandy, like the cheeks of so many French ladies, does not win its colour from Nature?"

"I am simply all amazement, Mr. Sidmouth," I re-joined, "that so much brandy *exists*. There must be enough in those waggons to keep London afloat for a year!"

"Or the members of White's,[7] at the very least," the gentleman replied ironically.

"And what organisation! What dispatch! The Royal Navy should observe these fellows' methods, the better to order their gunnery crews!"

"See there, the one in the blue cap, who stands aloof along the shoreline?" Mr. Sidmouth's face moved closer to my own, and his left arm extended before my nose, the better to distinguish his object. "*He* is Davy Forely, this crew's lander; and a better lander is not to be found along the entire Dorset coast."

"And what, pray, is a lander?"

---

[5] A spigot lanthorn is as Austen described it in the first chapter—a curiously shaped lamp designed specifically for signaling. It was tall, cylindrical, and entirely closed except for the spigot projecting from one side, the open end of which could be covered and uncovered by the signaler's hand, emitting a blink of light. It was frequently em-ployed by smugglers. —*Editor's note.*

[6] French brandy was considered "raw" when it hit English shores, because it was colorless. The smugglers would mix it with burnt sugar to give it the deep golden hue the English expected, and probably thinned it with water as well. —*Editor's note.*

[7] An exclusive men's club in Pall Mall. —*Editor's note.*

"The fellow employed by the smuggling captain to organise the men on shore," Mr. Sidmouth said patiently. "He it is that recruits them, and pays them, and makes certain they are loyal to the game."

"I had not realised it to be so sophisticated a profession, as to admit of hierarchies," I replied. "Your knowledge of the whole can hardly be to your credit."

He looked at me with some surprise. "I have known these men some few years, and may call them the most honest band of rogues in the entire Kingdom. Indeed, I have had occasion to depend upon their very efficiency and organisation. They have served my ends whenever needed, and saved my life more than once; and I should be churlish indeed, did I not offer them the praise that is their due."

"Mr. Sidmouth—" I began, in some perturbation at the import of his words; but my speech was stopped in my mouth, by the appearance on the shingle of a gentleman in a good blue coat, who leaned upon a cane, and observed the proceedings with an air of satisfaction—Captain Fielding, without a doubt, and beside him in the darkling dawn, a stranger to my sight—a short, spare man of wizened appearance, and heavy spectacles, and a protruding lower lip, whose gaze was bent upon the shore's activity with the bulbous intensity of a frog's. I had barely noted the Captain's arrival, in the company of this rare fellow, when the latter raised his arm as though in prearranged signal, and with a cry to harrow the bones of the very dead, a company of dragoons in the bright-hued uniform of the Crown descended upon the beach, bayonets extended, pell-mell into the crowd of burdened men.

"Good Lord!" I cried, forgetting myself in the tumult of the moment, "they shall be overrun!"

Sparing neither an oath nor a moment's hesitation, Mr. Sidmouth unloosed his horse, sprang upon its noble back, and threw himself down the Cobb to the shoreline's edge, his black hair streaming behind him. Full into the swarm of dragoons and struggling men he rode, lashing to the left and right with his crop. I stood open-mouthed upon The Walk, aghast at his activity; for the King's men were armed, and I assumed that Sidmouth was not, any more than the smugglers themselves should bear fire-arms—for to do so, I knew, was punishable by death. Clubs only they had in defence of their illegal trade, and these they brandished; but the threat of ball and powder proved too much, and even the hardiest of the lander's crew were soon forced to submit, and shuffled downcast from the surf past the triumphant Captain Fielding. I observed *that* result of the melee only at its close, however; for I confess the first object of my eyes was Geoffrey Sidmouth and the progress of his plunging horse.

He forged a path through the tumult, and rode to where the lander, Davy Forely, stood, shouting orders to his routed men; and in an instant, had grasped the fellow's shirt back and heaved him behind. With a cry and a lash, the stallion sprang forward, and broke from the chaotic scene; but Sidmouth was not to be let slip so easily. Captain Fielding had observed his course, and now harried a party of three dragoons to spring to the pursuit; and with weapons lowered and animal yells loosed from their lips, the men closed in upon the horse's hindquarters. Forely shouted, and kicked at the faces of the pursuing dragoons; the stallion screamed and reared as Sidmouth struggled with the reins; and as I watched, the master of High Down turned in the saddle, pulled a revolver from his coat, and aimed it, thankfully, in the air. A single ball was fired, and resounded above the duller noises of clubs and bitter oaths; and the dragoons, incredibly, halted where they stood. Mr. Sidmouth is plainly a gentleman, of a higher order than the smugglers' band; and, unlike them, his possession of a firearm could hardly cause comment; but the King's men were nonetheless amazed. One only shook himself out of his stupor, and levelled a blunderbuss; and though Sidmouth mastered the horse and attempted to flee the shingle, the dragoon let fire a ball. I saw Forely arch his back in pain, his teeth clenched in a terrible grimace; for an instant of suspended breath, I felt certain the lander should slip from the stallion's heaving flanks; but he proved greater than his wound, and clutched the tighter at Sidmouth, who kicked his horse up the slope with a furious oath. In a very little time, he and his clinging passenger gained the streets of town, the dragoons outstripped, and vanished from sight.

I heaved a shuddering sigh, and wondered at the racing of my heart; and attempted, as best I could, to quiet the chaos of my mind—until, recollecting how unseemly was my presence in the midst of such brutish behaviour, I turned and hastened back along the Parade towards the safety of Wings cottage. I cared not whether Captain Fielding had observed my silent form, high above the brawling men—I cared not what he thought of its purpose or propriety—I felt only the bitterest anger towards that gentleman, though for the life of me, I knew not how to reconcile it. The Captain had done what any man of decency and sound principles *should* do; he had observed the weighting of the cargo in exactly that spot by the Cobb, only the previous afternoon, and he had reported the same to the Revenue men at the nearest opportunity. Having received such excellent intelligence as Captain Fielding was able to provide, the dragoons should have been decidedly remiss in failing to apprehend the smugglers; but it smacked, all the same, of the setting of mantraps on purpose to break a poacher's leg—poor sport indeed, and reflective, in my humble opinion, of a man who delights in mastery at any cost.

"But Sidmouth is yet free," I murmured, as I opened our garden gate, "though he *is* the Reverend, without a doubt''; and I swung myself up the path, feeling a sadness and an exhilaration at his reprehensible daring. I opened the cottage door, and stepped inside, to my mother's open-mouthed regard—and stopped short, overcome with a blush.

"Whatever have you got about your shoulders, child? And where have you gone in such a state, so early in the morning?"

"I took a turn along The Walk, Mother," I replied, realising, as I did so, that a smuggler's cloak was yet warm upon my back. "It is the very soul of a September dawn, and I could not be kept indoors."

"Mind you wake Cassandra in time for the coach," she called after me, as I mounted the stairs, her puzzlement at my garb replaced by more immediate concerns. I fluttered a hand in the good woman's direction, and hastened towards the comfort of my room—the heady scents of pipe tobacco and brandy, lingering as they will in fine English wool, aflame in my lungs at every breath.

Chapter 8

Sense, or Sensibility?

IT IS ALMOST A SE'ENNIGHT SINCE I LAST TOOK UP THIS JOURNAL, AND much of import has occurred. I have had a letter of Cassandra in Weymouth, remarking upon the Royal Family's embarkation (which she and Eliza failed to witness, on account of a preoccupation with a milliner's wares), and the lack of ice in the entire town, which cannot have done her aching head much good. I had heard already of both eventualities, for Mr. Crawford had occasion to travel to Weymouth yesterday, and encountered Cassandra there— and his being able to assure us that she appears in good looks and improved spirits, somewhat outweighed the pain of our separation, which I am sure she feels as acutely as myself. But she sounds as cheerful as one might, who has been denied the delights of Lyme and her sister's company, not to mention the anxious attention of Mr. Dagliesh. Of *that* gentleman, whose spirits are quite sunk at Cassandra's absence, I had occasion to write—but forbore from doing so, in the knowledge that my dear sister and the surgeon's assistant are little likely ever to meet again. To convey tidings of his undiminished regard, and know how little it might avail Cassandra in her general loneliness and poor health, seemed nothing more than foolishness. And so when I answered her letter this morning—posted to Ibthorpe, where I believe Henry's carriage shall convey them this evening—I chattered on cheerfully about the ubiquitous dirt of Wings cottage, and the slovenly Cook, and my own poor efforts to supply Cassandra's place, and be useful and keep things in order. I told her a little of the manservant James, a willing and good-hearted young fellow, who is so earnest a student at his letters, that I have undertaken to supply him with my father's discarded newspapers; and of my own expedition to Charmouth in recent days, for the daring trial of sea-bathing.

It was then my occasion to ruminate on last night's Assembly—which, though pleasant, was not very full for Thursday; the Miss Schuylers were gone away some days, and though their return is imminent, I understand from Mrs. Barnewall that they think of quitting Lyme altogether in the coming week. I was actually honoured in Mr. Crawford's asking me to dance *twice*, that gentleman being moved to pity by the dearth of younger fellows in the rooms; though a new, odd-looking man, whom I judged to be Irish by his ease, and in the company of the Honourable Barnewalls, *might* have asked me—but came to the point of it only as I was quitting the rooms.

Mr. Dagliesh was present in the Assembly from the first moment, until called out by Mr. Carpenter to answer the pressing need of a child scalded in a pan of dishwater. At my entering the rooms, the surgeon's assistant was indeed the first acquaintance I perceived—for he hastened to my side, and took my hand so earnestly, and enquired what news I had of my sister—at which Mr. Crawford intervened.

"Her flight from your ministrations appears to have

done her a world of good, Dagliesh," Mr. Crawford said, with great good humour and a slyly conscious look for the blushing fellow; "I was so very fortunate as to encounter Miss Austen this morning with her party in Weymouth, and found her much improved. I was able to convey the happy intelligence to all her dear family only a few hours ago."

"Happy, indeed, to have been in so lovely a creature's presence," Mr. Dagliesh murmured, with a distracted air. "I am relieved to find that Miss Austen's removal did not increase the pain of her injuries."

"My brother Henry's carriage is so good, and his horses so gentle, that I am sure her passage along the coastal roads occurred without incident," I assured him. "We were sorry, Mr. Dagliesh, that you failed to make your own *adieux* to my sister; but her departure could not be delayed, as it depended upon the wishes and needs of others; and you *had* said you would attend her very early that morning."

The gentleman stammered, and looked confused; and indeed, seemed in such an agony of emotion, that I instantly took pity upon him. "But a surgeon's days are never his own to command, as my sister and I fully comprehend. You could not, perhaps, have come any earlier."

Mr. Dagliesh had appeared at Wings cottage, in all the disorder of extreme haste, some two hours after Cassandra's departure, and his disappointment at the fact suggested that he had been prevented from attending my sister by a sudden interference of events—and that he was quite put out by the loss of his farewell. From his present regret, I received a further conviction of my supposition's truth.

"I was called away suddenly—an injury of some moment—and with no other assistance available," he said, somewhat brokenly. "Not for anything but the direst circumstance should I have neglected to offer my compliments to Miss Austen. Pray convey them to her at the nearest opportunity, and I shall be the better for having attempted to make amends. I draw some comfort from the news that she is much improved; it is all that I could wish for."

"You are too good," I said gently. "I am sure that the knowledge of your heartfelt regard has furthered her recovery."

The poor gentleman was so much overcome by this notion, as to be rendered almost insensible for several moments; and though he collected himself enough to request my hand for the first dance, he was called away not long thereafter, and so our mutual expectation of felicity—mine, in being so soon solicited, and his, in the prospect of discussing nothing but Cassandra for a full half-hour—were all o'erthrown.

The circle was somewhat enlivened by the appearance of Miss Lucy Armstrong's father and mother—enlivened by the opportunity their presence afforded, of observing how heartily they are disliked by Miss Crawford. The Armstrongs have come down from Bath (by the terrible post chaise), expressly to retrieve poor Lucy from her summer idyll—and upon my word, idyll it must have been, with all its trials, in comparison to her usual society—for the parents are of a vulgar turn, quite apparent in Mrs. Armstrong's choice of gown, a brilliant yellow silk with black jet beads running the length of her very lengthy train[1]— unsuitable for September, and particularly for Lyme. The lady's manner does not improve upon further acquaintance, for when I visited Lucy yesterday morning—being desperate for female society in the absence of my dear sister—Mrs. Armstrong sat darning a sock the entire time

---

[1] The length of a woman's train increased with her desire for elegance; Austen usually ascribes a long sweep to her more vulgar characters, such as Isabella Thorpe in *Northanger Abbey*. —*Editor's note.*

I was present, and seemed quite given to conversing with herself, through a series of exclamations and sighs, regarding the poor quality of Miss Crawford's housemaid. I do not believe she heard above half a dozen words that passed. But my own mother is little better—being equally adept at self-distraction—and I must desist from mocking the habits of *others,* lest my derision come home to roost.

Miss Armstrong and I soon abandoned her parents for a walk along the Cobb, and the exercise and mutual pleasure in each other's society soon raised our spirits. The girl is a poor substitute for Cassandra or Eliza, but her understanding improves the further she flees from Miss Crawford's sharp tongue; she is conversable in a common way, though I perceive neither wit nor genius. Lucy is possessed of sense, and some degree of taste; and unlike her mother or aunt, her manners are most engaging. I must believe it is *this* quality—a general air of agreeability—that endears her to Mr. Sidmouth; for that he admires her—though to what degree I cannot be certain—is evident in the attention he continues to pay her.[2]

I had occasion to observe the gentleman rogue of High Down at the Assembly last evening, for Mr. Sidmouth appeared towards the close of the ball, and well after my father had departed with James and his lanthorn for Wings cottage—disappointed in his hopes of playing at loo, my mother being for commerce, and Captain Fielding moved to affect his attitude of *le Chevalier,* by gallantly acceding to her request that he partner her at the table. In the event, they divided the pot between them—a

[2] Much of this description of the past few days, and Austen's circle of acquaintance in Lyme, may be found almost verbatim in the surviving letter she wrote to Cassandra the same morning as this journal entry. A copy of that letter was not included in this journal, but can be found in the collected correspondence (*Jane Austen's Letters,* Deirdre LeFaye, ed., Third Edition. Oxford: Oxford University Press, 1995, Letter #39, page 92). —*Editor's note.*

testament, I fear, to Captain Fielding's superior understanding; for when my mother plays with another as equally prone to forgetfulness as herself, she rarely triumphs in so prosperous a fashion.

But now to Mr. Sidmouth—who, I declare, is possessed of the greatest *sang-froid*, in parading himself before the very society that must have observed his embattled flight a few dawns previous. He was as cool and collected as ever, bowing with frigid gentility in Captain Fielding's direction; and being prevented from partnering myself in the first two dances, by my engagement to Mr. Crawford, he soon made himself available to Miss Armstrong, who was glad enough to take his hand. He was all that could be desired in a partner; he danced well, did not confuse the figures, or trample her pale blue slippers; he attempted to converse, and from what snatches I overheard, kept the talk in a general way; but the fact of his attention seemed to overwhelm his fair partner. I observed that she spent the better part of the hour consigned to his company, with downcast eyes and a scarlet throat— Ah! The delicate sensibility of nineteen!

I wish I could find it in myself to envy Miss Armstrong; I should like to strike the attitude of a slighted heroine, and languish in forsaken love for one or another of the gentlemen thrown in my way; but she is too pale a figure for competition. I am convinced, upon reflection, that Mr. Sidmouth enjoys her company as he might that of a flower found along the roadside—there is little of heat or intensity in his regard. He is not the sort of man for an easy passion.

"Sidmouth!" Mr. Crawford cried, in approaching his friend at the dance's close. "How comes your lovely cousin not to grace the rooms this evening? And I do not recall that she was with us last week, or the week before, if it comes to that. It is too bad of you! We *must have* Mademoiselle LeFevre, if Lyme is to aspire to any real elegance!"

"I regret that my cousin is indisposed this evening," Sidmouth returned, with a slight bow and a formal air; "but I shall convey to her your sentiments, which cannot but be pleasing."

"And she *must* get out, eh? It has been an age since I have seen her—or, more to the point, been delighted by her singing! Come now. You cannot keep her at home in this stupid manner," Crawford said, with a jocular glance for me. "I am to have a smallish dinner party Saturday e'en—a sort of farewell for my Lucy—and you shall both come. Mademoiselle LeFevre's indisposition, I trust, will be but a trifling matter in four-and-twenty hours?"

"I may not presume to say. But I shall provide her with the opportunity to choose—and try whether the delights of Darby exceed those of High Down."

"Capital! I shall order a couple of dozen ducks killed on the strength of it—for Mademoiselle cannot give up a dinner at Darby; I am sure of it. The Austens, of course, shall be there"—this, with a bow for me—"and one or two others. Capital!"

And so Mr. Crawford moved on, issuing invitations as he went, and leaving me to the mercies of Mr. Sidmouth, who gave me a long look and the barest suggestion of a smile.

"You do not wear your sister's gown this evening," he observed, "and though the pink *was* becoming, and your own white muslin is more ravishing still, I should prefer to think of you always as you appeared a few mornings ago— like a siren on the rocks, your hair swept by the wind, and your arms wrapped close around a borrowed cloak."

I blushed hotly—and cursed my wayward cheeks, which are too frequently suffused with scarlet, and ever the bane of my existence. The frankness of Sidmouth's speech—

the warmth with which the words were spoken—almost unnerved me; but I recollected in time the nature of our parting that morning, and was strengthened enough to meet his eyes.

"I cannot think the episode too soon forgotten!" I cried. "Better you had saved your cloak to hide your shame! The reprehensible nature of your conduct—the blatant admission of your interest in the smugglers' affairs—and now, to *parade* your renegade self before all of Lyme, and with impunity—it is, in every respect, incredible!"

His countenance changed; and the dark eyes lost their intensity, and became remote. "I can find nothing for which to reproach myself," he told me. "I acted as any honourable man should, when a friend is endangered; and I should act in a similar way again, should circumstances require it."

"A friend! You call such a common criminal *friend*?"

"I do," he replied, with a set to his jaw. "I call any man friend who should not hesitate to lay down his life, if need be, in order to preserve my own. Davy Forely has risked as much, on several occasions I can number; and my own poor efforts to secure his freedom a few days past, are as nothing in the tally of obligation I owe."

"You amaze me, sir! Do the claims of a gentleman, of your very country—indeed, of everything affecting your respectability and position in life—have so little power to move you?"

Mr. Sidmouth bowed, and was silent; but that he struggled with conflicting emotions, I perceived in his countenance; and felt that my words, and the truth behind them, had succeeded in striking his hardened heart. Indeed, I believe he would have spoken, had Captain Fielding not approached at that very moment, and with the barest acknowledgement of Sidmouth's presence, requested my hand for the next dance—a cotillion.[3] I was enough possessed by my fever of indignation, to accept him with a very pretty grace; and when I turned to witness the triumph of my regard upon Mr. Sidmouth's features, I found him already across the room, and in the happy company of Miss Armstrong and Mrs. Barnewall.

I regret to say, that though Captain Fielding attempted to engage my attention the length of our half-hour, and exerted the full force of his intelligent person—though he paid me some fulsome compliments, and affected to place me above every other occupant of the room—that my thoughts were abstracted, more often than not, and my gaze *would* wander.

"You are not yourself, Miss Austen; you are decidedly not yourself," the Captain observed, after several unsuccessful trials at conversation.

"Pray forgive me, sir," I replied, with some remorse, and pulled my gaze back to his weathered face. "I am merely distracted by the remembrance of events I witnessed a few days ago."

"Ah. I recollect. You were there, on The Walk, when Sidmouth showed his hand; I observed you standing in all the appalled recognition of the import of his behaviour."

"I cannot deny that I was *then* as one amazed; but I am little reassured *now* by his appearance tonight! So easy as he seems, with all of Lyme in possession of his true identity, his unscrupulous way of life!"

"I agree that it is in every way incredible," Captain Fielding said soberly. "But I expect little else of a man

---

[3] A brisk dance characterized by intricate figures and frequent changing of partners. Other dances common to the country Assembly Rooms were the minuet—which generally opened a ball—the ecossaise, the contredanse, and a variety of Scotch reels and English country dances. The waltz, considered "fast," made its first London appearance by 1812, and the quadrille—a type of square dance with music in five movements of varying tempos—in 1816. —*Editor's note.*

like Sidmouth. His propensities are so very vicious—his principles so very depraved—that even the open acknowledgement of the evil is as nothing to him."

"Can he be so lost to everything?" I cried, unwilling to believe that any man might be.

"He can, and he is." Captain Fielding's assurance would have been more acceptable to my ears had it rung less with quiet satisfaction. "But Lyme shall suffer his sort of insolence only a little while longer."

I almost tripped in my movement through the figure, but recovered, and turned once more to face my partner. "You would apprehend him, then? Why did you not do so, that very morning of which we speak?"

"It would have won us only half our game," the Captain replied, in a lowered tone. "To take the Reverend, as we might have a few days past with but a little application, should be to leave his confederates abroad and capable of continued Free Trade."[4]

"But I thought the men were apprehended! There, on the shingle, and by the dragoons!"

"In the event, our effort was for naught," the Captain admitted unwillingly. "When the barrels were examined, they were found to contain only common beer, and from the Golden Lion. No, Miss Austen—the Reverend won in the last instance. Mr. Cavendish, the Lyme Customs man, believes the true cargo to have been retrieved during the small hours of morning; and the effort you witnessed at dawn—and which the dragoons thoroughly routed—was but a sham, a diversion for the law. We could apprehend no one, for the unloading of a cargo of beer; and indeed,

---

[4] *Free Trade* was the term smugglers applied to their business, since the purpose of smuggling goods into England was to avoid the numerous and costly taxes applied to a wealth of imported items. —*Editor's note.*

we were forced to make embarrassing amends, for the blows and injuries the labourers sustained.''

"I am all astonishment," I said faintly, though I felt a ridiculous desire to laugh; and I remembered Mr. Sidmouth's tousled appearance, and my conviction he had been out all that night previous. Truly the man was despicable. His bravado, his dash, knew no limits.

"But we shall have our man," Captain Fielding continued. "We have gained intelligence of a landing some few nights hence, and Cavendish will be waiting. A very little rope remains to Mr. Sidmouth, and I may fairly say there is a noose at the end.''

I understood the Captain's feeling of triumph; but I could not glory in his sentiments. The dance very soon thereafter being come to a close, I parted from the Revenue spy with something like relief, though I chided myself for the contrariety of my feelings. The weight of principle, of all that is *right*, must be said to be firmly on Captain Fielding's side. And yet I cannot be easy at his eagerness to place another man upon the scaffold. However much Geoffrey Sidmouth has cheated the Crown of its due, through years of clandestine importation, I do not think he deserves to die for it. But *what* do I see as the alternative? Is lawlessness to be permitted, simply because it is effected with a certain style? Jane, Jane! Where are your finer sensibilities? All o'erthrown, by a man with a golden tongue and a mocking glance?

I was sufficiently out of sorts with myself to summon my mother at the close of the dance, and plead with her for an early return home; and though I took comfort in the notion that I denied Mr. Sidmouth of my company as much as *his* was denied to *me*, by my quitting the rooms, I cannot suppose him to have felt equally wounded in the loss. Maddening man! Why will you not be banished from my thoughts?

Chapter 9

Le Chevalier Unhorsed

Monday, 17 September 1804

~

My hand is shaking as I pen these words, and I fear they must appear remarkably ill upon the page; I cannot credit the anxiety of my own mind, nor the truth of the news it has received—but steady, Jane! and consider your better self. Endeavour to be calm; to reason through events; to find amidst the discomposure of your senses, some resignation to all that has occurred—

I must return in thought, therefore, to Mr. Crawford's Darby, and the excellent dinner that gentleman composed in honour of his niece, Lucy Armstrong—for I shall better comprehend the *result* of violence, only once I have considered its *precipitation*. Banish, then, the quiet of Sunday, and the gentle service at St. Michael's, in Church Street; forget yesterday's bright weather, and my walk into Up Lyme, blest with sunshine and the first turning of the leaves; banish, too, the strange happiness occasioned by Mr. Sidmouth's attentions during Saturday's dinner party at Darby, of which more anon—such quiet concerns are all o'erlaid by this morning's news, of so terrible an import!

My father engaged a chaise Saturday evening to convey us the few miles up the Charmouth road towards Darby, which revealed itself to our sight as a pleasant house of recent construction, tricked out in red brick and white mouldings, with windows that bowed to Palladio, and a gentle lawn bordered by an orchard on the one side, and a horse-filled paddock on the other. It was a gentleman's country estate, pretty and well-mannered, with the first candlelight of evening shining from the doorway.

"Reverend Austen! And Mrs. Austen! A pleasure, to be sure!" Mr. Crawford cried, as he descended the stone steps to offer his hand, his sister simpering in his wake. He was quite magnificent in a red waistcoat, and his sparse hair shone with grooming. Miss Crawford, I observed, kept steadfastly to her habitual black, although in deference to the party, she had exchanged bombazine for the finest silk.

"Welcome to Darby, one and all," our goodly host continued with enthusiasm, "though I must declare myself quite put out at your skill with cards, Mrs. Austen—I suffered such a loss Thursday as must make me your sworn enemy at every future Assembly. Our differences shall be forgot, however, madam, for the length of this evening."

"The credit must be all Captain Fielding's," my mother replied with an effort at modesty; but I knew her to be quite puffed up at her success.

"Then Darby's card tables assuredly never shall be produced," Mr. Crawford rejoined, "for the Captain is within, and I shall spend the better part of the evening in preventing a like collusion."

The affable fellow helped me from the carriage and swept his eyes the length of my pale blue muslin. I confess to having taken especial care with my dress that evening, and of having abandoned my cap for the daring measure of a feathered turban very like my sister Eliza's, and obtained only a few days previous from Mr. Milsop.

"You are decidedly lovely this evening, Miss Austen. Darby shall be beside itself, we are all got up so fine! For you know," Mr. Crawford confided, "I have prevailed upon Sidmouth to bring his cousin, the bewitching Mademoiselle LeFevre; and I perceive them even now at the turning of the drive."

I looked over my shoulder, and espied a curricle,[1] with Mr. Sidmouth at the reins; a moment, and they were upon us. Mr. Crawford hastened to the curricle's side, the better to assist Seraphine from the conveyance, his aspect all admiration.

"Mademoiselle LeFevre! Darby is honoured indeed!"

"It is I who must profess myself to be so," the lady replied, with a quiet smile and downcast eyes. And such a voice! Like the sound of cool water slipping over stones, with a depth of peace in its faintly foreign accent. The drab garb of a common field labourer she had cast off, and the red cloak was left at High Down; tonight she stood arrayed in a sprigged white lawn with a modest train, as befit her age and station, her fair hair swept up and becomingly ringed about the brow. A circlet of pearls was twined in her hair, and a bright pink sash caught at her waist. I gazed, and admired, and strained despite myself for a glimpse of ethereal wings.

"Miss Austen, you will wish to be presented to Mademoiselle," Mr. Crawford cried, quite ignorant of our pre-

---

[1] A curricle was a light, fast equipage that held only two people, and was usually drawn by one or two horses easily managed by a male passenger. It was considered a smart carriage, usually owned by young men, rather like the sports car of today. Austen, for example, has Henry Tilney drive one in *Northanger Abbey*, to the utter transport of his companion, Catherine Morland. —*Editor's note*.

vious meeting; I extended my hand, a tentative smile upon my lips, uncertain how I should be received. But my hesitancy was all unwarranted; the girl took my hand in her own, her face transformed by the gladdest of looks; and bobbed a curtsey.

"Miss Austen, Reverend Austen, Mrs. Austen—I am happy to see you once more," she said simply; but I wondered at the change in her. Where once there had been coldness and indifference, a patent dislike of unwanted strangers, there was now an evident desire to please, and to be pleased in return. To what did we owe the warmth of such a reception?—the good offices of her cousin, perhaps?

But it required only the removal of our party from the stoop to the drawing-room, for a yet more astounding meeting to ensue. Our host led the way, and behind him ourselves, so that it was some few moments before Mr. Sidmouth and Seraphine observed the presence of Captain Fielding before Darby's ornate marble mantel—a delay that only sharpened the effect of surprise. I turned, in the act of taking a chair, and observed Mademoiselle LeFevre start and draw back, her cheeks overcome with blushes and her eyes at a loss for an object; Mr. Sidmouth's countenance whitened, and he stopped short in the very doorway, a wave of rage transforming his steady gaze.

"What is the meaning of this, Crawford?" he burst out, as Captain Fielding turned from the fire with a low bow— and at his poor host's bewilderment, and Miss Crawford's stiffened form, betrayed all his consternation.

There was a moment's shocked silence, with the party utterly at a loss for words. I observed Mr. Sidmouth narrowly, and knew that he struggled for self-mastery. Above the sharp hook of his nose, his eyes had gone cold with indignation, and the dark brow was decidedly furrowed. Whatever could it mean?

"Forgive me," he finally said, in a tone that was anything but penitent; "but I fear my cousin is indisposed. It will not be in our power to remain in your company this evening."

And indeed, Seraphine's complexion had lost all brilliancy, and her golden head drooped like a swan's. One hand clung to the door frame for support, and the other found strength on the arm of her cousin. At this last, however, she raised her head and gazed clear-eyed across the room at Captain Fielding.

"Whatever do you mean, Geoffrey?" she said, in a low but steady tone. "I am quite well, and only just arrived, and have no intention of departing so soon. It would be the grossest insult to the dear Crawfords' kindness."

"Are you certain, Seraphine?" Mr. Sidmouth enquired, in a voice I could barely discern.

The briefest of nods, and Mademoiselle LeFevre glided across the room to a chair near my own, at a safe distance from Captain Fielding's position by the hearth; and at the sudden appearance in the drawing-room of Miss Armstrong and her dreadful parents, just descended from their apartments upstairs, and the subsequent arrival of the Honourable Barnewalls, the attention of the company was thankfully diverted.

"My dearest Lucy!" Mrs. Barnewall cried, sweeping into the room before a gentleman I had never seen, and immediately concluded to be the elusive Mathew, heir to the viscountcy of Kingsland. "It cannot be true that you are leaving us! Sir—" she said, turning to a bewildered Mr. Armstrong with a pretty air of desperation undoubtedly assumed for the moment—"you could not be so cruel as to deny us your daughter's society! I declare, Miss Austen, is not he the cruellest of men?"

I was spared the dubious choice of an answer by Miss Armstrong's coming forward herself, to offer her thanks for such effusion in as collected a fashion as she was capable of. Mrs. Barnewall was clothed this evening in something resembling a Roman costume, which left one shoulder entirely bare and the other encased in masses of primrose-coloured silk; about her head she bore a circlet of silver leaves, the very likeness of Caesar. I had but a moment to take in the effect of this apparition; and then it was my occasion to be presented to the Honourable Mathew.

He is a curious fellow, ham-fisted and tongue-tied, with a decidedly red face and a figure made soft through dissipation. Just what I should wish for an Irish nobleman—part yokel, part dandy, in his fine wool breeches and gold-buckled shoes, the highest of white collars tucked up to his ears, and his hair worn raffishly short and curly about his broad, sweating brow. He drooped abruptly over my hand with an indistinct mutter, his eyes shifting round the room, and as swiftly retreated to the company of Captain Fielding as decency would allow. I observed the two men in close confidence, tho' the conversation appeared to be all on the Honourable Mathew's side.[2]

"Well, Sidmouth," Mrs. Barnewall cried with some asperity, as that gentleman stood protectively by his beautiful cousin, "and so you have brought the ravishing Mademoiselle into society again, and only a few weeks after her mysterious trouble! And how well she looks, too! I wonder what *le Chevalier* must feel on the occasion?" And with that she cast a knowing glance towards Captain

[2] Mathew Barnewall is described by Deirdre LeFaye, editor of the 1995 edition of *Jane Austen's Letters*, as having been a "missing heir" to the viscountcy of Kingsland, whose early life was spent as an illiterate potboy in the slums of Dublin. His claim to his property and title was in dispute at this time. Whether Austen was aware of Barnewall's history is unclear, but it probably accounts for her perception of the incongruities in his personal demeanor and character—a strange mix of crudity overlaid with hasty polish. —*Editor's note.*

Fielding, and awaited the effect of her words. But whatever their import, Seraphine proved equal to the tall Irishwoman.

"I *feel* very well, madame, I assure you," she replied, and with a slight nod in Mrs. Barnewall's direction, moved delicately to the French windows that let out onto the garden, as though absorbed in the decline of the season. I looked to Mr. Sidmouth, and found his gaze already upon me, with an expression so torn between tenderness and pain as to arouse the deepest suspicion of his thoughts. I wondered that Mrs. Barnewall did not observe it; but the lady had turned already to Lucy's mother, the redoubtable Mrs. Armstrong, and was engaged in offering false compliments on the woman's shocking red gown.

But my own curiosity could not be gainsaid, and speculation hounded me like a nipping dog the remainder of the evening. Though Mademoiselle LeFevre sustained an admirable composure, and Mr. Sidmouth retreated into a mute gravity, all enjoyment of the party for *themselves* was at an end. It could not be merely that Captain Fielding's disapprobation of their domestic circumstance had inspired such strong dislike, such discomposure of manner; and that *some other* episode lay among the three, I was firmly convinced.

But all my idle thoughts must be deferred for social necessity, though Mr. Sidmouth *would* place himself at my right hand once we had followed the Honourable Barnewalls to the dinner table, utterly confounding the slower Captain Fielding, whose game leg in this instance proved a decided encumbrance. Mademoiselle LeFevre, I observed, was safely seated between my father and Mr. Armstrong (whom I suspected to be quite deaf); and so the gallant Captain had no choice but to place himself between Miss Lucy Armstrong and my mother, at the far end of the table where Miss Crawford held sway. I found myself breathing a sigh of relief.

"And so, Mrs. Austen, I find that your dear child has been torn from the maternal bosom," Miss Crawford declared, in a very loud voice indeed, so that her words travelled the length of the table. "I *do* hope that you shall be blest with another sight of her. How you can find *any* enjoyment in Lyme, with the constant concern for Miss Austen's health that must daily plague you, I cannot think." The officious woman appeared insensible of the start her words gave my poor mother, and swept on in an ill-considered tide.

"How melancholy one's thoughts, in parting from a child in decline! What terrors, what palpitations! I am sure that if I had been blest with a daughter of my own— had Fortune proved kinder—I could never have suffered her to be taken from *me* in such a parlous state. I should sooner have thrown myself beneath the carriage wheels, than submitted to a like parting!"

My mother's looks were very nearly apoplectic, as though she waited *now* only for poor Cassandra to be brought into the room, a cold and lifeless form, in retribution for her parents' heedlessness; and so I hastened to interject some reason to the scene.

"We were so fortunate as to have very good news of my sister only a few days ago, Miss Crawford, and from Mr. Crawford himself," I said, leaning towards the nether end of the table. "I wonder he did not tell you of it? He met with my brother, Mr. Austen, and his party in the very midst of Weymouth, just after the embarkation of the Royal Family, which I understand my sister failed to witness, being preoccupied with the finery in a neighbouring shop window."

"Aye, so he told me," Miss Crawford said, nodding sagely. "It is ever such absence of mind, such regard for the smallest detail, that will herald a rapid decline. My own Mr. Filch was prone to spending hours in his hot-house, his poor gaze fixed upon the first tender sprouting of a prize tulip, in his final days. It is as though the soul would cling to the insignificant in life, at the very moment of parting with it. I would adjudge your sister's pre-occupation with the shop window a very malignant sign, Miss Austen. Very malignant."

Poor Lucy Armstrong was sunk in a misery of mortification, her cheeks flushed and her eyes upon her soup; her mother, happily, was engrossed in discussing horse-racing with Mrs. Barnewall, and those two ladies appeared to have heard nothing of what Miss Crawford had said. My mother, on the other hand, was completely devoid of animation; and I knew her to be suffering from terrors of the acutest kind.

"And what of my absorption in fossils, Augusta?" Mr. Crawford interjected impatiently. "Do you but wait for me to fall dead in the pit, the very victim of your worst predictions? It is utter nonsense!"

"So you may say, Cholmondeley, but time shall prove the right of it."

"Undoubtedly," Mr. Sidmouth drily replied, "for in the long run, we shall all of us be dead."

"Hear, hear," my father said quietly from his place by Seraphine, and devoted himself to the soup, which was admirably made.

"Miss Jane Austen," Miss Crawford continued, in an imperious tone, "may I be so bold as to enquire whether you are a needle woman?"

The question was so very unexpected, coming as it did on the heels of an altogether different topic, that I may perhaps be forgiven for starting, and letting fall my soup spoon.

"There, I have put the girl out of countenance. I suppose she never learnt." The old termagant could barely suppress a smile of triumph.

"Indeed, Miss Crawford," my mother broke in, with a look of mortification down the length of the table, "I think I may assure you that Jane is as pretty a hand with the needle as may be. She has the fashioning of all her sister's clothes."

"Then it should be as nothing to construct a few items for the St. Michael's Ladies Auxiliary," Miss Crawford replied, without hesitation. "We are collecting a contribution from all of Lyme's ladies, and should count ourselves honoured to include *yours,* Miss Austen."

"Now, Augusta—" Mr. Crawford interjected, with something less than his usual good humour.

"I am sure Miss Austen cannot mind it. It is a trifling enough affair, for a girl of *her* age, and as yet unburdened with the duties of a married woman."

It was the Honourable Mathew who served as my deliverer. Having heard nothing of what had passed, he emerged of a sudden from a brown study, and leaned across the napery to prod Mr. Sidmouth with a blunt forefinger.

"I say, Sidmouth, that was a demmed fine horse you rode the other day. Confounded the demmed dragoons in the handiest fashion. How much would you take for 'im?"

A sudden silence gripped the table, marked only by the slightest cough from Captain Fielding. If a cough could be declared *ironic,* then his was the very soul of irony. I could not lift my eyes to observe his countenance, nor yet Mr. Sidmouth's; but the air between us seemed to crackle with contained emotion. Did I imagine it, or had the master of High Down been paralysed at a word?

Then Mr. Sidmouth raised his serviette delicately to his lips, and the tension seemed to ease. "I should not have believed you abroad at such an hour, Barnewall. I trust you were merely returning *home* from the previous evening's entertainments, rather than already about your business for the day."

Mathew Barnewall threw back his head in raucous laughter, to the evident disgust of Miss Crawford. "Capital!" he cried, slapping his thigh with the greatest enjoyment. "You have the right of it, sir. But it makes no odds. What about the horse, man?"

"I should not part with him for a kingdom."

"You drive a hard bargain. I like that in a fellow." Barnewall glanced roguishly down the table to his wife, who regarded Mr. Sidmouth with an indulgent smile, as though he were a very small boy. "Perhaps I shall have Evie work upon you, eh? The woman can charm a cock out of a henhouse."

"I fear even such a talent would prove of little use in the present case, Barnewall," Captain Fielding interposed drily. "Sidmouth holds tenaciously to his dearest possessions. There is no wrath more powerful a man may excite, than to wrest from him that which he prizes." The two men exchanged a long look, and that the Captain spoke of far more than Sidmouth's horse, I felt convinced.

But it was Mr. Sidmouth who dropt his eyes first, seeming absorbed in the fork he turned in his hand. "Though Mrs. Barnewall may claim a stupendous advantage over poultry, and I *am* given to crowing on occasion, I beg to consider myself as anything but fowl," he said with a slight smile. "The horse is not for sale." With that, he turned away from the Honourable Mathew, as though the conversation were at an end, and bent his dark glance upon my countenance; but Barnewall was not so easily put aside.

"Come, come, Sidmouth! Having bested the dragoons at their own game, you cannot wish to engage them further! One would think you intended a swift escape from the country, and would keep the stallion at the ready!"

"And what do *you* intend for Satan?" Mr. Sidmouth

enquired levelly—halting the table at the very mention of the horse's evil name.

Mr. Barnewall hesitated, and looked about the dining-room, some of the wind drooping from his sails. "By Jove," he muttered, "I hadn't thought to buy a horse with such an ill-made handle. Might bring all the wrath of God upon the house."

"He intends to race him," Mrs. Barnewall said briskly in the continued quiet. "You know, Sidmouth, that Mathew is a formidable owner of a string of nags. He is quite the prop of the Jockey Club at home—to the detriment of our funds. He has excessive plans for Kingsland, does he ever come into his inheritance—and does he fail to squander it before he may truly lay his claim."

"I gather from your lady's words, Barnewall, that she fears your liberality, and should rather I *kept* my horse in Lyme, than sold him to you; and so much for her celebrated charm. We may consider the matter as settled."

"Now, now," Mathew Barnewall exclaimed, his scowl for his wife giving way to a fatuous smile, "don't force me to rob your stables!"

"If you did, my dear sir, it should avail you nothing," Mr. Crawford broke in, "for Sidmouth so prizes his horse-flesh, he has undertaken to mark them in a singular manner. You should not get far without discovery."

"Do you brand them, then?" Mrs. Barnewall enquired, her nose wrinkling with repugnance.

"Never," Sidmouth replied.

"He has his initials cut into their shoes!" Mr. Crawford declared, with a delighted slap upon his mahogany table. "No thief could fail to leave a telling trail behind him."

"Shoes?" my mother enquired, only now, it seemed, emerging from the fog of suspense into which Miss Crawford's words regarding my sister's fate had thrown her. "But cannot one merely exchange one shoe for another?"

I knew her immediately to have mistaken the *master's* shoe for his horse's, and to have stumbled upon a point all unawares; for Mr. Crawford seized at her apparent perspicacity with the greatest delight. "Assuredly, madam, and a clever ruse it would be—but even did the thief know beforehand of the shoes' mark, he could do nothing without a blacksmith; and horse and thief should undoubtedly be apprehended while still bent upon the forge. I consider it a capital idea."

This response so confounded my mother's understanding, as to silence her for the moment; and the conversation turned to other things.

My mastery of curiosity was rewarded as such mastery only rarely is—with Mr. Sidmouth's broaching the subject of his cousin in a very little while. The ladies had retired to the drawing-room, and at the gentlemen's following soon thereafter, bearing the scents of tobacco and excellent port about their persons, Mr. Sidmouth joined me before Captain Fielding should have the chance. Miss Armstrong had seated herself at the pianoforte, and Mademoiselle LeFevre stood at her side, her voice swelling with Italian airs; so captivatingly beautiful, and so clearly freed of all the evening's anxiety, as to make the heart sing with her.

"Your cousin is very lovely, Mr. Sidmouth," I ventured, with a glance at his brooding face.

He was engaged in studying Seraphine intently, and seemed almost not to have heard me. After an instant, his dark eyes turned back to mine, and he said abruptly, "I would ask of you a favour, Miss Austen. My cousin is too much alone. You will have guessed that she labours under the effect of some sad business; discretion, and a care for her delicacy, forbid me from saying more. I would ask only that you consider her gentle nature, her evident goodness—the fragility of her understanding—" At this he halted, for the first time in our acquaintance, completely tongue-tied.

"I do not pretend to comprehend your cousin's place in your household," I began slowly, "nor her entire relationship to yourself. But if I take your meaning correctly, you wish me to visit Mademoiselle LeFevre—to undertake a certain . . . intimacy."

Sidmouth had flushed at my initial words, and appeared in an agony of indecision as to his response; but now he bowed his head and touched a hand to his brow. "I cannot convince you of what you have no reason to believe," he said quietly. "Rumour and calumny are accepted of themselves, and a simpler goodness hardly to be credited. I know to whom I owe your hesitancy. But for Seraphine's sake I will say nothing of this here; I will merely trust in your goodness. You cannot turn away from a soul in suffering—your every aspect declares you to be a woman of sympathy and such warmth as is rarely met with."

Seraphine's liquid voice rose in the final tremulous notes of an aria—the cry, no doubt, of a woman betrayed and dying, as with all such songs—and fell away into silence. There was a moment's indrawn breath, a hesitation, and then a sudden patter of applauding hands.

"I shall call upon your cousin as soon as ever I may, Mr. Sidmouth," I said; and received a fervent look of gratitude in return.

I HAD OCCASION TO CONSIDER ALL THAT PASSED SATURDAY E'EN, while sitting this morning with my mother in the little breakfast parlour of Wings cottage—which I must confess is decidedly shabby, when exposed to the strong sunlight of morning.

"I *still* cannot comprehend, my dear, why Mr. Sidmouth should take his shoes to the blacksmith," my mother was saying to the Reverend Austen, whose head *would* droop over his volume of *Fordyce's Sermons*—when Jenny, our housemaid, threw open the door. Her fresh young face bore a look of alarm, and she twisted her apron in anxious hands.

"Miss Crawford, madam, and Miss Armstrong," she said, bobbing swiftly as the black-clad form of Augusta Crawford swept by her.

My mother stood up abruptly, her serviette dropping to the floor, while my father snorted to wakefulness and struggled to his feet. A chorus of salutation all around, which afforded me just enough time to notice the marks of weeping upon Lucy Armstrong's face; and then the ladies seated themselves without further ado.

"We do not come to you this morning merely for the pleasure of a social call," Miss Crawford began briskly, her hands gripping the reticule she propped upon her black-gowned knees; "no, I fear we are come with the saddest of tidings and the blackest of news."

At this, Lucy Armstrong could not stifle a sob; and drawing forth her handkerchief, buried her reddened cheeks in the sodden scrap of linen.

"Whatever can be the matter?" I cried. "Surely Mr. Crawford remains in excellent health?"

"Oh, Cholmondeley is as hearty as ever," Miss Crawford replied, with sharp impatience. "It is not *he* who was overturned on the road last night."

"Overturned!" my mother cried, her hand going to her heart; that she thought of Cassandra, and feared Miss Crawford's intelligence, I instantly discerned, and moved to offer her the assistance of my arm. But she struggled free of me and crossed with unsteady gait to Miss Crawford's chair. "Pray do not keep us in suspense!"

"Overturned, indeed," Miss Crawford said, with gruesome satisfaction; "and shot into the bargain."

"I think, Aunt, that the proper term is 'unhorsed,' "

Miss Armstrong interjected; but her faltering voice was heard only by myself.

"Shot!" my father ejaculated, removing his reading glasses.

"Through the heart." Miss Crawford looked to the shaken Lucy, her aspect all disapprobation.

"Of whom can you be speaking, Miss Crawford?" I enquired, with something less than my usual graciousness—for the picture of misery that was Lucy Armstrong suggested that it could be but one person. Surely only some injury to Mr. Sidmouth could have occasioned so much distress.

"Oh, Miss Austen!" Lucy cried, her reddened eyes emerging from her kerchief. "It is so very horrible! Captain Fielding is *dead*—and I have nothing now to live for!"

Chapter 10

Mr. Cavendish Pays a Call

17 September 1804, cont.

~

WHEN LUCY ARMSTRONG HAD BEEN MADE CALM, AND SENT UPSTAIRS
to rest upon my bed with a cool compress on her eyes, we
were able to satisfy our outraged curiosity in plying Miss
Crawford with questions. It required but a few to determine the nature of the evil so recently befallen Captain
Fielding; and not above four sentences sufficed for her
relation of what little was known of his untimely end.

The Darby household was only just preparing to depart
for town and some shopping this morning, when the sudden arrival of a boy on a lathered horse claimed their
attention. A man had been found upon the Charmouth
road not far from the house, it seemed, quite dead; the
marks of hoofprints round about showed him to have
been thrown from his horse, and the animal fled. It but
remained for Mr. Crawford to send the ladies on to Lyme
in the coach, and for himself to accompany the boy to the
scene of the disaster, and discover there the person of
Captain Fielding, to the routing of the unfortunate Mr.
Crawford's senses. The surgeon Mr. Carpenter, who

served as Lyme's coroner, his assistant Dagliesh, and a local justice by the name of Mr. Dobbin, were immediately summoned; the mortal wound to Captain Fielding's heart duly noted; and the conclusion reached that highwaymen had precipitated the gentleman's misadventure, since his purse was observed to be missing.

"And so we returned from Lyme to such a tumult!" Miss Crawford exclaimed. "My poor niece received the news with a pathetic sensibility; her mother fainted dead away; and my brother is even now shut up in his library with a bottle of claret for company. And since we knew you to be likely to discover the Captain's death before very long," she added, "we deemed it best to inform you as soon as possible, so that you might not hear it first upon the street, and receive a decided shock."

A shock it should have been; and I would be coldhearted, indeed, not to feel towards Miss Crawford some depth of gratitude for her present consideration, did I not believe her to find a despicable enjoyment in the spreading of her intelligence. I thrust such uncharitable thoughts from my mind, however, and saw in memory once more the weathered face of Captain Percival Fielding; his bright blue eyes, that could hold such warmth, or shine with steely command; his grace and forbearance in the face of a debilitating injury; his determination to prevail over Lyme's Gentlemen of the Night. Too young for such a miserable end, and taken too soon from the world; better, perhaps, that he had died while gallantly fighting the French off Malta, a few years past, than to have offered his life in defence of his purse. I felt all the tender emotion proper in the face of such a tragedy; but discovered, to my quiet relief, that I felt nothing more. My heart had been warmed by his gallantry, but my deeper emotions had remained relatively untouched.

"A highwayman!" my mother exclaimed, her colour draining away. "I had not an idea of it. That Lyme should be so beset with lawlessness is in every way incredible. I thank God that my dear Cassandra is safe in London. Do not you think, Mr. Austen, that we should quit this place as soon as ever may be?" She turned in some anxiety to my father, who for once appeared to give her fears some consideration.

Miss Crawford glanced around our cottage's small sitting-room with a calculating eye. "You *are* rather exposed to the street, my dear Mrs. Austen, in the placement of your windows. I should not feel safe, indeed, of an evening by the fire, without some stout barring of that door leading to the entry—perhaps you might have your young man thrust that heavy piece across the way?" She was intent upon a handsome, if somewhat scarred, secretary, that stood in a corner of the sitting-room, and which my father was in the habit of employing for his correspondence. "The windows might be effectively blocked, with the application of wood slatting."

"Come, come, Miss Crawford," my father interposed jovially. "If a highwayman were to prospect for riches in Lyme, he should hardly look to Wings cottage. We lack the sort of style to invite a concerted assault. I should imagine myself safer here," he continued, with a wicked gleam in his eye, "than were I an intimate of Darby—so lonely as you find yourselves, out on the Charmouth road, which we must assume the highwaymen frequent."

A highwayman indeed, I thought. I should rather believe it a smuggler's man, dispatched to foil the Captain's officiousness, and stealing his purse out of simple efficiency—for Fielding should assuredly have no use for it where his spirit had gone.

Or perhaps the monies were seized in an endeavour to effect the *appearance* of misadventure, the better to preserve the murderer's security.

At this last thought, which so smacked of calculation, I could not prevent Mr. Sidmouth's face from rising in my mind. With an involuntary sinking of the heart, I forced the image aside, the better to attend to Miss Crawford's intelligence.

"I fear, Mrs. Austen," the good lady said, with admirable self-command in the face of my father's teasing, "that the dear Captain was too good for us. He was just such a noble character—such a feeling and excellent fellow—as is taken too soon from this earth. It is ever the way. Once a man is prized, he is lost."

She leaned towards me with a rustle of black bombazine, the better to confide. "I feel for Lucy very much, you know, from detecting in her case something of my own poor history—though Mr. Filch *had* already proposed, and Captain Fielding had not. And my carriage was ordered some months at Mr. Filch's sudden death, and was to have been very fine indeed, with the intertwined devices of the houses of Filch and Crawford upon the doors.[1] But no matter." Feeling, perhaps, that I showed too much indifference to the vanished chaise, she returned her attention to my mother, whose aspect was all sympathy. "I comfort myself with the certainty that the Captain's loss shall blight dear Lucy's life, and that she shall die of a broken heart; and then they will be sorry."

"Of whom can you possibly be speaking, madam?" my father enquired, all bewilderment.

"Why, the men who took the Captain's life, of course!" Miss Crawford rose and shook out her dusky skirts. "I shall attend the hanging, and send news by way of Bath, that Lucy may find some comfort in it—however brief. Mr. Carpenter is to hold an inquest, you know, in three days' time at the Golden Lion; and I have every confidence that by then, Mr. Dobbin the justice will have

---

[1] Miss Crawford describes the common practice among genteel families of ordering the construction of a new carriage for a wedding—usually at the groom's expense. —*Editor's note.*

found his men. And now I must fetch my niece, and be on my way, for there is Lucy's packing to be thought of; she departs with Mr. and Mrs. Armstrong upon the morrow—though if she survives the journey home to Bath, I shall be very much surprised.''

And so the Darby ladies departed; and we were left to all the disturbance of disbelief, and conjecture, and sympathetic pity; though of my own dark thoughts regarding Geoffrey Sidmouth, I said nothing to my dear mother or father. The former was engaged in dispatching James about the secretary's removal, and considering how best to place it to advantage across the sitting-room doorway, while the latter devoted himself to humourous asides on the nature of highwaymen, and the likelihood that they should rob my mother of her *virtue* before her purse. I took refuge, for my part, in writing of all that had occurred to Cassandra, in the belief that it should effect some order in the sad tumult of my mind.[2]

18 September 1804

~

THE DAY BROKE QUITE STORMY, AS THOUGH ALL THE SEACOAST mourned the Captain's passing; and the inmates of Wings cottage lay late abed, hugging their dreams close against the rawness of the day.

From my bedroom window now, I may gaze upon the waves as they lash and turn against the Cobb, and know a little of what it must be to spend a winter in Lyme. The air, the sky, the sea are all one, in a turbulent greyness; a mournful picture, and rendered sadder still by the ceaseless crying of seabirds. Strange, that on a day of sunlight

[2] This letter no longer survives in the collected correspondence. Cassandra Austen is believed to have destroyed many of Jane's letters after her sister's death. —*Editor's note.*

and wind, the calls of the gulls can lift the spirit; while on a day of lowering clouds, they seem the very souls of the departed, returned of a purpose to haunt those who live where the earth ends, and the sea meets the limitless sky. But I would sink into morbidity, did I allow my thoughts to wander further; and I must shake myself loose, and venture into town, and find in idle activity some diversion for the perplexity of my mind.

For I cannot believe that Captain Fielding died by misadventure. There is a purpose in his death, as there was in the gruesome hanging of poor Bill Tibbit. That I find a motive for Mr. Sidmouth in the effecting of both murders, must be persuasive; and that I am alone in doing so, must astonish. For I am but a stranger to Lyme and its relations, while others, more intimate with the passions that animate their neighbours, should labour under a suspicion equally portentous. And yet no hint of such suspicions have I heard.

Further consideration in the solitude of my chamber, however, has given rise to the idea of Mr. Sidmouth, overcome with rage upon his arrival at Darby Saturday e'en. It must be acknowledged, however imperfectly it is understood, that Geoffrey Sidmouth bore Fielding a decided hatred—and his nature, I suspected from everything I had yet seen, was prone to violence. Seraphine was the first cause of the discord between the two men, for reasons that remained obscure to me; and though Sidmouth had mastered his rage for the length of a dinner, what might not have occurred on another night of waning moonlight, at a lonely turning of the road?

The master of High Down behaved in Fielding's presence as a man whose honour is offended; and from the Captain's contemptuous disgust of Sidmouth's treatment of Mademoiselle LeFevre, I could imagine him as likely to defend the lady at pistol point as any other military fellow with a lively regard for reputation. Though it be murder in England, duelling remains the gentleman's choice for the settlement of disputes; and where better to throw down a glove, than on a quiet stretch of road? But in any contest between the two, I should favour Geoffrey Sidmouth to prevail; and the Captain's ruined form would seem to prove the truth of my conjectures.

When confronted with such thoughts as these, I could wish my understanding less able, and my fancies of less persuasive merit. But having once parsed the riddle, what alternative may I choose? Do I thrust away the weight of my fears, as reflecting a woman's foolish misapprehension? Or do I consider with care the path of any further investigation, so decidedly necessary if guilt or innocence is to be proved? For the possibility of Sidmouth's innocence cannot be discounted; and indeed, though reason might construct a case for his culpability, I find my heart cries out within me that it is impossible. What, then, is to be done? For I cannot long survive the suspense of such conflicting emotion; nor the thought that I harbour a strange sensibility for a man who might very well prove a murderer.

(Here the writing breaks off, and is then resumed.)

I was disturbed in the very act of considering my future course, by the arrival of a visitor whose appearance and intentions may only be deemed fortuitous. Providence, assuredly, is a mysterious mover, and who is Jane to ignore its direction?

The sound of a carriage halting before the door, and the bustle in the entry that presaged a visitor, gave pause to my pen; and it required but a moment for the conveyance of a card, bearing a name strange to me—and yet familiar.

"Miss Austen, miss," Jenny broke in, as she peered around the door, "there's a gentleman below as wishes to speak with you. He's sent up his card, and very fine it is, too."

Mr. Roy Cavendish, the scrap of paper read. *His Majesty's Customs House, Lyme.*

I looked to Jenny swiftly. "The gentleman is even now below?"

Her white cap bobbed above widened blue eyes. "He's a King's man, in't he? Whatever can he want with you, miss?"

"And my parents?"

"The Reverend's showing him his chess set. The missus is darning a sock."

It seemed best to relieve the poor man directly. "Please convey my sentiments to Mr. Cavendish, and say that I shall attend him presently," I told Jenny, and gathered up my little book.

"IT IS A PLEASURE, MISS AUSTEN." ROY CAVENDISH BENT LOW OVER my hand as I halted in the sitting-room doorway. He retained, still, the unfortunate appearance of a frog that I had remarked while observing him from the Cobb, the very morning he had come to oversee the seizure of a smuggler's cargo—which seizure Mr. Sidmouth had effectively routed. But I noted that his dress was respectable, his figure neat, and his hand steady; though a repulsive moisture overlaid his palm, and his grip was reminiscent of something noisome cast up upon the shingle.

"The pleasure is mine, Mr. Cavendish," I said doubtfully, and sought my habitual seat. Despite the poor condition of the day, my father had deemed it wisest to seek the out of doors, and had prevailed upon my mother to accompany him, with the promise of tea and muffin on the high street. Mr. Cavendish took advantage of my ease to find a chair himself, and, flipping the tails of his coat over his legs, sat down with something of a flourish—quite at odds with his staid appearance.

"You will wonder why I am come," he began, "being a

stranger to yourself, and indeed, to most concerns that should preoccupy a lady."

"Indeed, I know not how to explain this visit—though I should not like you to believe it an unwelcome one, sir."

"You are all kindness."

I waited, believing the burden of conversation to be on his side; and Mr. Cavendish did not disappoint me.

"I shall turn directly to the point, Miss Austen. You will have heard," he said, tapping a black band high upon his arm, "of the death of the gallant Captain Fielding." At this, the Customs agent's countenance assumed a remarkable expression of mournful gravity, as though he had swallowed something inimitable to a frog's digestion. "His loss is a heavy one—for his King and country, no less than for his intimate circle."

"Indeed," I said, with circumspection. Let us try what Mr. Cavendish would reveal; let us observe how closely he guards his purpose. A gentle trap, delicately baited, should tell me much. "It is some time since I have been able to think of it with anything but indignation, sir. For such a gentleman, blessed with the noblest qualities, to be cut down by a common footpad! Are decent people no longer to move at liberty? Are we all to be victims of the rabble, as though we called ourselves anything but Englishmen?"

Mr. Cavendish's eyes protruded, and he leaned closer to study my countenance. "So they would have it in Lyme, Miss Austen, but in Lyme it naturally suits the purpose. I do not credit this tale of a footpad; I do not credit it at all."

"But the Captain was relieved of his purse!"

Mr. Cavendish offered an eloquent shrug. "A trifling matter. Any man intent upon taking the Captain's life should seize his valuables, the better to suggest a death by misadventure."

I had already determined as much in my own mind; if

Geoffrey Sidmouth (or anyone else) meant to disguise the nature of the Captain's end—since affairs of honour inevitably ended in the victor's flight to the Continent, if not his hanging—how better, than to turn out his pockets, like a common thief?

"Whatever do you mean to say, Mr. Cavendish?" I enquired mildly, with a view to encouraging his confidence. "That Captain Fielding had an enemy?"

An instant's silence, as the Customs man weighed his thoughts; but an instant only, and he had formed a resolution. "Have you heard, Miss Austen, of the Reverend?"

"I have. Captain Fielding himself related the chief of what I know about the man."

"I understood as much. That is why I am here."

"I confess I do not take your meaning, Mr. Cavendish."

"Do not trifle with me, Miss Austen. I know as much of your business regarding Captain Fielding as he might allow himself, as a gentleman, to reveal." The slight frown I adopted at this intelligence availed me nothing; Mr. Cavendish swept on with all the certainty of his purpose full upon his face.

"On the occasion of my final meeting with Captain Fielding, he informed me that he had admitted you to his confidence—a necessity precipitated by your own penetration. How much he may have betrayed himself, I cannot be certain; but he laid the credit entirely on *your* side, Miss Austen, in declaring that you had divined his business entirely from appearances, and had confronted him with your knowledge."

"I was aware that the Captain was engaged in affairs of a very serious nature, regarding the smuggling trade— that much is certain. He was not as he professed himself to be, a simple Naval officer living in retirement, and consumed with a passion for the cultivation of roses."

"You will have guessed, then, that the Reverend was his

object; and that in his pursuit of the Reverend, the Captain invited considerable peril."

"You would suggest, then, that Captain Fielding died at the Reverend's hand?"

The Customs man sat back in his chair somewhat abruptly. "I am certain of it. But I have no proof."

"And it is my understanding, Mr. Cavendish, that the Reverend's identity is all but unknown."

"Come, come, Miss Austen," he cried, with marked irritation, "you know what Mr. Sidmouth's display has been. Consider his abominable behaviour only last week, and before all of Lyme. His actions *then* declared him the smugglers' lord. He has been cleverness itself to date—his shipments follow no set schedule, being dependent upon the onset of foul weather, and the cover it provides; and there are others he employs, to captain the vessels and arrange the conveyance of goods, so that he is always far from the scene of a successful landing—but he *must* have the ordering of such agents at one time or another; and what is required is that we seize him in the very act. Once, then, in the clutches of the law, we might force him to an admission of Fielding's murder."

"And why do you tell me of all your plans, Mr. Cavendish?" I enquired, my heart sinking.

"Because, Miss Austen," he replied, rising and crossing to my side, "Fielding gave me to understand that you were an intimate of High Down Grange. It was his belief—and his anxiety, if I may speak frankly—that Sidmouth meant to seduce you as he has seduced his unfortunate cousin. The Captain's benevolence on your behalf was very great, young woman, and you should be cold-hearted indeed, did you turn from the memory of his goodness!"

This last was delivered in so abrupt a tone, as to make me jump where I sat; but I quelled my indignation, though my flushed cheeks surely betrayed my perturbation.

"You overreach the bounds of propriety, sir," I said, in a lowered tone. "I beg you will desist."

"Not until I have won your consent, Miss Austen, in a scheme of some importance to His Majesty."

"What can such schemes have to do with me?"

"Nothing—or everything, did you bear the Captain's memory some gratitude."

"Speak less of gratitude, and more of sense!" I cried.

"Very well." Roy Cavendish turned to pace before my chair, his head bent and his hands clasped behind him. "You are acquainted with High Down Grange. You have met, I think, Mademoiselle LeFevre."

"I have."

"It is in your power, then, to visit the household—to press your advantage—to discern the movements of its inmates, and discover, perhaps, the night of an expected meeting between Sidmouth and his henchmen."

I could make no reply.

Cavendish wheeled and gazed at me with penetration. "*You*, Miss Austen, might fill Captain Fielding's place— and with less danger to yourself, in that your gentler sex, and the inevitable presumption of good on your part, would render suspicion unlikely. *You* might venture where a man could not. And in so doing, you should perform a service very dear to the Crown, and to the memory of the excellent fellow who died in its service."

"You wish me to turn informer," I said clearly; but my hands clutched at the arms of my chair.

"No such despicable term as that," Mr. Cavendish rejoined, his thick lips curving in an unfortunate attempt at a smile. "You should serve rather as handmaiden to justice."

"A handmaiden," I said. "You are so convinced of Mr. Sidmouth's guilt?"

"I am. As surely as I stand before you now, Miss Austen, I may state that Sidmouth's mind alone has directed the foulest of deeds. The cleverness of the smugglers' work; the killing of Bill Tibbit upon the Cobb, so publicly and yet so secretly done; and now, the felling of the Free Traders' chief adversary, Captain Fielding—it cannot be coincidence only. Surely your heart cries out in a similar vein, Miss Austen. The Captain had moved close to his prey; and his prey turned predator in an instant. You cannot witness his death and be unmoved by a desire to avenge it."

I sat as though turned to stone, my eyes upon the sitting-room fire; and gave a few moments to contemplation. My despairing wish for Sidmouth's innocence met at every turn conviction of his guilt. Only a few nights previous, at the Lyme Assembly, Captain Fielding had declared him to be the very Reverend, and declared that the man was nearly in his grasp. He had believed himself assured of Sidmouth's taking; but his assurance was as dust. The master of High Down was a formidable foe indeed. Could I muster the courage to contest his mastery? Was the prize worth the risk—to my heart as well as my person?

And with this last thought, a wave of revulsion overcame me. It was impossible that I should harbour any sort of tenderness towards a man so recognised as lost to all morality—a man whose every energy was given over to the pursuit of wealth and unrestrained passion, regardless of law, regardless of cost. But I *did* harbour such an emotion; and I detected within it the refusal to credit Mr. Sidmouth's guilt. Much had been laid at his door—but still I could not find it in me to abandon him entirely. Was Mr. Crawford likely to exhibit such affection for a man whose reputation was entirely ruthless? And what of Seraphine? That she regarded her cousin as the source of all goodness was decidedly evident, regardless of the calumnies that surrounded them both.

If I were to settle the contest within my soul, however—if doubt and disapprobation were to be banished—I must have the truth. And Roy Cavendish's plan was as good an one for procuring it as any. The proof of my own eyes should serve to silence the warring voices within my heart. A delicate balance must be achieved, however, if my own pursuit of knowledge were not to run afoul of the Crown's.

I raised my head and gazed at the Customs agent evenly. "I shall do as you wish, Mr. Cavendish, on one condition."

"Name it."

"That I direct my own efforts. Your scheme depends upon my discretion; and a too-public converse between ourselves should ignite the suspicions of those we least wish to rouse."

He bowed his head.

And what if I discovered that Mr. Sidmouth was indeed capable of anything? Having gained the knowledge, how was I to act? I thrust aside *that* dilemma as trouble enough for another day.

"And one thing more, Mr. Cavendish." I rose to convey to him that our meeting was at an end.

"Miss Austen?"

"If you honour my reputation as a lady, you must never reveal the source of your information, do I succeed in obtaining it." I knew myself in that moment, and called myself a coward. For if I embarked upon a program of spying at High Down, and determined Mr. Sidmouth's guilt, I should be the means of bringing him to the scaffold, for the sake of all that I valued in society. But I could never bear to confront him, at his final day, with his knowledge of my betrayal full upon his face.

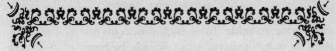

Chapter 11

Converse with an Angel

19 September 1804

~

ALL THROUGH THE LENGTH OF YESTERDAY THE WIND TORE ABOUT
Wings cottage—shuddering at the casements, howling
around the corners, and rattling the very door frames—
while the rain lashed at the roof, and sheets of salty spray
cascaded over the Cobb. I have never known what it is to
sail the seas, and feel the tossing of a fragile vessel in the
maw of a storm; and having witnessed the raging tide so
close upon my stoop, I am happy to leave such adventures
to my hardier brothers. The only consolation in foul
weather is to turn one's lock upon the street, and settle in
by the fire with tea and a good book—and hope that
Cook will devise a meal that comforts, as the day fades
into night.

But that meal, once taken, reveals itself as the high
point of an unendurably dull day; and the slow mounting
of stairs, while one's candle flickers in the turbulent air,
affords a moment to attend to the voices in the wind. My
sleep was certainly marked by their ceaseless crying—
though sleep itself was long in coming, and my tossing

and turning amidst the bedclothes a parody of the frenzied trees beyond my window. Such thoughts as roiled within my brain—of murder, and deceit, and a sinister smiling frog—would not be stilled, and required the full compass of the night for their consideration. I awoke from a fitful dreaming not an hour past dawn, and found the daylight sky turned peaceful, with the tattered remnants of cloud fading blackly at the horizon. Rivulets of water ran down Lyme's steep high street, to end in the calmer basin of the bay; and the first carters bound for the market were busy about the cobblestones. Peace after tumult, and with it, a clearing of the mind; I should take up the errand of returning Mr. Sidmouth's cloak, which he had placed about my shoulders some ten days before, and all but forgotten in a corner of my clothes press. I would attempt the few miles' walk to the Grange that very morning.

How very different were my feelings upon the present occasion, in approaching the old frame farmhouse high upon the downs, than they had been the night of my sister's misfortune! *Then*, my anxiety was active on another's behalf; but now, to my trepidation, I found it exerted entirely on my own. Deceit has ever been foreign to my nature, and the adoption of stratagems and disguise abhorrent; but truth and frankness would not serve in the present case, where so much of both were already prostrate upon dishonour's altar.

With firmer resolve, then, I redoubled my grip on Sidmouth's cloak and crossed the familiar courtyard, expecting every moment the onset of the dogs, or the boy Toby and his blunderbuss; but I was allowed to proceed unmolested today, and took it for a favourable omen. The courtyard itself was a confusion of waggons and harness, cast aside but not yet stored; and I remembered Roy Cavendish's words with a sudden chill. The Customs man had offered it as certain knowledge that the smugglers preferred to land their goods in the very worst sort of weather, the better to confound the Crown's dragoons; and assuredly last night had been highly propitious for any sort of skulduggery. At this further suggestion of Sidmouth's propensities, I confess my heart sank; but I determined to go forward, there being little comfort in turning back, as ever benighted by ignorance.

My arrival at the door occasioned another tremor—for what words should I summon, did the master of High Down confront me at his very portal, though I *had* committed to visit his cousin? The mere sight of Sidmouth should reduce me to a painful penury with words, so conflicted were my emotions towards himself. But I was spared even *this* trial; after some few moments, when I felt certain the entire household had been called away, the housemaid Mary answered my ring at the bell, and bade me come in search of Mademoiselle LeFevre.

I followed her down the cool stone hallway, and out a door on the nether end, and along a path to the kitchens—which, owing to a fear of fire, were separately housed. And there I espied the three dogs—Jasper, Fang, and Beelzebub, if memory served—in attitudes of languor about the kitchen door, and the sound of song emanating from within. It was assuredly Seraphine, her head bent over an ankle propped in her lap; and had it not been for a conviction that the foot was too small to be Sidmouth's, I should have turned and fled that very moment.

A sound I must have made, and her blond head came up; an instant's bewilderment, superseded as swiftly by recognition, and the ghost of a smile. "Miss Austen," Seraphine said quietly, and set down the shears she held in her hand; "what a surprise. And a pleasure. Please"— with that, a gesture towards the kitchen's interior—"be so good as to find a seat. I am almost finished my work here."

I entered, and found that the ankle was attached to Toby, and that his face and arms appeared singularly bruised. "Whatever can have befallen the boy!" I exclaimed, and received a surly glance from the fellow in question by way of reply.

"He has had a fall," Seraphine said smoothly.

"From the hay-loft," Toby added, with a quick look at his nursemaid. "Missed the ladder in the dark, miss, on account o' the lanthorn blowin' over in the storm. Quite a tumble I had, and my foot gone lame."

A hay-loft, indeed. To judge by the Grange's barn, such a fall should have succeeded in finishing young Toby, with a broken neck at the very least. More likely, to my mind, that he had taken a fall about the cliff, in the darkness of night and the confusion of a storm.

"I trust it is not broken?"

Seraphine shook her head and patted the bandage she had only just secured. "Our good Mr. Dagliesh has been and gone, and he assures us that Toby will be walking in no time. But until you are, young sir," she finished somewhat sternly, "you are to pay heed to Mr. Dagliesh's words. Rest and sit, or your leg will be the worse for it."

With a dark look and a mutter, Toby swung his ankle from Seraphine's lap and set it on the floor, barely disguising a whimper as he did so; and at that very moment, a shadow fell across the door and I turned to find Geoffrey Sidmouth standing behind me, his eyes intent upon my face and a pair of newly-whittled crutches in his hand.

"Mr. Sidmouth," I said with what I trust was my usual composure, and a bob of my bonneted head. "I am able to return your cloak at long last, with my deepest thanks. I have no excuse to plead for my neglect of your kindness these many days, but the usual absorption of a lady in seaside schemes of pleasure."

"There is no need for apology, Miss Austen—I might have sent a manservant, had I felt the cloak to be wanting—but your exertion in returning it is considerable, and not to be dismissed." And at that he bowed, though the hint of mockery in the gesture served to lessen somewhat its civility, and reached a hand for my burden. I gave over the cloak into Sidmouth's safekeeping; and saw that his thoughts had shifted already to the stable boy Toby.

"Come along, lad," he said, with a hand to Toby's head. "These crutches will have you to rights in an instant. Well do I remember my own turned ankles, from falling out of trees, Miss Austen," he added, with a look for me, "and tripping over fox holes; they were as much a part of childhood as the turning of the seasons. And fortunately I remember how to fashion a crutch, when need be."

Such gentleness, as he helped the boy to his feet! Such a tender concern for a stable lad's well-being, that he should whittle some support with his very hands! And how fond the look, as he watched Toby swing haltingly out the doorway, and cross the yard to the barn! Could such benevolence co-exist with the most vicious propensities? Impossible! But how, then, to explain the waggons about the courtyard, all speaking so eloquently of haste and necessity in the night?

My thoughts were disturbed by a sudden *Bump!* overhead, and the sound as of something rolling into a garret corner; I glanced up swiftly, and would swear I heard the shuffle of knees along bare floorboards, and then the very stillness of suspended breath. I looked to Seraphine for explanation, but she was bent over a cauldron hanging at the hearth; and if her cheeks were a trifle flushed, surely the heat of the fire might be taken as cause. Sidmouth, too, appeared insensible of the secretive movements above his head, being engaged in gathering up the cloth Seraphine had used for Toby's bandage; and I should have thought myself quite mad, did I not believe them both to have a purpose for assumed tranquillity.

I glanced about the kitchen, and observed a doorway in the far corner—concealing, perhaps, a staircase, and the way to the rooms above, where even now the Reverend's henchmen were foiled in their activity, by the appearance of a visitor below. The image of Davy Forely's grimacing face, glimpsed a week ago as he fled the dragoons on Sidmouth's horse, rose with conviction in my mind—was the lander even now recovering from his wounds, in hiding at High Down Grange? But to what purpose? For had not Captain Fielding divulged that no charge could be brought against the men, for retrieving a cargo of small beer? But *someone* was assuredly above, and keeping covert; Seraphine had pronounced my name quite clearly at my arrival, and Mr. Sidmouth equally so— a signal, perhaps, for the cessation of all movement in the garret. I must try what outright interrogation should reveal.

"I see you have visitors, Mr. Sidmouth," I said, and awaited his response.

He moved lithely to the doorway and peered out into the sunshine, as though in search of an arriving chaise. "I fear you are mistaken, Miss Austen. We must look solely to yourself for amusement this morning."

I allowed the slightest suggestion of confusion to cross my features. "But what, then, is the purpose of the waggons in the courtyard? I expected an entire party of pleasure-seekers upon my arrival—and yet could barely discover a soul!"

"We were about the hay-making yesterday," Sidmouth said evenly, with a look to Seraphine; "until halted by the onset of the storm. Had Toby been better fitted to his work, the equipages should hardly have been left standing; but his injury, and the pressing nature of my own affairs, necessitated their present abandonment."

He could not have known, of course, that Toby had declared his injury to be a thing of the night—and well after any waggons should have been put up.

"I hope your expectations are not all downcast, Miss Austen, at finding us quite alone? For we are generally so retiring at High Down Grange, that the addition of merely *one* to the circle is taken as a novelty. We are in your debt, you see, for this visit."

"And I feel it particularly," said Seraphine, turning from the fire, "for you know I see almost no one. I wonder, Miss Austen, if you would care to take a turn along the cliffs—the weather being so fine? We might converse at some leisure in the open air; and as such days will offer only rarely in the coming months, we ought to seize them when we may."

Though I had toiled fully two and a half miles uphill from Lyme in the previous hour, I surmised Seraphine to be seeking some privacy, if not my safe removal from the vicinity of the kitchen garret; and declared myself not antagonistic to the notion of exercise. While the lady went in search of her cloak, there being a brisk breeze off the sea, I settled myself into an empty chair; and so was left in the company of Mr. Sidmouth for some anxious moments.

"Let me repeat myself, Miss Austen, the better to show my gratitude, even at the risk of increasing your tedium," he began, his brown eyes warm in his harsh-featured face. "I am very much obliged to you for this visit. I know full well that you are come at my express request, made only a few nights ago—a melancholy night, in retrospect, given the events that followed hard upon our evening's enjoyment at Darby."

For a moment I knew not how to reply, surprised that he should mention even so obliquely the death of Captain Fielding.

"There is to be an inquest, I understand, at the Golden Lion," I ventured at the last.

"It will avail them nothing," Sidmouth said grimly, and threw himself into the chair Seraphine had vacated. "Fielding's murderer is long gone from the vicinity."

"You would credit, then, the notion of a footpad? You believe Captain Fielding to have died by misadventure?"

"Is there an alternative?" he enquired, with a knitting of the brows. "—For the Captain is unlikely to have done away with himself, Miss Austen, having first dispensed with his valuables."

"But another might have effected a similar appearance."

"To what purpose?" Mr. Sidmouth's voice was so quiet as to be almost inaudible, and his countenance was stilled and shuttered.

"To suggest that what was murder by *design,* was merely a perilous encounter with a highwayman—the better to divert suspicion, and throw into doubt all hope of confounding the killer."

"And why should any wish to trifle with Fielding's life in so terrible a manner?"

"Come, come, Mr. Sidmouth!" I cried. "*You* are a man of the world. *You* know what it is to inspire enemies, and to maintain a relation of enmity with another. Surely *you* may supply a myriad of reasons for such an extraordinary course. You bore the Captain too little love, not to wish him as much ill-fortune as he was unhappy enough to endure."

"Are you suggesting that I wished him dead, Miss Austen? Or, worse still, that in wishing him dead, I took measures to achieve my aim?" Mr. Sidmouth rose from his chair and crossed to where I sat, his powerful form overtaken by malevolence. I had an idea, of a sudden, what it should be to cross him in a matter of some importance to himself, and swallowed hard to overcome my fear.

"I suggest nothing," I replied.

"Miss Jane Austen of Bath *never* speaks to little purpose." He observed me narrowly. "You actually believe me capable of such foul conduct as Fielding suffered! Does my aspect betray me as so prone to violence, however just and warranted it might be? But no—" he said, wheeling about, "—it is unwise to enquire too closely of a lady whose aspect is so clouded with doubt. The answers should be too little to my liking."

"Mr. Sidmouth—"

"Say nothing, Miss Austen, for good or ill," he said harshly; "you cannot know the effect your words should have. I am too little master of my feelings in the present moment to meet either your contempt or your concern with the attention they deserve."

And with that, he left me—in such a state of perturbation, that I barely disguised my sensibility before Seraphine, who returned some moments later intent upon a walk.

"I MUST TELL YOU, MISS AUSTEN, THAT GEOFFREY ESTEEMS YOU highly. It is his fondest wish that we should grow acquainted; and I am so desirous of company in my isolation, that I welcome his interest, and the benevolence it has inspired. You are very good to weary yourself in seeking the Grange."

I studied Seraphine's beautiful profile curiously. She spoke so frankly of her retirement from society, as though it were a sentence imposed by a merciless court, that I adjudged her amenable to some gentle questioning.

"I cannot help asking, Mademoiselle—how come you to be here, so far from your home, and quite without friends?"

"Home is a mere channel away, Miss Austen, and Geoffrey the greatest friend I have ever known," she replied quietly. "But I understand what you would ask. France might as well be at the ends of the earth, for all the hope I have of returning—hope or desire, both being equally extinguished by my sad history. I have been in England nearly a decade, having fled the horrors of the guillotine at the age of fifteen."

"Your family suffered in the revolution?"

"Suffered!" Her lip curled expressively, and she turned to gaze out at the sea an instant, before resuming our pacing along the cliff's edge. "I saw my mother taken away in a cart, and my father; my three aunts, two of my uncles, and my eldest brother—all perished on the infernal machine."

"Good God!" I cried.

"Words cannot express the blood-lust, the mad desire for revenge, the senseless hatred that compelled the people in those days. It was the sort of frenzy only rarely witnessed by rational beings—thank God."

"But how came you to escape?"

She shrugged and averted her gaze. "My relations in England exerted their energies on our behalf—you should know that Mr. Sidmouth is the son of my mother's sister—and for once they were successful. We were smuggled out of the prison beneath a load of refuse, and borne swiftly to Boulogne, there to embark upon a ship bound for this coast; and here I have remained ever since, walking these cliffs that I might gaze towards France, and remember those who did not escape."

"You speak in the plural, Mademoiselle," I said tentatively. "Was there some *other* who escaped at your side?"

"My youngest brother, Philippe. He was but ten at the time."

"A brother! How fortunate that you should be left with *some* prop in the midst of tragedy—some confidant in sorrow! But where is your brother now, Mademoiselle? Away at school, perhaps?"

To my surprise, she shrugged, the faintest of smiles o'erspreading her lips. "Philippe has returned to France. He is with Napoleon's army there."

"With Buonaparte?" I could not disguise my incredulity. "But how is such a thing possible?"

"How might a victim of the revolution throw his strength and ardour behind its greatest opportunist, you mean?" Seraphine said, with a delicately-lifted eyebrow. "Well might you ask. My cousin and I have spent many long hours in contemplation of it." She exhaled a gusty breath and drew the collar of her red cloak closer about her throat. "I cannot rightly say. I loved Philippe as almost a mother—I clung to his sturdy boyishness, his indomitable spirits—until the moment when he disappeared in the night, taking only a few belongings and leaving but a few words. Perhaps I never understood him—what it was to grow up as a dispossessed child, aware of his family's noble history, and the ruthlessness of its decline."

"Women are more accepting of the vagaries of Fate, perhaps," I said thoughtfully. "We sit at home, and mourn in solitude, and find no outlet for our restless tides of vengeance. It should not be remarkable that a young man should wish to make his way in the world, and resurrect the glory of his name, by any means that offer. We cannot judge rightly, without standing awhile in his skin, and feeling all the burden of outraged youth."

"But you forget, Miss Austen," Seraphine replied. "I have stood there. I have felt the outrage. I have railed against the bitterness of Fortune, and shaken my fist at every sun that rises again to shine on the revolution's children, and I have hated Napoleon for his steady ascent. He climbs on the backs of the old aristocracy—who were cut down by men he has never disavowed, however little he formed a part of their schemes—and marries his generals to the orphaned daughters of the great. But I beg to hope, Miss Austen, that he will reach the height of power, only to discover that he has been ascending a scaffold—and that there is no escaping the noose."

I confess I was overwhelmed by the hardening of her tone and aspect; Seraphine seemed no longer an ethereal angel, but a woman clad in steel, and burnished by the sunlight thrown up from the sea.

"It would perhaps be justice," I observed, "did Napoleon fall as swiftly as he has ascended; but I do not believe it likely. Many years of blood and hopelessness remain, I fear, before vengeance may be done."

Seraphine turned a speculative eye upon my countenance. "That may be, Miss Austen; and then again, it may not. Time alone will tell."

"Assuredly," I said, in some confusion. For she spoke as though blessed with a more intimate knowledge of events than I should have credited in one so remote from their ordering.

We turned at the cliff's edge and walked on a few paces in silence, heads bowed against the fresh breeze off the sea. The pause in conversation afforded me the opportunity to recollect my true purpose in soliciting the mademoiselle's confidence—and for the space of several strides, I gathered my courage to speak. We could not labour on entirely in silence, however, without some end to our exercise being precipitated; and so I forced myself to broach a subject that could not but be distasteful to the lady.

"How calm the sea looks!" I observed, with a careless air. "Quite unlike the afternoon when Captain Fielding and I espied the smuggler's cutter abandon its cargo, not far off the end of the Cobb. On *that* occasion the seas were quite stiff, and the Navy ship that followed in pursuit made but poor progress, and came all too late behind."

There was a delicate pause. Then, with what I judged to

be an effort at composure, the mademoiselle enquired, "You were well acquainted with Captain Fielding?"

"Only a little. And you?"

"As you say—only a little," she said, with a quick smile, that as quickly fled.

"He seems to have been everywhere acknowledged as possessing an admirable character."

"Indeed."

A few more paces in silence, and I made another attempt. "However little you thought *yourself* acquainted with Captain Fielding, your well-being and happiness were clearly of some concern to the gentleman. He spoke well of you in my hearing on several occasions, and expressed some anxiety regarding your—situation—at the Grange."

"I do not doubt he mentioned my *situation*, as you put it," Seraphine said, her contempt flaring unchecked. "Captain Fielding was an officious and arrogant man, who little cared what damage his *concern* might do."

"You regarded his interest as interference?" I rejoined quickly.

She turned and studied my countenance quizzically, while I endeavoured to assume as clear an aspect of innocence as my own sense of guilt should allow.

"Would not *you* have done the same, Miss Austen, when a gentleman's meddling occasioned the worst sort of calumny, and the grossest of lies, to be heaped upon a cousin you esteemed as dearly as a brother? But how come you to wonder so much about the affairs of people, of whom you know so little?"

This was abruptness indeed; and I felt the chastening power of her words as severely as a lash. Groping for some justification, however, I fell back upon events.

"It is just that the Captain's tragic end, Mademoiselle, has thrown his whole life into question—do not you agree?" I gestured towards the road, just visible at the

176 ~ STEPHANIE BARRON

foot of the downs behind our backs, and emptied now of any conveyance. "How strange to think that the gallant Captain shall drive the Charmouth road no more, when only a week ago I sat beside him in his barouche. The suddenness of events is inexplicable; and the mind struggles for comprehension."

My excuses availed me nothing, however; Seraphine had stiffened beside me, and was grown as remote as marble—expressionless, opaque, and no doubt chill to the touch. My words might have been all unspoken.

I perceived no alternative but persistence, all the same. "The news was quite shocking, was it not?"

She stirred herself at last, but betrayed nothing of her emotion. "The news of the Captain's death? I suppose it was. Certainly I had not looked for it."

"But you found it not incredible?"

"I found it to be justice, Miss Austen, however curiously achieved," she cried, in some exasperation. "One cannot be otherwise than satisfied when justice is done."

Whatever I had expected, it was hardly this—an avowal of nothing and everything at once.

"I do not pretend to understand you, Mademoiselle. Had the Captain committed some infamy of which I am unaware?"

She studied the sea as though my words had gone unspoken, for the space of several heartbeats. I counseled patience to myself, and stood as still as a stone, reflecting that many a wild thing will come to eat from the hand, if a suitable caution is preserved. At length, however, I observed to my horror that silent tears were coursing down her cheeks; and it was perhaps more terrible still that she did nothing to impede their flow, or disguise their traces, so lost in contemplation was she.

"Mademoiselle LeFevre," I said, laying a hand along her red-cloaked arm, "whatever is the matter? What can he have done to you?"

She shook her head, and turned a watery smile upon my anxious face. "Never mind, Miss Austen. Whatever it was, it is past all remedy now, and all forgiveness. What *le Chevalier* did, was done in passion; and so his life has ended. There is nothing further worth asking."

Le Chevalier. That name again; and spoken now with a depth of bitterness that could not but make it ironic. To probe the girl's natural reticence would be unseemly, and beyond even *my* application; my gentle education had not taught me how to so offend propriety, even did I claim the pursuit of innocence as my spur. There were others— Mrs. Barnewall rose immediately to mind—who might shed some light on the matter. I managed, then, only to press Seraphine's arm in sympathy, and stand in an awkward silence; and so, I fear, I left her. She would not accompany me back to the Grange, being unequal, perhaps, to her cousin's scrutiny; and it may be that she found some comfort in gazing out over the sea, towards France and the turbulent past. But her figure lingers long in memory as I consider her, red cloak flowing in the wind, as still as a tower at the cliff's edge.

I HAD BARELY ACHIEVED THE COURTYARD BEFORE THE FARMHOUSE, and steeled myself for the tedious return to Wings cottage, when I espied a strange coach pulled up before the Grange's door. A man, whose appearance bespoke him a gentleman, stood aloof and grim at the horses' heads. Barely a moment upon the heels of this observation, the front door was thrown open, and a party of men exited, with Sidmouth in their midst. An expression of rage suffused the latter's countenance, and his bearing bespoke a wounded dignity; had not *these* apprised me that he went against his will, the manner in which the four burly fellows at his side secured his wrists and arms within their grasp, should assuredly have served as guide. In the grim huddle's wake came Mary, the housemaid, anxiously wringing her apron.

"Mr. Sidmouth!" I cried, aghast.

He found my eyes with an expression at once so ashamed and outraged it stopt all speech.

"Whatever has happened?" I enquired of the aloof fellow by the carriage. His eyes swept my figure with grudging interest, but he hesitated with his answer.

"I am Miss Jane Austen, a friend to Mr. Sidmouth's cousin, Mademoiselle LeFevre."

The gentleman's eyes shifted from my face to something at my back, and I turned to find Seraphine there, her expression one of horror as she gazed upon Sidmouth.

"Geoffrey!" she cried. *"Qu'est-ce que c'est tout cela?"*

At her appearance, the gentleman stepped forward and bowed. "Mademoiselle LeFevre, I presume."

Seraphine directed at his person the wildest of glances, and sprang towards Sidmouth's side, until prevented from reaching him by his captors' diligence.

"Some intelligence, for the love of God," I said, in exasperation.

"Mr. Dobbin at your service, madam." The gentleman removed his hat with a sweeping gesture. "I am appointed justice in Lyme, and am presently at High Down in that capacity."

"What business can you possibly have with my cousin?" Seraphine interjected angrily.

"Mr. Sidmouth has been seized on suspicion of the murder of Captain Percival Fielding, and will be held in the Lyme gaol until the inquest Friday next."

There was a gasp of horror from Mademoiselle LeFevre, and a swift glance of agonised sensibility for Sidmouth; it seemed almost to me as though she recognised, in one look, that he *might* have killed for her sake; and felt all the horror of her regret and culpability. That

Mr. Dobbin might read an equally telling truth in her countenance, I greatly feared. Her cousin, however, maintained a superior gravity that betrayed nothing—neither sensibility of Seraphine's doubt, nor confirmation of his guilt.

"And on what basis do you thus seize him?" I enquired of Mr. Dobbin boldly. My familiarity with the unjust imperilment of friends—so lately undergone at Scargrave Manor—gave me the courage to probe the law.

The justice's face closed. "I suggest you attend the inquest, madam, for the better satisfaction of your curiosity. And now I must beg leave to depart. The law may not be tarried, nor impeded in its course."

"Fiddlesticks," I muttered under my breath, and looked to Seraphine. Her every attention was claimed by her cousin, however, as he was hustled into the carriage in the company of two fellows, while the remainder stepped up behind. One look only I had from the master of High Down, as his head was forced below the carriage's sill; an intensity of purpose was in it, that spoke volumes without a word. I was to care for Seraphine as best I might, in Sidmouth's absence; and I felt the charge as surely as though it were his last.

I moved to take her arm, as the coachman clucked to his team; and found her stiff with horror and helplessness.

"Take heart, my dear," I said, with the falsest of hope. "Your cousin is not without friends. The first of these is Mr. Crawford. And though Justice Dobbin might pay little heed to the entreaties of a few women, he cannot ignore those of the first gentleman in town. To Crawford we shall go, therefore, as soon as ever we may."

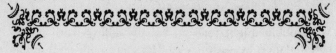

Chapter 12

A Signal in the Night

~

"I AM AFRAID, MISS AUSTEN, THAT THINGS LOOK VERY BAD INDEED for Mr. Sidmouth." Mr. Crawford turned from his decanter of claret with a sober look. "You are certain you will take nothing? Such an excellent wine as this cannot but be restorative. Even my sister acknowledges its healthful properties. And you have already endured much that is distressing—"

"Thank you, but no. I am already overly-fatigued, and fear it should unnerve me completely. You know, then, the nature of the evidence that would indict Mr. Sidmouth?"

Crawford bowed his head and hesitated an instant before answering. "I am ashamed to say that I do."

"Ashamed?" I gave a quick look to Seraphine, who sat white-faced upon the settee in the Crawford drawing-room. We were spared the thinly-veiled triumph of Miss Crawford, who had been on the point of paying a call at our arrival, and had tarried only long enough to express her sympathies to Mademoiselle LeFevre in as insufferable a manner as possible.

"Ashamed, indeed—for it was through my intelligence that Mr. Sidmouth was arrested."

"What!" Seraphine started to her feet, her eyes glittering and her aspect enraged. She would have leapt to Crawford's face, her fingers bent to claw at his eyes, had I not intervened; but though she struggled against me, her golden hair flying, her speech remained unfettered. "*You,* who are his dearest friend, would betray him so utterly? You would repay every kindness he has shown—all the days of good fellowship—with such lies as this? What depth of malevolence could have so turned your affection from my cousin?"

"No malevolence, my dear," Mr. Crawford protested, his countenance flushing deeply. "Only the conviction of my duty as an Englishman. For duty alone—and my respect for all the law upholds—could have prevailed in any contest of loyalty for Sidmouth. Had he been accused by another, on spurious claims, I should have defended him stoutly to the last; but the evidence of my own eyes threw in question the nature of the unfortunate Captain's end, and where my eyes bore witness, my tongue could not remain silent."

"Pray elucidate the matter, Mr. Crawford," I said quietly, as I helped Seraphine to regain her seat. The fight had drained from her slender form, leaving her beset with despair and trembling.

Crawford threw back the contents of his glass and sighed deeply, pausing to collect his thoughts; I knew then what his actions had cost him.

"You will remember, Miss Austen, during the course of Saturday evening last, when you and Mademoiselle LeFevre honoured us with your presence at dinner, that Mr. Sidmouth engaged in a lively debate with the Honourable Mathew Barnewall."

I looked all my bewilderment, and saw it mirrored in Seraphine. "But of course, Mr. Crawford. Mr. Barnewall wished to purchase Sidmouth's horse."

"The very Satan. So he did. Barnewall went so far as to jest that he should be reduced to robbing the Grange's stables, did Sidmouth persist in opposing him."

"And Sidmouth rejoined that it should avail him nothing, for his horses' shoes bore the mark of his initials."

"No, Miss Austen; I fear that it was *I* who voiced that opinion. You will remark that I knew full well how Sidmouth cared for his stables; and of how much value the horse Satan was to him. It was I who let slip the fact of the shoes being forged with a *GS* on their surfaces, and underlined that any who might steal one of the Grange's animals should leave a trail for all to observe."

Comprehension began to dawn, and I closed my eyes with a sudden weariness—the exhaustion of my hopes, perhaps.

"Of what importance is this in the present case, Mr. Crawford?" Seraphine enquired.

"Could you imagine, Mademoiselle, the tempests of emotion—of agonised doubt—undergone in the privacy of my study, on the very heels of the Captain's death, you should not look so harshly upon an old friend." Mr. Crawford threw himself down into an easy chair, his short legs extended before him and his hands resting upon his considerable stomach. His bald head shone with the effort of his communication. Miss Crawford had said that her brother spent the day of Fielding's discovery closeted in his study, with a bottle of claret for companionship; and I understood now the cause. Crawford had debated at some length before conveying his intelligence to Lyme's justice, as evidenced by the two full days between the Captain's death and Sidmouth's apprehension.

"I was the first man summoned to the scene by the boy who found Fielding's body," Mr. Crawford continued, "and for Sidmouth's purposes, there could not have been a worse coincidence. For I could not help but observe the hoofprints all round the Captain's still form, despite the trampling that his own horse had effected, in fleeing the very spot; and the fact of those initials—stamped deep in the mud at Fielding's very head—spoke more eloquently than even the blood upon the ground or the lily lying white upon his chest."

"Lily?" I cried, in sudden horror. The self-same flower had been found at the foot of Bill Tibbit's scaffold, at the very end of the Cobb. I little doubted, from Mr. Crawford's looks, that he was beset by similar fears. Had Sidmouth killed them both, and left the flowers as an inexplicable token?

"This is absurd," Seraphine spat out contemptuously. "Geoffrey is the very last man to kill another in so brutal a manner. You have been imposed upon, Mr. Crawford— and imperiled my cousin's life as a consequence."

"My dear Mademoiselle," Mr. Crawford said, with a pitying look, "who else but Sidmouth should have been riding such a horse?"

"Anyone," I broke in, "who hoped to incriminate him."

Crawford's face evidenced his confusion. "In order to throw suspicion far from the murderer himself, you would say?"

"Of course. Had you killed Captain Fielding, Mr. Crawford, should not you do the same?"

The ghost of a smile o'erspread the gentleman's features, and he nodded in acquiescence. "Perhaps, Miss Austen—though I should not place the blame upon my dearest friend."

"Assuredly not. You should choose your dearest enemy. And we may assume that Fielding's murderer has done as much." I rose to take a turn before the drawing-room fire, aware of the hope that dawned on Mademoiselle LeFevre's features. "I am more than ever of this opinion, I declare—for *had* Sidmouth wished to murder Captain Fielding, he is quite unlikely to have ridden Satan to the scene, from suspicion that the horse's hooves *should* be identified."

"But of course!" Seraphine cried, her countenance all animation.

"You may well have the right of it, Miss Austen," Mr. Crawford said, with a doubtful accent, "yet you do not account for the heat of passion. Your claims may only bear weight did the Captain's murderer *plan* his crime beforehand. But did the Captain meet his end of a sudden—in the midst, for example, of a fight all unlooked for, between two men of hot temper—the matter of his mount's shoes may have escaped the murderer's attention altogether."

Seraphine was cast down again in a moment—from a sudden conviction, perhaps, that the case was quite likely as Crawford had supposed. Geoffrey Sidmouth, as my own mind imagined it, was very creditably thrown into the role of sudden assassin, when the spur of his temper was placed in consideration.

"But would a man moved to such a sudden mortal blow carry a lily about his person, or leave it by the Captain in token of his sins?" I cried. "Depend upon it, Mr. Crawford. We are all grossly imposed upon. There is more to the matter than meets the eye."

"You may well be proved correct, Miss Austen," Mr. Crawford replied, his dejected form speaking all his misgiving, "but the Captain is unlikely to have known *two* men who bore him such enmity, as we know Sidmouth to have felt."

I could not charge Mr. Crawford with the betrayal of his friend, as Seraphine had done; he spoke only as Mr. Dobbin and the coroner might, in presenting the evidence at Fielding's inquest—and for any light to be thrown upon the matter, even the most distasteful of possibilities must be accorded a measure of thought. The darkest matters between the two men should be fully canvassed and understood, did we hope to find Fielding's murderer.

"Mademoiselle LeFevre," I said tentatively, with a look for poor Seraphine, whose face was lost in her kerchief, "I have no wish to increase your distress, for the idle satisfaction of my own curiosity; but it would appear that a better understanding of the affairs between your cousin and Captain Fielding, might materially improve Mr. Sidmouth's case. Is it in your power to reveal the cause of his profound dislike?"

Her angelic head came up, and her eyes sought mine with pain. "I do not know—I am not certain what may safely be said. I must speak with Geoffrey first."

"It turns upon the Captain's nickname, does it not?" Mr. Crawford gently enquired. "*Le Chevalier*. He won it through some service to yourself, I had understood."

"Service? *Service?* Is that what he called it?" Seraphine threw back her head with bitter laughter. "The English have a curious way with language, do they not? Mr. Crawford speaks of duty, when he should say betrayal, and Captain Fielding—Captain Fielding spoke when any man of honour should better have remained silent. From the *services* of our friends, my cousin and I have both of us been reduced to misery." She rose in a single fluid movement, swung her red cloak about her form, and turned to Mr. Crawford a countenance as remote as heaven.

"Thank you, Mr. Crawford, for the indulgence of your time; but I fear I must return now to the Grange. There is much to be done, and one less pair of hands to do it; and I hold my cousin's concerns too dear to neglect his business in his absence. You will forgive me."

Mr. Crawford cleared his throat, and sank his chin in his cravat, and seemed at a loss for words.

"May I offer my company, Mademoiselle, and my assistance?" I enquired.

Seraphine only shook her head. "You are kindness itself, Miss Austen, but I should like to be alone at present. We will speak again, I hope, in a few days' time."

That she envisioned some meeting by the Golden Lion, in the midst of Sidmouth's inquest, I little doubted; and felt a deep foreboding. A look for Mr. Crawford convinced me that the gentleman was similarly lost in thought; but he roused himself sufficiently to order his carriage, a measure of solicitude for which I was thankful, having walked my fill of Dorset's hills for one morning.

Our few moments' journey was rendered tedious enough in being passed in virtual silence, before Seraphine was deposited on the Grange's doorstep; and at the coachman's turning his horses' heads, I had a final glimpse of her—pale, upright, and clothed in fire, as she toiled her lonely way through the courtyard.

20 September 1804, in the wee hours

~

I COULD NOT SLEEP, TONIGHT, FOR TOSSING AND TURNING IN THE grip of tortured thoughts—all that I observed and witnessed today being fresh upon my mind. A thousand expressions and attitudes paraded before my wearied eyes— Mr. Sidmouth's warmth, as he handed the boy Toby his crutches; the face of Seraphine, as she stared across the sunlit Channel towards France; her tears, in considering Captain Fielding's mysterious behaviour towards herself; and her raging loss in the face of Sidmouth's seizure. Mr. Crawford, too, would not be banished from my mind—for such a heavy burden did he bear, in debating, as he must, his friend's guilt or innocence!

The heaviest share in sleeplessness, however, I must accord to the proper place, as arising from my own indecision regarding Sidmouth. In truth, I knew not what to think of the incriminating hoofprints. A plausible case might be made for another's having taken a mount from the Grange's stables, and done away with the Captain in Sidmouth's guise; but I felt all the truth of Mr. Crawford's conjecture—that none might harbour towards the Captain such enmity as the master of High Down.

—Or none, perhaps, than the smugglers and their lord, who undoubtedly bore towards the Captain a mortal grudge, for having bent his efforts to disturb their clandestine trade—but since all the world stood ready to proclaim Geoffrey Sidmouth the very Reverend, such an avenue led me nowhere.

Or did it?

I sat up in bed, transfixed by a thought.

Captain Fielding had supposed that Seraphine served as the Reverend's living signal, turning about the cliffs in her wide red cloak; he had offered it as his opinion that the very night that followed upon the heels of such a walk, should find the smugglers' landing. I had strolled with Mademoiselle myself this morning, and observed her stand like a stone on the cliffs above the sea, for whole moments together. No ship had I observed, it was true; but I had been much preoccupied with my own interrogation, and its effect upon the lady.

I threw back the bedclothes and reached for my boots.

The conjectures of a fevered brain, made less reasonable by lack of sleep, will bear all the weight of rational thought in the mind of the conjecturer, however ridiculous their merits might seem by the light of day. Full many a midnight thought have I entertained with alacrity, only to reject it over my breakfast chocolate as excessively disordered. Tonight, however, I was possessed of too much impatience to await the dawn; I felt I *must* know whether Sidmouth was the Reverend or no, and I knew with all the certainty of midnight that the answer lay upon the shingle below High Down Grange. That most ladies of gentle rearing and habits should rather die than venture alone through the darkness, I acknowledged; and set aside as irrelevant. I was not, after all, *most ladies*.

A glance through the curtains, to observe the waning moon, a few hours from its setting—and the hope that any smuggling band worth its brandy should be likely to await a greater darkness for landing. I might just have time enough.

And so, in the last extremity of caution, I clothed myself in my oldest dress—a serviceable brown wool, which should be some proof against the coolness of a September night, and the damaging effects of the downs—and let myself out of Wings cottage as quietly as I knew how.

THE WALK THAT WAS BRISKNESS ITSELF IN THE FULL LIGHT OF DAY, required nearly twice the time to effect in darkness and stealth; and the moon was fled from the sky indeed by the time I found the shore of Charmouth, and groped my way along its length. Mr. Crawford's fossil works I passed, and felt gratitude for its familiar humping of tools and rock, all shrouded now in canvas; passed, too, the path from the road above, where Mr. Sidmouth had pulled up the Crawford barouche—a day that seemed so long ago, I might have lived it in another lifetime.

I climbed up on a little bluff above the sand, to gaze at the rubble surrounding the fossil pits; and remembered the ammonite he had pressed into my hand—cool and smooth, like his strong fingers. Then I turned to the sea, and stared out over the endless black, as enormously empty as eternity itself. I had never before witnessed the curl of surf upon a beach at night, and was much struck by the white-green glow of the waters, as though some light from within the sea's depths would guide the waves to shore. The fresh wind clutched at my brown wool, and sent a chill through my body—unless it be the sensibility of my exposure to the elements, and the solitude of the night, and the possibility of a fate such as the Captain had found, that made me quail where I stood. Such isolation, as wrapt me round in discomfort! Well might I curse the power of midnight thoughts, that had sent me on such a foolhardy errand!

I turned back to the cliffs, and gazed upwards, searching for the light of a farmhouse or outbuilding, that might herald my progress towards the Grange; but the flanking bulk of the chalk heights foreshortened my view, and revealed nothing of the civilisation hugging its very edge. I stepped back, and farther back, until my boots sank well into the wet sand at the sea's margin; and craned myself to tip-toe.

And then I saw it—the short blink of a beam, as swiftly blinked out. An idea of Seraphine's curious lanthorn sprang to mind—its long, cylindrical spout debouching from one side, with a sliding cover of tin, so obviously designed for signalling. *Someone* above would make converse with a ship at sea. I wheeled, and strained to peer through the darkness—and was rewarded by an answering flare of light.

Not a moment should be lost, for they would be upon me with some swiftness. But where to hide myself?

Eliza's voice it might almost have been, from a light-hearted walk over a fortnight since, and ringing in my ears with her habitual frivolity—*A cavern, Jane, as foetid and dank as Mrs. Radcliffe should make it! Shall we venture within, at the very peril of our lives?*

I hastened myself back along the cliff wall, endeavouring to recall the exact location of the slight opening in the rock; had it been *before* the Crawford pits, or just after? Or was it well along the Charmouth shingle, almost to its end? Without the aid of the moon, I could make nothing of the fold and meander of the chalk; where deliberation and calm were required, I was maddened by a sense of urgency that would not be gainsaid; and so it seemed that I must have stumbled about the place a veritable age, when of a sudden I recalled the small rock cairn I had observed so many days ago, in walking with Eliza by the cave's entrance. A moment only secured it to my sight; and my relief at turning past it, and slipping within the protective blind, was little greater than my previous desperation.

I was forced to stoop in the entry, and felt the chill brush of moisture against my back; but the cave's sandy floor was dry enough, however little my eyes might discern of its depths. If the darkness without might be enough to terrify, it was nothing to the blackness within; and I groped my way like a blind woman robbed of her cane, with tentative step and arms outstretched. It remained only to find a suitable spot for sitting, since my purpose was to o'erlook the beach as best I might, while shielding myself from others' eyes; and to the left-hand side of the cave's opening, I found a large boulder with space enough behind to settle myself in a heap of exhausted brown wool, and schooled myself to wait.

To MY HORROR, I STARTED AWAKE SOMETIME LATER WITH AN AUDIBLE snort—and possessed not the slightest notion how long I had been slumbering. I was on my feet in anxious haste before the slight sound of oars turning in their locks stopt me at the cave's mouth; and so with caution renewed, I held my breath, and peered out into the night.

Two figures were huddled upon the shore, straining for a glimpse of something progressing over the waves— the very Seraphine, to judge by her length of dusky cloak, and the boy Toby, bent over his crutches. The mademoiselle's right hand was flung protectively around the boy's shoulders, while from her left depended an indiscernible object—the lanthorn, in all probability. I looked towards the sea for the object that engaged their full regard, and could just make out the form of a dory, breasting the surf well out from shore, where a hidden bar rose up in the night water. It was from thence the sound of oarlocks emanated.

I stood as still as caution might make me, and watched as the boat pulled nearer, revealing with the additional passage of a few moments the figures of four men—two at the oars, and two bent over the cargo. Brandy kegs? Or crates of goods, as various as the peoples of the Continent?

The boat slid to shore; the oarsmen jumped into the sea, and dragged their vessel high up on the sand; and to my surprise, Seraphine gave a stifled cry, and stumbled towards the dory's gunnels, her hand over her mouth in horror.

And at that instant, a group of men rushed from the cliff's foot down the shingle's length, and hurled themselves on the boat—dragoons, I thought at first, with a pounding heart, come to attack the Reverend's proxy—but it was clear they were known to the boatmen, and further observation revealed them dressed as rough fisherfolk, their faces blackened with soot to defy discovery. One, however, I recognised, to my intense surprise—for Mr. Dagliesh, the bashful surgeon's assistant, stood by the mademoiselle's side, while his fellows exchanged places with the oarsmen, and turned the boat back out to sea. Whatever did it mean?

I could spare no more attention for the dory's progress, however, the bulk of my interest being claimed by Seraphine, who knelt in a red-cloaked huddle over the vessel's beached cargo—which was neither kegs nor caskets, but the figure of a man, and quite insensible, from his attitude. The mademoiselle's shaking shoulders betrayed her to be silently weeping; and my curiosity was not greater than the sympathy her sorrowful attitude aroused. Dagliesh dropped to her side, and busied himself in attending the man; and the boy Toby leaned upon his staves, silently watching, with head bowed. His mistress looked up, and asked a quick question of Dagliesh, which was as fluidly and unintelligibly answered; and if my ears did not betray me, both had spoken in French.

Some grave mishap had overcome the smuggler's crew, that much was certain; and a wounded man—perhaps a dead man—had been brought to shore, and a team dispatched to serve as relief. Had the cutter been pursued across the Channel's length? Had it been fired upon, even, and stopt only long enough to send its casualties into English safekeeping? I shook my head in consternation. Such things were past my understanding.

The huddle of folk about the still form suddenly fell into disarray; Seraphine, with a wringing of her hands, turned to seek the path up the cliff's face, with Toby hobbling in tow; and the oarsmen, taking up their burden with a grunt, hoisted the unknown fellow to their shoulders and moved off into the night. No light had they, but for Seraphine's lanthorn; and if the cutter had indeed been pursued, it seemed likely they should spurn illumination for the protective cover of darkness. What a lonely trudge they faced to High Down Grange! And still more disheartening a night's watch, perhaps, over a man with little life left in him!

I turned back to the cave's interior, intent upon retaining my seclusion until the sounds of the smugglers' passage should have entirely died away, though my own spirits were so cast down, and my energy so sapped, that I should as lief have been gone on my own way home, the quicker to put the night's peculiarities behind me. The threat of discovery I could not entertain, however; and so

I counseled myself in greater patience, and ignored the cold that crept beneath my gown, and hugged my arms closer about my person. I envied Seraphine the utility of her thick cloak, and saw that I had much to learn of midnight skulduggery.

Perhaps a quarter-hour had passed, and I felt myself to be quite alone, and had just arisen with limbs aching from the cold, and ventured to the cave's mouth—when the sound of laughter and a stumbling foot stopt me dead. I drew breath, a wave of fear unaccountably washing over me, and found the courage to peer once more into the night.

Neither Seraphine nor Toby, nor yet one of the men so recently disembarked upon the shingle; but *two* fellows, quite rough in appearance, and strangers to my eyes. As I watched, one raised a bottle to his lips and tottered backwards, unmanned by spirits or the slope of beach or both; the other gave forth a burst of raucous cheer, and sang a snatch of a sailor's chanty. I glanced wildly about, and felt too swiftly the idiocy of my position—how alone I had made myself, and how unlikely a cry for help should *now* draw forth any aid from the Grange above—and cursed my too-active curiosity. It shall be my very death, I am sure, before the passage of much more time.

I drew back swiftly to the cave's interior, awaiting with bated breath the men's progress down the shingle; and clenched involuntarily at the rock wall to my back. The voices were approaching, amidst the tramp of heavy feet; their purpose was certain, and unswayed by any diversion, despite the fog of spirits that hobbled them. And so with suspended breath, and hands thrust behind to break any fall, I began to step noiselessly back into the cave. For I knew with a certainty that the men's object was my very place of hiding—and that all flight to the fore should be impossible.

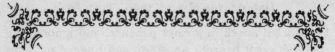

Chapter 13

Of Shoes and Ships and Sealing Wax

20 September 1804, cont.

~

A BEAM OF LIGHT DANCED IN THE CAVE'S MOUTH, AND I HELD MY breath, feeling my way backwards. One of the men—he who had earlier produced the bottle—had lit a lanthorn as they approached, and it was *this* that swung its welling arc of illumination ever closer to my feet. I took yet another step back, and felt my boot heel butt up against something hard—not the cave's nether wall, thank God, but the cool dampness of a very large boulder. I ducked around it, the better to afford myself protection, and found a narrow space behind just capable of admitting my form. Providence had not entirely abandoned me.

"Give us the bottle, Dickie boy," said a high-pitched, sneering voice; and with a guttural oath, his companion complied. The chink of glass against the lanthorn's metal, as the spirits changed hands; and then the contemptible sound of liquid coursing down a vulgar throat. "I 'ates the very sight o' such dank and nasty places, I do. I *still* says we should'uv gone 'round by the 'igh road. It's perishin' dark and wet in 'ere."

The lanthorn's light careened wildly up the rock wall opposite, and I assumed that Dickie had cuffed his partner about the head—which supposition was confirmed not an instant later by a howl of pain.

" 'Ere, now, what's the cause o' that?"

"I told you afore to shut up, Eb. Now *shut up,* I say. We've serious business above, and it's as much as our necks are worth, if the Reverend finds out."

" 'E's not a-goin' to find out," the man called Eb rejoined, in a wounded tone, " 'less you tells 'im, or I tells 'im, and that's not a-goin' to 'appen. We're snug coves, and do things proper. Care for a nip?"

"Put it away and stow your gaff." The light swung towards my place of hiding, and the tramp of feet approached; I could not prevent myself from cowering, I fear, in the recognition that I should be considered a terrible risk to the two, did they discover me. As the larger of the men—the one called Dick—passed within inches of my face, I closed my eyes in the certainty that I had been discovered; but he must have looked neither to the right nor the left, and eventually, the sound of footsteps ceased. I opened my eyes, but stayed still where I stood, my ears straining for the slightest sound.

The ring of metal on stone, and a lowering of the light; Dick had set the lanthorn down. A grunt of exertion, and a stifled oath from Eb, and then the squeak of poorly-oiled hinges—the men had heaved open a door! A passage must exist, hewn through the very rock, and leading deep into the downs. My heartbeat quickened, for I knew the men should toil onwards, leaving the cavern in peace; and the way to freedom and the road for Lyme should be entirely at liberty.

What an agony of conflicting impulses then assailed me! Though a heroine of Mrs. Radcliffe's or Charlotte Smith's should have gone determinedly through the door, and hazarded the horrors of the darkened tunnel without a backwards glance, I confess that I thought first of my deserted bed in Wings cottage, and the warmth of its quilts, and the comforting embrace of sleep. I longed to abandon the chase for another day, when Dick and Eb should be far from my thoughts and my person, and the chalk cliffs of Charmouth wear a happier aspect, in being gilded with September sun.

But Geoffrey Sidmouth had not the luxury of deferring what should be distasteful; to him there remained but a few days, before the coroner's parade of guilt; and I recollected that my object in journeying to the shingle tonight had been to learn something of the Reverend, in the desperate hope that he and Sidmouth were not one and the same. That hope was all but diminished—for Dick had invoked the Reverend's very name, and his familiarity with such a tunnel, placed at the Grange's foot, bore a decidedly unpleasant construction. If I was to learn the worst, then, and abandon all faith in Sidmouth, it must be effected *here* and *now;* I had no choice but to go on, when every fibre of my being screamed that I should turn back.

With indrawn breath and a quickened pulse, therefore, I ventured to place my foot before the sheltering rock, and eased myself back into the cavern's depths. A lighter darkness, and the stirring of air before me, showed the way to the shingle, and home; but with a pang, I turned my back upon escape and sought the nether wall.

I could discern nothing like the outline of a door; and feeling with trembling fingers across the rock face, I encountered something so squeamishly clinging and moist, that I nearly forgot myself and cried aloud, snatching my hands away in an instant. A nauseous smell, as of decaying fish—and I knew the stuff to be nothing more than seaweed, fresh from the shingle and rendered wet by the trickle of moisture that emanated ceaselessly from the rock walls on every side. An effective disguise, indeed, for a passage one does not wish discovered—for the casual observer should never surmise that a door lay behind, and an idle explorer should be immediately deterred by the stench and touch of the stuff. I drew breath, and the tremor in my limbs subsided; and in another instant, I had steeled myself to touch the foul weeds, and feel beyond them for the rough wood of the door. The latch was there, and mindful of the creaking hinges that had alerted me to the door's presence in the first place, I eased it open but a few inches, and squeezed myself inside.

The dimmest pinpoint of light before me, revealed Dick and Eb to have made considerable progress; and I immediately followed in their wake, thrusting all fears and doubts behind me in the distracting activity of my purpose. The tunnel's floor was uneven, and a sudden dip in its surface, or a sharp incline, could all but cause me to tumble; I turned my ankles too frequently for notice, and clutched at the walls to either side, being deprived of the steady lanthorn that must so comfort the ruffians before. A very few moments, however, and I wished even for the faint pinpoint first detected—for the tunnel must have turned, and the men and their light were hidden from view.

I toiled onwards, climbing ever more surely, until I came to a flight of rough steps; and eased my way up them, uncertain when the tunnel floor should resume.

"Eh, there, Eb, you've stepped on my foot," a harsh voice muttered, almost before me; and I crouched as swiftly as I knew how, hugging the very step—for at the stairs' end stood my two guides, and from the sound of their laboured breathing and puffs of effort, another tunnel door.

After some moments, it must have swung open, and the fellows were passed through, for with a *snick!* the tunnel was thrown in utter darkness, the encouraging lanthorn having vanished behind the door.

I climbed stealthily to the stairs' head, and took but a few steps until the tunnel's end was reached; and then, groping forward, I found a decidedly smooth wooden surface, and traced with my fingers the outline of a doorjamb; but no latch or keyhole could I find. The way was barred to me.

I swallowed hard, and turned about in confusion, and endeavoured *not* to consider the more usual inhabitants of such a subterranean passage—the scuttling rats, and the creeping spiders, of enormous size, that undoubtedly traversed the walls at either hand, or such nameless creatures as must give rise to shuddering dread—and wished fervently that I had chosen the cowardly way, of my bed at Wings cottage. For to what purpose had I journeyed so far, in the grip of such anxiety, if the men were now gone before, and the passage closed?

"Give us a 'and, Dick." I nearly jumped out of my skin, the high-pitched voice was so close to my ear; and a squeak must have escaped me, for there was a swift cessation of movement beyond the door, and a thrill of fear in the man's voice when next he spoke.

"Eh, Dick—joo 'ear *that?*"

" 'Ear what?"

"*That.* Some'at in the wall. Gives 'un the shivers, it did—like a strangled woman."

"Rat, more'n likely. Or maybe a ghost—'ow's that for a nasty bit o' cheer?"

"Dick—you don't think as the Cap'n—"

"Aw, for the luv of Jesus, Eb, com'eer and 'elp us shift a keg or two. We've not got all night, I reckon."

I leaned against the door, adjudging it to be cleaner than the tunnel wall, and listened intently. For some time the two men appeared to be engaged in serious labour—shifting what I supposed to be caskets, and tearing off the lids of kegs, from the sound of splintering wood; this, and the occasional oath at a bruised shin, were my sole amusements for what seemed an eternity. The chink of glass proclaimed the bottle to be passed, and a deep sigh the fact that it had been emptied; and still the search—for search it undoubtedly was—went on.

I found it in me to wonder, if the tunnel had indeed led to the very doors of the Grange, where the farm's inhabitants might be. Tending the wounded man, perhaps? Or were the men arrived at the very stables, and shifting about with only beasts for company?

"Eb! Eh, Eb—'ave a gander at this!" Dick exclaimed, after an interval.

A scuffle of feet, and a low whistle, followed by the nastiest of chuckles. "You s'pose as the swells really play cards like 'at? Indecent, it is. Fancy painting a Queen o' Hearts what ain't got no clothes on. Those Frenchies'll get up to anything."

And *this* was my reward for risk and wakefulness! I closed my eyes in wearied exasperation. I had long suspected the men were rifling a storage of smugglers' goods, but this last confirmed it. The rage for playing cards had so inflated the demand for them in England, that the Crown had imposed a tax upon the principal supplier—France—and rendered the game too expensive for most people's purses. French cards were often to form a part of contraband cargoes; but I had not formed a notion of what *sort* of cards they might be.

"Well, I'm *flummoxed*," Dick said, and from the complaint of a bit of wood, I knew he had seated himself on a crate.

"The Reverend's stuff ain't 'ere, nohow," Eb agreed.

I imagined the two of them scratching their heads, lost in a fog of spirits, and wished them more prone to babble and less to a complaisant silence. Had ever a keyhole listener heard less to the purpose than myself? It was not to be borne.

"What'll us do, Dick?" Despite his whiskey courage, there was a note of fear in Ebenezer's voice.

"Get out o' Lyme while the gettin's good," the other replied. "Now Sidmouth's in jail, we've bought oursels some time—His Honour's too distracted wit' the justice an' all. But we'd best make tracks afore he notices we failed 'im, or we'll land at the end o' the Cobb like Bill Tibbit."

The other man audibly swallowed, and to my horror, began to sob—a terrible sound in a grown man, however unnerved by drink and fear. My own spirits were little better—for Dick's words were too open to a painful construction, and their import had the power to sink my very heart—but I longed to hear them debate their dubious fate the longer, in the hope of learning more.

"Now, now, Eb—ain't I allus looked after ye?" Dick said, in an effort to comfort his fellow. "We're snug coves, like you says, and we'll work oursels out o' this pickle. Let's get on back to the beach afore daylight, and take the boat round to Pegwell Bay. It's a hop-skip from there to the London road, and we're out o' the Reverend's ken. You just buck up there, laddie, and trust in ol' Dick."

" 'Alf a tick—"

"Eh, what's 'at?"

"I'm not leavin' all *this* 'ere, you ninny. Us'll live a year in London, for the price o' these."

"Put 'em back, Eb," Dick said, with a certain menace. "I'll not 'ave the law on our 'ides, and the Reverend, too. Free Trade is one thing. Stealin's another. I've always kept the difference careful-like. A man'd 'ang for what you've got."

"But it ain't stealin'! This is contraband—"

"It ain't our'n."

"Aw, Dick—"

The sound of a blow, and a whimper, and some goods let fall, and Eb was brought to heel.

So absorbed was I in all that passed, that I barely attended to the approach of heavy feet, until with a click the door began to swing inwards. I flattened myself along the tunnel wall, and endeavoured not to breathe, though my heart was pounding painfully within my chest; and in another instant, the door was thrust hard against my person and the two men stumbled through. The heavy musk of liquor enveloped their passage. They were too lost in thought and spirits to notice that the door abutted something other than the tunnel wall; and indeed, in the welling shadows beyond their lanthorn's reach, little could be discerned. As Ebenezer went safely past, I gave a gentle push to the door, which swung closed behind the two men, to the satisfaction of a single glance from Dick over his left shoulder; and since I stood in the blackness just behind his *right*, I managed to remain undetected. What a fever of anxiety gripped my senses, however, while the three of us retained the same bit of tunnel! That the others could not *feel* the presence of a third, by some buried animal instinct, had the power to astonish me—so certain was I that my very breath cried out my betrayal.

But they discovered nothing, and were down the enshrouded flight of steps, and on into the tunnel's depths, before very many instants had passed—taking with them, perforce, their comforting beam of light. In a little while all was utterly dark. A decision was now before me: should I attempt to find the door's hidden mechanism, or turn back the way I had come—and face the dawn on Charmouth beach? That way, assuredly, lay the easier path of least resistance; but I had come thus far, and would gladly return to Lyme possessed of the knowledge of *whose* storeroom the men had invaded.

I ran my hands the length of the door's face, and pressed its wood determinedly; but the portal remained unmoved. Perplexed, I paused for consideration. Neither Dick nor Eb had appeared to expend any remarkable energy, in forcing the way; and neither was possessed of inordinate cunning, as a puzzle lock might require. Abandoning the wood, therefore, I felt along the jamb's length, and was rewarded by a small knob, of very little protrusion, and roughly the size of a shilling. I pressed it, and was unsatisfied; pulled it, and was confronted with an open door.

All was darkness beyond the sill, and discernible within it, the huddled shapes of a quantity of goods, spilled about in hasty confusion. The men had not troubled to restore order where they had bestowed their chaos; and as I stepped into the room, my boots met splintered wood. After so many hours in utter gloom, my eyes could see nearly as well as by day; and I took a moment to look about me curiously, content from the example of the two men's easy search, that the room was safe from surprise.

The room had no windows; it must, therefore, be a cellar—beneath the Grange's barn, perhaps? Or a greater excavation still, a floor below what passed for cellars in the farmhouse itself? I must trouble to move with caution, until I learned better whose manor I invaded. But what riches this storeroom held!

I strained in the darkness to put names to the huddled objects, and was rewarded with a king's ransom of goods. There were brandy kegs by the dozen, and deep casks of fragrant tea—the best China leaf, too dear for the humble Austens' housekeeping—and rough sacks of coffee beans, and pounds of chocolate; exotic spices, from Malabar and the Canaries; the finest Spanish lace; a snorting wealth of sneezing snuff; coal, coffin-nails, hair-powder, and sealing wax; and in one extraordinary chest, all disordered at the tunnel's very entrance, a quantity of newly-strung pearls. Cool and silken to the touch they were, and I understood now Eb's unwillingness to let them slip, and felt a strange respect for the stalwart Dick's refusal. The morality of the Gentlemen of the Night was indeed passing strange.

I stood up, and let the pearls drop back in their chest, a frown of puzzlement creasing my brow. Something was missing. What could it be? What had the two besotted fellows sought and failed to find?

Silk.

But of course. *Silk,* so necessary for clothing a beautiful woman as vanity and fashion dictated; silk, that draped the costliest windows on the most breathless streets of the country's principal towns—most precious of tissues, its sheen unrivalled, its colours brilliant, its sinuous length wrapping the kingdom from north to south—*silk.* Spun principally on the Continent, and in the south of France, and taxed within a hair'sbreadth of everyone's life, and thus a smuggler's fortune. I had owned only *one* silk gown in my entire life; but I had not yet learned to despise its glorious folds.

And so the Reverend was a silk trader—*a Man of the Cloth.* The sobriquet's sly pun bespoke a certain clever-ness—a tendency to flout convention, and turn the com-prehensible on its head; both qualities quite native to Mr. Sidmouth's character. And my very own Eliza had de-clared Sidmouth a frequent traveller to France, where his cousin Seraphine must provide a valued service, in speak-ing the language fluently. I little doubted that whatever her *professed* distaste for Buonaparte, or the depth of her wounds from the revolutionary past, that with a brother well-placed in the Imperial army, she was not disinclined to cross the Channel on behalf of Sidmouth's interests. From Roy Cavendish I had it that the Reverend employed agents—and who better to employ, than Seraphine? Was this the source of the enmity between Captain Fielding and High Down Grange? Had he discovered that Made-moiselle LeFevre was but a pawn in her cousin's game, and endeavoured to separate them, for the preservation of her liberty?

I sat down on a keg and put my head in my hands. The

night's burden of knowledge was all too heavy, and my store of sleep too small. There was nothing more to be done, than to discover my whereabouts, and effect a return home—by the road, if all within the Grange were yet abed, or the tunnel, if need be.

There was a staircase at the room's far side, and I quickly sought it, and in the greatest stealth and trepidation, turned the doorknob at its head, expecting at every instant to be set upon by Sidmouth's dogs. But all was quiet; and a delicate light streamed over the threshold as I swung wide the door—dawn had come to the cliffs above the sea. I waited an instant, listening for some sound in the stillness, and then stepped into sunshine and looked about me, blinking in disbelief.

For I had emerged from a gardener's shed, and found myself in a ruin—a prettyish sort of place, surrounded by rosebushes now long past their bloom, and the arched forms of wood nymphs trapped forever in unyielding marble.

Captain Fielding's wilderness temple.[1]

---

[1] Austen's description of the tunnel corresponds to several discovered in recent years throughout the coastal towns of the Channel counties. Some lead to landing areas from the cellars of inns, which often served as smugglers' central meeting places and storage areas for contraband; others, from manor houses on the cliffs above; and still another, from a family vault in the crypt of a church—used to store brandy barrels, no doubt, instead of dead ancestors. —*Editor's note.*

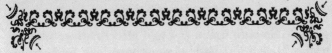

Chapter 14

Setting a Course

20 September 1804, cont.

~

"How very provoking of Mr. Sidmouth to get himself arrested," my mother was saying, in some vexation, as I descended the stairs to the breakfast room. "For he is certain to hang, so Miss Crawford tells me, though he seemed to be overflowing with admiration for our dear Jane. I declare I never saw a more promising inclination, Mr. Austen—excepting, perhaps, Captain Fielding's—but that came to nothing, and Miss Crawford assures me in any case that he intended to make his proposals to her niece. But, there it is—the poor man died before he could speak, and Miss Armstrong is denied even the interesting circumstance of mourning a proclaimed lover."

"Indeed," my father responded drily. "To mourn for a gentleman one may only claim as an acquaintance, lacks something of verisimilitude."

"A sad business altogether," my mother resumed, having heard, one imagines, the sense of her husband's words, without their subtle derision. "I shall never speak of Mr. Sidmouth again, as I told Miss Crawford only yesterday. He is a very undeserving young man, and his want of consideration for the feelings of others is truly abominable—and I suppose there is not the least chance of Jane's getting him *now*. Ah, my dear, here you are at last!"

As I claimed my place at table, my father peered at me over the top of his spectacles, and remarked at my wearied countenance.

"You are not lying awake of nights, my dear, in consideration of Sidmouth's affairs?" he said, with a brief smile. "It is something indeed, for a girl to pine after a gentleman in gaol; it lends a certain style to her attitude, and renders her remarkable among the circle of her friends; but I should hope my stout Jane not unduly affected in her *finer* sensibilities."

"No, Father," I replied, and knew not where to look.

"Mr. Sidmouth is one of the most undeserving young men in the Kingdom," he said, with an air of evident enjoyment, "or so your mother assures me. The very worst of men, I understand, for having shot the gallant Captain—or for failing to petition your hand *first*—I am not quite certain which. But one assumes he had his reasons, for both his trifling actions."

"I cannot believe a man should act as he has done, *without* a very good reason," I rejoined.

"Ah, there you would debate philosophy, my dear—and I never entertain philosophy before breakfast. It *is* unfortunate, all the same. I cannot find out that anyone in town believes Sidmouth innocent; and so he shall probably hang; and yet I liked the man. He had a sound understanding, and a forthright temper, and a dignity of purpose that was not unbecoming. Jane," my father broke off, "I am sure you are indisposed. Your aspect is decidedly weary for one who has lain so long abed."

I endeavoured to reassure him, and divert my mother's

attention, in pleading the probable onset of a cold (nothing very remarkable, when I consider the manner in which I spent the better part of the night); and was accordingly counseled to keep to my room, and partake frequently of warm lemon-water. I made no objection to the plan, perceiving some benefit in quiet reflection; for I have much to consider. A few pleasantries over chocolate and rolls, then, and my mother's petitioning me for an opinion as to the trimming of a hat she purchased yesterday for Cassandra, and in a very little while I found myself alone once more, and established over my journal and pen.

To say that I was astounded at finding myself in the Captain's garden is perhaps to say too little. With what disbelief, did my eyes encounter the familiar landscape, and how, with a mind revolting against the evidence of its own perception, did I cast about for understanding amidst the utter routing of my sense! Every precept I believed to be founded upon rock, I must discard as so much baseless sand; and those cherished notions of my own ability, as a canny student of *character*, I must vigorously disown. They are the product of vanity, and being acknowledged as such, deserve their sudden abandonment.

The revelations of the wilderness temple have forced a revision of all that pertains to Captain Fielding's affairs, and the conclusions I drew—was intended to draw—from his words and actions. His extensive establishment of the gardens—over so short a period of residence—becomes more comprehensible when one considers the labour so necessary to the excavation of the tunnel and storerooms, and the secreting of their purpose amidst a quantity of greenery. (I must endeavour to find the labourers who effected it, since the Captain assuredly did not.) His behaviour, too, on the first occasion of my visiting the wilderness temple, now bears a different construction; for the Captain's anxiety at Cassandra's indisposition is revealed now as a fear of discovery—and I recall, with all the clarity of the remembered day, his haste in summoning the ladies from their stopping-place, and his closing the tool-shed door, before ever he enquired as to the extent of my sister's distress. I wonder I did not remark upon it before—how a gentleman encumbered by a wooden leg, should choose the greater exertion of crossing the little pavilion entirely, on such a trivial errand.

But what, exactly, did he endeavour to hide?

Are the goods stored below the temple but a repository of the Crown, and the representation of contraband seized on behalf of the Revenue men? —Or are they symbols of a duplicity more sinister still, in being the fruits of *Captain Fielding's* clandestine trade, achieved amidst the odour of sanctity he wore like an epaulette? If the former, then assuredly Roy Cavendish should know of the goods' existence, and I had but to apply to the gentleman for a full disclosure. I could not feel myself to be easy with this notion, however; for why should such contraband not be immediately transferred to the Lyme Customs House, and thence to London? For what possible purpose should it be retained in hiding?

At the thought of Mr. Cavendish's unfortunate countenance, his oily manner, his effort to twist my affections and obligations to his own ends—I could not flatter myself secure. For all I knew, he might well have colluded with the Captain himself, and the two embarked upon a profitable enterprise, in the seizing of others' hard-won cargoes without the knowledge of the Crown. They might summon the dragoons, and take possession of kegs and caskets, without a single remark other than a smuggler's curse; and none in Lyme be the wiser. I could credit Mr. Cavendish with such nefarious behaviour, though I knew him not at all; there is something in his manner that does not inspire confidence.

I will keep my own counsel for a time, until I know what may safely be said in his hearing.

But Captain Fielding? Could so noble a gentleman be so wanting in principle?

His knowledge of the smugglers' operations must tell against him. He understood the nature of captains and landers, and their preferences in coastline and weather; his very home afforded a likely spot for the observation of all their traffic, being sited on rising ground. I imagined that he possessed, as any Naval fellow might, a sound spyglass for scanning the horizon; and he was better placed than many to anticipate the disposition of Royal Navy ships, and the strength of their pursuit, in foiling Channel crossings. Valuable intelligence indeed, if one but put it to the purpose; but what motivation might the Captain have had, to so betray his trust?

I summoned to memory his weathered face—the bright blue eyes, the boyish shock of hair; and could find there no hint of malevolent purpose. But when I considered again his broken figure—the indignity of his affliction, his dependence upon a cane—my heart perceived another sentiment. Captain Fielding had sacrificed a great deal, in the height of his powers, and lived to see all his hopes blighted; denied advancement, denied glory, denied a lifetime his youth had toiled in the making— and given, perhaps, very little by way of gratitude or pension. Had he died off the coast of Malta, he should have won a place in glorious history, and been saluted by his comrades for valour and example; but as it was, he merely suffered for the winning of ignoble retirement, with a lifetime of regret and thwarted purpose before him. A terrible bitterness, coupled with a weary cynicism, in observing the considerable profits of Free Trade, might be little enough to effect his transformation—from gallant officer of His Majesty's ships, to roguish profiteer.

I must consider, finally, what he himself had avowed— that the skills of many a smuggling captain were so very great, given their familiarity with the most challenging coasts in the very worst of weather, that the Royal Navy placed their value above many more reputable veterans. Why should not Fielding, then, have turned his talents to use? —He had been denied a Navy ship; but why not purchase another vessel, more secretive and private, and range his wits against the best the Navy had to offer? For this, Roy Cavendish should be unnecessary, except in that by gaining his confidence, and affecting to labour on his behalf, the Captain might hope to secure himself from suspicion.

And with this last thought, I turned to Geoffrey Sidmouth, and felt there a bewilderment of emotions. If I credited the Captain with so great a duplicity—such depth of cunning as he must command, for the accomplishment of his aims—then very little further was required, to suspect him of establishing a rival, for Cavendish's pursuit and the better deflection of his own guilt. Why not choose for scapegoat a man he hated, and make him the very picture of the notorious Reverend?

But was Fielding, then, the Man of the Cloth?

From the tool-shed's contraband stores, it would appear unlikely; I had pierced the sense of the riddling name, and surmised the Reverend to deal in silk, of which there was none below. Dick and Ebenezer, my companions of the night, had spoken of the smuggler as living still, and his attention diverted by Sidmouth's misfortunes. Is Sidmouth, then, the Reverend? Or is there another, unnoticed by Fielding, who yet plies his trade in Channel silks?

I threw down my pen at this juncture, and paced about

the room, in an agony of confusion and hopeless thoughts—for my sense is as tangled as a ball of yarn beset by a litter of kittens. It is enough to have put down what I surmise or fear, and to acknowledge what I do not; and to admit that I am very far indeed from the truth of the matter. I must wonder *less*, and enquire *more*, before I shall know how to think.

I HAVE SPENT THE BETTER PART OF THE PAST HOUR, IN REVIEWING those journal entries that bear some mention of the Captain and Sidmouth; and a few nuts have I gleaned that might direct my future purpose. The matter of *le Chevalier* must be elucidated, if the source of Fielding's enmity towards Sidmouth is to be understood; and as Mademoiselle Seraphine is unlikely to assist me, I must look to others for enlightenment. From Mr. Crawford's probing of Mademoiselle LeFevre, I must assume that he is equally in the dark about the matter; and so I shall not waste my time at Darby. Mrs. Barnewall—who first spoke the name in my hearing—might be better solicited.

Second, and perhaps more important, I was reminded of Bill Tibbit, the unfortunate fellow hanged at the end of the Cobb. I persist in believing his death is no mere coincidence—that the same hand that raised his gibbet, fired the shot that killed the Captain. To understand the one is to begin to know the other. The mere presence of a white flower near the body of each would counsel that the deaths are not unrelated; and the two men were assuredly known to each other. The very night following Tibbit's hanging, at the Lyme Assembly where Captain Fielding was introduced to my acquaintance, I learned from Fielding himself that the dead man had been in his service, in pursuit of odd jobs. Is it too far from belief that Tibbit might have laboured at the tunnel, in the company of some others (Dick and Ebenezer come to mind), and

212 ~ STEPHANIE BARRON

been too swift to reveal his understanding of its purpose? Might he have gone so far as to blackmail the Captain, and met his end as a result?

Dick and Eb are undoubtedly far along the London road, if their drunken resolve of last night did not desert them; and I should not know how to find them anyway, did I determine to break silence, and reveal what I knew of their movements. But Bill Tibbit has a widow, if Captain Fielding spoke rightly; and a woman bereaved has often the loosest tongue. To the Widow Tibbit, then, I must go, when once her lodgings I have found out.

A GLANCE THROUGH THE WINDOW REVEALED THE DAY TO BE QUITE fine; and my few hours' reflection had restored my strength and spirits considerably. I was not, it appeared, to submit to the indignity of a cold; my brown wool had done me a service in this regard, as in so many others; and, upon listening in vain for the sound of my mother and father below, I concluded my parents had believed me abed, and sought the out-of-doors. I might depart, then, unremarked; and so I gathered up my Leghorn straw, and threw a serviceable wool shawl about my shoulders as proof against the late September wind, and descended the stairs in all the briskness of my purpose.

In the sitting-room I encountered poor James, intent upon his task of nailing some considerable pieces of wood across the windows looking out upon Broad Street. I waited in sympathy while he grunted and heaved through his exertions. Such a flush as o'erspread the young man's countenance, and such beads of perspiration as shone upon his face! For he must support the wood with one hand, while hammering with the other, and the exercise was decidedly an awkward one. I considered suggesting he call for Jenny, and petition her aid; but fearful of exciting his contempt, in questioning the manliness of his strength and vigour, I stood mildly by and waited until he should have done.

"There, miss," he said, rising to his full six feet, and easing his powerful shoulders; "that should please the missus."

"Indeed," I said, "as every form of kindness you exert on our behalf has done. We are indebted to you, James, for such labour freely offered, and with such good humour."

He blushed furiously, and cast his eyes about the rug, and was made so clearly ill at ease by my praise, that I hastened to give him opportunity for diversion.

"I wonder, James, if you are acquainted with the Widow Tibbit."

"Old Maggie?" he ejaculated, with an air of surprise. "Whatever d'you want with Maggie Tibbit?" Then, as if recollecting his place, he blushed once more. "Leastways, it's none of my business, beggin' your pardon, miss. You'll have your reasons, I expect, as I don't need the knowing of."

"But you *do* know Mrs. Tibbit, then?"

"All of Lyme knows Maggie," he said, with something of a smirk. "She lives down in Hull cottage, along the river."

"The River Buddle?"[1]

He nodded, curiosity in his eyes. The River Buddle district is a famous place in Lyme, and not for charitable reasons.

"Miss Crawford was so good as to think of the Tibbit children," I said, with a casual air, "and gathered some clothes among her tenants. I offered to take them to the widow, with our sympathies and compliments."

---

[1] *The Buddle* was the name given to the mouth of the Lym river, from which Lyme derives its name. —*Editor's note.*

"Then you'll be giving Old Maggie more consideration nor half the town," James declared, "but that's like your ways, miss, if you don't mind my sayin'. A zample to us all, so Jenny was sayin'; and I'm of her mind."

A zample, indeed.

Chapter 15

By the Buddle's
Noisome Banks

20 September 1804, cont.

~

THE RIVER BUDDLE—WHICH I SHOULD SOONER CALL A STREAM—
begins in the sweet grass of the high downs above Up
Lyme, and ends in the salt freshness off the Cobb; but its
narrow banks are crowded with a huddle of housing, and
the district bears a very ill reputation. So much I had
already known; but more salacious details were imparted
to me by Miss Crawford, when I called upon that lady in
the guise of charity, to solicit clothing for the bereaved
Tibbits—for I should not like to appear in the neighbourhood without a clear purpose, lest my visit to the widow
excite local speculation.

"Maggie Tibbit?" Miss Crawford said, peering at me
over her spectacles as I sat in the Darby drawing-room. "If
the woman had been possessed of sense, she should have
married anyone but the man she did; and having committed *that* folly, she should have determined to bear fewer
children. There are no less than *five*, you will understand,
and all of them decidedly ill-favoured."

"But deprived, nonetheless, of the support of a father," I had rejoined mildly. "Winter *is* coming on, Miss Crawford, and the condescension of the ladies of St. Michael's could hardly be better bestowed. Consider what Mrs. Tibbit's anxieties must be—and how slim the wretched woman's resources—with so many pitiful mouths to feed!"

"Aye, Maggie's resources are slim enough," Miss Crawford rejoined with a snort of contempt. "She has but one, as I'm sure you'll observe, do you persist in this foolish errand."

I made no reply, but awaited the outcome of Miss Crawford's benevolence; and in an instant, she had tidied her needlework with an air of decision, and bestowed upon her visitor another withering look.

"I will turn over some part of the clothing we hold in store, against the needs of such pathetic objects, but I cannot undertake to pay the call in your stead, Miss Austen," she told me severely. "I truly cannot. It would appear to countenance such behaviour as Mrs. Tibbit pursues, with the church's approbation. Soon all of Lyme's degraded women will be knocking at our doors."

"Indeed," I replied, with a demure look and inward rejoicing; for I had no wish for Miss Crawford's company, nor the discovery of her sharp ears, as I plied my questions. It but remained to follow her creaking black skirts into Darby's offices, and to have her turn over a quantity of clean linen, dutifully mended by the dutiful Lucy Armstrong (now returned to Bath in the company of her parents), and to enquire of Miss Crawford the approximate ages and sex of the Tibbit progeny. Despite her disinclination to involve herself in Maggie Tibbit's affairs, that charitable dame revealed herself well-acquainted with them. She could recite with dispatch the intelligence I required. I paused but to wonder what knowledge of *my* life she had amassed all unbeknownst; and then with the profusest of thanks and my bundle of clothing, I was handed into my hack chaise, and sent speedily on my way.

The stench of the Buddle embraced me well before I encountered its ramshackle cottages; for the river here is little more than an open sewer, that churns all manner of refuse and human waste along its course, to end in the beaches and the sea. The odours that arise from its banks must be overwhelming in the stagnant heat of summer; but I was preserved from the most unhealthful effects, by a brisk breeze and the application of a kerchief, liberally doused with lavender-water, to my nose. I had wisely donned a simple and sturdy gown—my old grey muslin, of a military cut, with the charcoal braid—my brown wool being quite sandy about the hems, the result of my Charmouth adventure, and possessed of a great slit in its backside, acquired somehow in the course of that midnight wandering. The Leghorn straw I had left behind, as too fashionable and frivolous for a charity errand; a sober closed bonnet I had adopted instead, which afforded the added benefit of shielding my features.

The cobbles of the street were few, and gaping holes pocked its surface; I saw where last week's storm had carved a rut along the verge, and the soil was much eroded. Picking my way with care, therefore, I searched about for a not unfriendly face, intending to ask the way. Several fellows lounging in doorways I swiftly discarded, as bearing too fearsome an aspect, or appearing too befuddled by drink to answer *any* enquiry with sense; but at last I espied a matron, with a market-basket over her arm and a cap upon her head, and an apron both tidy and white despite the squalor of her environs; and deemed her a suitable guide.

"Excuse me, madam," I said, with a bow at once stately

and condescending, as befit my role, "would you be so
good as to direct me to the Tibbit lodgings?"

The woman halted in her course, and stared at me with
outrage; and then, depositing a mouthful of phlegm on
the paving stones at my feet, continued along her way
with a sweep of skirts.

I stared after her, all amazement, then glanced swiftly
about the street. We undoubtedly had been observed; and
yet, the faces of the Buddle's intimates bore a carefully-
shuttered ignorance. Whatever could such behaviour
mean? And how was I to discover the valuable Maggie, if
her neighbours proved so taciturn and hostile?

"If ye be wantin' the Tibbits, ye've not far to go, miss."
The voice came at my very feet; and with a start of surprise, I looked down upon the bent back of a cripple, in
truth not above the middle age, but from his rough appearance and apparent ill-health, seeming as ancient as a
relic of Shakespeare's time. He leered up at me, head
craned at an awkward angle, his gnarled fingers gripping
a stave. Involuntarily, I took a step backwards, and
clutched tighter at my basket of clothing—for I should
not like to be taken unawares by a footpad in just such a
caricature, who would leave off his martyred stance and
turn his cudgel upon my head.

But no blow did I receive—only a cackle of laughter,
and a rattle of indrawn breath. "Ol' Sam's long past cha-
sin' the likes of ye, miss. The rheumaticks've got 'im. Not
but what ye ain't a sweet bit o' goods, and right to keep
yer wits about ye."

"The Tibbits?" I managed, by way of reply.

The creature swung his head farther down the road.
"The red 'un, with two winders what looks out onto the
street. Ye'll find it, certain sure. It's got a dead pullet
nailed to the door."

I should have hastened from him as fast as my legs
could carry me, but that he shuffled nearer, and held out

a withered palm, grinning repulsively through all his rotten teeth. I had just enough command of my wits to find my purse, and drop a coin at his feet. This he swiftly gathered up; and his laughter followed me the length of the narrow lane.

I thus found the Tibbits' abode, and judged it to be occupied, from the squeals and cries of children within, which were all too frequently punctuated with slaps and the swift onset of tears. It was a poor sort of place, constructed of odd bits of timber, and with a roof in sad need of pitch, and a facade that wanted paint, and a frame too prone to precarious tilting; almost I might have thought it poised to slide into the river at its back, and should misgive the effects of another storm upon its eroding foundations. The river here was narrow enough, that the houses perched on the opposite bank were but a strong man's leap away—so that the effect of the massed housing was more evocative of London's stews, than of Lyme's cheerful cottages.[1]

To my horror, a chicken indeed adorned the Tibbits' door—and had for some time, to judge by its decayed appearance, and the foul smell that drifted from its carcass (now, do not be suspecting me of a pun, I entreat). Traces of rotten vegetable matter I also discerned upon the portal's surface, and wondered at the tyranny to which the Tibbits were subjected. Was not the loss of a

---

[1] Austen here describes a feature of the River Buddle district that was apparently not without design. Geoffrey Morley notes in his book, *Smuggling in Hampshire and Dorset, 1700–1850* (Newbury, Berkshire: Countryside Books, revised edition, 1994), that this was the traditional smugglers' quarter of Lyme, and that the proximity of the housing served as a useful means of escape. When a smuggler's home was to be searched, its occupants often fled out the back windows to the houses on the Buddle's opposite bank, taking their contraband with them. —*Editor's note.*

father, in so public and horrible a manner, tragedy enough?

Squeamish in the extreme of knocking upon such a door, I turned to a window, but found that nothing was visible through its oilcloth; and so, after an instant's hesitation, I was reduced to calling towards the house.

"Widow Tibbit! Pray come into the lane! I would speak with you a moment!"

A sudden silence greeted my words—a listening silence, I was certain—and then I heard the sound of chair legs pushed back from the table, and a hoarse whisper hissed: "You there, Tom, give a look through the winder and tell us 'oo it 'tis. If it be that hussy Sue Watkins, you 'eave this tater at 'er 'ead!"

This last intelligence caused me to feel no little dread, and from my knowledge of small boys, and their relishing of any opportunity for battle, to consider a retreat to the porch opposite. Tom's appearance at the window, however, prevented my flight.

" 'Taint 'er," he reported over his shoulder; and I breathed a sigh of relief. " 'Tis a lady."

"A *lady*? What, wi'out a carriage?"

The sound of feet rapidly coursing towards the door, and a swift pull to its handle, that set the crucified pullet to jiggling; and I was as urgently waved inside by a woman I assumed to be the very Maggie I sought. Without a second thought, I mounted the two steps and eased past her, blinking somewhat as my eyes adjusted to the cottage's poor light.

"Maggie Tibbit, at yer servus," the woman said, bobbing.

"Miss Austen," I replied, and met the timorous stares of five very dirty children. One had a hand in its mouth, another hitched continually at his trousers, and the youngest took one look at my fine figure and burst into tears.

"There, there, Jackie boy," said Maggie abruptly, as

she scooped up the screaming child and unceremoniously offered it her breast, "the lady won't bite you."

The Widow Tibbit was a blowsy-enough figure, as I had half-expected from the nature of Miss Crawford's disapproval. Her dark curls were undone about her face, and she was arrayed in a dressing gown of soiled silk, though the morning was well-advanced. There was *rouge* upon her cheeks, which might have benefitted from a bath, as should the rest of her person; and a dark substance trailed down her front, that I adjudged to be snuff—though what use a *woman* might have for such a substance, I could hardly imagine. On her feet were satin slippers that had once been red, and once very dear; and from the cloud of fumes she breathed in my general direction, I knew her to have been indulging in brandy.

The woman was a walking advertisement for the smuggler's trade; and that her larder should boast some excellent if contraband tea, though not an ounce of oats for her children's porridge, I swiftly surmised.

"Mrs. Tibbit—" I began.

"Plain Maggie'll do, now Bill's been done for," she replied, and knocked the child from her breast with a casual blow that immediately set it to wailing. "What bizness 'uv ye got wit me?"

I lifted the basket of clothing from my arm, and opened its lid. "I thought your children might benefit from these few things collected by the women of St. Michael's."

"That Crawford bitch 'ave sent you, bain't she?" Maggie's countenance darkened and she advanced upon me pugnaciously, her protuberant lower lip revealing some very poor teeth indeed. "Reckon she's cackling summat fearsome, in all her black feathers, now old Mag's out on the street."

Somewhat disconcerted, I took refuge in a backwards step and a folding of my gloved hands. "I received the clothing of Miss Crawford, assuredly, as she manages St. Michael's good works—but the desire to visit, and to bestow these things upon your children, was entirely mine, I promise you, Mrs. Tibbit."

The widow pawed through the clothing, scattering chemises and shirts with a careless disregard for the dirtiness of her floor; but in considering the grime that covered her children's bodies, I recollected that the linen should not long survive in a pristine state, and forbore to vent my outrage. The scattered goods disappeared amidst a tangle of youthful limbs, like meat torn asunder by starving wolves. " 'ere!" cried the eldest, whom I recollected to be Tom. "You've never brought us shoes!" His expression of disgust might as readily have greeted the rotten pullet nailed to his front door, and in truth, the worn leather boot he held aloft bore an ill-begotten air. But Tom need not have worried—the shoe was snatched from his fingers by a fellow urchin of indeterminate sex, arrayed in what appeared to be a fisherman's overall many sizes too large; and borne from the house with a triumphant cackle. Tom dashed into the street in pursuit, a fearsome oath emanating from his childish lips. Their mother reached for a bottle resting on the worn oak settle and took a long draught. To my relief, she did not think to offer me a similar hospitality.

"The things'll do," she declared, and thrust the empty basket aside. "What I wants to know, miss, is why you come—when us's strangers to each other."

"Who could be unmoved by so much misfortune, as you have lately endured, Mrs. Tibbit?"

"Oh, most o' Lyme—and that's a fact," she rejoined sardonically. She spared a moment to place little Jack upon the floor, and shoo the remaining two urchins towards their fellows in the street. Then she turned to me with a calculating air.

"But my troubles is none o' yer concern, miss. What you want o' me?"

Any further attempt at explanation on my part was immediately forestalled by the street door's being once more thrust open, to reveal a massive fellow with a belligerent face leering upon the stoop. "Eh, Mag," he said, by way of salutation. "I've brought you summat nice."

"Not now, Joe. I've company."

"Company?" The fellow spat out the word like a wounded animal, and slid into the room without need of further invitation. The newcomer was burly and forceful, a fisherman from the look of his callused hands and the odour that pervaded his person, and he was clearly all but overcome with the anger engendered by his fears. It required all my fortitude not to flee through the open door, so menacing was his aspect; and yet, some sensibility that Maggie Tibbit should not be left alone with such a man, urged me to stand my ground.

"Is that Matt Hurley slidin' up yer skirts again, and Bill not dead a fortnight?" Joe advanced upon his object, his broad hands clenching convulsively.

"You cared little enough for waitin' yersel, for all yer talkin'. Now get out. I've a *lady* to visit."

As if acknowledging my presence for the first time—though how he could have overlooked the alien fact of cleanliness in that squalid room, I do not know—Joe swung his head around and met my gaze. An instant's mortification ensued, before the fellow pulled off his cap, and shifted uneasily on his feet; and then, blushing bright red, he backed his way to the door.

"I'll be leavin' yer, Mags, until a better time, beggin' yer pardon, miss," he said, and felt behind him for the latch.

"You'll be leavin' me for good, Joe Smollet—and good riddance to ye," Maggie shot back, lifting high her youngest, the baby Jack. "If I could count the days you've promised me that length o' silk, as you knows I've a need fer, and taken your bit o' cuddle—''

"I've got that silk right outside, I have, all done up in paper, like," Joe protested, halfway to the street.

A calculating look o'erspread the slattern's features. " 'Ere now, Joe, don't be so 'asty," she called. "You just leave that parcel 'ere, so's it don't go wanderin' with the first cove as passes by, and I'll tend to you proper, I will."

Joe shot me a glance of embarrassment, but was nonetheless unequal to the force of Maggie's charms. He ducked back inside to deposit something wrapped in heavy brown paper in the entryway. "See you, Mags," he said, with a sheepish nod for me, and thankfully pulled-to the door to the street.

" 'E's not a bad sort, is Joe." Maggie swooped down upon the package and shoved it under a truckle bed that sagged in one corner, its covers askew. "Woman's gotta live, don't she, and all these mouths to feed?"

"Indeed," I said. "A length of silk should go far in filling your children's stomachs."

"S'not like I'm a-goin' to *wear* it." She sat back on her heels, face black with mistrust.

"You would sell it, then?" I enquired, as suddenly enlightened.

"Joo interested?"

Here was an opening to goodwill, indeed. I surveyed the widow's countenance and considered what I could afford. "I should like to see your silk, Mrs. Tibbit."

The package was swiftly drawn forth, somewhat dusty from its brief repose beneath the bed, and the fastenings undone for my benefit. Maggie pulled out a quantity of glorious stuff, of a peach-coloured hue much like Eliza's silk, and but wanting a feathered turban to complete the effect. I felt my heart lurch—what a thing it should be, to own such a gown!

"And the usual price of Mr. Smollet's goods . . . ?" I enquired.

Maggie smiled, and then, as if recollecting her poor teeth, raised a hand to her lips. "That's rare stuff, that is."

"I could find as good in the shops of Pound Street."

"Not for what I'll charge ye."

"Which would be?" I looked at her over the fabric's edge.

"Five guineas."

I thrust the stuff in her arms and picked up my reticule. "Ridiculous. I am no fool, Mrs. Tibbit, and should never pay for the privilege of acting like one."

"Three, then, and that's my final offer," Maggie said without a second thought.

I measured out the silk according to the span of my arms, and found it to be roughly fifteen yards; enough for a gown with a ravishing train, the very essence of elegant attire. With Eliza's suggestions as to cut and fashion, it should all but make my winter balls—and I knew as well as Maggie that three guineas was but a fraction of what I should pay at Mr. Milsop's, for silk more legitimately won. If my conscience was besieged at this notion, I comforted myself with another thought—three guineas should go far in feeding the little Tibbits, if the sum survived their mother's fondness for the bottle.

"Done at three guineas," I said, arranging the silk in careful folds, "if you will tell me how you came by this stuff."

Her eyes shifted, and she snatched back the fabric. " 'ad it off'uv Joe, same's you saw yersel."

"And he had it for services rendered, I imagine, to the Reverend himself."

The effect of my words was extraordinary, and beyond my expectations. Maggie Tibbit all but collapsed upon the bed, my precious peach stuff crushed in her hands, and began to shake in an alarming fashion.

"Mrs. Tibbit!" I cried. "I fear you are unwell!"

She gestured desperately beyond me, at a loss for words.

I whirled about, and espied the brandy bottle still open upon the settle, and fetched it to her side. Several swigs having been consumed by the woman, she recovered her senses enough to fix upon me baleful eyes, and say with authority, "We never mentions that Reverend's name in this 'ouse."

"But he is known to you?" I crouched down at her feet, the better to fix her gaze.

"Hah!" she ejaculated. "As if the Reverend'd be known to the likes o' Maggie Tibbit. *No one* knows 'oo 'e is, much less *me*. But my Bill knew," she added darkly. "My pore Bill saw 'is face, I reckon, just afore 'e died."

"You believe the Reverend responsible for your husband's hanging?"

She nodded and affected a melancholy air.

I hesitated—aware, at the moment, of the depth of my ignorance. "Mrs. Tibbit—forgive me—but was an inquest into your husband's death recently held by the coroner Mr. Carpenter?"

Her head shot up, and her eyes glittered with malice. "Death by misadventure," she pronounced. "As if I don't know what '*at* means. It means they ain't askin', and nobody's steppin' up to tell. There's no justice for the likes o' us, miss. *That's* for yer coroner!" And she spat into a corner of the room.

"But how is it you believe your husband a victim of the Reverend?" I probed, after an instant's painful pause.

"I *knows* as he was. All on account o' that ship what went aground last spring, and Bill never the same since."

"Aground?" At this, I did not need to affect surprise. "One of the Reverend's vessels?"

The widow nodded. "The *Royal Belle* it was. Bill worked as spotter, see, at the Lookout over to Puncknowle way.[2] He was s'posed to work the signals that night, and a powerful foggy one it was. But somethin' musta went wrong, acos he never left the Three Cups. The *Belle* was grounded and lost with all hands aboard. Some local boys was among the crew, and some Frenchies, too, from the clothes they was wearing when they washed up on Chesnil beach. The Reverend never forgive my Bill for tarrying over 'is tankard, and he 'ad 'is blood fer it."

With a cursory look for dirt and a stifled sigh at the inevitability of stains, I drew forward the room's one good chair and settled myself near the widow. "What happened the night of the ship's grounding, Mrs. Tibbit?"

She shrugged, and ran a broad hand through her unbound hair, the impudent belligerence overlaid, of a sudden, with profound weariness. I knew then that for all her swagger, Maggie Tibbit had not done with mourning her murdered husband. I silently pressed her hand. "Bill 'ud never speak of it," she said. "No matter how much I asked. Swore he'd made a mistake, is all, same's ever'body else, and cryin' wouldn't make it undone."

"But did he *know* he was to work the smugglers' signals that night at Puncknowle? And was his staying at the Three Cups a deliberate omission, or merely an oversight?"

[2] Maggie Tibbit is presumably referring to the two-story structure set upon a knoll between West Bexington and Puncknowle. It was built as a signal tower for the Sea Fencibles, the local militia arrayed against a seaborne invasion by Napoleon; it commanded a view beyond Portland and Weymouth to the east, and over Bridport to Lyme Regis and Lyme Bay some seven miles distant. Signal fires would have been lit to warn of enemy ships approaching the coast, which ran straight and clear at this point, making for easy landing. —*Editor's note.*

"Folks 'round 'ere would 'ave it he did it for blunt,"
Maggie said.

"For—blunt?"

"Coin. Money. That he was paid to ground the *Belle*,"
the woman explained patiently. "But my Bill'd never do
that. He'd friends on that cutter, and they never come
back. Tell *that* to Nancy Harding."

"I'm sorry, Mrs. Tibbit, I don't—"

"Nancy's the bitch as nailed the pullet to my door.
Wouldn't give 'er the pleasure o' takin' it off, I wouldn't.
It can stay there, and look as foolish as Nancy 'ersel, by my
mind."

I sat back, thoroughly at sea. "And why should the
woman do such a thing?"

" 'Er son Bob was on the boat. Just fifteen, 'e was. I'm
not sayin' as she ain't got a right to mourn, same as all o'
them—but a *chicken*?"

"The grounding occurred last spring, you said, and yet
your husband's hanging came only two weeks ago. How
do you account for it?"

She shrugged, and pulled herself to her feet, the soiled
dressing gown sagging about her hips. "Screwin' up their
courage, more'n likely. Nancy Harding was, for certain
sure—it took 'er long enough to show my Bill for a coward. She only stuck that chicken there the night afore he
got took."

"As a sort of—signal?" I enquired, with sudden inspira-
tion.

"Dunno."

I paused for reflection, and allowed the sense of this to
sink in. "You speak of your husband's being taken. Did
his murderers come to this very door?"

She shook her head and her eyes filled with tears. " 'E
was at the Three Cups, same as always, 'cept that night 'e
din' come 'ome. I reckon they bamboozled 'im on the

street, when 'e 'adn't much fight in 'im, and strung 'im up when no one was to see."

Remembering the image of that fateful dawn—the surf crashing whitely over the gibbet and its terrible burden— I shivered involuntarily. How horrible to meet one's end at the hands of neighbours, and to know that pleas for help will avail one nothing, when the weight of community opinion has condemned one already to death! I understood, now, the positioning of the gibbet—Bill Tibbit had been executed in the very midst of the furious waters, in a manner to recall the deaths his carelessness had caused.

"Who is likely to have served your husband so rough a justice, Mrs. Tibbit?"

She eyed me warily over the lip of her brandy bottle, which must be fast approaching its dregs. "Why d'you want to know all this? What's my Bill to you?"

I hesitated, as if in consideration of her trustworthiness, then leaned a little closer. "You may have heard of Captain Percival Fielding," I began.

Her eyes lit up, and she licked her lips with avidity. " 'Im what got popped out on the Charmouth road."

"Exactly so."

"And?" She was all enthusiasm for the intelligence.

"I was on terms of some intimacy with the Captain." I cast my eyes downwards, to suggest a nearer interest than I felt. The attitude was not lost upon my interlocutor.

"Sweet on 'im, eh? And lookin' fer answers?" Maggie slapped her thighs with relish. "Sad to say, miss, but you won't find 'em near my Bill."

"Your husband never knew Captain Fielding?"

"Not as I could say."

I allowed my disappointment to be obvious. "I had thought it possible your husband performed a job of work for the Captain. . . ."

"And if 'e did?" Maggie replied, crossing her arms over her ample chest. "There's still no call to kill 'im."

"But *did* your husband do some work for Captain Fielding—in his garden perhaps?"

She shrugged, with infinite disregard. "Makes no odds. My Bill drank what little 'is labour fetched, and me never the wiser."

I cast about for another approach. "Did your husband claim any of the local men as particular friends, Mrs. Tibbit?"

"A few," she replied. "Leastways, until the *Royal Belle* went down."

"And might he have worked in tandem with them?"

"In what?"

"Might they have gone out to work together?"

Her expression of bewildered irritation cleared of a sudden. "Matt Hurley," she declared.

"The man who"—I hesitated, then found more acceptable words—"the man whom Mr. Smollet seemed to find so objectionable?"

"The very one," she replied, with a gleam of satisfaction in her eye. " 'E's a rare one, is Matty. Likes to set 'imsel up as foreman o' the crews, what stands out on Broad o' Mondays, waitin' on people's fancy."

This took a moment to decipher. "The local men wait in gangs on Broad Street of a Monday, in the hope that someone will purchase their labour?"

"That they do. Matty styles 'imsel a gang 'ead, 'e does."

I had seen such groups of men loitering about the street corners, and thought them merely idle rogues, never realising there was a purpose to their inactivity.

At this interesting juncture, a knock unfortunately came upon the door, and the dim shape of a head appeared through the window's stained oilcloth. Joe Smollet, I supposed; and Maggie should be little likely to turn him away again. Very well—I should take my leave. But a few questions yet remained to me.

"Where might I find Matthew Hurley?" I enquired.

"The Three Cups," the widow said, with a dubious look; "not that a lady like yoursel 'ud go to the pub o' nights." She crossed to the window and squinted through its murkiness, waggling her fingers. "I'm much obliged to yer fer the kids' things, miss, but I've bizness that wants attendin'."

"I understand." I rose and brushed absent-mindedly at my skirts. "Have you any idea, Mrs. Tibbit, why a white flower should be left near your husband's gibbet?"

"A white flower," she said, staring. "What white flower?"

"A lily, I believe. You knew nothing of it?"

"Not a whisper. Coo, that's odd, that is. What'd they go puttin' a flower by Bill fer?"

"I cannot imagine," I replied, "though the act itself bears a decidedly melancholy aspect."

Maggie reached for the door latch and pulled it meaningfully—to suggest, I suppose, that the interview was at a close. I stepped over little Jack, who was rolling about in the dirt with a tomcat of ferocious appearance, and opened my purse.

"The price of your silk, Mrs. Tibbit," I said.

She turned over the peach-coloured stuff with an expression of regret, but deemed my three guineas to afford a deeper satisfaction; and so we parted, equally pleased with our bargaining. I had learned from her a little to my purpose, but hardly enough; it remained to locate the resourceful Mr. Matt Hurley, an errand for another day.

BUT THE MOST CURIOUS EVENT OF THIS MORNING'S ACTIVITY occurred as I was wending my way out of the River Buddle district. For it was then I observed the approach of a carriage, that bore a familiar coat of arms upon the door, and within its depths, a lady much veiled, as I observed upon her leaning out the window in converse with her tyger. Mrs. Barnewall, if I was not utterly mistaken, and her carriage pulled up before Maggie Tibbit's very door.

Chapter 16

The Night in Question

Friday, 21 September 1804

~

"MY DEAR," MY MOTHER SAID INTO MY EAR, AS WE SAT TOGETHER amidst the better part of Lyme's residents in the main room of the Golden Lion, awaiting the commencement of the inquest into Percival Fielding's death, "Miss Crawford looks very fine indeed, in her black silk and illusion veil. I do not think she could have had *either* of Mr. Milsop—though he styles himself so very high, there is *that* about his shop that defies real elegance. I wish our Cassandra were here to see it. Miss Crawford's veil, I mean. But then, *she* is free to wander about the shops of London—Cassandra, I would speak of now—Dr. Farquhar having pronounced her quite recovered; and I *do* wish she might write to us of sleeves, and whether they are to be long or short this season; but she *will* not, being much preoccupied with Eliza's circulating-library. I do not understand her indifference upon such a point—"

"Mother," I interceded, as the good lady paused to draw breath, "I wonder if Miss Crawford is not to be called up by the coroner? For the care her attire has demanded, would suggest some benefit in display."

"Indeed," my mother replied, laying a hand over my own in agitation. "And yet, *we* were as well acquainted with Captain Fielding—though *Miss Crawford* would have it he was to beg for Miss Armstrong's hand, and not yours, as I had thought. Why are not *we* to be called?"

"I imagine we can have nothing of particular intelligence to offer the coroner," I replied firmly, and patted my mother's cold fingers. My father harrumphed, censorious of our chatter, and at that very moment Mr. Carpenter appeared—coroner and surgeon of Lyme, and the superior of our friend Mr. Dagliesh—and strode importantly down the aisle. All rose to offer him the respect that was his due.

Joshua Carpenter was a portly gentleman of jovial countenance and a ponderous wig, of somewhat outdated fashion. He was dressed in rusty black—rusty, from its apparent long use and sad neglect—his collar was wilted, his shirt-sleeves frayed, and his coat collar bore the signs of a nuncheon recently consumed. When he turned and surveyed the uplifted faces of the crowd, however, I detected a gleam of amused intelligence in his eyes, and a contemptuous curl of the lip, as though he understood well that *gossip*, rather than justice, was the hope of nearly everyone assembled. He glanced at the twelve men of the jury—all strangers to my eyes, and drawn, it seemed, from local folk—who sat composed and cowed upon two of the inn's long benches, and nodded to the one appointed foreman.

How similar was this scene to the one I witnessed two winters past, at an inn in Hertfordshire, when another man had died all untimely! Painful memories could not but intrude as I contemplated my surroundings. And yet—how *different*, in the figure of Mr. Carpenter, and the mood of the crowd, and the degree of interest I felt in the outcome. For though my anxiety was roused on Geoffrey Sidmouth's behalf, and my heart aflutter at the prospect of seeing once more his harsh and brooding features, I knew better this time what I should expect. I had been an innocent, and had hoped for justice, when my dear friend Isobel, Countess of Scargrave, was accused of murdering her husband; today I was unlikely to be so sanguine. Appearances should tell against the master of High Down, and I little doubted that, the inquest speedily concluded, he should be held until the next session of the local Assizes,[1] and then sent to London to be tried for the murder of Captain Percival Fielding.

Unless, of course, I discovered something to his benefit betweentimes.

Mr. Carpenter called for order, and at that moment there was a rustle of consciousness and low-muttered talk from the rear of the room; turning, I perceived Mr. Dobbin, the Lyme justice, and his burly fellows, as they led Geoffrey Sidmouth into the assembly. Behind them came Seraphine, her head high above her long red cloak, and the boy Toby on his crutches; and the mutters swelled into a roar. What pity I felt for the mademoiselle, at that moment! The mixture of pride and despair that overlaid her countenance! A confusion of emotions could not but grip her, at such a time.

"This inquest is now convened," Mr. Carpenter declared, in a voice plummy and deep, as the Grange folk found their seats; and he called first a young fellow of rough appearance, who stated his name as Ted Nesbitt, of Smallwood Farm, not far off the Charmouth road. It was this Nesbitt—a lad of perhaps fifteen—who had discov-

[1] The Assizes are preliminary sessions held locally throughout the United Kingdom, in which a suspect is charged, indicted, and remanded for trial. In Austen's time they were held quarterly. —Editor's note.

ered Captain Fielding's body; and with many awkward pauses, and scratchings of his head, young Ted related for the assembly's edification how he had all but stumbled upon it.

"Lying at the edge of the road, the dead gentleman was, and near hid by the tall grass, that part of the field not having been mown yet in the hay-making. I'd have passed him entire if the horse hadn't started, and even then I took him for a lot of cast-off clothing."

"And what did you then, Mr. Nesbitt?" the coroner enquired.

"Made sure he was dead, I did—*which* he were—and took off for Darby as though the Devil himsel' were arter me."

"Was the gentleman known to you?"

"He were Captain Fielding," the lad said stoutly. "I'd seen him about, us being neighbours of a sort; but my folks don't mix wit' the quality, sir, and I can't say as we ever exchanged more nor a hullo."

Mr. Crawford next appeared. His bald pate shone with anxiety, his aspect was set and disturbed. He said little more than was necessary for the grim intelligence he must impart—namely, that he had attended Nesbitt to the body, and ascertained to his shock that the dead man was Percival Fielding, and that he had certainly been murdered; and that done, he had fetched Mr. Carpenter and his assistant, William Dagliesh, and the Lyme justice, Mr. Elliot Dobbin.

"Did you note anything particular about the corpse or the scene that might assist this enquiry, Mr. Crawford?" the coroner asked, with an air of complaisance.

There was an instant's painful silence; and I observed Mr. Crawford's eyes drift towards Geoffrey Sidmouth's position in the rear of the room. "I did, sir," he replied, and his jaw set firmly on the words. "There was a chaos of hoofprints in the mud about the corpse."

"From this, we are to assume that the deceased was mounted at the time of his death, or very nearly before."

Mr. Crawford bowed, and hesitated, and then continued with reluctance, "That is not all we are to assume, Mr. Carpenter."

"I see," the coroner replied slowly, his voice like cut velvet. "Then perhaps you may enlighten us, Mr. Crawford. Why should these hoofprints concern us?"

"They were of a singular kind. They bore the initials *GS* clearly stamped within them."

"*GS?*" The slightest of frowns beetled the gentleman's brow. "And can you conjecture, Mr. Crawford, what these letters might signify?"

Poor Crawford appeared to debate the point within himself. "I took them to mean that the horse belonged to a gentleman of my acquaintance." "Presumably a gentleman whose initials are GS?" Mr. Carpenter suggested. "Yes." There was a fractional pause as the coroner adjusted his frayed lace cuffs. "I must ask you, Mr. Crawford, which gentleman among your acquaintance may lay claim to those letters of the alphabet?" "Geoffrey Sidmouth," Crawford replied, his voice barely audible.

"And why should this be so?" The coroner glanced about the room as though seeking some support. "Why should not these hoofprints and their damning marks belong to some other person?"

"Because I knew Mr. Sidmouth to make a practise of having his blacksmith etch those initials on his mounts' shoes."

"I see," Mr. Carpenter said, and sat back in his chair. That he had been apprised of this intelligence well before the proceedings, by the efficient Mr. Dobbin, I little doubted; and that his behaviour on the occasion was intended for effect, I perfectly understood. The fellow had surely missed his calling—he should better have trod the boards of Drury Lane, in the guise of Falstaff. I expected him to call Sidmouth without delay, and end the sad business; but Mr. Carpenter was nothing if not thorough. The coroner had set aside the afternoon for the canvassing of Percival Fielding's death; and he was not about to quit his glorious stage so well before dinner. He now bade Mr. Crawford stand down, and called Mr. William Dagliesh in his stead.

Poor Dagliesh took his place at his employer the coroner's right hand, and was sworn, and looked everywhere but in the eyes of his friend at the back of the room; but his moment of martyrdom was brief. The surgeon's assistant stated what Mr. Carpenter already knew—that the Captain had been dead some hours by the time they were called to examine the body; that Fielding had lost a quantity of blood, from the wound in his heart; and that he had witnessed Mr. Carpenter extract a ball from the wound itself, which he should judge to be a simple lead one such as was commonly used in a gentleman's pistol.

"And could you state the approximate hour of the Captain's death?"

"From the condition of the body, I believe we agreed that he had died sometime during the evening before."

"But you cannot state when?"

"I cannot."

"Have you anything further?"

Mr. Dagliesh hesitated, and looked finally to Sidmouth; and as if emboldened by the sight of his friend, assumed a sterner countenance. "I should simply like to add, sir, that I may vouch for the behaviour of Mr. Geoffrey Sidmouth," he said, in a voice so strengthened by his purpose it seemed to fill the room. "I believe him incapable of the despicable actions that the presence of his horse's hoofprints might suggest; and moreover, I will freely admit that I was in his company the entirety of the night in question, and parted with him only at dawn, when Captain Fielding's death had already been effected many hours."

Mr. Carpenter studied his assistant's face when the speech was done, his own expression unfathomable. "You are on intimate terms with Mr. Sidmouth, Mr. Dagliesh?" he enquired.

"I am."

"The safeguarding of his person, then, is a near concern of yours?"

"Would I call myself friend, were it otherwise?"

"And have you another witness who might vouch for the gentleman's whereabouts?"

"Is not my word enough?" Mr. Dagliesh cried, his face reddening with indignation. I closed my eyes upon the sight, remembering my own poor hopes of sincerity and goodness two winters past, when Isobel's life hung in the balance.

The coroner smiled. "For myself, perhaps," he said, "but I fear the jury might demand a greater proof. Could you delineate for us all your movements on the night in question?"

Mr. Dagliesh blushed, if possible more hotly, and his eyes shifted again to his friend. I turned, and surveyed Mr. Sidmouth's countenance. I read there what I can only take to have been a warning.

"Honour forbids it," the surgeon's assistant finally replied, "but I may assure you, sir, that our activities were such as should not disgrace a gentleman."

A low ripple of laughter greeted this unfortunate attempt, and I saw a knowing glance pass between two members of the jury. I adjudged Mr. Dagliesh's effort to have hurt, rather than aided, his friend. His words should be dismissed, as the desperate fabrication of a moment, and Mr. Sidmouth's fate be sealed. But from the look that had passed between the two, I should rather say that Dagliesh was *forbidden* to speak to his friend's defence, than that he lacked the means.

Mr. Carpenter released his unfortunate junior, and Dagliesh fled with relief and a dignity somewhat impaired. As he hastened down the aisle, he cast upon me a look so beseeching as to be eloquent in its silence. I felt he begged, then, for the indulgence of being believed, however little he might reveal as proof of his assertions; and for my part, I certainly *wished* to grant his request. But the coroner had called Mr. Dobbin; and all my attention was claimed by the justice.

Mr. Dobbin related in a concise and easy fashion, as though in converse of the weather, the disposition of Captain Fielding's body upon the Charmouth road, and the probable flight of his horse; the single shot to the Captain's heart, and the presence of the aforementioned hoofprints. It was for Mr. Dobbin to add, however, that the Captain's purse had been seized, and a white lily laid in the grass near his corpse—and undoubtedly not by chance.

At this, the coroner surveyed Mr. Dobbin shrewdly.

"Just such a flower was recently found near *another* body, was it not?"

"It was, sir—by the late William Tibbit, who was hanged on the Cobb last Thursday fortnight."

"And do you think the two deaths are linked?"

"I cannot yet say, sir."

"I see." There was a pause, and a significant glance for the jury, most of whose members attempted to look sensible of the coroner's meaning, and failed.

"You observed, Mr. Dobbin, the hoofprints by the body."

"I did, sir."

"And did they speak with as much meaning to *you*, as to Mr.—er—Crawford?"

"Mr. Crawford's being at the scene empowered that gentleman to share his convictions and fears."

"Yes, yes. And what did you then?"

"Not wishing to appear over-hasty in a matter of such gravity," Mr. Dobbin began smoothly, "I enquired first of the local blacksmiths, of which there are three; and discovered that none of them had forged a like shoe for anyone. —Excepting, that is, Mr. Geoffrey Sidmouth."

Mr. Carpenter reached a hand to his fleshy jowl, and caressed it reflectively. "And then?"

"I determined that Sidmouth's horse, at least, must have been at the scene, and deemed it appropriate to enquire of his stable lad whether any mounts had been absent on the evening in question. He assured me, with some defiance"—at this, I glanced at poor Toby, and saw him starting from his chair, and wincing in pain at his ankle's unequal attempt to bear his weight—"that the horses were well-guarded within the stables the entirety of that night." Mr. Dobbin paused, the better to unleash his effect. "All, that is, except Mr. Sidmouth's particular mount—a black stallion by the name of Satan. It seems Mr. Sidmouth departed High Down Grange on horseback just after supper—around eight o'clock—and returned only with the dawn. The stable boy would not, or could not, say where his master had been."

The sensation aroused at this revelation was decidedly excessive; though I should have thought the crowd to be blessed with such particulars, by way of the intimacy of milliner's stall and publican's room, well before the inquest. I looked for Sidmouth, and found him unbowed in the midst of his captors; but Seraphine, in her chair beyond Mr. Dobbin's men, appeared very unwell indeed. Her golden radiance was dimmed, her gaze unfocussed—the angel's wings as clipped as a captive swan's.

When the stir of interest had died away, the coroner continued. "And as a result of this information, Mr. Dobbin," he said, "you arrested Mr. Geoffrey Sidmouth, pending the outcome of this jury's deliberation?"

"I did."

"You may stand down."

"I would beg to suggest, sir," the justice interposed, "that Miss Augusta Crawford be requested to give evidence. She has information that has only lately come to my attention."

Mr. Carpenter raised an eyebrow in Dobbin's direction. "Indeed? Then she shall be called. Miss Augusta Crawford!"

It was as I had suspected; Miss Crawford had found a place for her tongue in the midst of the proceedings, and appeared well-satisfied with the fruits of her ingenuity, as she advanced upon the jury in a rustle of black silk. Her high cheekbones were sharp, her mouth severe—but her eyes, I thought, held a sparkle of malice as she stood in her place beside the coroner, and they were fixed upon Mademoiselle LeFevre.

"You are Miss Augusta Crawford, sister to Mr. Cholmondeley Crawford, of Darby?" the coroner began.

"I am."

"And what have you to relate that should be of service in these proceedings?"

"It is in my power to offer an account of the events that occurred at Darby the evening *before* the evening when Mr. Sidmouth murdered Captain Fielding," Miss Crawford replied, with some importance of manner.

"Madam!" Mr. Carpenter ejaculated. "Mr. Sidmouth's guilt in this matter has not yet been determined." He turned to the foreman. "Pray disregard the lady's words. Madam?"

"Mr. Crawford and I had several guests to dinner that evening—"

"—being Saturday last?"

"—being Saturday last; and among them were Captain

Fielding, Mr. Sidmouth, and his cousin, Mademoiselle Le-Fevre." At the mention of Seraphine's name, Miss Crawford could not contain an expression of lively scorn, that should certainly have discredited her intelligence, were *I* the coroner; but Mr. Carpenter's countenance remained impassive.

"The deceased and Mr. Sidmouth were on such terms as might encourage social intercourse?" he enquired.

"So my brother and I assumed," Miss Crawford replied, "from understanding that the Captain had preserved the mademoiselle from an adventure of some danger to her person, and was thus due, one would think, the deepest gratitude from all who held her welfare among their dearest concerns; but imagine our amazement, when Mr. Sidmouth betrayed himself as anything but pleased to see the Captain, and went so far as to question my brother's motives in having invited them both!"

"Miss Crawford," the coroner probed with the faintest suggest of irritation, "what is it you would wish this panel to understand?"

The lady stared at him open-mouthed, as though dumbfounded the fellow should be so obtuse. "Why, my good sir!" she rejoined. "Is not it apparent? Mr. Sidmouth bore the Captain a grudge! The mademoiselle treated her cousin with excessive coldness—the result, I imagine, of his having *caused* the very misadventure which required the gallant Captain's assistance, or so I understood, from something the Captain once dropped; and that she *preferred* Captain Fielding to Mr. Sidmouth, caused in him an enormity of rage, the result of which we saw first in our drawing-room, and not two days later, upon the Charmouth road!"

"And how would you explain the fact of the dead man's purse having been stolen? Surely you would not suggest that a crime of passion was also one of calculation?"

"I suppose Mr. Sidmouth to have been covering his tracks, by suggesting some common footpad had killed the Captain."

"But, my dear lady," Mr. Carpenter said smoothly, "it would appear that *covering his tracks*, is exactly what Mr. Sidmouth did *not* do." He paused to appreciate the full effect of his little joke, then took up his pen with an air of dismissal. "I fear this is all conjecture, Miss Crawford. It cannot put our enquiries any forwarder."

"You ridiculous man!" that lady cried. "Do not you see that Fielding was killed in a duel over the mademoiselle's honour?"

"You may stand down, madam," the coroner replied distantly. "Mr. Geoffrey Sidmouth!"

Miss Crawford spluttered, and looked all her outrage; but she was conducted from her place nonetheless, and suffered a momentary quailing of her courage, in being forced to pass quite close to the very Mr. Sidmouth she had just maligned, as he approached the coroner's table. He gave her neither a look nor a word, being intent, it appeared, on the maintenance of his gravity, amidst the tide of chatter his passage engendered. I could not detect in the noise, however, any evidence of ill-will towards the gentleman, despite his damning appearance of guilt; and it struck me forcibly that Geoffrey Sidmouth retained his reputation among the folk of Lyme, and a measure of gratitude, however heinous his offences. A curious community, indeed, that could treat a Maggie Tibbit with such contempt, and a Geoffrey Sidmouth with unrelenting tolerance.

Mr. Carpenter gave the gentleman at his right hand a cursory glance, neither severe nor benign. "You are Mr. Geoffrey Sidmouth, of High Down Grange, are you not?"

"I am."

"And what answer can you give, Mr. Sidmouth, to the

conjectures so lately put forward by Miss Augusta Crawford?"

"I would suggest that the lady pay greater heed to her own affairs, and less to those of her neighbours, or she shall utterly lack for dinner partners," he rejoined mildly, to some laughter; but from knowing Sidmouth a little, I judged him to be checking his temper only with the greatest difficulty. A muscle at his temple had commenced to pulse, in a distractingly involuntary fashion.

"And did you, sir, bear a *grudge* towards Captain Fielding?"

"I certainly bore him little affection."

"That is frankness indeed, from a man so imperilled by circumstance as yourself," Mr. Carpenter said, in some surprise.

"I make it a practise, sir, to offer honesty when such is possible."

"When it is *possible*—but not, you would have us understand, on every occasion?"

"Can any man assert such consistency?"

"It is a common-enough profession."

"But to *profess* honesty, and to practise it without fail, are entirely different talents. Rare is the gentleman who allies them both."

My father leaned towards me and winked. "One for my philosopher," he observed softly.

"So we may take it as settled that you harboured towards the Captain a healthy dislike. On what was it predicated?"

"Upon matters of a personal nature."

"Having to do with Mademoiselle—"

"—LeFevre."

"LeFevre. And would you care to elucidate, Mr. Sidmouth?"

"As I have stated, these are personal matters. It should

be a violation of every conception of honour, did I canvass such things before the common crowd."

"I see." From his expression, Mr. Carpenter clearly did *not* see. "And will you state your movements during the course of Sunday evening last?"

"I was away from home."

"This panel is aware of that. And were you riding your black stallion"—at this, the coroner peered narrowly at his papers—"the unfortunately-named Satan?"

"I was." From Mr. Sidmouth's expression, it pained him to let slip even so small a sentence.

"In the company of the surgeon's assistant, Mr. William Dagliesh?"

"Yes."

"Mr. Sidmouth," the coroner ejaculated, in evident exasperation, "if we are to have any hope of placing your guilt in doubt, you must give us some means of proving your innocence! Will you not tell us your movements on the night in question?"

There was an instant's silence, and Sidmouth's eyes met mine with a sudden flaring of intensity, so that I felt my heart lurch; then his gaze moved beyond me, to the back of the room. I knew whose face he sought; and turned, despite myself, to look for it.

Seraphine had risen, as slow as a spectre rising from the grave. "Tell them, Geoffrey," she said—though her voice was so caught in her throat, the sense of it may not have reached him. "Tell them," she cried, in a firmer accent, and clutched at a chair for support.

"You know that I cannot," he rejoined. His voice was infinitely gentle—the very quiet of despair, I thought. "Sit down, my dear, before you fall."

"Is there something you wish to say to this panel, madam?" the coroner asked, rising to gaze at the mademoiselle. She nodded briefly, unable to look at her cousin.

"Say nothing, Seraphine!" Sidmouth interposed with sudden fierceness. "There can be no cause for such sacrifice. I will not allow it! Say nothing—I beg of you—that you will not recall years hence, with vast regret!"

"Oh, Geoffrey—" she said, in a breaking wail, and swayed as I watched. In an instant, Sidmouth had sprung from his place, and coursed down the aisle to her aid; but Dobbin's men were before him, and barred his path, in evident alarm that he meant to flee. He was seized, and maddened by the seizure, as Seraphine crumpled to the ground in a faint; and the room was in an uproar in an instant. Between Sidmouth's efforts to fight loose of his captors, and the shouts of those around him, even Mr. Carpenter's gavel rang out unheeded in the tumult.

At last the gentleman was subdued, and the lady borne from the room into the street, the better to revive her; and the jury dismissed, for the consideration of the case. In but a few minutes they had returned, with hanging heads, and avowed their belief that Captain Fielding had died at Geoffrey Sidmouth's hands. And so the master of High Down was taken away, half-mad with anxiety for his cousin's state, and thrown once more into the foetidness of Lyme's small gaol.

Miss Crawford alone could look triumphant, as the assembled crowd filed away. She was afforded no congratulations; and indeed, most of Lyme's worthies avoided her like a manifestation of the plague; but she had seen enough to confirm her wildest conjectures. From Seraphine's behaviour, could anyone doubt that *she* was the cause of all the Captain's grief? Or that her cousin bore her such love, as would counsel killing to preserve it?

Chapter 17

Playing at Cat's-Paw

21 September 1804, cont.

~

SUCH EVIDENCE OF SIDMOUTH'S GUILT COULD NOT BUT BE
convincing. I should have felt the merit of its claims more
forcibly, however, had I not perceived that *some other* consideration had silenced his friends and himself, and that
the better part of Sidmouth's struggle throughout the
proceedings, had been to *prevent* a matter coming to light,
that should assuredly have cleared him of the murder, but
at a personal cost he was mysteriously unwilling to endure. Proof of innocence through revelation, was an avenue closed to us; proof of *another's* guilt must, therefore,
be the avenue pursued. I did not stop to ask why I felt
myself to be the chosen pursuer; it was a matter that did
not admit of choice. Someone had murdered Percival
Fielding, for reasons that remained obscure to me; and
someone wished the world to believe Sidmouth had done
it in his stead. In such a case, could *any* stand by, and
observe injustice triumph? *Jane* assuredly would not. But
what, in fact, was to be done? A bewildering array of paths

branched from the ground at my feet, like the turnings of a wilderness maze; how to embark upon the proper way?

"Well," my father declared, as he stared about the rapidly emptying room; "well, indeed. It might be advisable—do not you agree, my dear Jane—to offer the mademoiselle what assistance we may, for she is decidedly bereft of friends at the moment, and some Christian solicitude should be as balm to her distress."

"You are all goodness, Father," I said, somewhat absentmindedly; for my thoughts were employed in the consideration of other matters, against which Mademoiselle LeFevre's indisposition must be weighed as slight. It was imperative *not* to set a foot wrong at so critical a juncture, when every hour might have bearing on Sidmouth's fate. I bent my thoughts accordingly to a review of the facts, and set aside for the moment all extraneous conjecture.

Geoffrey Sidmouth was assuredly abroad on the night in question, and that he rode his stallion Satan, we knew from the statements of both the surgeon's assistant Dagliesh and Toby the stable boy. The marks of hoofprints bearing his initials were clearly stamped in the mud by Fielding's body. Therefore, if it were conceivable that Sidmouth was *not* Fielding's murderer, then I must find that *another* had stolen the horse on the night in question, while Sidmouth was otherwise engaged; or that someone else from the Grange had ridden forth that night, despite the stable boy's words to the contrary; or that a different animal altogether had been similarly shod, and ridden to its fatal errand. Mr. Dobbin would have it that the blacksmiths in town were above reproach, and that their negatives of having forged such shoes for any but Sidmouth might be taken as truth; but I was not so sanguine. Regardless of the motivations in the case—the mysterious business between the Captain and Seraphine, the presence of white flowers by the corpses, and the matter of the Reverend's identity—the horseshoes were the crux of the affair.

"Will you accompany us, Jane?"

I looked up to find my father already on his feet, my mother by his side, and both serene in the certainty of doing good. Their purposeful faces reminded me that Seraphine had very nearly revealed the nature of her trouble, before fainting away, and that all might be speedily concluded, were she *now* persuaded to speak. I rose from my seat without a word, and followed hastily in my father's train.

POOR SERAPHINE LAY PROSTRATE IN A CHAMBER ON THE LION'S FIRST floor, her wild mane of hair flung out on the straw mattress, a compress to her head. One of the inn's maids-of-all-work leaned mistrustfully in the doorway, torn between the claims of gossip-mongering and those of legitimate work; but the subject of her baleful study might almost have been turned to stone, so oblivious was Mademoiselle LeFevre of anyone's presence. She stared fixedly at the ceiling above her head, her lips moving continuously in what might pass for a prayer—but knowing a little of Seraphine, I rather imagined it to be a curse. Her hatred for Sidmouth's enemies, and her driving need for vengeance, should be fearful to behold; and I respected as well as feared her for it. I would not care to find myself on the wrong side of her will.

"Forgive me, mademoiselle," my father said gently, as he approached her doorway, "but we would wish to offer some consolation in your distress. Is there aught that any might do, to ease the discomposure of your mind? Some sustenance, perhaps, or a conveyance home to the Grange?"

"Mr. Austen!" my mother cried. "The poor thing cannot be left to her own devices in such a house! So lonely as it finds itself, in the very midst of the downs, and so melancholy in its current atmosphere! Such reflections, as must overwhelm her! I am sure, Mademoiselle, that you should better come to us. We might send our Jenny to the Grange for your things, and make you as comfortable as can be." My mother appeared well satisfied with her speech, until a moment's reflection brought the inevitable cloud.

"—Providing, that is," she added, "you do not mind making shift to room with Jane. For, you will understand, we have but two bedchambers. It would be some return," she concluded, brightening, "for your kindness in taking our family in, not a few weeks ago, after our own dreadful misfortunes—though I should not like to suggest that being overturned, and being charged with murder, are at all the same thing."

"You are very good, Madame Austen," Seraphine replied, her gaze steadfast upon the pale plaster above, "but it is not in my power to accept your invitation."

"Not in your *power*? But, my dear—how can it not?"

"Mother—" I said, in an attempt to intervene, "Mademoiselle LeFevre may wish for the reflection so necessary at such a time, and so dependent upon solitude."

"Indeed, *madame,* I have obligations that *must* be met—the needs of a farm being unrelenting—and though I value your kindness and consideration"—at this, the angel's eyes slid downwards to meet our own—"I must decline your entreaty to remove from the Grange."

"Well!" my mother declared, dumbfounded.

I recollected, then, the midnight landing from the smugglers' cutter, and the muffled burden borne up the cliffs at Seraphine's direction. Was an unknown fellow even now recovering from his wounds beneath the Grange's roof? Was this why Seraphine could not desert her post in Sidmouth's absence?

"As you wish, my dear," my father said, with a mild nod, "but may we offer you *some other* relief?"

"Pray for me, my good sir," Seraphine replied, "and for my cousin, Mr. Sidmouth. I fear that neither of us shall be long for this world."

I glanced at my father, and motioned the maid from the doorway. "Fetch a pot of tea for the mademoiselle, and be quick about it," I said. "How long should the lady have lain here, without a drop of restorative by her? I cannot believe you did not think of it before."

"There's no tea to be had," the maid replied, without shifting from her place. "Stores'uv been low these three days past, and what wit' the 'quest today, tea'uv been all drunk up."

"Then do you run to a shop and purchase some, you stupid girl," I said briskly, and handed her a few shillings. "Be off with you."

The slattern dropped a curtsey, and scurried away, her expression turned sour. I seized the opportunity of her absence to close the chamber door as firmly as I might. I did not choose for the entirety of Lyme to overlisten my conversation with the mademoiselle.

"Your cousin's circumstances are so very bad," I observed, as I turned back towards the bed with an effort at complaisance—for I was curious how my apparent indifference might provoke the lady, and what turn of conversation it should bring. "I wonder that he bothered to deny his guilt at all, considering how many are the proofs against him." Without waiting for a reply, I looked to my father. "When, sir, did you declare to be the next sitting of the Assizes?"

"I did *not*, that I can recall," the poor man replied, in some surprise, "but I believe I heard them to be held in Dorchester, in but ten days' time."

"So Sidmouth must endure another ten days in the Lyme gaol," I said thoughtfully. "Unless it be, of course, that *some other* comes forward, and admits a part in the Captain's murder. But who else can have had so much reason to kill the man? It does not seem very likely. We may take it, then, that Sidmouth has but a few weeks more to live; for the Assizes once concluded, his trial and execution shall be speedily achieved. You know that they are in the habit, at Newgate, of hanging the convicted only a day or two following their condemnation."

"Jane!" my mother cried. "Remember where you are, my girl! Have you lost all sense?"

But Seraphine's attention was gained—her expression more pained, and less remote—and so my cruel object was won. Her face, always pale, was almost translucent, and her eyes were gone glassy from shock.

"Get out," she said, her fingers clenched upon the bedsheet. "Get out, before I serve you with violence."

"As you did Captain Fielding?" I replied, drawing forward a chair, and seating myself companionably by her side, to my parents' consternation. "Was that the thought of the moment as well—or did you *plan* your assault upon his person?"

Seraphine's beautiful face was working, lost between outrage and confusion, and I hastened to profit from the moment.

"I have the idea of it well," I continued. "Yourself on a horse, perhaps in pursuit of a surgeon for one of the smuggling men kept hidden in your attic—you will recall that I could not help but hear their movements, the day I visited you at the Grange, the very day your cousin was seized by Mr. Dobbin." At this, a redoubled expression of shock seized her features, and something very like fear. (I saw no reason to mention the wounded man borne from the beach the night of Sidmouth's arrest, for *his* appearance was well after Fielding's death, and my knowledge of him *must* be explained. It was enough to alert her that I knew of the attic's use.)

"You are coursing down the Charmouth road, intent upon your purpose, but with one ear cocked for sounds in the underbrush—for you, a woman alone in a lonely place, should not like to encounter a brigand. It was in consideration of this that you carried with you one of the Grange's pistols, and kept it hidden beneath your cloak. Imagine it," I said dreamily, my eyes fixed upon Seraphine's countenance. "The moonlight—on the wane, but strong enough for a general glow, as the night before, when we all dined together at Darby—and the sudden appearance of Fielding's horse, from the entrance to his drive. It is a white horse, is it not? He rode it to call upon us at Wings cottage one day, and looked every inch *le Chevalier*." At this, Seraphine could not contain a shudder. "The horse and rider must have shone in the moonlight like an apparition.

"Did he hail you, eager for the conversation you had denied him the night before? Did you pull up in alarm? And at what moment did you fire the ball, so clear into his heart? When he leaned close to kiss you?"

"This is madness," Seraphine hissed. "You know it is madness."

"Do I?" I replied, with a look for my father. "I know only that Geoffrey Sidmouth would rather die than reveal what might clear his name—and I can think of no one for whom he might offer such a sacrifice but *you*, mademoiselle. Who better than yourself, to have taken a horse from the Grange's stables, and counted on the stable boy's silence—for that Toby adores you, is readily apparent. He might even now believe that you simply went for the surgeon, as you had intended—and as you undoubtedly did, once the Captain lay dead upon the road, and his horse fled for home. And so Toby said nothing to the justice, Mr. Dobbin, regarding your midnight errand—for the fact of the men's existence in your attic is something to keep hidden. Is it not?"

"I see that you know altogether too much about our affairs, Miss Austen," Seraphine rejoined. She had pushed herself upwards on the pillows, and looked at me directly, without animus or anger. "But I think you do not know quite enough. You make leaps before you know the distance to be covered, and so you fall into the abyss, yes?"

"Jane was ever a foolish, fanciful girl," my mother broke in. "And she is forever writing her fancies in a little book, and secreting it beneath a table linen whenever I enter the room. She is not to be thought of, I assure you, mademoiselle, so pay her no mind."

"But I fear that I must," Seraphine replied, with a sudden smile for my mother. "Your daughter's fancies might be taken for truth, did I fail to address them. And so, good sir, and gentle madame, would you be so good as to leave us alone for a time? It is best that we speak in private."

I cocked an ear towards the passageway, and gave a look to my father. "If I am not very much mistaken," I said, "that is the maid returned with the Green Leaf I bade her purchase. Do you go, my dear father, and take some tea with my mother. I shall not detain you above a quarter of an hour."

"Very well," my mother said grudgingly. "I cannot deny that I should relish some refreshment. But, Jane," she whispered low in my ear as she passed, "do you be careful. She *is* French, after all, and may very well be a murderess, and must possess arts you can know nothing of."

"I SHALL NOT KEEP YOU ABOVE YOUR QUARTER-HOUR," SERAPHINE began, without meeting my gaze. "I like your company too little to prolong its enjoyment."

"Our *tête-à-tête* might be concluded in a moment. A

word alone shall suffice to end it. Did you kill Captain Fielding, Seraphine?"

She permitted herself the briefest of laughter. It was a brittle, a heartbreaking sound. "And what, now, do I answer? If I say *no*, you will not believe me; and if I say *yes*, I will not believe myself. But I cannot avoid the one or the other; so *no* it must be, Miss Austen. I did not kill the Captain." I expected her to look at me then, to convey the sincerity of her words; but she did not. The very sight of my countenance must be odious to her. "I have been moved to wish for his death in the past; and I admit that his death, once achieved, caused me no pain. —Until, that is, my cousin was taken for it."

"And why should I believe what you say?" I enquired gently.

She shrugged. "Why should you believe otherwise?"

"Because I am committed to a pursuit of the truth," I replied, "and must consider every possible alternative. I will leave no stone undisturbed, until I have found the meaning behind Fielding's death, and may know whether your cousin is guilty or no. My heart whispers that he is not; he had not the look of wilful deceit, in all his assertions to the coroner—his was rather the appearance of intentional restraint."

"And so you would have me stand in his place." Her expression of amusement was scathing. "I would gladly take it for him, if he would let me. I would give my life for Geoffrey, Miss Austen!" she cried, with a passionate look. "And even you, who must bear him some love, could never say as much."

"I? *Love?* That is absurd," I replied, excessively stung. "I am merely an Englishwoman, who pays the notion of justice the most profound respect. I would not have your cousin falsely accused, and hang for a crime he did not commit."

"Noble words," Seraphine said, with something like a

sneer, "but false words nonetheless. You Englishwomen are all the same—cold, and unwilling to admit in the brain what the heart knows to be truth. Well, Miss Austen, I am *French*. And I say you are in love with my cousin. I am not afraid to look the truth full in the face. But I hate you for it."

"Hate me if you will, Mademoiselle. Believe what you will. It is no concern of mine," I rejoined, with an effort at calm. "I care only for the facts. Were you within the Grange's walls, the night of Fielding's murder?"

"Why should I answer you?"

"Because the more knowledge I have, the more likely that I will find the truth; and that can only help us all. Even did I prove your cousin guilty, we might draw comfort from the certainty. Would you rather continue in ignorance, and allow blind luck to determine the outcome?"

"No," she said reluctantly. "Though you will understand that the truth makes not a particle of difference to *me*. I care nothing for your justice. I care only for Geoffrey. But if the world believes him guilty, he shall certainly die. I am not so wilful I do not see the danger."

"Will you answer me, then?"

The need for hope and the desire to thwart me struggled for mastery in her face. "I was within the Grange all night. I did not stir beyond its doors, as the housekeeper, Mary, may vouch. You were correct, when you said we had guests abovestairs. She and I were much occupied in tending to them."

"A smuggler's crew?"

She shrugged. "Perhaps. You saw yourself what a friend my cousin has been to them."

"A friend? Not their leader?"

She did not answer.

"How many horses are stabled at the Grange, Mademoiselle?"

"Eight," she answered, without hesitation. "A matched pair for the curricle, and Satan, of course; four draft horses for the farm; and my own mount."

"And do all bear the same sort of shoes?"

"Stamped with Geoffrey's initials, you mean? Of course. Any of the horses might have left those prints."

"Any, that were the same size, and bore the same weight," I replied thoughtfully, "for the height of the horse and the heft of its mount, must severely affect the impressions."

"That is true!" she cried. "Geoffrey is a tall, well-built fellow, and Satan the same. Not every horse could make a print like that stallion's, when Geoffrey is upon him."

"Not, for example, yourself."

"No," she replied, with a bitter smile. "My Elf is a dainty lady. The draft horses, however, with a man astride, might manage it."

"There is also the curious affair, Mademoiselle, of the white lily."

"Yes," she murmured, her gaze shifting. "It is curious, indeed."

"Have you any notion what it might signify?"

"I fear that I do not. It is simply one more confusion amidst all that is bewildering."

"I wondered if it might not refer to the Captain's name."

"His *name*?"

"Yes. *Le Chevalier*. The title Fielding won from his service to you."

She winced. "I do not pretend to understand you, Miss Austen."

"A French flower for a French knight," I said patiently. "Is not the *fleur-de-lys* a white lily?" A symbol of a country's trampled greatness, like the absurd title Fielding bore. But what, then, was the significance of the flower left by the hanged Bill Tibbit?

"I wonder, Miss Austen, that you think you might affect the odds in this way," Seraphine said, breaking into my thoughts. "For what can a woman do, in a proceeding so determined by men? Had not Geoffrey better stand his chance, in a world in which he is at least an equal, unlike ourselves?" But for the steadiness of her sombre gaze, I might almost have believed her to be mocking me.

"I have never been willing to admit that inequality," I told her. "I spend the better part of my life endeavouring to redress it. But no matter. If *all* did but bend their efforts to determining your cousin's guilt or innocence, some resolution might speedily be found. I do but contribute my part, as I am sure Mr. Crawford will, and even Mr. Dagliesh."

"I have seen enough of their parts today."

"Their hands were tied."

"Then I do not want their hands further in the matter," she rejoined with animosity.

"Very well," I said. "But that cannot prevent you from sharing what you know with *me*. I cannot emphasise enough, Mademoiselle, that some part of the conviction of your cousin's guilt arises from the general perception that he hated Captain Fielding. What possible reason can he have had, for doing so?"

In her look of contemptuous dismissal, I fancied I read the same disdain her long-dead mother must have shown the guillotine. "I am not inclined to tell you, Miss Austen, and certainly not without Geoffrey's approval. It would seem too great a betrayal."

"And if your cousin dies as a result of your silence, you foolish girl?" I cried.

"He will not."

"But of course he will!"

She shrugged, all of France in the gesture, and stared into the middle distance. I saw that whatever influence I had held over her mind, had begun to slip away.

"You were ready enough to speak this afternoon, before the coroner," I threw out, in one final attempt. "You very nearly *then* revealed everything to do with your affairs, and gladly, in an effort to save your cousin's neck."

"But as you saw, Miss Austen," she replied with chilling calm, "my cousin did not wish it. It was *his* words that stopped my mouth before Mr. Carpenter, and yours shall certainly never loose it."

"Tho' you hazard the risk of sealing his guilt?"

"Even so. I must trust in Geoffrey's determination of what is right; and further importuning must be useless. I must beg you to cease. We have spoken long enough."

I saw from her looks that she was quite determined, and so I rose with a sigh, and turned for the door.

"You shall have but a few days for the consideration of your cousin's fate," I said, "when every hour is precious. If ever you determine to seek some assistance with your burden of confidence, know that I stand ready to help you bear it."

"And if you, Miss Austen, can ever admit what you feel for Geoffrey," she replied, "then we shall both know where we stand. But until then, I believe I shall keep my own counsel."

"And I shall pursue my own path," I said, with some asperity. "For the cause of justice will not suffer indifference, Mademoiselle."

"Justice, Miss Austen?" she said mockingly; and turned her head away. But her laughter followed me down the length of the passageway, and I confess it disturbed me more than I should like. There was too much of Eliza's knowing in it.

Chapter 18

The Sagacity of Fathers

21 September 1804, cont.

I FOUND MY FATHER ENSCONCED IN A DIM CORNER OF THE LION, HIS
book open upon his lap. My mother had long since departed the inn to pay a call upon an acquaintance—an
intelligence I received with some relief, as I had feared
her too-eager canvassing of Seraphine LeFevre's affairs in
so public a place. I could now avail myself of my father's
advice without concern for interruption; and so, as he
gathered up his things, I suggested we take a turn along
the Cobb. A dubious proposition for one of my father's
unsteady gait; but the day was fair enough, and the wind
not of a strength to overwhelm. He appeared surprised at
the suggestion, but ready enough to seize the opportunity
for exercise; and thus we set off, companionably arm-in-
arm.

"And so, Jane—what is *your* opinion of this sad business of Sidmouth's? I should enjoy a share in your
thoughts at the present; for I know that your acquaintances among the great have taught you much about scandal and violence," my father began. That he referred to

Isobel Payne, and her nephew Fitzroy (who were even now upon the point of uniting once more the titles of Countess and Earl of Scargrave), I immediately understood.

"I fear that my singular experience of two winters past prepared me for nothing in the present case—unless it be a greater tendency to question the truth of *everything* I hear, and to assume that the persons appointed to safeguard the law, are little likely to look beyond the most obvious construction of events," I replied. "But I would gladly share my intelligence, Father, if you will promise in return some measure of perspicacity."

And so, as we coursed the length of the breakwater's stone, I told my father all that I had learned of the infamous Reverend and of Mr. Sidmouth—who might, or might not, be one and the same man. I did not neglect to mention my dubious commission from Roy Cavendish, nor the curious movements in the Grange's garret, nor the appearance of a wounded man on the Charmouth shingle, nor my own midnight adventure in the cavernous tunnel, nor my interview with Maggie Tibbit. When I had done, the good man was lost in silent contemplation for some few minutes; and when he had sufficiently roused himself from thought to pay his companion more heed, he turned to me with an expression of wonder and—dare I say it—respect.

"My dear Jane," he said. "My *dear* Jane. I knew you for a lady of fine understanding and natural courage; but I dared not hope you possessed such faculties of determination and initiative. Forgive me if I must observe that they seem rather the part of one of your brothers, than a member of the weaker sex. I am not *entirely* assured that the affairs of either Mr. Sidmouth or the Captain required so *much* active benevolence on your behalf—and at such risk to your person—but I will not pain you with suppositions regarding your motives. Only tell me,

Jane"—and here he hesitated—"are you *quite convinced* of Sidmouth's innocence in the Captain's death? For I should not like you to suffer for what you will discover."

"I am convinced of nothing, dear sir," I replied, "and do not imagine me to harbour such tender emotions towards the gentleman in question, that my senses should be entirely routed if I find my labour has gone only to confirm his guilt. I may congratulate myself upon a clear-sighted view of his character. Sidmouth is forthright, but self-serving; loyal to those he values, but indifferent to the broader claims of society. His temper is mediated only with difficulty, though I could not charge him with *unwonted* meanness of spirit. And though I know no real evil of him, I cannot profess a complete confidence in his motives or aims. I hear such conflicting reports of him, as should bewilder a finer understanding than my own. There—have I satisfied your anxiety?"

"For the moment," my father replied. "But tell me, Jane—could you ever love a man you regarded with such ambivalence?"

"Must love, then, be *blind*, in your opinion?"

"Not blind—but preferably unalloyed; and best bestowed upon a worthy object."

I hesitated before I answered him; for I knew from the kindly tenor of his words, that my father's whole heart was in the subject. "I am not now in love with Mr. Sidmouth, Father," I said with remarkable firmness, "and I do not know that I could ever be, or that the question should even be put to the test, in the event that he returned such feeling. And since the gentleman promises fair to *hang* before he should have time for a tender dalliance, you may set yourself at ease."

"Jane! You cannot jest in such a matter!"

"Matters have come to such a turn, my dear sir, that I may fairly do little else. But I *will* be serious. I *will* promise you to take what care I can in the business. I shall not plunge whole-heartedly into a matter that might offer only harm, without judicious thought beforehand."

"That is as I should expect of you, my dear," my father replied, with a pat to the hand he held close in the crook of his arm. "You were ever a girl whose heart was ruled by her head."

Was I? I thought fleetingly; *and is that to be preferred to a head ruled by the heart? I cannot be entirely certain.*

"Father—" I said, with a purposeful effort at changing the subject, "—what should, then, my next step be? For so much cries out for elucidation, that I am in a confusion as to my proper path."

We had reached the end of the Cobb, and lingered to feel the freshness of the spray; and I knew with a sinking of the heart that autumn was advancing, and winter coming on. The sea air was sharper than it had been only a few weeks before, and I shivered as I drew my shawl closer about my thin muslin gown. We had but a little of our Lyme sojourn remaining to us; but Geoffrey Sidmouth had fewer days still. I must not be a spendthrift with time.

"You have declared the horseshoes to be the crux of the business," my father said thoughtfully. "And since you are unlikely to have success where Mr. Dobbin did not, I should counsel against a useless review of the Lyme blacksmiths. Your appearance in their midst, and in pursuit of such information, should only arouse suspicion against you, and excite the attention of the local tradesfolk."

"Very true."

"Let us consider, my dear Jane, whether any of the people hereabouts might spurn the Lyme trade, and engage a private smithy for the maintenance of their beasts."

"No one in our acquaintance is likely to require such a service," I objected. "Even Mr. Crawford has a modest stable, as we observed only a few days ago."

"But the Honourable Barnewalls have gone in for horses on a larger scale, have they not?"

"In *Ireland*, perhaps," I said doubtfully, but my father waved away such temporisations with surprising vigour.

"Forgive me, Jane, if I beg to speak from greater knowledge," he said. "I have known a few of your race-mad fellows in my time. They are never far from horse-flesh if they can manage it; and from Barnewall's conversation the other evening at Darby, I should adjudge him to be perpetually in a fever of acquisition over *some* mount or another. You will recall he wished to purchase Sidmouth's Satan; and undoubtedly he has snatched up a horse or two—or *ten*—in the course of his visit to Lyme. Have you paid a call on Mrs. Barnewall, Jane?"

"I have not," I replied, with new respect for my father's turn of mind.

"It is very remiss of you, when one considers the attentions she has shown. I should not have thought you capable of such rudeness."

"Indeed. And I might solicit her excellent taste, in the matter of my new silk—for Mrs. Barnewall *is* the very soul of fashion, and would appear well-acquainted with Maggie Tibbit's wares."

"And perhaps even with the woman's manner of obtaining them," my father finished smoothly. "I should think a visit to the Honourable Barnewalls highly profitable."

We turned with some reluctance from the vivid view of the bay, and had the wind at our backs for the remainder of the way home. It was a slow walk, and marked only by desultory conversation, for my father was much fatigued; and I was far too preoccupied with his perspective on the matter, to spare a thought for much else. The Honourable Barnewalls had their fingers in every piece of this pie; and I wondered I had not troubled to notice it before. It was *she* who had first introduced *le Chevalier* to my acquaintance, and *he* who elicited the valuable intelligence that Geoffrey Sidmouth marked his horses' shoes. It should take less than a few hours for a private smithy to render a Barnewall horse similarly shod; and the Honourable Mathew had enjoyed the span of a day, between learning of the Grange's brand and the murder of Captain Fielding. Could he have so wished to obtain the stallion Satan, that he resorted to theft and murder to do it? It seemed incredible. But might there exist *some other* motive in the matter, that should make the death of Captain Fielding, and the guilt of Geoffrey Sidmouth, in every way delightful to the peer-in-waiting?

For Mrs. Barnewall was familiar with the River Buddle district, and the Tibbit household; she clearly spent a fortune on dress, and her husband a fortune on horses; and yet, they continued to live in a style that suggested a comfortable income. Could it be that Mathew Barnewall—stupid, vulgar, utterly uninteresting Mathew Barnewall—was the very Reverend himself?

But my interest in the Barnewalls' affairs, though quickened by my father's observations, must await another day's satisfaction; for the afternoon was much advanced, and my father wanted his dinner, and I confessed to feeling much fatigued in my own right, and to be longing for the quiet of Wings cottage, and my too-long neglected *Watsons*. The fitful attention I had paid poor Emma in recent days, had left my heroine marooned in the midst of a fairly tedious ball—albeit her first in her adopted neighbourhood—and at the mercy of a small boy, who had been dancing with her far longer than was necessary, owing to my scattered wits. And so, I sat down once more before the fire in the little sitting-room—having crossed through the scullery in order to reach it, the doorway to the hall being now permanently barred by the bulk of the oak secretary—and applied myself to my writing with every intention of industry.

It would not do, however; in a very little while my attention wandered, from the odious Lord Osborne and the bland Mr. Howard, and the still less amusing Tom Musgrave; they were all of them pale substitutes for Geoffrey Sidmouth, and my emotions were all alive to the dangers that so threatened that gentleman, and over which I had but little power. He was at once more *real*, and more vividly engaging, than anything my imagination might summon—and thus a person unique in my experience. For I have generally found the creations of my pen more pleasing, and arguably better company, than the bulk of the men thrown in my way.

With a sigh, I closed up my ink bottle, and gathered up my little papers, and submitted to a dubious glance from my father. "Your efforts do not engage you, Jane?"

"No, Father. The words come only with difficulty this evening."

"Then I trust you are off to bed."

"I believe I *shall* retire, if you have no objection."

My father gave a look to my mother's comfortable countenance, which bore the ghost of a smile as she laboured over the stitching of a child's undergarment (which should go, no doubt, to St. Michael's Ladies Auxiliary, of which she had become a temporary member), and nodded. "I trust that tonight, at least, you shall endeavour to *sleep*," he said, with a slight warning in his tone; and I knew that he thought of my nocturnal ramblings along the Charmouth road, and the mortal danger they had invited.

"But of course," I replied, with as much innocence as I could muster; and made my way back through the scullery.

It was as I gained the hall, however, and would turn towards the stairs, that I encountered our valuable James. He was engaged in trimming a lanthorn set into an alcove in the entryway. It *would* smoke, despite our best efforts, and we had all but despaired of its utility, and determined to abandon it for another, of more recent vintage; but I observed to my delight that James had succeeded where less able hands had failed. He is genuinely a master of all things domestic. At my appearance, he stood to his full height, and turned to me with an expression of deference. Such an opportunity for confidence—and beyond the ears of my mother—should only rarely offer; and so of a sudden I seized it.

"James," I said, in a barely-audible whisper and with an eye for the barricaded sitting-room door. "I would speak with you in private."

He looked over his shoulder, as though my parents' eyes might bore through even the oak secretary, and nodded conspiratorially. I turned back into the scullery—but it remained the province of Cook and Jenny, who were setting the bones from dinner to boil—and felt myself in a quandary. Did I exit the front door, my father should hear, and believe me gone on some mysterious errand; I should not put it past him to follow, and leave my mother in some confusion as to his purpose.

"The back garden, miss?" came a whisper from James; and indeed, it should be the very thing. I slipped past him, and mounted the stairs, while he followed along behind—as was entirely proper, for he served to valet my father in the evenings, and was generally engaged at this hour in setting out his nightclothes, and arranging his toiletries upon the washstand.

Wings cottage has a peculiar charm, in being built into the rising ground at its back, so that the first storey might almost be another ground floor. With a door just off the first-floor hallway, the back garden is suitable for ladies' use, being accessible to the bedchamber and dressing-room; and indeed, my mother and Cassandra had sat here in the sun of a morning or two, while Cassandra was recovering, and enjoyed the gentle breezes, and the last of the summer's flowers, nodding from the bank. I had not had time to give the garden much thought; but I was pleased to find that two wooden chairs remained upright in the grass, despite the storms of the past week, and that today's sun and wind had entirely dried them. I took one with alacrity, and gazed up at the heavens; the first stars had begun to make their appearance, though the sky as yet held light. We Austens are determinedly unfashionable, and *will* dine early; and so the sun had barely set, though we were some hours already pushed back from the table.

"How may I be of service, miss?" James enquired, with an uneasy glance over his shoulder for ears beyond the doorway. He had remained standing, and could not but feel the awkwardness of the arrangement; for indeed, there was the faintest whisper of an assignation about our presence together in the garden. I should not like him to seem less than at ease, and so paid him the respect due to his situation.

"I shall not keep you long," I began, in a lowered tone. "Are you perchance acquainted, James, with a fellow by the name of Matthew Hurley?"

"What—Matty the Nob?" he rejoined, with a broad smile. "We all knows Matty. There's nothin' he can't fix nor find, for a price—and it's allus too high. What you want wit' Matty, miss? Leastways—" he amended consciously—"if I'm not bein' impertnunt."

"You will remember that I had an errand to Mrs. Tibbit." I leaned towards him, the better to inspire confidence. "About the clothes for the Tibbit children."

"Right you are, miss."

"It seems that Mrs. Tibbit believes her late husband is owed some monies by Matthew Hurley, for some job of work they recently performed together; and though the manner of her husband's death must throw suspicion upon *all* his former activities, not to mention confederates, I felt it my duty as a Christian to pursue the matter on her behalf."

"Bill owed some money?" James snorted in disbelief; "I reckon 'tis the other way 'round. But I guess you're wantin' the way to Matt Hurley, is that it?"

"In truth, James," I said, with a pitiful expression of dependence, "I had understood that the fellow keeps such low company, that it should be a penance for any lady to seek him out. I had rather hoped that *you* might enquire of Mr. Hurley as to the particulars of his dealings with Mr. Tibbit. He might prove more forthright to a man of his acquaintance, and a native of his town known to him some years, than he should to a lady and a stranger."

James shrugged. "If 'tis important to you, miss, I'm happy to oblige. But I can't see rightly why you pay such mind to Maggie Tibbit. The truth's as scarce as teeth in *her* mouth, beggin' your pardon, miss; and from the manner of his death, I reckon Bill Tibbit got what he was owed."

"I gave the woman my solemn vow, for she was much disturbed in the matter—and indeed, she has many mouths to feed, and might feel the want of coin severely." I hesitated, wondering how openly I might direct the course of James's enquiries. "I gathered that the labour was a matter of digging, performed for the late Captain Fielding—and that Maggie Tibbit might have gone to the Captain himself, but for his sudden death."

James did not respond for a moment, and his eyes narrowed shrewdly. "They've been a number of sudden deaths, to my thinking," he finally said thoughtfully, "and none of 'em too well explained, for that matter. I'll see what Matty Hurley has to say for himsel'. You just place your cares in James's keeping, miss, and think no more about it."

I thanked him, and pressed a few pence into his hand, which he blushingly accepted, though only after profuse entreaty; and I sent him on his way. As I watched him go, I gave thanks for the Jameses of this world, and their easy access to places a lady should take care not to visit. He is very likely to form his own construction of matters, but little likely to divine the truth of my purpose—suspicion being far from his nature, and detection beyond his power. I have observed that men will quite happily believe they are rendering a *service* to a lady, where they might baulk at being made a mere pawn; and yet it is the latter that is so often the case.

And with that thought, the face of Seraphine LeFevre rose unbidden before my eyes. The equivocations of this afternoon did not sit well upon my mind. I could not be easy in her character; I mistrusted her motives, and her purpose was unclear to me. Did she tend the wounded at the Grange tonight, as the stars shone from a darkening sky? Or had my suspicions unnerved her—and sent her out on the beach to a dark green boat, and a hard row against the tide, and a cutter waiting to sail for France— leaving Sidmouth alone in a stone-hearted gaol?

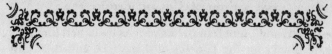

Chapter 19

Tête-à-Tête
at Wootton Fitzpaine

22 September 1804

~

LAST EVENING'S STARS PROVED AS LITTLE TO BE RELIED UPON, AS THE
conflicting reports of Sidmouth's character; for this
morning dawned still and wet, with a thick fog rolled in
off the harbour, and all the town's bustle and business at
once magnified and muffled by the impenetrable cloud. I
gazed at the lowering gloom with displeasure. If any hoofprints yet remained at the site of Captain Fielding's misadventure, they should be utterly marred by rain, and
offer little in the way of suggestion as to the murderer's
comparative size and strength. *That* door was closed to
me; but others might yet be opened.

It was decidedly *not* a day for paying a call; and so I was
hard-pressed to explain the energy of my resolve to wait
upon the Barnewalls this afternoon, at my mother's ex-
claiming over the poor nature of the day, and declaring it
fit only for remaining indoors by a comfortable fire. Indeed, she began to talk so much of an early removal from
Lyme, it being evident that the closer weather of autumn
was hard upon us, and the fair golden days of late Sep-

tember fast in decline, that I seized upon her mood and avowed as I *must* pay the call, as we might determine to be off at any moment, and the Barnewalls sadly neglected. I was forced to exaggerate here the level of attention the lady had paid me, from the necessity of painting an object worthy of serious consideration; but eventually gained my point. A hack chaise was summoned; my father handed me in with a wink; and in less time than I should have imagined possible, I was on my way to the Barnewalls' residence. It was a slow trip, owing to the fog, and elicited many a grumble and curse from the coachman; but I benefited from the solitude and tedium of the occasion, in reviewing my purpose in paying such a call.

I knew from rumour, and something Mrs. Barnewall had dropt, that they had taken an excessively large establishment some few miles out of Lyme, near the village of Wootton Fitzpaine.[1] This is a small habitation, tucked into a valley between two hills, with an ancient ruin on the one and a lovely growth of woods crowning the other. One or two well-kept farms, and a cruciform church, in some need of repair, form the major part of the village; and as I eyed the belfry of the latter, I could not but think that it should make an excellent signal tower, did someone have need of conversing with ships at sea. I had neither time nor inclination to explore its utility, however; the one truly fine house in Wootton Fitzpaine was my object, and I could spare only a thought for the scattered settlement it overlooked.

Wootton House proved to be an excellent modern estate, its limestone construction dating not earlier than the middle of the last century, and well-fitted-out by its own-

---

[1] Wootton Fitzpaine is a small village some three-and-a-half miles northeast of Lyme, between the forested Wootton Hill and Coney's Castle Hill, on which sit the ruins of an Iron Age settlement. —*Editor's note*.

ers, who were absent in London, and who had leased the place to the Barnewalls through their Dorset agents—or so Mrs. Barnewall informed me, within a few minutes of my arrival at her door, having seen me divested of my pelisse and hat, and begun the necessary civility of showing me around the house. If my call occasioned any surprise, she was equal to it; and ascribed my attention to the weather, which should render even the most resourceful unutterably stupid, did they remain within doors too long. Or so she said; though I observed a book laid down at my entrance, and a comfortable lap rug thrown aside, and knew that I had discomfited my hostess a little.

She was dressed today in a remarkably decent gown of French blue wool, with a full bodice and sleeves, and very little ornamentation; I was surprised to observe that the cut followed the lines of no ancient civilisation, as her gowns so often did; it had virtually the effect of a cowl, and rendered her slanting eyes, and pale face, and dark springy locks, the more interesting for its severity. And so I assumed her to be effecting the mood of the cloister, so suited to the general atmosphere out of doors; and decided that this was as much a sort of trumpery as her Roman or Egyptian garb.

We began with a parade through the principal rooms, all very fine, and done in excellent taste, with silk draperies and mahogany furniture—so curiously formal for Lyme, that I adjudged the present owners to be little in residence there, and to have simply repeated their usual style of city living, in their country place. As we walked, Mrs. Barnewall informed me that she had been a full six months in command of the house, and that though they intended a removal to Ireland in but a few weeks, her husband had determined to renew the lease the following spring, and spend the better part of the summer season in Dorset.

"I am excessively disappointed," she declared, "for I

had *longed* for a London season, or perhaps a trip to the Alps—though the renewal of hostilities between England and France might make such a journey difficult. I could have been happy with Easter in Bath, and spent May and June in London, with a daily parade along Rotten Row, and devoted my industry to the direction of a legion of dressmakers—and retired to someone's shooting lodge for August and September. But it is not to be. Mr. Barnewall is not to be gainsaid. To Dorset we shall return. I hope that we may find you here as well, Miss Austen— for I *depend* upon good society, in such retirement. You think of returning, I hope?"

"I cannot undertake to say," I replied, "my time is at my parents' disposal, I fear, and I go and come as they choose to send me. But I wonder, Mrs. Barnewall, at your engaging a residence so long, in a town and amidst a society for which you show so little affection. What can it be, that so fixes your husband's interest here?"

The lady burst out laughing. "This is frankness, indeed, Miss Austen! Have you learnt to admire Lyme *less*, now you have suffered it the *more*?" She slid her arm through mine and urged me along a gallery, painted pale yellow and overlaid with plaster figures and garlands in the best Adam manner, designed for the parade of portraits of people utterly unrelated to my hostess. She seemed to think nothing of living amidst another family's ancestors, though *I* should find it decidedly strange. The stern faces in oils might have been so many *objets d'art* on a shop-keeper's wall, for all the mind she paid them. "I fancy we are of the same opinion, more often than not; for though you profess the usual proprieties, and are careful to keep your face as demure as any chit of fifteen, the most delicious absurdities *will* escape your mouth, whenever you open it!"

I felt I had only echoed her declared sentiments, and said so.

"But that is the wonder of it! Can you be insensible that the majority of ladies should have ignored my obvious dislike of this place, and uttered some commonplace phrases in praise of its ugliness, and avowed themselves blessed in such an habitation? But pretence and hypocrisy are not for Miss Austen. You are a valuable acquaintance indeed; and to your friends, must be irreplaceable."

We had come to a staircase, and ascended it to a broad landing, with a window in the style of Palladio that rose to the height of several storeys.

"This must be lovely in fine weather," I ventured.

"Indeed. It overlooks the rear of the house, and the walled garden, and to the right, in the distance, Mr. Barnewall's stables. Or rather, the *owner's* stables, which Mr. Barnewall has seen fit to employ rather more fully than has been their wont."

I was reminded sharply of my purpose in paying this call, which object had been overlaid with a surprising level of agreeability, so unexpected in such a quarter, and lulled to quiescence by the warmth of my companion. But I shook myself from complaisance, and turned to a subject of nearer interest than my own frankness and value as an acquaintance, however delightful those observations had been.

"Mr. Barnewall, I understand, is an avid horseman."

"Oh! Avidity is too gentle a descriptor, I assure you. It was at the races that I was first introduced to my future husband; at the races that he proposed marriage to me; and at the races, very nearly, that we were married—Mr. Barnewall having a horse in the running on the very morn he was to be at the church, and most anxious to know the outcome of the match. Our wedding trip was rather an excursion about the breeding capitals of Europe, and instead of Sèvres, or a trunkful of dresses, I returned from my three-months' tour in possession of several cunning little mares. We are all for horses in Ireland,

I assure you, and while in Dorset must spend the better part of every afternoon riding out to visit one or another of the local stock farms. Whenever I *do* get to London next, I am sure I shall be amusing myself in whatever fashion allowable, while Mr. Barnewall eats, drinks, and sleeps in Tattersall's arms."[2]

The view beyond the window, which on a good day should have offered so much for my edification, remained resolutely blank. Blacksmiths by the score there might be, all pounding away at the hooves of a veritable herd of horses, and the cloud of fog that enveloped the Barnewall stables should reveal none of it to my sight.

"Such a hobby must require a considerable retinue for its maintenance," I observed circumspectly.

"And a fortune in expense," my companion returned, with a knowing glance. "I am sure you are too good to voice such a thought aloud; but it remains true, nonetheless."

"How many animals have you at present?"

"Some thirty mares, and two or three stallions, and one or two foals. But that is nothing, I am afraid, to what we maintain at Ireland."

"How extraordinary! And what shall you do with them when you depart for that country?"

Mrs. Barnewall shrugged. "As we are to renew the lease of Wootton House, we shall engage to keep the horses here, and their stable boys with them. Our manager, Mr. Farnsworth, is a true gem—or so my husband says; and in our absence he shall ensure that every possible measure is taken for the animals' comfort."

"But what consideration must be given, to every aspect

---

[2] Tattersall's was the most famous of the horse auction houses in the London of Austen's day; it was also known for its betting book, kept in an anteroom, and forming the secondary occupation of the gentlemen who frequented the place. —*Editor's note.*

of the horse's life!" I cried. "What supplies of fodder, and attention to tack, and endless trips to the farrier and the blacksmith!"

"As to the farrier, he comes to us, my dear," Mrs. Barnewall replied in some amusement, "and the estate has its own smithy. But enough talk of horses, or you shall be wanting a visit to the stables; and I confess my slippers are unequal to the remains of the black frost. You shall have to endure your impatience regarding the beasts, another day."

I cared little for the denied stable visit; it was enough to know that the means to make a shoe existed on the property, and that Mathew Barnewall was indeed a desperate addict of horseflesh in all its forms. But I could not yet see him resorting to murder, however important a horse might be, in order to obtain it. For tho' Geoffrey Sidmouth's goods might be forfeit, and Satan sold, were he condemned for a murder that Barnewall committed, it seemed a circuitous route to the business.

If murder had been done, and a horse from Wootton House its agent, then the motive must be far more serious and deadly indeed. Nothing less than Barnewall's entire manner of living must be at stake—and *there,* were he indeed the Reverend, I might find a reason for Captain Fielding's killing.

"And now, Miss Austen, will you take some refreshment in the morning room? Though I confess it bears a rather chilly aspect today."

I assented to the suggestion with alacrity, and descended the stairs in Mrs. Barnewall's train. After a passage through a central hall, from which several corridors sprang, and the selection of one of these, we proceeded past the open doors of several drawing-rooms and a dining-parlour before achieving the morning room. It was a cheerful place, being painted a pale green, and draped in a flowered stuff of a similar hue, and bearing about its cornice the figures of several cherubs, all engaged in staring down at us with the most puckish of expressions; it was at once more intimate, and less formal, than the part of the house in which I was originally received. Here Mrs. Barnewall should conduct her correspondence, and have her second cup of breakfast chocolate, and say yea or nay to the cook's choice for the day's dinner, and take up what needlework or sketchbook should suit her fancy. A pianoforte stood at one end, backed by an excessively large pier glass, that whichever performer chose to essay the keys, might have an admiring audience of *at least* herself. I could not help an involuntary exclamation as I perceived the instrument, for my music had been denied me throughout the length of our travels; and my delight did not go unnoticed by my hostess.

"You are a proficient, I presume?"

I shook my head regretfully. "An aspirant only to that title, and sadly in want of practise from a summer's worth of neglect."

"Pray, delight me with your skill, Miss Austen. Music is above all things my preferred activity."

"Then I should rather hear yourself, and avoid embarrassment."

"Oh! I never learnt, I am afraid—and so should hardly stand in censure upon your performance."

After a moment's hesitation, I drew off my gloves, and seated myself at the piano, and attempted one of the simple airs I so loved to play for my sister, of a quiet morning in Steventon, so many years ago.

"It *is* a plaintive melody," Mrs. Barnewall observed, when I had done; "but perhaps you merely echo the weather."

"Perhaps," I said with a smile, and rose from the instrument. "I may confess to a longing for my sister, who is the dearest creature in the world to me, and denied me by the misfortunes of which I know you have heard."

"Indeed!" Mrs. Barnewall cried, as she threw herself carelessly into a settee. "The famous overturning. An event almost as thoroughly discussed by the Lyme worthies as Mademoiselle LeFevre's unfortunate accident only a few weeks before."

"Her unfortunate accident?" I replied, feigning bewilderment. "What accident was this?"

"Why, my dear, you *must* have heard of it—the Miss Schuylers talked of little else the length of their stay. Not that they are possessed of such faculties as should provide them with frequent diversion, it is true—they were much dependent upon the affairs of others for their edification and amusement. But I recollect. *Your* business of the overturning, and the hanging of the man on the Cobb, quite put all thought of the mademoiselle and Captain Fielding out of our minds for a time."

"It was the Captain who caused Mademoiselle LeFevre's accident?"

"No, no—it was *he* who rescued her. Hence his affectionate name of *le Chevalier*." My confidante reached for an exquisite porcelain box that sat upon a Pembroke table near her seat, and to my amazement, drew forth a pinch of powder on the tip of her forefinger, which she inhaled as elegantly as it was possible to do. At my inability to conceal my surprise, she smiled devilishly. "Would you care for some snuff, Miss Austen? Or is the daughter of a clergyman a stranger to this, as to so many other vices?"

"I do not believe I should find it agreeable." My voice sounded priggish, even to my own ears. "How can you find it so?"

"It clears the mind wonderfully," she said, and sneezed.

"Indeed?" I confess the practise is new to my experience. Though my brothers James and Edward are both fond of their clay pipes, they take care never to smoke them within doors, and as it is my father's view that tobacco is a dangerous addiction, I was hardly exposed to the fumes in my infancy. Even Henry, however—charming, foolish, light-hearted Henry—has avoided the fashion for snuff. Though there are some who have partaken of the substance for years, I may fairly state that only recently has it become the rage to carry the little boxes about, and change them according to whether one is at home or in society, or abroad of a morning or an evening. I had *never* witnessed a woman consuming snuff—even my flamboyant sister Eliza.[3]

"I failed to discover the meaning behind *le Chevalier*," I said, with an effort to appear rueful. "I fear I have not your penetration, Mrs. Barnewall, and the Captain *did* appear indisposed to discuss the matter."

"That is like his natural reticence," she replied softly, and sighed, her snapping dark eyes momentarily clouded. I had not considered that the lady might consider herself in mourning. Such obtuseness should be unforgivable, had I not believed her too light in her attachments to regard the poor Captain with anything like tenderness. But I am too prone to a hasty judgment of the characters and impulses of others; it may be fairly declared my chief failing.

"The tale does him no dishonour, I trust?"

"Hardly." She adjusted a cushion at her elbow, and settled in for a long chat. "It was a few weeks before your

[3] There were numerous varieties of snuff in Austen's day, rather as there are of herbal teas in our own, and different blends were chosen according to the mood of the consumer or the time of day. The Prince of Wales kept varieties from all over the world in his snuff cellar, though he disliked snuff itself, and contrived never to inhale it however many times a day he went through the ritual. His mother, Queen Charlotte, consumed from the age of seventeen only one blend—of tobacco, ambergris, attar, and bitter almonds. —*Editor's note.*

arrival, Miss Austen, about the middle part of August, I should say. We had all been in attendance at the Thursday night Assembly, though the crowd was rather thin, the summer people in general having departed for country estates to the north. There was nothing like a moon that night, as I recall, and so for those of us who travelled into town by carriage, the drive home was a slow business. Captain Fielding had *not* been in the rooms—indeed, I had thought him away from Lyme on some business—and his absence deprived the ball of a good part of its gaiety.

"Mr. Barnewall and I had agreed to follow Mr. Crawford to Darby, for a late supper and some cards, being little inclined to retire early, despite the ball's having closed a full hour before its usual two o'clock. And so our carriages travelled in train, up the Charmouth road towards Mr. Crawford's estate—until with a 'Whoa!' the equipage in front was pulled up, and in a moment Mr. Crawford had descended, and then my husband must be impatient to know what was toward, and we were all out in the road in the middle of the night, with only the light of a lanthorn to show the scene.

"And what a scene!"

"Mademoiselle LeFevre?"

She shook her head. "Captain Fielding, unhorsed and with the lady quite insensible in his arms. What a picture they made! Her long red cloak, trailing from unconscious limbs, and the fall of her extraordinary hair across his arm; his face bruised and weary, and himself standing upon a wooden leg, and endeavouring to bear her homeward, without benefit of assistance or even his horse! Had we not arrived at the very moment, I cannot think how things should have gone; but we did, and commended him for his gallantry, and managed them both to their respective houses."

"But what *had* occurred?" I cried, in some exasperation.

"We had it from the Captain—whom we chose to convey homeward, while the Crawfords took the mademoiselle—that the lady had been abroad on horseback, well after midnight, about some errand of her cousin, Mr. Sidmouth—only fancy!—and that her horse had startled, and bolted, and thrown her to the ground; at which point she was fortunate in the Captain's happening upon her on the road, at his return very late from business in Dorchester. Only think! Our carriages might have run over her body in the dark, as she lay insensible, had he not appeared to act as saviour!"

"Perish the thought!" I said, with suitable fervour. "But why, then, had the Captain's horse *also* run off?"

Mrs. Barnewall leaned closer, her eyes once more brilliant with animation. "I understood from Fielding that he was unhorsed in the animal's act of leaping over the mademoiselle's still form, as the beast came upon her in its way. It was thus he made the discovery of her."

"I suppose Mr. Sidmouth was very grateful," I observed, with conscious stupidity, "to have his cousin so safely restored."

"Mr. Sidmouth seemed rather to despair of his errand's having gone awry," Mrs. Barnewall replied, "but that is ever his way. He should rather have all the world trampled underfoot, than have his own business interrupted; and the poor little Frenchwoman is but a cog in his larger affairs. She is capable, I suppose, and dutiful in her bidding, and there her utility ends. But we knew of this only later, when it became apparent that there was a grudge between Sidmouth and the Captain—the result of which we have all unfortunately seen."

"And what do *you* believe is Sidmouth's business?" I enquired of her tentatively. "He is much abroad, in France, I hear—though perhaps not so much of late."

"Because of the war, you would mean?" She sat back against the cushions, one delicate forefinger to her reddened nostrils. "Aye, that is very bad for business, I have no doubt. I myself intended to purchase a lovely length of silk, promised me by one of the Free Traders hereabouts, and I find it is not to be had. The controls at the ports are much stronger, I hear, and the Royal Navy less amenable to turning a blind eye, no matter how much brandy is waved beneath their noses."

"Whatever would you speak of, Mrs. Barnewall?" My brow was furrowed, my countenance the very picture of confusion.

"Why, the Gentlemen of the Night, of course! The Reverend's men, who keep us all in silk and snuff, and playing cards and sealing wax. You *will* have heard of the Reverend—as I recall, we discussed his exploits at your very first Assembly."

I studied my acquaintance's expression—the slanting eyes, sparkling with fun—or was it calculation?—the determined smile, which might hide a mind curious to know how much I had guessed of her affairs—the impenetrable facade of a carefully composed woman, betraying nothing of her true mind. She had allowed me to know that she was familiar with the smugglers' habits, that she patronised them for their wares; and had even referred obliquely to Maggie Tibbit's silk. One might almost think that she knew of my visit to the woman, and my own purchase of the stuff—as perhaps she did. For the first time I was afraid in her presence, from knowing myself to be in waters too deep for steady footing.

"I did not know that people in my acquaintance were aware of the clandestine trade," I said slowly.

"Aware of it? But, my dear, they *run* it," she replied, in some amusement. "Whatever do you think Sidmouth's business is? His errands for the little LeFevre? His grudge against the Captain, whom we all know to have been opposed to the Trade? Depend upon it, Miss Austen, the Captain's death—however conveniently it might be ascribed to an *affaire de coeur* over the *petite* mademoiselle—was a matter of business. And if I adjudge Sidmouth rightly, he will dispose of the coroner's charge in similar terms. He will disappear, of a sudden, from his Lyme gaol, and take a swift ship for France, where he shall be given up for dead; but in a little while, in a different town, on another part of the coast, the Reverend will reappear."

"You are very intimate with the gentleman's business, Mrs. Barnewall," I observed.

"Am I?" She laughed mockingly, and reached for her snuffbox with the archest of glances. "I must say I find the gentleman irresistible. But then, most women do, do they not, Miss Austen? I daresay you have fallen victim to Sidmouth yourself, on one or two occasions."

"If I have, I should be the very last to own it," I said firmly, and rose to take my leave. "It has been a most enjoyable afternoon, Mrs. Barnewall; I regret that I visited Wootton House only at the close of your stay in these parts. I should like to have seen it in finer weather."

"Then do not stay away, while yet we both remain in Lyme," she rejoined, with perhaps an equal level of insincerity; and so we parted—two women of self-sufficient habits, and little inclination for the society of females, and yet driven together by a mutual need for confidences gained. I had come to Mrs. Barnewall with the intention of soliciting intelligence; but it was only at our parting that I knew her to have received me with an *equal* aim in view. I felt that I had been carefully managed from my first step inside her hall; but the *why* of it eluded me.

Chapter 20

The Watcher
in the Doorway

Sunday, 23 September 1804

~

IT WAS NEARLY THE HOUR FOR DINNER WHEN I RETURNED TO WINGS cottage from Wootton Fitzpaine yesterday afternoon, but the fog had lifted under the influence of a light breeze, promising a shift in the weather; and so I seized a few moments of liberty to slip down Pound Street to the linendraper's, of a mind to view Mr. Milsop's latest sketches of evening gowns, so important to the effect of a good length of peach-coloured silk, and to consider whether a demi-turban[1] or a feather should be better suited to my headdress; and with such pleasant fancies dancing before my eyes, and banishing all thoughts of smugglers, their wives, and their purported bloodlettings, I very nearly ran down poor Mr. Dagliesh, who was engaged in conversing with a rotund lady of middle age, not five paces from Mr. Milsop's door.

[1] This was less a turban than a length of material—often lace—tied around the crown and knotted at one side of the head, in a somewhat Turkish fashion. —*Editor's note.*

"Miss Jane Austen!" he cried, with a flourish of his hat and a hasty bow. "I hope I find you well?"

"Very well, Mr. Dagliesh," I replied, with a nod for his companion, who paid no heed to ceremony and made her lumbering way on up the street, leaving me to enjoy the gentleman's undivided attentions. "I am relieved to see you in excellent health."

"Had you any reason to fear for it?" he enquired.

"Oh! No reason at all—though I guessed you were so much in demand, and in the middle of the night, too—about the shingle and the downs, in attending to all manner of wounds of a sudden received, whose victims have not the luxury of appearing by the light of day—that I thought you must soon be quite broken down."

He started, and gave me a narrow look, and with a foolish smile, said that the demands of a country practise were sometimes unmanageable.

"Particularly when one is under the obligation of attending to one's friends," I continued. "The demands of a stranger might be put off to another day; but the necessity of one's intimate acquaintance may not be gainsaid. And there has been so much of that sort of thing in Lyme, of late! A lady thrown from a horse here, a shot to the back there, a skirmish at sea that might leave a man at the mercy of Fate—I wonder you have slept at all, from riding to the Grange."

"Miss Austen—" he began, and then halted in confusion.

"I know now why you could not be summoned, the very night of my sister's unfortunate injury—for you were undoubtedly in attendance upon some smugglers' band, deep in the folds of the Pinny, or secreted in a convenient cave. And nothing is plainer than your failing to appear the morning of her departure for London, to pay your respects. It was the very morning that Mr. Sidmouth routed the dragoons, just below the Cobb, and even *I* observed Davy Forely the lander to have been shot. Was it Mademoiselle LeFevre who cared for him there, in the kitchen garret, against the Preventy Men's discovery?"[2]

"I could not undertake to say," the surgeon's assistant replied. "It was not *there* that I attended him, certainly. But tell me, Miss Austen—would you have a man die of a wound he did not merit, when a surgeon could easily be called? Is there some *wrong* you might find, in my ministering to such unfortunates? For to heal *is* my calling in life."

"No wrong, Mr. Dagliesh—unless it be that your care for the local criminal set prevents you from attending to those more worthy of your attention. Had my sister died of her injuries, I should look with less gentleness at the manner in which you spend your evenings."

"Heaven forbid!" he cried, with a sensible look. "And how does your sister? She continues to mend?"

"As swiftly as we might have hoped—her *London* physician having *no other* claim upon his time and attention, that might prove more remunerative."

"You are severe upon me." He turned his hat in both hands, worrying at the brim. "But money has not been my object, though you *would* have my motives solely mercenary. I may go so far as to assert, Miss Austen, that neither my conduct, nor that of those I have attended, merits such censure; but honour forbids me saying more." His look, when he raised his eyes, had something of pleading in it, and a circumspection I should not have guessed Mr. Dagliesh capable of. "There is a nobility in the most common of men, Miss Austen, when they are spurred to act from principle; and I have found that the

---

[2] The *Preventy Men* was a common name for the officers of the Board of Customs. —*Editor's note.*

appearance of what is wrong may often cloak, conversely, a very great good."

"As I am sure the opposite is true," I rejoined, somewhat tartly, "with all manner of evil parading itself as circumspection and propriety."

"That has ever been the case," he said, with some gentleness. "The wonder is that we should still be equally as fooled." And with a civility, he left me—though less happy in my designs upon peach-coloured silk.

IT WAS AS I RETURNED FROM POUND STREET TO WINGS COTTAGE, that I first noticed the presence of a man to my back. He appeared to find interest in shop windows at exactly the moment I turned to gaze at something on offer; and resumed his slow stroll in my train whenever my interest was satisfied, and my own walk recommenced. Upon first perceiving him, I was puzzled; then alarmed; and finally, determined upon calculation. Though I had half a mind to confront him with questions, the possibility that I but succumbed to an over-active imagination, could not be discounted; and so I turned instead into a local purveyor of comestibles, in search, ostensibly, of tea. I knew the shop to let out onto an adjacent street at its rear; and upon learning that no tea was to be had in all of Lyme—a curious notion, that—I exited by this latter way. Imagine my dismay, upon perceiving the gentleman as yet behind! For he had assuredly pursued me to the shop's interior, and thence into the adjacent street.

I had no desire to alert him to my awareness of his presence, by attempting blatantly to lose him; and so, with my head down and my feet purposeful, I made as swiftly as I might for Wings cottage. A hurried ascent to my room, to dress for dinner—and to observe the gentleman posted in the street below, arranged so very casually in a doorway, for all the world like one of my brother James's Loiterers.[3]

I wonder what shall become of him? Does he intend to remain there the rest of the night? And who has set him upon me—and for what possible reason? Is he, perhaps, one of Roy Cavendish's men, intent upon learning the direction of my enquiries, since I have been so rude as to avoid communication with the Customs man himself?

I was unsettled the length of dinner, and could make only the most cursory of replies to my mother's many suppositions regarding Wootton House, and my father's observations of the history of Wootton Fitzpaine's church.

And now, alone with my pen and paper in the clear light of a Sunday morning, with little of activity before me other than the writing of a long-overdue letter to my poor Cassandra, I am incapable of so simple a task, and must rise continually to peer out at the street, in as stealthy a manner possible, in search of an unknown watcher.

Monday, 24 September 1804
~

NOT LONG AFTER BREAKFAST THIS MORNING, AS I SETTLED DOWN IN the sitting-room to mend the slit in my brown wool, and mull over all that I knew of Lyme's tangled affairs, I was startled to find in the depths of my workbasket, a bit of paper—its edges sealed with a drop of tallow. Opening it in some wonderment, I discovered it to be a missive from our man James, written painstakingly with a bit of lead, and looking something of a scrawl.

Dear Miss, it ran, *I will be seing Matty Hurley as you askt it*

---

[3] Austen's brothers James and Henry, while students at Oxford, established the literary journal *The Loiterer*, to which Austen herself may have contributed the occasional letter. —*Editor's note.*

being my free day. Do you come to St. Michael's church at 3 o'clock. I hope as this will serve. Yours respeckfully James.

I had but to waste the better part of the morning, then, in fitful bursts of work, and occasional glances from the scullery window—which revealed no watchers waiting in doorways; and indeed, I am forced to wonder if my fancies did not run away with me Saturday e'en, in being surfeited with all manner of preposterous schemes.

St. Michael's being but a short walk down Broad to Bridge Street, and from thence, after a brief look at the sea and Broad Ledge, which was visible now at low tide,[4] up Church Street, I had a very little way to go. I set out not long before three o'clock, accordingly, in my demure close bonnet and with a basket of clothes depending from my arm; for at my mother's hearing that I intended visiting the church, she *would* charge me with delivering her contribution to the ladies' auxiliary, and was only persuaded with difficulty against accompanying me herself.

St. Michael's is not a handsome edifice; and that may be attributed, perhaps, to it being two churches at once— a late Norman one, and the present building, which dates from the sixteenth century. It sits nobly upon a cliff, however, and seems quite suited to the spirit of Lyme, with all its peculiarities. I should not *wish* a more regular building to take its place; it seems, indeed, to have been a part of this coast forever.

I stood a moment on the stoop of the church, and glanced back the way I had come; and shivered to think

---

[4] Broad Ledge was originally a part of Lyme proper—medieval maps of the area suggest it once was crowded with houses—but was later inundated by the sea, and is now visible only at low tide. It serves as a reminder of the shifting nature of the Dorset coastline. —*Editor's note.*

that I detected a figure lingering behind; but it must have been an effect of the sunlight, a chimera of sorts, for when I blinked to observe a second time, the figure was no more. I pushed open the church's heavy oak door, and stepped into the cool dimness of its vestibule.

All was hushed, and the few supplicants scattered amidst the pews, too bowed in prayer to attend to my arrival. I looked about for James's broad shoulders, and could not find them; and so, after a moment, I progressed up a side aisle and took my place among the reverent. The church bell tolled the hour.

After fifteen minutes of silent contemplation, I determined to search for James outside the church; and made my way once more to the vestibule. It was *there* I encountered Miss Crawford, as staunch as a general the afternoon of a battle. She stood to one side of the vestibule itself, in the Auxiliary's anteroom, in an imposing black cap arrayed with jet. Her nostrils were pinched as though in reception of a noisome odour, but her bony hands fairly flew among the ordered piles of cast-off clothing. She looked up as I hesitated on the little room's threshold, and under the command of Miss Crawford's gaze, I could not but drop a curtsey.

"Good afternoon, Miss Austen," that lady said sharply over her spectacles. "I understand you were at Wootton Fitzpaine on Saturday. You should have informed me of your visit prior to having paid it, and I should have charged you with enquiring of Mrs. Barnewall *when* she intends to make her contribution to the ladies' auxiliary. My brother tells me she is to leave the country soon; and it should be a very shabby thing, if in all the bustle of making ready, St. Michael's were forgot. But no matter. I was not to know you were to go—and on such a foggy afternoon, too!—and so I shall have the trip to make over."

"My apologies, Miss Crawford. I could not imagine you

to have an interest in that quarter, and thus could not be expected to inform you of my plans."

"Expected! Hardly. The *young* are never *expected* to treat anyone with consideration. But never mind. I see you have your mother's things in that basket."

"I do, and I send them with her compliments."

Miss Crawford paused to examine a tiny nightdress, of fine cambric, overlaid with my mother's excellent satin stitch; and sniffed audibly. "The seams might have been straighter; but then, one never gives as much care to things for the poor, as for one's own; and I suppose her eyes are weak, at her age."

"I shall inform her of your gratitude," I said drily, and turned for the door.

"Do you remember, Miss Austen, to tell her of the ladies' tea, to be held at Darby on Saturday," Miss Crawford called sharply after me. "It is meant as a kindness to the good-hearted women who do so much for the unfortunates of the parish. It is a vast deal of trouble, to be sure, but I count it as nothing. It is the *least* that I may do. It is to be a very fine tea."

"Though, perhaps inevitably, *tealess*," I observed.

"Whatever do you mean to say, Miss Austen?"

"I had understood there was not a leaf to be had, in all of Lyme."

"But that is hardly the case at *Darby*, I may assure you." Miss Crawford spoke with an air of smug complacency. "My dear brother is never at a loss for tea—but then, we may consider him as having resources, that should be denied a mere *visitor*, such as yourself."

"Indeed we may," I rejoined, in some amusement at her vanity, and quitted the church and Miss Crawford together.

I made my way to the little churchyard, and found James with his back against a headstone, and a burly man, quite ill-shaven, at his side. The latter discarded a bit of grass he had been twirling between his teeth, and pulled himself to his feet. He had no hat to hold, and so stood with his head slightly bowed, awaiting my notice—a balding fellow, with a crooked nose, a perpetual dimple in one cheek, and a rough warmth to his gaze. Despite his attitude of deference, he had a confident air, as though life held no mysteries beyond his understanding.

"Miss Austen, miss," James said, with the barest suggestion of anxiety in his aspect. "We thought as you weren't coming."

"I was somewhat detained by church business," I replied. "I take it you are Matthew Hurley?"

"Matty'll do just fine, miss."

"I've been a-tellin' Matty here how Maggie Tibbit'd have it 'e owes her money," James began, "and Matty— well, you tell Miss Austen, then."

"I don't owe Bill Tibbit nothin' nor a curse," the fellow said comfortably, "and haven't done, since he ran the *Royal Belle* aground."

"The ship's loss does seem to have turned all of Lyme against him," I observed.

"It did that. He were paid to lose the *Belle,* and three fine young men o' town was lost with it." Mr. Hurley paused a moment to clear his throat, and as abruptly spat.

I glanced at James's untroubled countenance, then turned to his companion. "It was the Reverend's ship, I understand."

"Now, 'oo be tellin' you that?" Matty Hurley said, with a narrowed eye.

"Maggie Tibbit. She said that her husband had been a regular spotter for the smugglers' crews, and that he lingered too long over his tankard, when he should better have been gone to Puncknowle and the signal tower."

"It's right convenient she should think so," the man replied, "but that warn't the truth of it. Bill were *paid,* and he met 'is end fer it, as did the feller as paid 'im."

I looked from one to the other with a growing apprehension. "You cannot mean—that is to say—Mr. Hurley, would you have it that *Captain Fielding* paid the man to ground the *Belle?* And that he lost his life as a result?"

"I ain't sayin' here nor there," the fellow asserted, his eyes shifting. "It's a deep business, as no lady should concern hersel' wit. But Maggie Tibbit oughter know better."

This was a thought to give one pause, indeed. The Captain must have believed the ship to be engaged in smuggling, and attempted to thwart the trade in a ruthless manner, considering the consequences. And yet, if the doomed ship was not the Reverend's—

"How can you be so certain that the *Belle* was *not* the Reverend's, Mr. Hurley?"

"Let's jist say as I was a-waitin' on the Chesnil beach for 'er to land, and had the pulling of the bodies out o' the surf," he replied darkly. "I hope I may never see another such a sight, as long as I may live. Terrible it was, and Nancy Harding's boy but fifteen."

"But what can a ship have been doing, in so clandestine a manner, if *not* to smuggle contraband?"

Matty Hurley shrugged, and flicked a glance at James, who turned back a bewildered countenance. "You'll be a stranger to Lyme, miss, and all our 'fairs," Matty offered. "I'm not sure yer needin' to know. Just settle as it was a matter o' some importance, as three young coves and a passel of Frenchies give their lives for, and not a thing to do with brandy barrels or kegs o' snuff. Bill Tibbit was no good, and a traiter, and we're well quit of 'im, whatever 'is Maggie says. You can tell 'er so for me." He turned away, of a conviction, no doubt, that our discussion was at an end; but I could not suffer him to leave in so sybil-like a manner. A cloud of conflicting thoughts held converse in my mind, but through them all I grasped at one. The man had declared that the boat was *not* the Reverend's; but I knew of one other household, at least, that was much given to signalling ships at sea.

"Matty," I said, reaching a hand to detain him, "did the *Royal Belle* belong to Mr. Geoffrey Sidmouth?"

The astonishment that overlaid his hardened features was a spectacle to behold, and should have elicited my delighted laughter, had not I perceived his underlying consternation, as having betrayed perhaps too much. "Never fear," I assured him. "Your secret is safe with me—though from your words, I must declare it a rather open one, since most of Lyme seems admitted to it."

"Just the folk o' the Buddle district," Matty said grudgingly, "and only them as are trusty."

"So it was *Mr. Sidmouth's* ship that ran aground," I said thoughtfully, "as a result of Bill Tibbit's carelessness, or design. And Bill Tibbit died for it, as did Captain Fielding. That *does* alter the complexion of Sidmouth's case. For his motives and his natural reticence about the matter, become all too clear."

"I thought she come here on a matter o' Maggie Tibbit's," Matty protested, with a glare for James.

"She did!" the poor man rejoined, in natural dismay. "Miss Austen?"

"No matter," I replied. "There is another of whom I had better enquire, and leave Mr. Hurley in the clear." I turned and looked towards the horizon, in an effort to judge of the time—for of a sudden I had a notion to conduct a further piece of business in the hours remaining before dinner. It could not be far from half-past three; and we generally dined at five. It should just do.

"You have been very helpful, Mr. Hurley, and I thank you—for what you would not, as well as what you might, impart." The wretched fellow shifted from one foot to the other, and looked desperate to be gone, his native confidence fled. I reached into my reticule and retrieved several coins, which I pressed upon the two men, who bobbed their thanks, however doubtfully. For my part, I affected a desire to return to the church, that they might be freed of my presence, and go about their business, as unmolested as I preferred to go about *mine*—for I had no desire to be observed, in making my way, as I must, towards the grim stone keep that served as Lyme's gaol.

Chapter 21

Final Confession . . .

24 September 1804, cont.

~

RATHER THAN HUGGING A LONELY STRETCH OF COASTLINE HIGH above the turbulent seas, bereft of civilisation and the comforts of humanity, as should befit a prison in Lyme, the gaol where Mr. Sidmouth was held sat in the very midst of the town, with a stock in front and a cubby for the watchman; I should move under the keenest observation as I approached the place, but could not find it in me to care, as my errand seemed too urgent to admit of delicacy. I knew not whether the gentleman was permitted visitors—but deemed it likely that what persuasion might not produce, the application of coin should speedily acquire.

The watchman—a smallish fellow clothed in nankeen, with a sharp nose, watery eyes, and a perpetual habit of sneezing—rose from his stool as swift as a street tumbler, and danced a bow before me.

"Gordy Trimble at yer service, ma'am, though what service ye might be seekin' *here*, 'tis beyond me to say," he offered by way of introduction.

"I am Miss Jane Austen," I said with dignity, "and have come with a basket of victuals from St. Michael's Church—a gesture of charity towards the poor man detained within those walls." I had retrieved my mother's basket from Miss Crawford after parting from James and Mr. Hurley, in the thought that the ladies' auxiliary should hardly require it as mightily as *I* should. In making my way towards the gaol, I had tarried only long enough to purchase bread and cheese, and a few apples, to put in its depths.

"*Poor* man? Never thought as I'd hear His Worship called poor, ma'am, and that's a fact. And him been stylin' hissel' so fine. Ah, well—the world's gone topsy-turvy, it has, and Gordy Trimble's not the one to make the right of it." He reached a hand to the basket handle, and I saw with a start my mistake.

"I should like to deliver the goods myself," I told him firmly.

"Eh, now, you'll not be thinkin' I'll have the eatin' of 'em before him?"

"Assuredly not—that is to say—I should like to speak with Mr. Sidmouth a moment, since he is so soon to be taken away," I faltered.

The little man's face creased in a wicked smile. "Sweet on him, are ye? Half o' Lyme is in the same state, or I'm not Gordy Trimble. The parade o' ladies as has been through that door would make a priest blush, it would. Not to mention the mademoiselle. Fair spends her days here, she does—though I'll not be lettin' her sit by him that long. Leans in the doorway, mooning like a sick calf, until the sun's about down; then hies hersel' off to the Grange, for to attend to the milking."

"Is the mademoiselle within at present?" I enquired, in some apprehension. I had not thought to encounter Seraphine when I hastily undertook my errand.

"Nay—you'll be havin' yer five minutes to yersel, I

reckon," the watchman replied. "But no more." He peered into the basket and poked a finger around the victuals. "Wouldn't want you bringin' a knife or a pistol to my prisoner, now would I?"

"Mr. Trimble!" I cried, "*I* am a clergyman's daughter." I sailed past him to the door of the small keep—a square, whitewashed building with a thatched roof—and waited while he jangled his keys. Mr. Trimble retained a quantity of them for a man with only one room and one prisoner to guard. I could hear the slight sounds of scuffling, and a length of chain dragged along the floor, from beyond the heavy oak; Sidmouth must be alerted to visitors, and be rising to his feet.

The door swung open, and emitted a cloud of dust from the hay that served as flooring; I sneezed, and understood now the gaoler's streaming eyes. How did Sidmouth stand it? But I had not another moment to consider it, for the heavy door closed behind me, and I was thrown into the dimmest complicity possible with the man. A warm stillness to the air, and a slightly sour smell, of too much humanity confined too long in so slight a space; it should surely drive one mad, for too many days together.

The hay rustled not five feet from where I stood. "Who is it?" he enquired, in a tone of some doubt; and I knew that backlit in the open doorway as I must have been, my features were obscured to him. "Not Seraphine. But a woman."

"Miss Austen," I replied—and was surprised to hear how strongly my voice emerged. My heart was aflutter, and the palms of my hands grown moist; such anxiety, over so simple a purpose! I had visited a prison far worse than this, and faced evils of a sterner nature; and yet, today, I might have been as weak as a child, and as ill-formed for such an experience.

A short laugh, harsh in that stillness, and yet tinged

with amusement. "Miss Jane Austen of Bath, in the very midst of Lyme gaol! To what a turn have matters come! I should rise and welcome you with a proper bow, madam—but that I cannot rise at all, at the moment. I hope that you will forgive me, and ascribe my poor manners to the proper cause."

A faint shaft of sunlight fell from a slit placed high in the wall to my back; and as my eyes adjusted to the dimness of the room, I discerned the darker shape against the stone that must be Sidmouth's form. A manacle was clasped about each ankle, and bolted to the wall so that he was denied a range of movement, though his arms as yet were free. I took a step towards him.

"What possible reason can you have, for so exposing yourself to the opprobrium of Lyme society, in seeking me here?" the master of High Down continued easily.

"I have brought you some victuals," I said, laying the basket at his feet, and sinking low myself. I dared not sit, for fear of the state of the straw, but rocked about on my ankles. "But I will not deny, Mr. Sidmouth, that this food is as a mere pretext, for gaining entry enough to speak with you. I am come on a matter of some urgency."

"A welcome change," he rejoined drily, "since all urgency, I fear, has fled from my days. It is extraordinary, is it not, Miss Austen, how the perception of time will shift, according to the measure of one's duties? In having none to perform, I find myself equipped with so much time, that I might effect a revolution in men's affairs, did I but have the freedom—for I pass a year in every day, or so it seems."

"And yet the days still pass," I said crossly, "and the number you command grows short. I myself have but five minutes. We must not waste them in philosophy, sir. But your talk of revolution *does* inspire a thought—not of war and tumult, but its alternative—a world of reason and order, however imperfect it might have been. Mr.

Sidmouth, I have been turning over in my mind a welter of conflicting thoughts—for I have heard such varied accounts of your business, as confuse me exceedingly. Some would have you a smuggler, the very Reverend, in fact; while others would call you simply a rogue. Much time and penetration on my part has gone to find the meaning of the business. But I believe that I have."

"Then pray enlighten me, Miss Austen, for I am told that a few sentences will suffice to sum up the matter." I could not discern his expression; but I caught the flash of white teeth, and the glitter of his eyes, and imagined him smiling sardonically. "It seems that Captain Fielding was in love with my cousin, and that I grew so enraged at her indifference to me, that I killed the man. What better resolution could there be?"

"I must pay you the compliment, sir, of believing you more the master of your energies than such a construction will allow. That conclusion to the sad affair pays no attention to the presence of a white flower near Captain Fielding's body—a white *lily*, more to the point—nor does it incorporate the death of Bill Tibbit, hanged on the end of the Cobb, with another such bloom at his feet. When I discovered that Tibbit had run a ship aground—and that a number of Frenchmen had died as a result—I knew at last the nature of the Grange's trade."

I paused, to allow my words their full effect. "You have been smuggling Frenchmen between England and France, have you not? And *Royalist* Frenchmen, I would assume from the foundered ship's name and the speaking symbol of the *fleur-de-lys*. But such men are unlikely to find a happy reception on their native shores, now Buonaparte is emperor. Indeed, I cannot imagine them to be returning with anything like his health and safety in mind. Are you a trader in assassins, Mr. Sidmouth?"

There was an astonished silence; and then Geoffrey

Sidmouth's chains rattled. I felt cool fingers slip over my own, and drew a startled breath.

"How come you to know so much?" he asked quietly.

"You have been hardly as secretive, or as careful, as you might have thought," I replied. "The mooring ring at the end of the Cobb bears the marks of green paint, from the skiff you keep on Charmouth beach; in the act of erecting a scaffold, the boat must have brushed against the stone and the ring, and left its tell-tale sign. I am further assured of this, from having viewed the boat itself, in a later walk upon the shingle."

"Many people own such a boat, and might paint it green; and the marks of wear be everywhere upon its surface."

"Do you deny that you own such a boat?"

After a grudging instant, he said, "I do not. You have been well-informed, Miss Austen."

I shrugged. "It must be impossible to employ so many men, upon so precarious a business, without *some* of them tending to talk. And the grounding of your ship last spring—for which I understand Bill Tibbit paid with his life—has turned the emotion of the townsfolk against him, and made them more likely to air their grievances, out of a mixture of injury and pride."

"The *Royal Belle* was a heavy loss." Sidmouth paused, as if uncertain how much to say. "As a result of Tibbit's treachery, seven men aboard it died; and all of them true-hearted and brave, and my dearest friends."

"There are five Tibbit children who must feel a similar desolation," I replied.

A silence fell between us, and in the distance I heard the voice of Gordy Trimble, skylarking in sunlight. I looked down at my gloved hand, and saw Sidmouth's fingers still upon it; but a curious heaviness had taken hold of me, in knowing him to be guilty beyond the faintest doubt. I had held out hope for his goodness so long; and though I knew Tibbit's hanging to be a form of retribution—a life taken for so many lives unjustly lost—I could not shake the chill that had overcome my body. There was Captain Fielding to consider. How many deaths were necessary, in payment for blood already spilled?

"I am thankful for this, at least," I said, faltering. "I thought you likely to hang unjustly—and the weight of it should have haunted me all the days of my life. But I will be reconciled the better, in knowing that Tibbit's blood is indeed on your hands—and on Percival Fielding's as well, for having paid the man to ground the ship. But I cannot understand what should have urged the Captain to such a ruthless act! Did he believe you to traffic in nothing more than contraband?"

"I cannot say." Sidmouth's voice was heavy, and his fingers slid away from my own. "I did not know for a certainty that he was behind the fellow Tibbit—but your stating it now must be the fruit of further knowledge."

"And so you *killed* him, though you doubted his complicity?" I was all horrified amazement, and my shock must have throbbed in my voice.

"*I,* killed Percival Fielding? But I *never* killed the Captain, however little love I bore the mincing scoundrel!"

"But, indeed, you must have!"

"Indeed, I did not!"

"But the horseshoes—the white flower—"

"I must assure you solemnly, Miss Austen, that I was standing for the better part of the night some six miles distant, on Pucknowle hill, awaiting the signal of a ship most anxiously desired, which failed, however, to appear! And that Mr. Dagliesh was with me, from the direst necessity, and will vouch for my presence the entirety of the night Captain Fielding was murdered."

A memory of the scene I had witnessed on Charmouth beach, the very night *after* Fielding's killing, flashed before my eyes.

"The boat that landed the following night—with the wounded man—it was for *this* that you waited?"

"How come you to know of it?"

"I was a witness to its arrival."

"But *how*?" Sidmouth's voice was hoarse.

"You must know of the cavern, on the Charmouth shingle. I had hidden myself in its depths, the better to observe unmolested the movements on the beach—for after your arrest at the hands of Mr. Dobbin that morning, I felt I *had* to probe the truth of matters more. For *he* seemed little inclined to do it."

"The cavern—" Sidmouth hesitated. "You explored its fullest extent?"

"You would mean the tunnel? You knew, then, of its existence, and its end point in Captain Fielding's garden?"

"I did. In point of fact, the tunnel predates the Captain's tenancy of that house, it having been built for another gentleman more inclined to clandestine trade, who has since fled these parts, Miss Austen. You will understand that the Gentlemen of the Night have long held sway about this coast—some hundred years, in fact—and Fielding's house is at least as old. He may have prettied the place a bit with his wilderness temple, and bits of antique statuary, but the way carved through the cliffs was not his enterprise to claim."

"And yet," I mused, "he may have employed it for just such a clandestine purpose. I found the storeroom filled with what appeared to be contraband goods, a fact that has much puzzled me."

Sidmouth's laugh was short. "Since Fielding styled himself a prop of the law, you would mean, and affected to be so much in the Customs man's confidence? But tell me this, Miss Austen. How do you think that Fielding supported his customary style? On a Naval pension?"

"I assumed him wealthy from the seizure of prizes,"[1] I replied. "You would ascribe it to smuggling?"

"Not smuggling. No. I believe Fielding to have become wealthy through the consideration of others, more benevolent to his circumstances. For certain Gentlemen of the Night, a small expression of gratitude for silences kept, and discovery averted—a cask of the finest Darjeeling, let us say, or a barrel of French brandy—might seem a gift well-placed."

"Bribery," I said slowly. "It has a certain aptness. We may assume him to have sold what he could not consume himself, and thus been in a way to supplement his income."

There was a smallish pause, as I mulled over the Captain's duplicitous character.

"The cavern I understand; but how came you to discover the tunnel at all?" Sidmouth enquired.

"In following two men within its depths." I was deliberately vague; I should not like to admit to Sidmouth *now* that I had expected Dick and Eb to be making for the Grange. "I felt sure their business was suspect, and thought to discover its nature in pursuing them. In the event, I found only what bewildered me. I must conclude *now* that they sought to retrieve some tribute previously given to Fielding—for they canvassed the storeroom with thoroughness. But their activity was for naught; they quitted the place in some disappointment."

The master of High Down did not bother to express his astonishment on this point; he had done with such effu-

---

[1] Throughout the Napoleonic Wars, Royal Navy officers—if they survived—frequently made considerable fortunes from the taking of enemy ships and their cargoes. Austen's naval brothers sent frequent news of such booty, and she describes this sort of swift advancement in *Persuasion*. Captain Wentworth begins his career in 1802 a man without fortune, and by 1814 is a wealthy one. —*Editor's note.*

sions. I had no longer the power to surprise him. "And did they, too, witness the landing of the boat?" he asked, in some concern.

I shook my head. "They appeared on the shingle *after* your curious skiff."

"It was *La Gascogne,* the boat you saw once on the very beach; and it bore my cousin Philippe—Mademoiselle Le-Fevre's brother."

"The one who serves Napoleon?"

"The one who *served* Napoleon—as a spy for the Royalist cause—and nearly gave his young life as a result. If there can be any consolation for myself at such a time, it is in learning from Seraphine that the boy will survive. Had he not been encamped in Boulogne, with the forces readying the Monster's invasion of England, he should never have escaped when finally he was discovered. But escape he did, if gravely wounded; and though the boat was delayed by storm, it landed successfully a day later—in Charmouth rather than off the Chesnil bank. Dagliesh at least was present, though I could not be."

I drew a tremulous breath; such turbulence as this man endured! Such passion, for a cause so beyond himself! And to end, now, with the end of a rope—but he had accepted such a possibility, undoubtedly, when first he undertook to commerce in the unseating of emperors, however upstart.

I sat back on my heels. "But if *you* did not kill Captain Fielding—who, then, fired the deadly ball?"

Sidmouth shook his head. "I do not know. I have expended a world of thought upon the subject—for the Captain's murderer took great pains to incriminate me utterly. It betrays a certain knowledge of my household, and my particular habits, that cannot but be troubling, as well as a desire to see great harm devolve upon myself."

There was a knock upon the door. "Yer five minutes be ten, Miss Austen! Out wit' ye!"

"Another moment only, pray, Mr. Trimble!" I called, and turned swiftly to Geoffrey Sidmouth. "It pains me to broach so intimate a subject, and which cannot but be painful to you; but I must voice my darkest thoughts and have done. Is it possible—can you find it in your heart to believe—that Seraphine might have done the murder in your very absence?"

"*Seraphine?* That is preposterous!"

"I do not mean to say she should have killed the Captain from a desire to incriminate yourself," I said hurriedly, over his words of protest. "She may have happened upon him of a sudden, and feared a renewal of those events that proved so disturbing to her, but a few weeks before; and so fired upon him, in a belief she acted in self-defence, and then fled the scene. At such a moment she was unlikely to think of the horseshoes."

"But the lily," Sidmouth rejoined. "It should be no one's custom to travel abroad at midnight in possession of such a flower."

"Perhaps she bore it with her, on some errand to one of your Royalist men hidden about the countryside, and only laid it near the Captain in the thought that he was behind the grounding of the *Royal Belle,* indeed."

"I suppose that such a case is possible," Sidmouth said slowly. "For it is difficult to account for the horseshoes otherwise. You make a very convincing argument, Miss Austen." He raised his head, and I perceived again the glitter of his eyes. "I wish it might be less so. But it is of no matter. I have taken on myself the burden of that death; and perhaps it is only justice that I should stand for Seraphine, as someone else has undoubtedly stood for me, in the matter of Bill Tibbit."

"Bill Tibbit's death shall never be pursued," I said dismissively. "It will be ascribed to a feud of the fisherfolk, and left to lie. Mr. Dobbin, the justice, will only exert himself in a matter of quality—such as the Captain's. I understand, now, the agony of Seraphine's mind, in the very midst of the inquest. You had a suspicion of the truth, did you not, and so urged her to keep silent?"

"I had no notion—indeed, I wished her only to say nothing of where I had been, or Dagliesh either, the night of Fielding's death, from anxiety that *all* our plans should be o'erthrown. But upon reflection, I find it not unlikely that events should have occurred as you have said. Seraphine had reason enough to hate the Captain, and fear his appearance on a lonely road."

"What *did* occur between them?" I enquired curiously.

Another knock from Mr. Trimble.

"I shall be with you directly! I pause only for my basket!" I called.

"I see no reason to deny you the intelligence," Sidmouth said, "from knowing I may depend upon your complete discretion."

"I was told that Fielding recovered the lady after she suffered a fall from her horse, and was attempting to carry her to the Grange, when he was overtaken by Mr. Crawford's equipage."

A flash of teeth that betokened a grim smile.

"He had drawn her out to the road itself, with a falsely written message—a plea for help from one of our Royalists, hidden in the Pinny," Sidmouth said. "A drawing of a white lily was sent with the note; and it arranged to meet in a lonely spot not far from the Grange, in the early hours of the morning, when the moon should have set." He paused to draw breath.

"You have seen that road at night; you know full well how little aid might be found, did one suffer a mishap. When Seraphine arrived, Fielding was waiting; and she knew him to be attempting her discovery. She fled from him, and was upon the point of escape, when his horse overtook her own—and he dealt her such a severe blow to the head with his whip handle, that she fell unconscious from her mount's back. It is solely by the grace of God she avoided a more severe injury still."

"But what can have been his purpose?" I cried.

"We think it probable he wished to detain her some time, in an effort to win that intelligence from her, that should be so deadly to our cause."

"But why? What reason can Fielding have had, to so disturb your activity? He was an officer of the Royal Navy! Should not the downfall of Napoleon be in the interest of *all* who claim a part in that noble institution?"

"All, who are not presently dependent upon the Monster's purse," Sidmouth replied grimly. "I have believed Captain Fielding a spy of the French for many years; but it was only in recent months that he allowed himself to show his hand, in his attempts to discover my methods. He styled himself an agent of the Revenue men, as he took care that all of Lyme should know; but his treachery had as its object far more than Free Trade. It has ended with his life."

Mr. Trimble could no longer be thwarted; and I made as if to go, my aching ankles almost numb from the conditions to which I had subjected them. I could not but think that I should never see Geoffrey Sidmouth again, and emotion *would* rise; but I hurriedly removed the bread and cheese and apples from the basket, and placed it over my arm, and was on the point of turning away, in despair of ever making an audible *adieu;* when Sidmouth's hand closed over my own, as tightly as a vise.

"To have you leave without a word will tear the very heart from my body," he said harshly. "However little approbation you accord my actions—despicable, unjust as they may seem—do not deny me the gentleness of your pity! One word of farewell, for God's sake, to a man whose fate is so uncertain!"

I stared at him wordlessly, all but overcome; and in an instant, he had pulled me down beside him in a crushing embrace, made more awkward by the presence of his chains. I felt myself enmeshed in iron, and closed my eyes against the force of it, until I felt his lips move warmly over my own.

"Must you surely die, then?" I said brokenly.

"It seems I must," he replied, in some bitterness of spirit, "—unless it be that chaos reign, and fire cover the earth, and these bonds be loosed by hands more powerful than my own. But do not cry, dear Jane! Perhaps we shall meet again—be it only beyond the grave!"

I felt the sharp prick of tears to my eyelids, and thrust myself to my feet, unwilling and unable to linger more. At the gaol's entry, I turned for one last glimpse of Geoffrey Sidmouth.

"There may be men with a greater claim to unblemished reputation," I said, "but none to bravery. It is something, indeed, to know myself your friend. *Adieu*, Mr. Sidmouth—and courage! in that most mortal hour."

And so I knocked upon the portal, and emerged into daylight, and the curious eyes of Gordy Trimble—and let the little gaoler think what calumnies he might.

AN INVOCATION OF FIRE, AND OF CHAOS UNLEASHED. I HAD THOUGHT it a pretty speech, from a man in contemplation of his fate, and gave it no more consideration than I should a verse of Cowper's—stirring words, to be sure, and well-phrased, but with little of prophecy about them. I made my slow way home, and endured a listless dinner, my thoughts unabashedly pensive; for the few moments I had spent in Sidmouth's arms were calculated to send any woman's principles to the winds (yes, *even* a clergyman's daughter), and at the thought that I should never see him the more, I could not but be melancholy. My father observed me narrowly, but forbore from interrogation; and even James—though ignorant of the cause of my languor—had something of sympathy in his tone as he bade me good night.

"You are returned, then, from your day of liberty?" I said, my hand on the stair-rail. My parents had preceded me to bed, leaving me to close up the house in the man-servant's company, with only a tallow taper between us to light the way. If there *was* the thinnest paring of a new moon, a bank of clouds had sufficed to hide its light, and the night beyond the windows was very black. "I hope it was not *entirely* a slave to my service."

"Not a'tall, miss—though I'd count it no hardship if 'twere."

"I am deeply grateful for your energy and intelligence, James."

He blushed scarlet, and knew not where to look. A sudden recovery of his memory, however, gave him relief in providing a purpose. "Beggin' yer pardon, miss, but there's one thing as we forgot to talk of, with Matty Hurley this afternoon."

"Indeed?"

"You were wonderin' 'bout his work on the gangs, if I recollect."

"I was."

"And whether he ever worked wit' Bill Tibbit on a job for the Captain wot's dead." James threw home the front-door bolt with a satisfying thud.

"You need not concern yourself with enquiring further of Mr. Hurley, James," I began, "for I learned something to advantage this afternoon that makes all such questions of the Captain's garden irrelevant."

James shrugged. "Don't need to *enquire further*," he replied. "Me and Matty's talked o' it already. He never worked wit' Bill at the Captain's, him havin' chose his own folk, on the quiet-like, and kept 'em paid proper. Seems as if Bill spent three or four months up

Charmouth way, when he warn't drinkin' in the Three Cups."

My interest was piqued despite myself, though the tunnel was no longer an object of mystery. "And did Captain Fielding engage only the one man?"

James shook his head. "There was one or two others. Dick Trevors, and Martin Clive maybe, and old Ebenezer Smoot, 'im with the high voice and the soft 'ead."

"Dick and—Ebenezer?" My voice, I confess, was tremulous.

James nodded, and paused at the foot of the stairs, preparatory to leaving me for the evening. "Marty died o' the fever last May, and I 'aven't seen Dick lately, come to think on it, nor Eb neither."

"I believe they are gone to London," I said drily, remembering their fear of the Reverend and his vanished silk, "on rather pressing business. The result of having mislaid something of value to their current employer."

"They've never gone and filched from Mr. Crawford?" James exclaimed, in surprise.

"Mr. *Crawford*?"

"Aye. They've been a-workin' them fossil pits, and his bit of a smithy, most o' the summer now." The manservant scratched his head in wonderment. "Dick and Eb, run off with Mr. Crawford's property! There's something like. Now what they want with them bits o' stone, then?"

Chapter 22

. . . *and Absolution*

25 September 1804

~

MR. *CRAWFORD*, THE EMPLOYER OF DICK AND EBENEZER—MR.
Crawford, whose passion for fossils allowed him unquestioned observation of the Charmouth coast, and a presence for labourers on each and every day, and a
cavernous excavation where he might easily have constructed a hidden room, for the purpose of secreting
contraband—Mr. Crawford, whose demeanour and reputation assured him an unquestioned propriety, the better
for conducting his nefarious business. Mr. Crawford, who
never lacked for tea, or the best of brandies, and whose
sister went about clothed in a dressmaker's dream of
black silk; Mr. Crawford, whose fortune seemed so easy,
despite his open hand to friends, and the liberality that
too often placed others in his debt—a debt, perhaps, that
might purchase goodwill and silence, did those friends
think to question his activities.

Mr. Crawford, who clearly knew of Sidmouth's habit of
marking his horses' shoes, and was quick to tell the entirety of his dinner guests the fact, only a day before Cap-

tain Fielding met his untimely end. Mr. Crawford, whose friendship with Sidmouth might make him privy to the man's concerns, and cognizant of the import of a white lily left by the dead man's feet; and whose sadness at discovering the very hoofprints that should betray his friend, must disarm the suspicions of all—particularly Mr. Dobbin, the justice, who could not be expected to believe such a gentleman in any way involved in a crime of passion. Mr. Crawford, whose forge at the fossil site might readily have served to craft such a set of shoes, well before he undertook to murder the man whose relations with the Lyme Customs officer, Roy Cavendish, had quite disrupted his lucrative trade.

Mr. Crawford the Reverend, and Percival Fielding's murderer. It strained even *my* propensity for cynical calculation.

I sat down upon the lowest step in an attitude of shock, the lighted taper dropping from my nerveless fingers. James could not suppress an exclamation of anxiety, and fell to his knees by my side.

"Dear miss!" he cried. "Are you unwell? What can I have said?"

I reached a shaking hand to ward off his concern. "It is nothing, James—nothing—a mere trifling indisposition. I shall be myself in a moment."

"A glass o' water, mebbe?" He dashed into the scullery and rummaged about in a cupboard, reappearing instantly with a saucerless teacup filled to the brim. "You drink that down, now, miss, and you'll be right as rain."

I brushed his hand aside and rose, my faculties all but routed. "I must be off at once," I said. "I must speak with Mr. Dobbin!"

"At such an hour?" James's voice was doubtful, and I saw from his look that he thought my senses quite fled. "He'll be a-bed, surely, or close to it."

"That is as nothing. The man must be stopped."

"What man, Miss?"

I ascended the stairs as hastily as I knew how, in search of a bonnet and cloak, paying little heed to my father, who emerged from his bedroom in nightshirt and cap, his countenance overlaid with wonder.

"Are you intending to pay a *call*, my dear? And in the middle of the night?"

"It is not above ten o'clock," I replied crossly, and turned from him in haste. "I do but go to Mr. Dobbin, and shall return directly."

Comprehension dawned on my father's face. "But do you know the proper direction? Had not I better accompany you?"

At this, I paused—for indeed, I had not the slightest idea of where the justice of the peace was to be found. "I shall have James to accompany me," I said, with an air of decision that brooked no reply. "He will know the way, and may serve as greater protection in case of need. Do not alarm yourself, Father, and endeavour to disguise the truth to my mother. Inform her I have been called to the side of a sick friend—Mrs. Barnewall, if need be—at the lady's request."

"Are you certain, Jane, that such activity is *required* of your benevolence?"

"Justice demands it, Father. I shall not be long." I gave him a swift kiss, and received his hand on my head in blessing, and turned from him in a swirl of my wool skirts.

It was as James and I stepped out upon the threshold of Wings cottage, and turned up Broad towards the center of Lyme, that the glow upon the horizon—so incongruous in so dark a sky—astounded our senses. We stood aghast, our purpose forgotten at the sight of the blaze, and smelled the sharp odour of wood and tar upon the wind.

•　　•　　•

"Fire! Fire!"

All was chaos, with the old wooden buildings at the center of town aflame. Fire licked at the stone pavements, and found no purchase, and so turned to leap greedily from thatched roof to thatched roof, in a crackle and volley of sparks that suggested a riotous celebration, as though the Devil himself had determined to hold a party. Several of the principal buildings along Silver Street were ablaze, and a long line of men were engaged in swinging buckets from the town's main cistern; but the water was as a drop to the throat of a dying man; it had no power to stem the course of events, except in that it allowed the onlookers to feel comfort in the activity of refusal.

"How did it start?" James cried hoarsely to a passing man.

"Dunno," the fellow replied. "Does it matter?" and he handed my manservant a sack of burlap and a stout shovel. "Get you to the fireguard, there, and join in the diggin'. If the flames come near, beat at 'em with the sack."

James did not hesitate; in an instant he had disappeared into the thick cloud of smoke and townspeople collected near the blaze; and I was alone at the periphery of Hell.

I gazed in horror, remembering Sidmouth's words of but a few hours ago—*unless it be that chaos reign and fire cover the earth*—and that swiftly, I felt I *knew* how the blaze had begun, and the object of so much general diversion. Did the townsfolk exert their energies in an hour of true crisis, they should be little likely to guard the gaol. The Royalists had done as their leader predicted. Fire rained down from the heavens, and chaos reigned;[1] and in the midst of it all, I knew that Sidmouth was fled.

---

[1] This description of the Lyme fire appears nowhere in Jane Austen's surviving letters to Cassandra, and it is probable that it is

I turned away from the prospect of Silver Street, and ducked down a narrow alley towards the whitewashed stone keep. The fire was at just enough distance from the gaol, and threatened so valuable a number of shops, as to ensure complete distraction. A very few moments sufficed to bring me to Gordy Trimble's cubby; and to find it deserted, and the doorway beyond flung wide. I did not bother to look within; for I knew I should find the manacles burst, from the blow of an axe, and the prisoner gone into the dark.

I turned—in the grip, at the moment, of indecision; and nearly collided with a gentleman at my back.

"Miss Austen!" he cried, and despite the disorder of our surroundings, did not neglect to bow.

"Mr. Crawford!" I replied, in a tremulous tone—and wished, of a sudden, for James by my side. "The blaze has brought you out, I see!"

"How could it not? I observed the light of the flames from Darby's high position; and waited only long enough for Miss Crawford to put up some bread and cheese, before mounting my horse and hastening to town. You cannot know, I realise, that we are very much prey to such blazes, here along the coast; a similar fire not a year ago quite nearly levelled the lower part of town; and every man's aid must be necessary at such a time."

His earnest face was as good-natured as ever beneath the balding pate, and he betrayed not the slightest hint of his propensity for evil, nor the incongruity of us both, as we stood many streets away from the conflagration he had

---

among those that Cassandra is known to have destroyed before her own death, as too revealing of Jane's personal life. A reference to the flames *does* appear in letter #57 in the LeFaye edition of *Jane Austen's Letters,* which LeFaye attributes to the November 5, 1803 fire known to have occurred in Lyme. The account of a blaze recorded here, however, some ten months later, may in fact be the one to which Jane refers in letter #57. —*Editor's note.*

hastened so far to combat. I forbore from suggesting that he might find his way closer to the flames, from fear of arousing his suspicions; and endeavoured to appear as though my anxiety were active only on the crisis's behalf.

"But what do you here, Miss Austen—at such a remove from both your home and the blaze together?" he enquired, bending nearer. Did I imagine it—or did his tone bear a sharper construction?

"I began by observing the activity in some proximity," I attempted, "but found the heat from the flames and the noise of the townsfolk to be too great; and so sought relief in this removal. I hardly know where I have got to."

"Indeed," Crawford said. "I think you have fetched up quite close to the Lyme gaol." And at that, he peered over my shoulder into the yard beyond, and his eyes widened. "I see that Sidmouth's friends—if, indeed, he retains any—have profited from the confusion, to effect his escape. Mr. Dobbin must be informed!"

I turned about, and pretended to as great a surprise as Mr. Crawford, though I imagine neither of us saw anything very unexpected; and delayed only a moment to speed the gentleman on his way to the justice of the peace.

"Do you hasten, Mr. Crawford, sir, lest the villain be lost in the general alarm!" I cried, with as much fervour as my desire to be rid of the man allowed. "With such criminals about, I believe I shall make my way back to Wings cottage, and take refuge there with all my dear family, until a general order is restored. I declare, I had not an idea of such terrifying adventures—such utter disregard for propriety, or such a propensity for revolution—when I undertook to travel to Lyme. Our sojourn in this place has been one long trial of fortitude; I wonder that *either* you or your good sister can long sustain a residence in the place."

"It is possible," he replied, "that we shall seek a removal in the near future—for I may admit that Miss Crawford's views are very similar to your own, Miss Austen. But I hesitate to send you off so very alone—I fear that perhaps I should accompany you—for great are the misfortunes that might befall so gentle a nature as your own, in the general recklessness of these streets."

"I would not delay your errand for the world!" I cried, with energy. "Only consider the consequences!"

"Indeed," he said, in some hesitation; and I felt him to have anything *but* the justice's house in view. His object, rather, should be to see me safely out of the way, before proceeding himself in pursuit of Sidmouth; for Crawford's plans had been too carefully laid to be put so awry. Sidmouth must serve as scapegoat for Crawford's crimes; and if the man were lost as a result of the fire, and never appeared again, so much the better. I knew, of a sudden, what Crawford intended. He would make his way to the beach below the Grange, there to search for Sidmouth as he awaited removal by boat; his friend had no reason to suspect Crawford's motives, and did he appear in the guise of aid, should welcome him with open arms. It but remained to thrust a dagger through his heart, or turn him over to the justice, and complete his betrayal.

Sidmouth must, at all costs, be warned.

I bobbed a curtsey to Crawford, and summoned the falsest of smiles. "I shall be quite all right, I assure you," I said, and turned away. "I should never sleep easy, Mr. Crawford, did you not hasten to Mr. Dobbin this very moment. God forbid that Jane Austen should stand in justice's way!"

I RETURNED WITH HASTE TO WINGS COTTAGE, IN THE EVENT THAT Mr. Crawford followed; for I knew not how narrowly he suspected my motives, or my presence by the gaol, and I would wish to preserve the *appearance* of credulity in Mr. Sidmouth's guilt and an innocence of my intended plan. But I knew that Crawford should spare a very little time, and should be mounted on horseback, and must lose nothing to delay. And so I tarried only long enough to discard my cumbersome cloak and bonnet, don my stout boots, and mount the steps to Wings cottage's back garden—there to slip once more into the night. It was but a scramble up the hillside, and a furtive ducking through the yard of a neighbour, before I found my road; and in a very little while, my hand pressed to a stitch in my side, I was hastening across the exposed expanse of Broad Ledge at low tide, and down into the little cove of Charmouth beach.

THE ROYALISTS SHOULD NOT HAVE CHOSEN TO SET THE TOWN alight, and free Sidmouth from his chains, only to keep him in hiding several days—no, there was a plan behind all of this, and a purpose, and I little doubted that I should find a party upon the beach, in expectation of the arrival of a ship offshore, and a signal light that should go unremarked against the broader glare of flames to the west. That Crawford might assume as much—or look for Sidmouth to return to the Grange, and from thence make his way down the cliff side to the shingle, seemed equally likely. I had not a moment to lose.

Caution must be my guide, however; and so, as I drew shuddering breath at the eastern foot of Broad Ledge, my shins much abused by my passage and my gown spattered with sea spray, I attempted to calm my racing heart. I could not know for certain the route Mr. Crawford should take; but his own familiarity with this bit of coast, and the proximity of his fossil digs, must make him a knowing adversary. I strained to make out the beach's foreground, and observed no movement; but for safety's sake, I turned into the cliffs, and began to creep my way up the shingle.

Nothing but the soft susurration of waves upon the shore, did I have for comfort in the darkness; that, and the light patter of raindrops that had begun to fall from the clouds above—slowly at first, and then with a mounting urgency, as though the very heavens wished to save the houses and shops of Lyme, in letting fall a healing flood. My turn of mind was grown quite biblical, I reflected—a propensity for which I must blame Geoffrey Sidmouth, and the discord his circumstances had unleashed. I placed a careful foot upon a rock, in an effort to leap a small sea-pool, and found I had miscalculated; the rock o'erturned, with a sharp *clink!*, and I stopped in horror of discovery.

Nothing greeted my misstep, however—no leap to alarm, or sudden gunshot, or cry of warning torn from an anxious throat. Had I miscalculated? Was Charmouth beach empty, and Sidmouth lost in the mouth of the Pinny, and far from the effects of Crawford and my warning together? Or—and at this, I felt a shudder of apprehension—was Crawford better apprised of his friend's whereabouts, and I had lost both Sidmouth and the opportunity to effect his salvation?

I found my fingers were trembling, and willed myself to complaisance with an effort; but it was not fear that had so unnerved me, but *cold*—for I was wet through to the skin from the combined effects of rain and spray, and my hair hung in wet rat-tails about my face. I looked the very part of castaway, and must find some shelter soon, or catch my death.

The cave, I thought; *of course. They shall have hidden themselves in the cave, and await the signal of the ship, and be all but invisible to my wandering eye.*

But did Crawford know of the cavern as well? No, I

could not believe him ignorant of a feature of the landscape he had occupied so long.

The gentleman's fossil pits were before me; I longed to explore their depths, and find there a storeroom, and a quantity of silk of exceptional quality; but such things were better left to the light of day, and Mr. Dobbin's men. It remained now for me to pass the entrance in as much safety as possible, against the possibility that Mr. Crawford was even now about; and so, despite the cold, I pulled my clinging skirts into a girdle around my waist, exposing my stockinged legs to the elements, and fell to the sand on hands and knees. A stealthy crawl along the shore, with many a pause for safety, and the pits were nearly passed; when a soft nicker nearly startled me out of my wits, and I looked up to find a horse tethered to a rock not three feet from my head. —A dark horse, nearly invisible on such a night, and undoubtedly Mr. Crawford's.

But where was the man himself?

A shudder, part cold and part terror, overcame my body, and I laid my face against the sand. Did he find me here, I should assuredly be lost.

"Miss Austen," came a voice from above, "and in so abject a posture! Can this be the light angel of old?"

I raised my head slowly, in fear for my life—and gazed squarely into the eyes of Lord Harold Trowbridge.[2]

IT IS NOT FOR ME HERE TO RELATE THE JOY WITH WHICH I GREETED his narrow, calculating face; nor the shock and relief I felt, nor the questions I plied—for I was denied all such, in being grasped roughly by the arm, and dragged into

---

[2] Lord Harold Trowbridge—rake, scoundrel, second son of a duke, and spy in the service of the Crown—made his first appearance in Austen's journals while both were at Scargrave Manor, the home of her friend Isobel Payne. —*Editor's note.*

the safety of a cairn, and held with rapidly beating heart against the wet wool of Trowbridge's greatcoat.

"Make no sound," he commanded in a whisper. "It is as much as your life is worth."

I nodded once; and in an instant, observed the confident pacing of a man across the shingle with a cocked pistol in his hand, some twenty feet from the rocks behind which we sat. *Crawford.* Quite careless of discovery—or confident that he should prevail against it.

"He is making for the cavern," I breathed. The slightest pressure of Trowbridge's hand warned me against further speech. We waited, with breath suspended, until Crawford had achieved the mouth of the cave—and startled us with a sudden cry.

"I say! Sidmouth! Are you there? It's Cholmondeley Crawford. I've come to offer my assistance!"

I stole a glance at Trowbridge. "The man is Sidmouth's enemy."

"I know."

"But how?"

"I have had you followed for some days," he whispered in reply. "Having observed to whom you spoke, I merely spoke to them in turn. What you have deduced, I have seconded. Crawford is the Reverend, and hopes to put Sidmouth in the way of settling his score with the law." He rose to a half-crouch, and peered around our sheltering stone. "He is being ushered within. We have not a moment to lose. I doubt not that the law follows hard upon his heels, and that he expects to hold Sidmouth and his men at gunpoint until he might hand them over to the dragoons, and pose as hero of the day."

"But are not the Royalists armed?"

"It shall avail them nothing, if they are taken by surprise. Stay here in safety, and do not move until I return." He took a step out from the rock, but I clutched at his coattails immediately.

"You would not leave me here!"

"I have no choice, Miss Austen," Lord Harold said impatiently. "You must find your fortitude where you may."

"I am coming with you."

"You cannot."

"I must," I insisted, and rose to my feet. "If you do not allow it, I shall scream at the full pitch of my lungs, and bring Crawford down upon you."

We had parried closely before, but never in the presence of such mortal danger. Tonight Trowbridge was neither amused nor incensed at my insistence; he merely calculated a measure past it, and handed me his pistol. I had never held such a thing before, and had not the slightest notion of how to discharge it.

"It is loaded with ball," Trowbridge said. "Keep it pointed in the air, and fire at will if the dragoons approach. In this you should be performing a dearer service, and prove less of an encumbrance, than if you dragged at my heels. Not another word!" he commanded; and was gone as swiftly as a star at sunrise.

I gave him a few moments; observed his lean form scuttle along the beach with bent back and arms akimbo, for all the world like a retreating crab; and then turned as noiselessly as I might, and began the slow ascent up the cliff's face.

I DID NOT EXPEND MUCH THOUGHT IN RESOLVING LORD HAROLD's presence upon Charmouth beach, or his admission that he had had me followed. Sidmouth's support of the Royalists, as I had already divined, had as its object the destruction of Napoleon's reign; and that Harold Trowbridge, servant of the Crown, should be behind the Grange's projects, should hardly astonish. Tho' the Royal Navy stood vigilant against invasion, and the Sea

Fencibles[3] were roused along the coastline, how much more easy should all of Britain sleep, if the tyrant were torn from his throne, and France no longer in thrall! What lives should be saved, at the expense of this one life! *Others*, did they know of it, might speak with shock of statecraft so dishonourably conducted, behind the veil of proper diplomacy; and were the Royalists unmasked, and Lord Harold's part in their skulduggery exposed, he should bring down upon his head only the usual measure of disapprobation his activities generally enjoyed. But I may, perhaps, look more kindly on Sidmouth and his men, for having *two* brothers much exposed to the caprice of war; and count as nothing the cloak and the dagger deployed to secure their continued health and safety. In truth, I quite admired His Majesty for undertaking such a course.[4]

After perhaps ten minutes of struggle, I gained the cliff's head; and from there, it was but a short scramble to Captain Fielding's garden, and the wilderness temple. I glanced swiftly around me—at the still shadows cloaking

[3] This was a sort of coastal militia, of fishermen and small craft superintended by naval officers, arrayed against possible channel invasion from France. —*Editor's note.*

[4] What Jane suspected was in some part true. By 1804 the British government was actively supporting French Royalist plotters who found refuge on English shores by providing them with bank drafts in the millions of francs; and a certain Captain Wright allegedly carried three separate shiploads of Royalist insurgents to French shores throughout 1803 and early 1804. All were discovered, tried, and, in the main, executed. "I may fairly say," Napoleon later recalled, "that during the months from September, 1803, to January, 1804, I was sitting on a volcano." The assassination attempts culminated in Napoleon's unwarranted seizure and execution of the Duc D'Enghien, who was of Bourbon descent and falsely accused of aspiring to Napoleon's throne, in March 1804; but from Austen's account, it would seem that Royalist efforts continued well afterward. —*Editor's note.*

the empty house, and the rank-upon-rank of dormant rose bushes, and the discerning eyes of the stone wood nymphs—and without a second thought, secure in such isolation, I plunged into the tool-shed and made for the tunnel's very mouth.

THE DARKNESS OF THE PASSAGE WAS AS ABSOLUTE AS I REMEMBERED; I felt my way down the initial flight of steps, and along the sloping ground, with as much haste as discretion allowed. I could not recall with certainty how many minutes were required for the completion of the distance; but that it should be far less than the *ten* demanded of a direct assault upon the cliff's face, I confidently assumed. And indeed, a little over half that time had elapsed, when I found myself confronted with the wooden door, and the faint line of light at its edges, that proclaimed me come to the cavern itself. I placed my ear against it, and stood as still as a mouse.

"At the very least, Crawford, allow Mademoiselle Le-Fevre to go free," came a grim voice; I recognised Sidmouth, and knew that his every illusion regarding Crawford's purpose must be now o'erthrown. "She has done nothing to deserve arrest, and her brother is wounded, as you may plainly see. Send them out to the boat—at pistol point, if need be—and keep me hostage to their word. I may fully vouch that they shall depart without a backwards glance, if I so command it."

"Do you think me a fool? Should I allow a boat to land, and armed men with it, before the dragoons are come? I have not spent a decade in flight of the law, to fall victim to another rogue. No, Sidmouth, you shall remain within, and the signal go unsent, and the boat remain offshore."

There was a faint groan of suffering—from the injured Philippe, I supposed. It was because of the boy that I had assumed Sidmouth would seek hiding so near to the

Grange, rather than in the wilds of the Pinny, or simply flying along the Crewkerne road. He was not the sort to leave his ailing cousin, and since any attempt at removal by waggon should delay them insupportably, they *must* go by boat, and be borne swiftly out of harm's way, or die in the attempt.

There was a rapid cursing in French from Seraphine, and the sound of a woman spitting.

"You may rest easy, Mademoiselle," came Crawford's voice. "By my lights, we have not long to wait."

Where, oh, where, was Lord Harold?

"What was that?" Crawford's voice held a note of apprehension. "A sound, like a rock falling." A pause, during which I assume the Reverend peered cautiously from the cavern's mouth. "Not the dragoons—they should have no need for stealth," he mused. "Some *other*, then. Sidmouth!"

Footsteps crossed the cavern swiftly, and I heard with a shudder a cry of pain from Seraphine and the cocking of a pistol. "Your beloved dies, unless you speak the truth. What manner of man is beyond the cavern mouth? Is it Dagliesh, your black dog? Or one of your lily-bearers, perhaps? Out with it!"

"You had better keep your ball for the defence of your prize," Sidmouth drily rejoined, "than spend it in terrorizing my cousin. I have no notion who might be beyond."

He spoke strongly, with much of bravado; but there was something like hope in his voice. A sudden in-drawing of breath, and an ill-suppressed whimper from Seraphine, was his only reward.

A gunshot rang out, and I jumped, in a fever of anxiety that Crawford had carried out his ruthless aim; but even as the thought occurred, I knew the ball to have been fired from some distance, the beach beyond, perhaps, and not from within the cavern. It must, it could only be, Lord Harold. There was the sound of a scuffle, and a dragging of a body across the floor of the cave, and then Crawford's voice was very nearly at my ear.

"The girl comes with me, Sidmouth, as proof against your aims. If I am pursued, she dies—even if I must die with her. But if your man outside makes no attempt to follow, you have my word that she shall live."

I knew with sharp certainty that Crawford intended some retreat up the very tunnel whose doorway I commanded, with Seraphine as his hostage, and I felt my heart race. I pressed myself against the tunnel wall, my breath suspended, and raised Lord Harold's pistol high in both hands. I should have only one chance, or be overcome.

The door was thrust wide, and Crawford backed into the passage, his left arm hooked about the throat of Seraphine, who struggled futilely, with rolling eyes; and in his right hand, an upraised gun, that trembled with a cowardly anxiety.

So much I saw, before I brought the butt of Lord Harold's pistol down upon his skull, with all the force in my slender frame and a guttural yell that shocked even *my* overwrought senses—and Crawford swayed a moment on his feet, then crumpled to the ground.

What hullabaloo did then ensue! It was Sidmouth first who vaulted into the passage, followed swiftly by one or two men I judged to be French, and in their train, Lord Harold Trowbridge, with something very like amazement on his narrow face, and a touch of amusement in his cold grey eyes. Seraphine had sprung free, and thrown herself in Sidmouth's arms; but it was to me he looked, over her golden head, and spoke all his astonished gratitude.

As for myself—the apprehension of the moment having given way to energetic activity, I found myself with tremors now renewed, and a shaking at the knees, and all but crumpled to the insensible Mr. Crawford's side; but found support, at the last, in the strong arm of a French stranger, who helped me from the tunnel and into the comparative freedom of the cavern's depths.

"My compliments, Miss Austen," Lord Harold said briefly, joining us. "Mademoiselle—the signal?"

"The boy has it," Seraphine managed, from the folds of Sidmouth's shirt.

Trowbridge turned to Toby, who leaned in a shadow on his crutches, and held out his hand for the spout lanthorn. He waited only for the striking of a match, and was as swiftly gone to the beach.

A groan, and I turned to observe Mr. Crawford regaining his wits; and saw that he was firmly trussed in rope, with his hands bound behind.

"Leave him," Sidmouth tersely ordered his companions. "Lord Harold shall deal with him. Let us bear Philippe to the beach. If the dragoons come before the boat, at least we may make our stand in the open, and die nobly at the last." He gave a shake to Seraphine, who released him with a sigh, and bent to the task of removing her brother, who lay on a litter in the very midst of the cave. I drew a deep breath, and passed a hand over my draggled locks. The flight had been planned with extreme simplicity; a few sacks only lay about the floor, filled, I supposed, with but a change of dress and provisions against the journey. I reached for one, and carried it to the cavern's mouth.

Trowbridge stood upon the shingle, careless of all who might observe him, a pocket glass to his eye, his every fibre straining towards the horizon. "The boat!" he cried. "It advances!"

The rain that had begun perhaps a half-hour before had become a veritable storm—*smugglers' weather,* I recalled with a half-smile—and the suspense that characterised the skiff's approach was such as I hope never to endure again. Twice, it was nearly capsized, but for a manful pulling at the oars, as it attempted to breast the surf at the bar; and once, an oarsman was swept overboard with a terrible cry, and was only retrieved by his mates with difficulty, at the loss of several moments' precious time. But at last it achieved the beach, with Lord Harold and Sidmouth running into the surf to their thighs' height to aid its approach; and the Frenchmen bent to Philippe's litter.

At that moment, Seraphine gave a cry. I turned to observe her uplifted hand, pointing back along the cliff's edge; what seemed an army of men was descending the road to the fossil works, swarming over the beach and heading in our direction. The men sprang to the boat; Lord Harold heaved with all his wiry strength at the prow, and Sidmouth swung Seraphine to safety amidships. He turned, half-standing, half-kneeling, in the boat, and searched for my face.

"Jane!" he cried. "What we owe, nothing might repay! God keep you, all the days of your life! And may you find the happiness denied to *me,* with your loss—"

I could not answer, for the tears streaming down my face, and slowly raised a hand in salute. Lord Harold surged out into the waves; the oarsmen bent to their burden, and with an agonising slowness, the boat turned towards the open water beyond the bar, fighting, fighting, against the storm.

A ball whistled over my head, and in some shock and surprise, I turned towards the shot. A rough hand pulled me backwards, and Lord Harold dragged me to the cavern's mouth.

"*This* time, Miss Austen, I beg you will do me the honour of respecting what I say," he said, with much labour of breathing, the result of his exertions. "*Stay here,* and do not make a sound, and if we are very fortunate, you may survive this debacle."

Chapter 23

Jane's Afterword

~

A VERY FEW WORDS WILL SUFFICE TO CONCLUDE MY TALE.

The dragoons attempted, and failed, to impede the flight of Sidmouth's boat. After a frantic quarter-hour of firing poorly-sighted blunderbusses across a heaving sea, they gave up the effort, and stood at the water's edge in a degree of ill-humour and rainswept soddenness, that should have been amusing to behold, did not I find myself in so precarious a position. I espied Roy Cavendish, on the periphery of his troops. The Customs man's arms were folded, his hat brim dripped with the dispiriting rain, and there was an expression of dismay on his countenance. I suspected his foul temper would descend upon *my* head, did I appear.

It was then that Lord Harold advanced upon them.

He had left me at the mouth of the cave, confident that the dragoons might persuade me to caution where his influence could not. With customary coolness, he had torn a length of rag from his white shirt, and affixed it to his pistol end; then he hauled poor Crawford to his feet, and forced the man to serve as shield for their advance through the pelting showers. It remained only to wait until the dragoons' fury was spent, and Sidmouth safely out of the way; and so Lord Harold did.

"Ahoy there!" he cried, waving his makeshift flag of truce as he thrust the reluctant Crawford before him. "Your commander, I pray!"

Cavendish started from his abject ruminations, and stepped forwards to meet the men; and a parley ensued, in the lowest of tones, that seemed to invert the Customs officer's very world. Disbelief o'erspread his features, and something very like shock; and he took a step backwards from Cholmondeley Crawford in utter amazement.

Roy Cavendish was not a man of the Crown for nothing, however—and in a few moments, he had dispatched a squadron of dragoons from their fruitless position on the beach, to retrieve what dignity they might, in a search of Crawford's fossil site; and they discovered there a quantity of silk and other fine stuff, all imported without benefit of the King's custom—and perhaps, most important, a set of horseshoes made crudely on the fossil forge, and marked clearly with the initials *GS*.

The intelligence thus obtained, and a few low words regarding *statecraft*, and *His Majesty's government*, from Lord Harold Trowbridge, ensured that no Naval cutter should be loosed in pursuit of Sidmouth and his party. But all this it was my privilege to learn later, once Crawford was borne away to the Lyme gaol (all threat of fire in that quarter being now contained), and the dragoons dispersed. At Lord Harold's suggestion, Roy Cavendish made it his business to inform the justice of the peace, Mr. Dobbin, of Cholmondeley Crawford's murderous deceit.

It was then that Lord Harold retrieved me from my place of seclusion, and looked with concern upon my sodden clothes and ravaged face.

"Miss Austen! I have been wretchedly in neglect," he said, with the first suggestion of anxiety I had ever observed throughout the length of our acquaintance. He doffed his dripping hat and held it awkwardly over my bedraggled curls. "You shall catch your death of cold from your exposure this e'en."

"I care little for that," I said wearily, brushing his hat aside, "only I should dearly love a proper cloak, and some conveyance home, as I am falling down with fatigue."

He hastened to swing his greatcoat from his shoulders, and flung it about my own, and without another word, led me to his good dark horse still tethered at the fossil pits; and with the utmost gentleness, he bent to provide a hand for my mounting. I hauled myself onto the horse's back, with less than my usual grace—being anything but a horsewoman in the best of times—and Lord Harold sprang, with something more of lightness, to the saddle before me.

We paused an instant to gaze through the curtain of rain, and out across the waves, where, like a scrap of torn fabric, the sail of a cutter showed against a lightening sky. It moved swiftly, and as we watched, disappeared from view.

"Where, then, do they sail?" I asked, after a moment.

"Not to France, assuredly." Lord Harold's voice held an unwonted sobriety. "The country is grown too hot for men of their persuasion. The cutter will bear them to Liverpool, I believe—and it is their intention *there* to secure passage on a ship bound for America."

"*America?*" I felt the pain of parting redouble with all the swiftness of a blow to my heart. "I shall never see him again."

"I fear not," Lord Harold said quietly. He clucked to the horse, and turned its head, and commenced a slow jog towards Lyme.

And so we rode in weary silence for a time, with nothing but the soft patter of raindrops and the first tentative birdsong to cheer our way. My thoughts were torn between exultation at the party's escape and a regret so profound I could hardly speak. Until, with something more akin to his usual raillery, Lord Harold observed that I must take greater care in the forming of my acquaintance.

"For, Miss Austen," said he, "though I will not say that I *disapprove* of your predilection for characters such as Sidmouth, or your habit of dining at the home of smugglers, I confess that my nose is quite turned, at finding my success so spoilt, in being dependent upon your penetration. You will quite ruin my reputation, if word of this gets out; and I shall be reduced to offering you employment."

"—Which I should as readily decline," I replied. "At this moment, sir, I want nothing more than the safety of my room, and a hot toddy, and a warm brick wrapt in cloths between the sheets. How it *does* rain! I will never be without my bonnet, in future, no matter how many borrowed greatcoats I may acquire."

"You have a most vexatious talent for intrigue," Lord Harold insisted, with utter disregard for my ideas of bricks and toddies. "Most unusual, in a woman. I shall be constantly looking over my shoulder, in future, from a fear of finding you behind."

"Then you shall run headlong over my foot, my lord," I rejoined with spirit, "for I shall assuredly stand before."

About the Author

STEPHANIE BARRON, author of the critically acclaimed *Jane and the Unpleasantness at Scargrave Manor* and *Jane and the Man of the Cloth,* is a lifelong admirer of Jane Austen's work. She lives and works in Colorado.

If you enjoyed Stephanie Barron's *Jane and the Man of the Cloth*, you won't want to miss any of Jane Austen's sleuthing adventures. Look for the first, *Jane and the Unpleasantness at Scargrave Manor*, at your favorite bookstore in paperback.

And turn the page for a preview of *Jane and the Wandering Eye: Being the Third Jane Austen Mystery*, now available.

Jane and the

Wandering Eye

Being the Third Jane Austen Mystery

By Stephanie Barron

Wednesday,
12 December 1804
Bath

~

A ROUT-PARTY, WHEN DEPICTED BY A PEN MORE ACCOMPLISHED THAN MY own, is invariably a stupid affair of some two or three hundred souls pressed elbow-to-elbow in the drawing-rooms of the great. Such an efflorescence of powder shaken from noble wigs! Such a crush of silk! And what general heartiness of laughter and exclamation—so that the gentler tones of one's more subdued companions must be raised to a persistent roar, rendering most of the party voiceless by dawn, with only the insipid delights of indifferent negus and faltering meat pasties as recompense for all one's trials.

So Fanny Burney has described a rout, in *Cecilia* and *Camilla;* and so I should be forced to record my first experience of the same, in a more modest volume I entitle simply *Jane,* had not Fate intervened to render my dissipation more intriguing. For last night I endured the most fearsome of crushes—a post-theatrical masquerade, forsooth, with myself in the role of Shepherdess—at no less exalted an address than Laura Place, and the Dowager Duchess of Wilborough's abode, with attendant hundreds of her most intimate acquaintance.

And what, you may ask, had Miss Jane Austen to do in such company? So my father gently enquired, at the moment of my setting out from Green Park Buildings (where all my dear family have been situated but two months, having lost our former lodgings in Sydney Place to the infamous Coles), my brother Henry at my side, a most formidable Richard the Third, and his wife, Eliza, done up as Marie Antoinette.

"Why, Father," I replied, with a wave of my Shepherdess's crook, "you must know that the invitation is all my brother's, procured with a view to amusing Eliza, who must have her full measure of Bath's diversion during so short a visit to the city, and in such a season. Bath at Christmastide may yet be called a trifle thin, in requiring the larger crowds of Easter to lend it style; and if Eliza is not to be thoroughly put out, we must seize our diversion where we may. A masquerade, and at the express invitation of a Dowager Duchess, cannot be let slip. Is not this so, Henry?''

"Indeed,'' my brother stammered, with a look for his elegant wife, who appeared to have entirely swallowed her little dog, Pug, so pursed with false innocence was her mouth. Eliza is but a slip of a lady, tho' in her present towering headdress, complete with ship's models and birds of paradise bestowed about her heavily powdered curls, she bid fair to rise far above her usual station.

I must confess to a greater admiration for Eliza's queen than for Henry's king—for though both may be called cunning by history's judgement, Eliza has the advantage over Henry, in having at least *seen* Marie Antoinette in all the Austrian's former glory, and thus being capable of the incorporation of that lady's vanished style in her present dress; while Henry is dependent upon the merest notion of humped backs and twirling moustachios, or a general reputation for squintyness about the eyes, for the affectation of his villain.

"And our own dear Madam Lefroy is to be in attendance at the Duchess's party as well, Father,'' Eliza added. "It is to form the chief part of her final evening in Bath—she returns to Hampshire on the morrow—and we cannot part without some notice on either side. I am sure you would not wish us to neglect so amiable a neighbour, so dear a friend. For who shall say when we shall meet again?''

"But are you even acquainted with the Duchess, my dear Jane?'' my father asked, in some bewilderment.

"Assuredly—'' Henry began.

"—*not*,'' I concluded.

"That is to say,'' my brother amended hastily, "the acquaintance is entirely *mine*, Father. I have performed some trifling service for the Wilborough family, in the financial line. The rout tickets came to me.''

"I had not an idea of it, my dear boy.'' The expression of pleasure that suffused my father's face, at this indication of his son's advancement in his chosen profession of banking, made the falsehood almost worth its utterance.

"But now we must be off,'' Eliza interjected firmly, "or lose another hour in search of chairs, for our own have been standing at the door this quarter-hour.[1] It has quite struck eleven, and how it snows! Do observe, my dear sir, the unfortunate chairmen!''

Bath's climate is usually so mild as to escape the advent of winter, but this night at least we were subject to a fearsome blast. And thus, as my father clucked in dismay from the drawing-room window, all benevolent concern for the reddened cheeks and stamping feet of the unlucky fellows below, we hurried down to the street, where indeed our chairs had been idle already some minutes, and settled ourselves comfortably for the trip to Laura Place—or would have, had not my Shepherdess's crook refused the conveyance's close accommodation. This small difficulty resolved, by the abandonment of the offending object on the stoop of Green Park Buildings, the chairmen heaved and hallooed, and off we went—with only the occasional bobble to recall the untidiness of the snowy streets, and the likelihood of a yet more strenuous return.

I profited from the brief journey, by indulging in a review of the causes of our exertion, for pleasure was unfortunately the least of them. However circumscribed my usual society in Bath—which is generally limited to my Aunt Leigh-Perrot's insipid card parties, and the occasional indulgence of the theatre when my slim purse may allow it—I am not so desperate for enjoyment as to spend a decidedly snowy midnight done up as a Staffordshire doll, in a gay throng of complete strangers more blessed and happy in their mutual acquaintance. Nor are Henry and Eliza so mad for rout-parties as my father had been led to believe. My brother and sister[2] had succumbed to my entreaties for support, and had gone so far as to prevaricate on my behalf. From an awkwardness of explanation, I had deliberately withheld from the Reverend George Austen the true nature of our visit to Laura Place. We were gone in the *guise* of

---

[1] In Austen's day, it was the custom to travel about the streets of Bath and other major cities in hired sedan chairs carried by a man fore and aft.—*Editor's note.*

[2] Eliza de Feuillide was both Jane Austen's cousin and the wife of her brother, Henry, but Jane usually refers to Eliza simply as her *sister.* It was a convention of the time to address relatives acquired through marriage in the same manner as blood relations.—*Editor's note.*

revellers, indeed, but laboured in fact under a most peculiar commission.

Lord Harold Trowbridge, my dark angel of recent adventure—confidant of the Crown, adversary of whomever he is paid to oppose, and general Rogue-about-Town—is the Dowager Duchess of Wilborough's younger son. He is also in the throes of some trouble with a lady—nothing unusual for Lord Harold, although in this instance, the novelty of the lady's being not only unmarried, but related to him, must give the mendacious pause. In short, his niece, Lady Desdemona Trowbridge—an Incomparable of the present Season, a girl of eighteen with all the blessings of fortune, beauty, and breeding to recommend her—has thrown off the protection of her family and friends; has left all in London whose interest should form her chief consideration and care; and has fled to the Dowager Duchess in Bath. The agent of her flight? The redoubtable Earl of Swithin, who claims an interest in the lady's future happiness. In short, the Earl has offered for her hand—and caused the fair Desdemona considerable vexation and grief.

Lord Harold observed the flight, and respected his mother's wishes to leave the girl to herself for a time; he remained in London, and restrained His Grace the Duke from summoning the chit immediately back home; he forbore to visit Laura Place himself, and urge the reclamation of sense; and when the Lady Desdemona showed neither an inclination to quit her grandmother's abode, nor to suffer very much from her voluntary exile, being engaged in a delightful round of amusement and shopping in the weeks before Christmas—he applied, at last, to *me*.

My niece is a lady of excellent understanding, Lord Harold wrote in his barely legible hand, *but possessed of the Trowbridge will. She is headstrong, and entirely capable of acting against her own interest. I am most concerned that she not fall prey to the basest of fortune hunters—whose attentions she might unwittingly encourage, from a misplaced sense of pique, or an inclination to put paid to Lord Swithin's plans. Is it impossible—do I ask too much—that you might observe her movements for a time, my dear Miss Austen? And report what you observe? I wish chiefly to know the nature of Desdemona's acquaintance—in whose circle she spends the chief part of her days—and the names of those gentlemen upon whom she bestows the greatest attention. You would oblige me exceedingly in the performance of this service; for tho' Her Grace might certainly do the same, she is, as you may be aware,* not the strictest judge of propriety.

And as the letter supplied a direction in Pall Mall— White's Club, to be exact—and the very rout tickets formerly mentioned, I could not find it in me to refuse—if, indeed, at present I could refuse Lord Harold anything. It is not that I owe him some great debt of gratitude, or harbour for the gentleman a more tender sentiment; but rather that where Lord Harold goes, intrigue surely follows—and I confess I have been insupportably *bored* with Bath, and the littlenesses of a town, since my return from Lyme Regis but a few weeks ago. The Gentleman Rogue and his errant niece presented a most welcome diversion.

And so to Laura Place we were gone.

I DO NOT BELIEVE I EXAGGERATE WHEN I DECLARE THAT THE DOWAGER Duchess of Wilborough's establishment was ablaze last e'en with a thousand candles. Light spilled out of a multitude of casements (the original glazing of which must have exacted from the late Duke a fortune), and cast diamond-paned shadows upon the snowy street; light flowed from the open entry-way at every chair's arrival, like a bolt of silk unfurled upon the walk. A hubbub of conversation, too, and the clatter of cutlery; a voice raised hoarsely in song; a burst of laughter. The faintest strain of a violin drifted to the stoop.

Henry paid off the chairs and presented our cards to the footmen, but I found occasion to dally at the very door, almost deterred by the glittering hordes I glimpsed within— until an exclamation from Eliza thrust me forward. I had trod upon the foot of Marie Antoinette.

The foyer was a wealth of pale green paint picked out with pink and white, the colours of Robert Adam. Pink and green silk lined the windows, and a bust of the Tragic Muse loomed before a pier glass opposite—Mrs. Siddons, no doubt, and taken from the painting by Reynolds.[3] I gazed, and beheld myself reflected as Shepherdess, a forlornly bucolic figure amidst so much splendour. Eliza pinched my arm.

[3] Sarah Siddons (1755–1831) was the foremost tragic actress of Austen's day. With her brother, John Philip Kemble, Siddons dominated the London stage at this time, where it is probable Jane had seen her perform.—*Editor's note.*

"As near to Old Drury as may be, my dear," she murmured.[4]

"Indeed," I replied. "The Dowager Duchess may be living in relative retirement, but she has not yet foresworn her passions."

"Let us go up," Henry interposed with impatience. "There is a fearful crush at my back!"

The rout was intended, so Lord Harold had informed us, as a tribute to the principal players of Bath's Theatre Royal[5]—and the present evening's performance being just then concluded, the tide of humanity spilling into Laura Place from the direction of Orchard Street was decidedly at its flood. The staircase, a grand curve of mahogany, was completely overpowered with costumed bodies struggling towards the drawing-room; I hooked one arm through my brother's, and the other through my sister's, and so we stormed the barricade.

Let us pass over in silence the travails of the next quarter-hour; how our gowns were torn, and our headdresses deranged; what injuries to slipper and glove. Better to employ the interval in relating the chief of what I know about the Dowager herself—the barest details of Her Grace's celebrated career.

I have it on so good an authority as my dear mother's dubious memory, that Eugenie de la Falaise began her ascent as a pert young chorus girl in the Paris comic opera; from thence, with a comely ankle and a smattering of English, she rose to Covent Garden; and it was there the Duke of Wilborough—the *fifth*, rather than the present, Duke—fell headlong in love with the lady. Wilborough was already past his first youth; he had seen one Duchess into her grave, and her stillborn son with her; and thus it should not be remarkable that he might establish the beautiful Eugenie

[4] Robert Adam's renovation of Old Drury Lane Theatre in 1775 featured pale green and pink paint with bronze detailing—which the Dowager Duchess apparently emulated. Old Drury was pulled down and replaced by a newer building in 1794. This building burned to the ground in 1809.—*Editor's note.*

[5] This was the original Bath theater on Orchard Street, where Jane was a frequent patron. Its company divided performances between Bath and Bristol, playing houses in each city on alternate nights—Tuesday, Thursday, and Saturday in Bath; Monday, Wednesday, and Friday in Bristol.—*Editor's note.*

privately, or offer unlimited credit in the most fashionable shops, and a smart pair to drive her about Town, in return for the enjoyment of her favours, as Lord Derby once did with Miss Farren.[6] But Eugenie had a greater object in view. She wished to play at tragedy.

That she was unsuited for Isabella, or Lady Macbeth, or even the role of Portia in *The Merchant of Venice*, need not be underlined. *Twelfth Night*, perhaps, or *She Stoops to Conquer*, may have shewn her talents to advantage; but at the Duke of Wilborough's intercession with the Drury Lane director, Lady Macbeth she played—and opposite no less a personage than the redoubtable Mr. Garrick.

The performance—there was, alas, only one—was declared to have been lamentable. The outraged patrons hissed and shouted, threw all manner of refuse from theatre pit to stage, and forced the curtain down in the very midst of Lady Macbeth's celebrated walk. Eugenie de la Falaise was mortified, and disappeared abruptly from public view, never to return to the London theatre.

We cannot in justice fault the fifth Duke for having married her. He may be forgiven the indulgence of his folly. The pity, the generosity, the rashness her ruined career may have excited—we can have only the merest idea of how they worked upon his sensibilities. Eugenie was, it is said, a beautiful woman at twenty-four; and though she is now a grandmother these many years, and Wilborough long since gone to his reward, she is no less a formidable a presence.

I say this, having found my eyes directed to the Dowager Duchess upon first gaining entrance to her drawing-room. Tho' possessed of fully seventy years, and requiring the support of a stout cane she clutches tightly in one hand, Her Grace commands immediate attention. Her narrow features and shuttered aspect recall the face of her son, Lord Harold; but where the effect is often forbidding in the latter, it may be declared devastating in the former. A lesser man than the Duke of Wilborough—accustomed as he was to the power of doing as he liked—would have braved greater scandal in pursuit of such a woman.

And scandal there was. His Majesty George II is said to

---

[6] Elizabeth Farren was a member of the Drury Lane company during the 1780s and the recognized mistress of the Earl of Derby, who made her his second countess at his first wife's death in 1797.—*Editor's note*.

have interceded in the match, which condescension was stoically declined. The Duke's political fortunes may subsequently have suffered. Certain of his acquaintance may have cut him dead. But others, made more valuable through the passage of time, accepted his bride; and accepted no less the heirs she pragmatically produced.

Bertie, who succeeded his father, bears the greatest fidelity to the Wilborough line, in character as well as countenance; Lady Caroline Mulvern, *née* Trowbridge, is the unfortunate picture of her Trowbridge aunts; but in the face of Lord Harold, the impertinent among society's loquacious have gone so far as to question paternity. Lord Harold is so clearly Eugenie's son, that the late Duke might have had nothing to do with his fashioning.

The Dowager stood in the midst of her fashionable rout last e'en arrayed in the form of Cleopatra—an Egyptian robe and a circlet on her brow, with a velvet mask held before— and beside her stood a girl so very much of Eugenie's stamp, albeit some fifty years younger, that I knew her immediately for the Lady Desdemona, Lord Harold's errant niece. She was robed to perfection as none other than *herself,* having ignored the general command of fancy dress; and her quite ordinary appearance amidst the general excess of baubles and plumage rendered her as exotic as a sparrow in Paradise. I could trace no hint of her mother, Honoria, or her apoplectic father, Bertie, in her narrow and elegant face, and wondered whether her character was as French as her countenance.

"Jane," Eliza cried, her visage incongruously marred by the mask that covered fully half of it, "Henry *will* have me to dance; and though I confess the heat and crush make the prospect an indifferent one, I cannot find that sitting down should be so very agreeable *either.* Can you forgive us our desertion?"

"Go, my dear, and make as frivolous a figure as your murdered Queen may support. I shall do very well in idleness here. I find I have an excellent prospect of Lady Desdemona."

"Where?"

"She stands beside the Duchess."

"Ah," Eliza said, with the driest satisfaction, "in the figure of an *ingénue.* She might readily be Cecilia herself, and prepared to thwart a cavalcade of admirers, whose costumed obscurity can only encourage impertinence. Let us call her Virtue, and have done."

"Indeed? I had thought her merely to disdain all pretence or disguise. And burdened as I am with so hot and ungainly an outfit—" I surveyed my multitude of muslin underskirts with a shake of my bonneted head—"I cannot in justice criticise. I fairly long for an exchange."

"Perhaps. But does her abhorrence—or wisdom—reveal a niceness of temperament and taste? Or may we judge her merely to spoil sport?"

"I cannot undertake to say, without a greater knowledge of the lady."

"Then find her out, my dear Jane, and I shall be content to think as you do. It saves me a vast deal of trouble in thinking for myself." And with a smile and a care for her overpowering headdress, Eliza left me to Lord Harold's business.

I began by surveying the company—a torrid blend of the comely and the grotesque, their colours garish and their accents brazen, relieved somewhat by the solitary interval of an elegant figure, composed against a doorframe or supporting a distant wall—engaged, it seemed, in an activity similar to my own. A Harlequin I espied, resplendent in a suit of black and red, in the closest conversation with a stately Queen Elizabeth; and a fearsome Moor, all flowing capes and harshly graven features—though *not* in attendance upon my particular Desdemona. More than one visage I detected, that when deprived of its domino might daily grace the pages of the *Gentleman's Magazine,* or one of Gillray's drawings for the *Morning Gazette.* The Prince of Wales's henchmen, Lord Moira, and the beetle-browed Mr. Fox, I named in silence; and a forbidding personage well-launched upon her middle years, whom I suspected of being none other than the notorious Lady Jersey. She wore no costume, and held court at the far end of the drawing-room from that commanded by Moira, being sadly out of favour now that Mrs. Fitzherbert was returned to the Prince's side.[7]

---

[7] James Gillray (1757–1815) was the foremost caricaturist in aquatint engravings, which began to make their appearance in the London newspapers in the 1780s. The engravings generally made sport of fashionable scandals or political missteps, much as do present-day political cartoons. Lord Moira and Charles James Fox were noted Whig politicians; Countess Frances Jersey, although a grandmother in her fifties, was a scheming and unscrupulous woman who had

A full quarter-hour of observation, however, could not betray to my sight the predatory horde whose idea had so excited Lord Harold's anxiety. Two men only approached the Lady Desdemona—yet *another* Harlequin, suited this time in diamonds of alternating black and white; and a fellow who might well have been Henry VIII, tho' of a corpulence supplied by tailor's padding. These two seemed as intent upon conversation with the Dowager Duchess, as with her lovely charge.

"And are you, too, of the Theatre Royal?" came a voice at my shoulder; and looking up, I beheld a Knight in the semblance of armour, complete with visored head, his identity secure in mystery.

"Of its occasional box alone," I replied, "but I may confess to admiration for good, hardened, professional acting. Are some part of the company present, then?"

"The masquerade is in their honour."

"So I had understood. But with so many figures in fancy dress, how is one to divine the true player from the false?"

My companion bowed. "You merely posit, madam, the oldest question of mankind."

I studied the visored face, which revealed nothing of the gentleman within. Could it, in fact, be Lord Harold, making sport of circumstance? The voice betrayed an echo of the Gentleman Rogue's tone. But no. He should hardly engage my offices on the Lady Desdemona's behalf, had he intended to form one of the party.

"I wonder, sir," I began again, "that you can think me a member of such exalted company."

"I merely tossed at hazard. You might be exalted in any number of ways—as I might myself. We appear as utter strangers the one to the other; but indeed we might claim the deepest intimacy, and yet pass in ignorance, so impenetrable is our garb."

"And the most accomplished actress herself must go unremarked."

"There, madam, you betray a charming innocence of accomplished actresses. It is the first rule of the stage that to go

served briefly as the Prince of Wales's mistress in the 1790s. She had displaced the Catholic and twice-widowed Maria Fitzherbert, whom the Prince secretly and illegally married in 1786, but by 1804, Mrs. Fitzherbert was once more the Prince's companion of choice.—*Editor's note.*

unremarked, is to go presently into the wings. Observe the Medusa in scarlet."

I looked about, though the compass of both bonnet and mask rendered all vision partial.

"By the fireplace, in converse with the bearded Pierrot."

I observed then an extraordinary woman, all vibrance and fire, her flowing black hair and tattered raiment the very soul of madness. Her beauty was such as to astonish. Her costume, however, barely merited the word, in leaving more of her person exposed than it disguised. The effect *must* draw even the most jaded attention. She had flaunted custom, and wore no mask. Whether her conversation was as engaging as her person, I could not discern; but as I watched, the bearded Pierrot threw back his head in hearty laughter.

"That is Miss Conyngham," my companion remarked.

"*Maria* Conyngham? I had not an idea of it."

"Her brother is beside the Duchess."

I turned to look for Her Grace.

"The Harlequin?"

"Henry the Eighth."

"So *that* is the famous Hugh Conyngham! I wonder I did not observe it before! Who can see his present self, and fail to trace his tragic Hamlet? His murderous Macbeth? His pathetic Gamester? The nobility of suffering is writ in every line of his countenance!"

"With charcoal, if not by nature," the gentleman observed.

"And are you then a player, sir? Claim you some acquaintance with the pair?" It was absurd in me, I own, to cry such admiration at Conyngham's discovery; but so much of my meagre purse has gone to furnish *his*, in supplying the coveted seat in a box for the actor's performance, that I may be excused my excesses of enthusiasm. I have invested as much in Conyngham as Henry in all his four percents.[8]

"I have not that distinction," the Knight replied with an inclination of the head. "I may claim the accomplishment of dancing only, and that with indifferent skill. But I must beg for the indulgence of your hand, fair Shepherdess, or suffer

---

[8] These were the government's public funds, one of the few reliable investments in Austen's day, which generally yielded annuities of four percent per annum.—*Editor's note*.

the charge of impertinence, in having monopolised your attention too long.''

I hesitated, with thoughts of Lord Harold, and the necessities of duty; but a glance at the floor revealed the Lady Desdemona, all smiles and animation, going down the dance with her partner opposite. The White Harlequin, it seemed, had prevailed in his suit; his appearance of attention to the Dowager had been rewarded with the hand of her granddaughter. Lady Desdemona's eyes were bright, and her complexion brilliant; but how, I thought with vexation, was I to report her partner's name? For a masquerade is ill-suited to espionage; conjecture only might supply the place of the man; and I should be reduced to outright eavesdropping, if I were to learn anything to Lord Harold's purpose. To the dance floor, then, with the greatest despatch.

I bowed, my own mask held high, and took my suitor's proffered arm; and found to my relief that armour may be formed of cloth, however shot through with silver, and pose no impediment to a country dance, though it reveal nothing of the Knight within.

A FULL HALF-HOUR OF HEATED EXERCISE PROVED INSUFFICIENT TO THE fulfilment of my schemes, however; it was impossible to over-listen anything to Lord Harold's purpose in so great a throng; and so, with a civility on either side, I abandoned my partner for a comfortable seat in the supper-room near Henry and Eliza. I had divined only that the White Harlequin made a shapely leg and was a proficient in the dance, with a vigorous step and a palm decidedly moist, as he handed Lady Desdemona along the line of couples. She seemed happy in her choice of partner, and moved in a fine flow of spirits; *he* was a spare, neat figure possessed of a hearty laugh and a general conviviality, who comported himself as a gentleman; and what was visible of his hair was brown. There my researches ended.

The delights of cold fowl and buttered prawns, white soup and ratafia cakes, were all but consumed, and Henry had embarked upon the errand of refilling our cups of punch, when I began to consider of Madam Lefroy. Anne Lefroy has long been our neighbour in Steventon, being established in the rectory at Ashe these two decades at least; and though she is full five-and-twenty years my senior, she remains my dearest friend in the world. The claims of friendship had recently drawn her to Bath—her acquaintance with the Dowager being of several decades' standing—and the previous fortnight spent in her company had been one of the most delightful I could recall. Our tastes are peculiarly suited the one to the other, and there is no one's society I should more eagerly claim in good times or in bad.

It was Madam who refined my taste in poetry, who improved my ear for music, who taught me that cleverness is far more than mere surface wit. From Madam, too, I learned that even *ladies* might converse about the nation's affairs—for as Madam feelingly says, when so great a figure as Mr. Sheridan confuses a parliamentary bench for Drury Lane, how can *we* be expected to respect the difference?[9]

Anne Lefroy was to leave us on the morrow—but we had intended a meeting in Laura Place. The crush of bodies and the bewildering array of fancy dress had quite disguised her from my sight. I craned about in search of her glorious hair—when a muffled ejaculation from the direction of the fire demanded my attention.

Two men—the White Harlequin and my unknown Knight—were arranged in an attitude of belligerence, although the effect was rendered somewhat ridiculous by the incongruity of their costumes. The Knight had removed his helmet, revealing a fair head and a sharp-featured face that *must* be vaguely familiar; and he now glared boldly at his masked opponent.

"You are a blackguard, sir, and a liar!" he cried.

The Harlequin swayed as he stood, as though influenced by unconquerable passion, or an excess of spirits. And at that moment, Lady Desdemona intervened.

"Kinny! You will apologise at once! Mr. Portal meant nothing by his words, I am certain of it. I will not have you come to blows!"

"I'd sooner fall upon my sword than beg pardon of such a rogue," my Knight exclaimed; and as if in answer, the Harle-

[9] Richard Brinsley Sheridan, the noted Georgian playwright of *The School for Scandal* and owner of the Drury Lane Theatre, was also a member of Parliament. Sheridan first came to Jane's notice in 1787, when he made a four-day speech against her family's friend Warren Hastings, the former Governor-General of Bengal, during Hastings's seven-year parliamentary trial for impeachment.—*Editor's note.*

quin thrust Lady Desdemona roughly aside. She cried out; it was enough. The Knight rushed swiftly at his opponent.

A scuffle, an outburst of oaths—and the two were parted by the actor Hugh Conyngham and the stern-looking Moor.

"Gentlemen! Gentlemen!" Mr. Conyngham exclaimed. "You will look to your conduct, I beg! This is hardly what is due to the Duchess!"

My Knight, his countenance working, drew off a silver glove, and dashed it to the floor. The White Harlequin struggled in the Moor's arms, determined to pick it up.

But it was Hugh Conyngham who bent to retrieve the glove. He tucked it deftly into his Elizabethan doublet. "No challenge, my lord, I beg," he muttered, with a look for Lady Desdemona.

Eliza craned on tiptoe for a clearer view of the scene. "But how droll!" she whispered. "An affair of honour! And can the lady be the cause?"

Lord Harold's niece turned and quitted the supper-room in considerable haste, her eyes overflowing with tears. As if released at a command, the scandalised guests sent up a buzz of conversation; and the Duchess moved to follow her.

"Stay, Grandmère," called my Knight; "I shall go to Mona. Have Jenkins show this blackguard the door." And with a look of contempt for the White Harlequin, who sat slumped in a chair, he sped swiftly in Lady Desdemona's train.

My knight, the Dowager Duchess's grandson? Then was he, in fact, Lady Desdemona's brother, and the heir to the Wilborough dukedom? There was a something of Eugenie's sharpness in his features, and I could imagine him as almost his uncle's twin in another twenty years.

The Duchess halted in her path, leaning heavily upon her cane, and glanced around the supper-room. "Jenkins!" she called, her voice low and clear. "Send round the wine, if you please. I shall attend to Mr. Portal." And grasping her cane with one hand and the White Harlequin with the other, she led him unprotestingly away.

"I might almost think it a set-piece of the stage," said a wry voice at my back, "did not my familiarity with a lady's tears argue its sincerity. What think you, Jane? A lovers' quarrel? Or something deeper?"

"Madam Lefroy!" I turned in delight, and held out my hands. "Do my eyes misgive me? Or is the magnificent Elizabeth reborn in the form of Ashe?"

The masked figure of Queen Elizabeth, whom I had observed earlier in conversation with the Red Harlequin, seized my fingers and laughed.

"As you find me, my dear Miss Austen!—My dear Mrs. Henry! And how do you like the Duchess's party?"

"I may forgive her the disadvantage of a large acquaintance, however much it ensures I shall be crushed, now that there is a touch of scandal to the evening," Eliza declared mischievously. "Of what else might I speak in the Pump Room tomorrow?"[10]

"Eugenie should never forgo a chance to set the town to talking—but I wonder if the Lady Desdemona is quite of her way of thinking? She seemed much distressed."

All discussion of the interesting episode was forestalled, however, by my brother's return. Henry carried a chair with effort in one hand, and a glass of punch in the other; and the result of his exertions, in having raised a fine dew along his forehead, did little for his Richard.

"My poor Henry," I exclaimed. "Your benevolence for naught. I have secured my dear Madam Lefroy, as you see, and will leave you to your lovely Antoinette, and the comforts of iced custard."

[10] The Pump Room was one of the social centers of Bath. It adjoined the King's Baths, near the Abbey and Colonnade in the heart of the city, and was frequented by the fashionable every afternoon. There they would congregate to drink a glass of medicinal spring water presented by liveried pump attendants; to promenade among their acquaintance; and to peruse the calf-bound volume in which recent arrivals to the city inscribed their names and local addresses. Austen describes the Pump Room to perfection in *Northanger Abbey*, in which Catherine Morland and Isabella Thorpe make the place their second home.—*Editor's note.*